The Tempting Voice

Paula Chaffee Scardamalia

ACKNOWLEDGEMENTS

It's not always easy to respond to even the most tempting of voices when it comes to getting a story on the page, so I am so very grateful for all the help, encouragement, and support I had for this story.
Many thanks to Win, Misty, Rona, and Delia of the Sunday Writing Circle. Always there to cheer me on and offer help and suggestions. Thanks, too, to Misty for recommending Rowan Prose Publishing so my book could find a home.
Thank you again to Win for keeping my website working its own magic.
And thank you to editor Katie O'Connor and publisher Kelly Moran for being such effective and magical Muses.

Dedication

To Bob, the most tempting, supportive, loving, inspiring Voice in my life. Without you, I wouldn't be able to see the myth and magic at work everywhere.

Chapter 1

As the Ferrari's car doors winged up, Nik crawled out from beneath them. They were moving too slowly to suit him. Normally, he enjoyed this modern-world-imitation of Pegasus, winged offspring of Poseidon, but he had no time for its mechanical magic today.

He hoped Juliette, the eighty-year-old mortal who was his client, was well. He'd tried calling her several times in the last two days with no answer. Not like her. Not like her at all. He clicked the button on the car's key fob, but didn't watch them wing down, instead ran down the stone-paved path to the door of the three-story house where she lived. Even when she was busy working on her next book, she would answer the phone when he called, since she was of that generation. At first, he was relieved. Their relationship in the last months felt more like grandson and grandmother than the professional one of his usual mortal assignments. Not good.

And now? He had a bad feeling. He could have asked his mother and her sisters to use the scrying pool, but he wanted to check on her himself. The breeze off the ocean whisked through his hair. He smoothed it back. Hammered silver clouds hung low and the strong breeze spurred white horses in the sea beyond the cottage. He loved when the wind and water were a little wild. Another time, he'd be tempted to shuck his shoes and socks and go wading. Instead, he raised the door knocker. Cast in the shape of a turtle, it was a symbol for the endearing old woman of protection, persistence and long life. He knocked several times, shifting back and forth as he tried to wait a reasonable time before knocking again.

He waited. One minute. Two. He knocked again, harder, cocking his head to listen for footsteps or a voice. Nothing. A chill sneaked up his spine, compelling him to pull out his seldom-used key to the cottage. She wanted him to have it even though she was usually here whenever he arrived for a visit.

Pushing the door open, he called out, "Juliette?" He walked into the open living area with its floor to ceiling windows framing the sea. She wasn't on the deck or the beach in front of the cottage, and inside, everything was tidy. But the silence. Where was she? He leaped up the stairs to the second floor.

"Juliette?" Her bedroom door stood open, the bed neatly made, but she wasn't there. The bedroom he used when he stayed with her and the other bedroom were empty as well. Hoping he was wrong; he opened the door to the third-floor stairs and raced up them two at a time. Stopped. Took a breath. The old woman sat slumped over her desk, unmoving.

"Juliette!" he whispered. He didn't want to know. But he knew.

Swallowing, he reached out and touched the arm that rested on the desktop, her fingers slightly curled, her pen lying just beyond their reach, a few handwritten pages spread out beneath her. Her skin was cool. He slid his fingers to her wrist. No beat of life. He hated this. As a Voice, he wasn't supposed to get attached to his mortal clients, but that didn't mean the deaths were easy for him, especially this one.

He pulled his cell phone from his breast pocket and dialed, hoping the one he needed was currently in the mortal realm and would answer. Three rings. He was just about to hang up when—

"Nikos? That you?"

He sighed. "Yes. You're needed at Juliette's. She's gone. Alone."

Silence. Then, "I'll be right there."

"I'll call the lawyer. He can handle the rest." He delivered the message of Juliet's death to her lawyer's secretary so she could tell her boss and he could inform the family. It wasn't Nik's job to deal with family, undertakers, and medical personnel with too many questions he couldn't, or wouldn't, answer. He hung up just as Hermes materialized, dressed in silver tunic and hose. His white hat with its white crane feather brushed the sloped ceiling of the room as he bent his head to gaze at the old woman.

His face softened. "Even though she never knew exactly who you were, Nikos, or what you did for her, this mortal honored us well. She understood how doing something with creativity and love breathes life into the universe, and she did it with passion and fullness of heart."

Nik nodded; throat tight. She'd honored them and her creative spark so well that, with his help, she'd amassed a healthy sum of money.

"Juliette," Hermes said loudly, and held out his hand, "come! Your time here is done. Come with me, dear mortal."

Nik curled his fists as, slowly, the bright, yet almost transparent form that was Juliette's shade rose from her body.

"Madame," Hermes said, tipping his head to her, a rare courtesy not granted to many.

Her shade hesitated, looked around, down at her body, then placed her hand in Hermes'. He flashed his gaze to Nik. "Will you stay until..."

"Nik!" Juliette's shade interrupted when she turned to see whom Hermes was talking to. "It is you, dear boy. I always believed that you were more, did more, than you shared with me. Thank you everything. You were a light in my life..." He could have sworn she twinkled at him, "and the inspiration for so many of my heroes."

Nik swallowed, "I'm sorry I was not here when you..."

She reached for his face. He barely felt her hand.

"I was in my own world, Nik. I was happy. You have your work, I had mine." She gestured at the paper on her desk.

"Mortal, time to go," Hermes said, tugging at her hand.

"Please, a moment.," She turned back to Nik, "Promise me one thing?"

What could she possibly ask of him now?

"If I can."

"Promise me you will do for my granddaughter as you did for me. And I don't mean make her money."

"What?"

She looked at Hermes who smiled at her and back at him. "I know what you are now. What you can do. Please, work your special magic on MJ. Deep inside, my granddaughter is at war with herself, and has been for years. I did what I could when she was little, but I haven't been able to help her since... Well, she needs someone to encourage and support her creative dreams. Someone who isn't an old woman. Will you help her as you helped me? Please?"

"I can't make that promise, Juliette. Apollo..."

"Won't mind," Hermes spoke over him, flashing a grin. "Give the lady her promise, Nikos. We must depart."

Troublemaker. Anything to annoy Apollo. Why should Nik help the granddaughter? From all he'd witnessed, she was—how did the mortals put it—a lost cause.

"What was in her heart as a child is still there, Nik." Juliette's shade reached a hand to his heart. "Please?"

Apollo might not mind, but Erato, Nik's mother would. He wasn't thrilled either. After the last centuries, he was tired of being a Voice, always in service to someone. But the hopeful look on Juliette's face... Reluctantly, Nik nodded.

"Bless you, Nik."

Hermes winked at him, then looked at Juliette's body. "You'll stay until...?"

"Of course."

Hermes clapped him on the back. Then he and Juliette's shade faded from the room. All Nik could do now was wait for the undertakers, then he'd return to Mt. Helicon and break the news to his mother, of his promise to help Juliette's granddaughter, MJ.

If that was possible—even for him.

MJ sighed heavily as she sank into a chair at her grandmother's mahogany dining room table in the old house that Gran and Gramps lived in after their only son was grown and gone. No tea party beneath the table today, her Gran dressed as a fairy godmother serving hot chocolate with tiny marshmallows and dry ladyfingers for dipping. Instead of the sparkly crinoline princess dress her grandmother had stitched for her when she was five, MJ wore a simple black sheath similar to her mother's. Her long hair was neatly pulled back and braided. No glittery gold paper crown made with Gran's help. No more magic or make believe or their private game of "What if?" No Gran.

Across the table with its light coating of dust, her mother sat, a model of ladylike demeanor, every hair in place beneath her black, brimmed hat and veil, her lipstick fresh, hands tucked in her lap, avoiding the dust.

MJ straightened in her chair, clenching her hands in her lap, and swallowed again. Don't cry. Don't cry. Seated next to her, her father reached over and squeezed her hands lightly, then returned his hand to his lap. Slumped in his chair, his tie was askew at his throat, his hair stuck up in places, and he looked every bit the middle-aged professor. Weariness and sorrow etched lines around his eyes and mouth.

Her mother's lips tightened before she turned her sharp regard to the lawyer. "Well, Mr. Lewis," she said and cast another impatient glance at her watch. "What are we waiting for? Let's get this over with so we can go home, and my husband can rest."

Mr. Lewis cleared his throat and straightened the papers—the will, MJ presumed. "We are waiting for Mrs. Montague's man-of-affairs."

"Her what?" Her mother's eyebrows arched under the veiled brim of her hat.

Mr. Lewis adjusted the knot of his tie, "That is what Mrs. Montague called her business manager and financial advisor. Her little joke."

"Of course she did," her father whispered to MJ.

"This is no time for jokes." Her mother glared at Mr. Lewis.

"No, no, of course not." The lawyer ducked his head, "I do apologize..."

A man's voice said, "Apologizing for me, Mr. Lewis? I can do that myself."

MJ jerked her head in the direction of the archway of the dining room where the man stood. She blinked. *Wow! No wonder her grandmother called him her man-of-affairs. If she had a business manager who looked like him, she'd call him other things as well. Hottie came to mind.* Smiling at the possibility, her first smile in the long, sad day, she took in the long dark hair that brushed the collar of his steel grey suit, the strong lines of his clean-shaven jaw, the wide mouth with its full lower lip and— The lips quirked and MJ flicked her gaze up to his eyes, eyes fastened on her, eyes like dark honey that seemed to take her measure. Her heart beat a little faster and she darted a glance at her mother. Thankfully, she was looking at the stranger, too, but with irritation.

The lawyer stood and gestured to the man. "Mr. Montague, Mrs. Montague, MJ, this is Nikos Stefanopoulus, the late Mrs. Montague's business manager."

"And friend, I like to think." The man stepped forward, hand outstretched to her father. "My sympathies, Mr. Montague. Your mother was a fascinating and imaginative woman, and I will miss working with her."

Friend? He sounded as if he knew her better than MJ as of late. Guilt curdled in her stomach. Why had she let so much time go by?

"Mrs. Montague." He nodded at her mother. "MJ. I do apologize for my tardiness. And please, call me Nik."

He called her MJ, just as her grandmother had, not Marie Juliette as her mother insisted on doing. Narrowing her eyes at him, her mother said, "Mr. Lewis, now that Mr. Stefanopoulos is here, perhaps we could get started."

"Of course, of course." He waved a hand at Nik, who took the empty seat next to the lawyer, smoothing his grey-on-black striped tie to his chest. The lawyer looked at her father.

"Your mother's estate is in fine order. There are no outstanding debts except of a minimal amount on her two credit cards. As you might expect, since you, Mr. Montague, are her only child, she left most of her estate to you, along with this house and its furnishings."

"Most?" Her mother's tone was sharp.

"Er, yes, she left a few small bequests to organizations she supported and—"

"And this is where I come in," Nik interrupted.

MJ looked at him, then out the window to her left at the blue sky, instead of his striking features. She couldn't ignore the charm and attraction of the man, but her mother would not be happy with her for checking him out. Was he really just Gran's advisor?

"Mr. Montague," that whiskey-smooth voice continued, "your mother hired me to manage income and investments from her recent career."

What? Her gaze shot back to him.

Her mother leaned forward. Her brows drawn together. "A career? What kind of career? Do you know anything about this, Thomas?"

Her father opened his mouth to say something, but her mother barreled over him. "What? Did she knit afghans and sell them on that website, what's-its-name?"

MJ refrained from shaking her head. Knitting was not her grandmother's style at all. Or was it? After all, except for brief visits with the family at holidays, she hadn't spent any real time with her grandmother for... She swallowed against the persistent ache in her throat. She'd lost the one person in her life who loved her without measure, who encouraged her imagination and wildest dreams, even if it had gotten her in trouble. But how had she had a career if she had become as "dotty" as her mother implied?

"Martha, please, let Nik tell us what he is here to tell us." Her father dragged a hand down his face. Her mother sat back, crossing her arms and fixing her gaze on Nik, who had taken a card from his pocket. He looked at MJ.

"From the beginning, your grandmother intended that whatever success she had in her career," he held up his hand as her mother opened her mouth to speak, "which I will tell you more about in a moment, she intended it to be a legacy for you, Ms. Montague."

God, she wanted to crawl under the table. Her grandmother had thought of her even though MJ had done little in the last few years to warrant it. Sensing her distress, her father reached over and again covered her hands with his.

"What is this legacy?" her mother snapped. "Just tell us so we can go home."

The advisor flicked a glance at her mother, then turned his attention back to her, "Mrs. Montague's legacy includes the income from the stories she wrote and published over the last ten years..."

Remember, MJ, "once upon a time" are the most magical words in the world.

"...that paid for the purchase and maintenance for her second home where she spent most of her time in recent years writing, her cottage on Block Island. Her income also grew into a nice, as she called it, nest egg for her senior years." He reached inside his suit jacket and pulled out a small but bulky, blue envelope. "The cottage, the nest egg, the continuing income from royalties is all yours, Ms. Montague, if you meet one condition. In order to receive the legacy in its entirety, you must first spend the summer at the beach cottage on Block Island."

MJ closed her eyes. Sun and sand and sea flashed enticingly before her, but—

"Impossible. Marie Juliette has a dissertation to finish," her mother said.

The vision evaporated as MJ opened her eyes. Her father gripped MJ's hand tighter as her mind tried to process possibilities. Could she take so much time away from her research when she was already behind? Obviously, her mother wouldn't be happy if she did. But how could she possibly refuse her grandmother's last gift to her? Her last request? Surely, she could make this work.

She turned to the hunky man-of-affairs. "When you say spend the whole summer, do you mean I can't leave at all or that I have to spend most of my time there?"

"Marie Juliette, you cannot possibly—"

He interrupted her mother again. Brave man. "I know you are in the middle of research for your dissertation." How did he know that? "Your grandmother always thought some time at the beach might help, but she didn't intend for you to feel imprisoned there. You can, of course, leave the cottage for short periods of time to return here, but only for two or three nights at a time, according to your grandmother's wishes and the terms of the legacy."

Her mother frowned at her then turned to him. "Ridiculous! Of course, she can't spend her summer there. She has responsibilities here, practical matters to attend to. Typical."

He turned to her, brows raised.

"Tell him, MJ," her mother ordered, pointing at Nik, her brow raised, fully expecting her to comply. Like she always did to keep her mother happy.

Embarrassed, she wanted to crawl under the table, tea party or no tea party. She felt eight-years-old again. Torn between mother and grandmother. Her grandmother wanted to give her something, had thought of her even after all this time. Her mother expected her to do what had been laid out for her. Finish the dissertation, get her degree, and take up a full professorship at the same university where her mother was just steps away from becoming dean. Dare she deal with her mother's opposition? But the place where Gran wrote and wanted to share with her? MJ imagined her grandmother urging her to go. *The second most magic words, MJ, are 'What if?' With those magic words, almost anything is possible. Never doubt that.*

Her father said firmly, "Let her decide, Martha. The bequest is hers."

Hers. Away from her mother. Away from the university. Away. "I'll do it." She straightened, then forestalled her mother's next words. "Bad enough I allowed so much time to pass without visiting her. I didn't even know about the cottage. Did you, Dad?"

When he shrugged, she continued, "I will honor Gran's wishes, then I will decide what to do about this legacy."

The man looked at her, brows slightly raised. Was he surprised?

"Your grandmother," her mother emphasized the word because she hated it when her daughter used 'Gran', "with her usual disregard for the demands of the real world, did not stop to think how this would inconvenience others—and for what? A small little cottage with more dusty antiques?" She waved her hand at the antique pieces in the room.

Before she could disagree with her mother, Nik spoke up again, "I always found Mrs. Montague to be smart, generous, and considerate." *Was that a tic at his jaw? Was he angry with her mother? Wow, Gran had a champion, a knight ready to do battle for her. What would that be like?* "She had reasons for her request," his voice interrupted her imaginings, "which I will discuss with Ms. Montague at the cottage."

He pushed the card he had pulled from his jacket across the table to her. She reached to take it from him and almost yanked her hand back at the jolt that ran up her arm when his fingers touched hers. His eyes narrowed. "The address and phone number of the cottage are there, and I've written my cell phone number on the back. Will you need directions?"

Drawing the card back, she drew a breath as she shook her head, "I'll just plug it into my car's GPS.

He shoved the small blue envelope at her next. "These are keys to the cottage."

She took that too, feeling the bulk of the keys inside. "When do you want me there?"

She looked up from the card just in time to see his eyes with that assessing look in them again. Why? He cleared his throat. "The sooner, the better, Ms. Montague. Shall we say this Saturday?"

She nodded, caught in his gaze.

"Marie Juliette," her mother said, "You cannot possibly be serious about doing this."

Nik didn't take his gaze from her and she forgot to breathe. "I'll look forward to meeting with you then. I will let Mr. Lewis finish his business with you. Again, my condolences, Mr. Montague. Ms. Montague, please text me or call me when you are on your way. Good day."

He rose, shook her father's hand and left. She dragged in a breath. He had dominated the room and her mother. She blinked. Her father sighed, "Is that all, Mr. Lewis. Is there anything else I need to know or any other papers I need to sign right now?"

"Just a few more items here..."

MJ kept her gaze on her hands. She didn't want to see her mother's face, that look, whether of disappointment or anger.

"I think that is everything." The lawyer stacked his papers. "I'll send you a copy of everything for your records. Once your daughter meets with Mr. Stefanopoulos at the cottage, he'll send me a copy of the codicil about it, its contents, and the financials. I'll see you get a copy of all that as well." He rose and held out his hand to her father who stood to shake it.

"Martha, shall we go?" He pulled out MJ's chair for her. "I'm beat. It's been a long day."

MJ tucked her hand into the crook of her father's arm and walked with him out to the car. Her mother's irritation beat a staccato rhythm with her heels on the pavement as she followed behind. Even with all the childcare Gran provided for MJ when she was little, her mother had never been a fan. She settled into the front passenger seat of their car without a word, shoulders rigid. MJ slipped into the back seat, remembering with awe how that irritation hadn't quelled Gran's advisor one bit. She closed her eyes, recalling his intense regard, and his surprise when she agreed to investigate the legacy. She'd surprised herself. Where had she found the courage to risk her mother's disapproval?

A summer at the beach. Maybe she'd finally be able to focus on her research and get her dissertation done. The deadline drew close and she was having a hard time getting motivated. If her grandmother's cottage had a water view, she'd soak up every minute of it while she worked. In truth, it would be easier to work without her mother constantly checking on her. Yes, a summer at the beach sounded perfect.

But, she hoped, not too good to be true.

Chapter 2

MJ pushed through the door of The Hub, the popular hangout for the university's professors and students. In spite of the air conditioning, the temperature inside was warmer than outside. Students sat around dark wooden tables and in booths, shoveling in fries and slurping sodas. She recognized many of the men, professors, filling the bar stools and eating with gazes glued to the Red Sox baseball game on the TV above the rows of bottles behind the bar.

Her friend, Neri, stood at the far end of the bar, hair frizzing around her face, her cheeks flushed, and a towel thrown over her shoulder as she spoke with one of the men. MJ walked to an empty stool and sat down. Neri smiled at her as she walked by, said something to the man, wiped the spot in front of him with her towel and then came over to MJ.

"Give me a hug, you. I haven't seen you for a while."

MJ stood back up and stretched over the bar to do as her friend commanded, feeling the knots in her stomach loosen just a little.

"How did the meeting with your adviser go?" Neri asked.

The knots tightened back up. She shrugged. "Oh, you know. The usual. Am I certain I want to continue with this line of research? Am I really going to be finished and ready to defend at the end of the summer semester? Etcetera, etcetera. I spun him a story about how everything is on track and how much easier it will be to stay focused now that I am done teaching and grading papers for the semester. I didn't tell him about Gran dying and that I have to spend the summer on Block Island. Not that he'd care."

"Sorry to hear about your grandmother." Neri covered MJ's hand with her own. "How are you doing? And why are you spending summer on the island?"

MJ shrugged again and waited to respond until Neri had poured her a glass of tonic, dunked a slice of lime into it, and set it in front of her. She took a sip. "Thanks. The stay on the island is because I inherit her cottage and the rest of a legacy from her if I spend the summer there. I'm meeting Gran's man-of-affairs there to find out what the rest of the legacy is."

"Oooh, on an island with a man-of-affairs? Tell me more."

MJ smiled at her friend. "He was her financial advisor, but he is hunky"

"Hunky, huh?" Neri leaned over the bar and whispered, "Opportunities to take pics with your phone and send them to me?"

MJ thought about the man's dark skin against his pristine white collar. His eyes... She shook her head. "He's there for business. Nothing else. I think he shocked my mother, though, because he pretty much ignored her."

"Still, the beach, a hunk?"

MJ smiled. "Business, remember? And my dissertation. Let's not forget that. Mother sure won't," she said the last under her breath. "Anyway, he needs to go over stuff with me. And as soon as he's done, I'm putting my head down and finishing the Big D. I need to get it, and Mother, off my back."

"Are you sure you want to spend the summer on the island. Seems like there is always too much to do and not enough time to do it?"

And Neri would know. She worked harder than anyone MJ had ever met, including her mother.

"I can't complain. Look at you, holding down two jobs while working on your degree. How's the job at the art museum?"

Neri shrugged, "It's fine. What do you want to order? You are going to eat something, aren't you?"

MJ ordered a cup of soup. The knots in her stomach were loosening, but not enough to eat anything heavy, as she knew from experience. Every time she met with her adviser, she ended up feeling stupid, inept, and incapable of writing a worthy dissertation, let alone finishing it on time. She suspected he was a bit of a misogynist. Unfortunately, departmental politics and schedules made him the only choice she had had.

Neri slid the cup of chicken noodle soup and the packet of crackers in front of her. "Anything else?"

"No, I have to get back and pack." She leaned over to breathe in the aroma of chicken, cream, and thyme. *Ahhh.* She slipped that first spoonful into her mouth and savored the flavor and its heat, tracing its way to her stomach. One spoonful followed another, and soon the knots in her stomach were gone with the soup. Neri served up a drink to one customer, cleared an empty glass off the bar, then rang up a customer and sent him on his way with her smile—which disappeared as soon as he turned away.

"Neri," she called to her friend, who had moved further down the bar to remove empty dishes.

"Why don't you come with me—to the island—for a few days?" Having Neri with her would help mitigate some of her grief. Her friend had a talent for coaxing a laugh from her. Plus... "You could use a break."

Neri shoved her confusion of curls back behind her ears and shook her head, immediately setting a few of the curls free again. "I'd love to, then I could meet Mr. Man-of-Affairs. But I can't, not right now at the end of the semester. Possibly later." They grinned at each other. MJ rose, reached across the bar to give her friend another hug, handed her the bill and cash for the meal with a generous tip.

"Let me get you your change."

"Keep it. Put it toward your travel fund."

"Have fun," Neri called as MJ headed toward the door. But did she know how to have fun anymore?

"Marie Juliette, you can't afford to go traipsing off to the beach. I'm sorry about your grandmother, but you need to work on your dissertation, especially since you decided to include those forgotten novelists."

MJ paused her packing to rub at her forehead. She'd "decided" to include that bit at the behest of her mother who said it would add verity and weight, but didn't say researching them would slow her down. All week, her mother came up with one argument after another for not going to the island. Truly, it would be easier to just give in—as usual. But Gran... She straightened and shook her head, turning back to her dresser. "I owe this to Gran."

"Ridiculous, you don't owe her anything, Marie Juliette. She's dead. Don't let her hold some old cottage by the ocean over your head to make you do what she wants."

MJ's fingers tightened on the bottle of lotion she intended to pack in her toiletries case, surprised at how badly she wanted to throw it. But that would be unladylike. Instead, she thrust the lotion into the case, and silently counted to ten. Her hairbrush and comb went into the bag, then she zipped it closed. Did she have everything? She scanned the room.

Her mother sat down on the bed next to her, smoothing her skirt. "This isn't like you, Marie Juliette, to go haring off, when you have important work to do. For what? To spend your summer at some ramshackle out-of-the-way beach cottage on some loopy old woman's whim. The place is probably overrun with vermin."

Her mother shuddered at the thought. Well, that should keep her away for a while, at least. MJ opened her mouth to respond, but her mother talked over her. "That dissertation deadline is looming and it's highly unlikely that the committee will give you any wiggle room because of the passing of your grandmother. Now is not the time to get sentimental."

MJ took several deep breaths. Honoring the gift of someone you'd loved and lost was sentimental? Couldn't her mother give her a hug, sympathize with her feelings and send her off, telling her to work hard but have a good summer? She remembered Gran's warm hugs. *No, don't go there.*

When she didn't say anything, but only closed her suitcase and zipped it, her mother added, "And I don't trust this so-called financial advisor. Why did your grandmother even need one? He was probably bilking her of the little she had. I don't like that he's going to meet you there alone. What if he tries something?"

She sighed. What decade did her mother think they were living in? Did she expect the sophisticated Mr. Stephanopoloous to go on a rampage? Remembering that mouth and those shoulders, she sighed. Heck, would she mind if he did?

"Why don't you just have him put the cottage up for sale and be done with it? Besides, it's not as if you two had a close relationship."

Anger made her mouth move before she thought. "Of course not. I just met him a few days ago."

Her mother surged to her feet. "That's not funny, Marie Juliette. I am only looking out for your welfare, as a mother should."

Now she played the mother card? MJ was a twenty-five-years-old adult. A bit late for the mother card when her apparent priorities over the years always seemed to be career and reputation. MJ figured she maybe came in third behind her father. She took a deep breath.

"Why do you think I'll sell the cottage?"

"Why not? When you get your degree, you are sure to be offered a position in my department at the university. You can't commute from the island, and you'll probably be too busy to spend much time there."

She was so tempted to point out that her mother wasn't dean yet. Her stomach knotted at the thought of her mother being her boss, so she shoved it away.

"I can't decide what to do with the cottage until I see it. It would be foolish to turn down the income, as well."

Her mother shrugged off her concerns. "A shack and a few hundred dollars, I'm sure."

"Nevertheless, I can't sell what I don't own. So off I go."

She lifted her suitcase to the floor and raised the handle, then wheeled it past her mother, who followed her to the front door of her apartment. Her wheeled laptop case was there, already packed with laptop, research folders, and several books.

"I suppose I'll have to come to the island to check out real estate agents with you and help prepare the cottage for sale. I'll see if there is a hotel nearby."

The knots in MJ's stomach tightened. She shrugged. "Suit yourself, but you may want to wait until I've had time to settle paperwork and such with Gran's financial advisor. I won't be able to make any decisions until then. After that, I need to focus on the dissertation, remember? I appreciate the offer, but it's not necessary. I'm a big girl. I'll handle this."

Her mother shook her head. "A big girl, a responsible adult, would make the decision to stay here." She picked up her leather purse from the small table near the door. "I'll call you soon to see how you are coming along." She walked through the door MJ opened. As her mother drove away, MJ loosened her grip on the doorknob and took another deep breath. To think of being hours away from her mother for days or even weeks.

She pulled her car keys from the basket hanging next to the door and after closing and locking the door behind her, towed the luggage to her car, a bright red Mini Cooper. She loved the little car, and how easy it was to maneuver and park, especially in the limited space at the university. Plus, the gas mileage was great. She opened the trunk and lifted her bags inside the small space, then stopped to listen to a cardinal calling from a nearby pine. Smiling, she slid inside and buckled up, then turned the key, input the address of the ferry that would take her to Block Island into the GPS, and drove out of the complex. Within a few miles, she relaxed her grip on the steering wheel.

Maybe if she'd gotten her priorities straight years ago, the close relationship with her grandmother wouldn't have remained broken. But she'd do her best to honor her grandmother's last wishes. In spite of everything. And everyone.

"I'm coming, Gran."

Thalassa, and her two sisters, stared intently down into the small tidal pool encircled by rough black rocks. Her older sister, Pelagia, pointed at the image, rippling slightly in the water. "There she is, lost, just as we planned. My work with the currents obviously messed with her four-wheeled chariot's compass."

"Car," Thalassa corrected her. "You know this, Pelagia, so why do you insist on calling it a chariot?"

Pelagia shrugged. "There is no magic in the word."

True. The word served as a reminder that the world had moved on in all these amazing ways, while she and her sisters remained stuck on the island of Elpida. The name meant hope. What a joke. She and her sisters had lived on the island for so long that it was now called Sirenuse. The hope of getting off it grew dimmer every century.

She blew out a breath. They would never get off if she let the heat of her anger guide her. They had work to do.

Pelagia said, "Thalassa, blow upon the water—gently, mind. We want a fog, not a storm."

As Thalassa bent over the water breathing her warm breath upon it, Pelagia told the youngest sister, "Leucothea, put a small spell on this woman to make her sleepy."

"But, she'll crash, maybe die. I do not want to harm her."

Thalassa looked up as her older sister curled and uncurled her hands. "Patience, sister." They both knew that the youngest of them had a tender heart and fascination for mortals, forgetting and forgiving the evil they did.

"Fine, then make her tired," Pelagia said. "Tired enough that she'll give up searching for the old woman's cottage and find an inn instead. Her failure to appear will insult Nikos so he will change his mind about working with her. I'll continue to confuse the chariot's compass."

And that was what was important. Thwart Nikos so he quit trying to help every mortal who imagined they could create like the gods. Then maybe he would return.

Thalassa blew that thought out as she blew gently on the water. Pelagia leaned over the pool and slowly moved her hand counterclockwise. Though relegated to this island of rocks and cliffs, and the salt waters of the oceans, far from the abodes of others, they still had their magic and their songs. The Muses hadn't been able to take those from them, believing Thalassa and her sisters confined to the island and its environs. The sisters, though, had discovered they could travel anywhere there was saltwater, and guarded their secret.

As they worked together, Pelagia sang. Softly at first, like the fog creeping in to surround the woman in her car. Deeply, like the dark of the night sky. Discordantly, like the fatigue and confusion the woman should be feeling as Leucothea whispered her spell.

The Muses may have taken their wings, but...

Wings or no wings, they were still Sirens.

Nik climbed reluctantly from the car, recalling his last time here and how much Juliette enjoyed riding in the car with him, along the island's winding roads, as a much-needed break from her writing. No other car was in the driveway or parked on the verge so he assumed the granddaughter wasn't waiting for him.

The car door closed with a soft thunk that spoke of its solid craftsmanship. It may not be Greek, but Italian was close enough, and he was grateful for Juliette's encouragement to buy it. Cars were just one of the mechanical inventions of mortals that he loved. The speed, the rumble of the engine, the luxurious comfort of the ride was a big improvement over the disorientation of portals or the challenge of staying on Pegasus' broad back. He should have said no to her donation to its purchase, but he couldn't deny her the pleasure of it, even if it had aroused feelings of not just gratitude but closeness, connection. As if he were her grandson. But he didn't want to dim her smile, or deny himself of one of the few freely given gifts from a mortal.

Just to be sure, he knocked on the door, but no one answered. MJ had not arrived yet. Good. He didn't want to keep her waiting. From what he'd seen at the reading of the will, if MJ was anything like her mother, she would not appreciate his tardiness. But then, if she was like her grandmother... The granddaughter surprised him when she accepted the condition of the legacy. The way the mother tried to control the discussion, he was convinced MJ would cave to her mother's concerns and demands, and braced for the disappointment of Juliette's earnings going to a charity instead of her granddaughter. Of course, he would be off the hook then and able to take an assignment that didn't carry so much emotional resonance for him. Or, better yet, not take any assignment.

He checked his watch. She should arrive soon—unless she changed her mind. He checked his cell phone for a message from her. Nothing. The late afternoon breeze carried the scent of ocean and freedom to him, so this time, he slipped his polished Italian loafers from his feet, pulled off his socks and stuffed them inside, turned up the cuffs of his slacks, loosened his tie and strolled toward the beach. The sand was still warm under his feet, but a cool mist from the pounding waves kissed the tops. He stood, hands in his pockets, watching the sea.

It looked different here than on Mt. Helicon. He inhaled deeply. Under normal circumstances, he would have had a break to visit with his mother and his aunts, to take it easy for a while before receiving another assignment, but these weren't normal circumstances. The white streak in his mother's hair reminded him of that. Too, this was the first time he'd ever worked with two individuals from the same family line, one right after the other. Juliette's legacy to her granddaughter left no room for delay, and Marie Juliette was going to be a challenge.

"I don't know what I did," Juliette said one day as they talked about her intentions for the cottage and the rest. "We used to be so close. We had such fun together, playing dress up and telling each other stories. Until her mother arrived one day to pick up MJ and accused me of confusing her daughter by letting her spend too much time playing make-believe. Apparently, something happened at her school that, according to her mother, indicated MJ didn't know when to stop playing make believe, something that embarrassed them both. When I asked her what happened, she just shook her head. After that, she never asked me to take care of MJ again. And when I offered, or wanted her to come for a visit, she never came alone. Tea parties under the table with her mother watching every move killed all the fun. After a while, her mother was too busy. Or MJ was."

He curled his toes in the sand, remembering the pain and sorrow in Juliette's voice, the tears in her eyes. He'd wanted to reach out and hug her, but he was supposed to be her business manager, not her family. Instead, he took her hand for a moment and then went back to recording instructions for her lawyer. Despite the separation, Juliette wanted her granddaughter to be happy, and she'd done what she could to give the young woman time to explore the possibilities. As he continued to write, Juliette had laid her hand over his, "What would make you happy, Nik?"

His breath caught in his chest. Had anyone, even his mother, ever asked him that question before? The power of the question was so big that he was tempted to give a throw-away answer, "World peace and a trip to Disney."

For centuries, he'd served his mother and Apollo as intermediary between Muse and mortal, a gateway to ideas and inspiration, to stories. Through walking in their dreams, through little nudges, and sometimes direct suggestions, he transmitted the inspiration and ideas to his mortal clients to write stories that commanded large audiences of readers or, in the case of playwrights, viewers. He'd been endlessly fascinated by the mortal ability to take one idea, one theme or inspiration and go off in a million different directions. Truly, it still astounded him.

Gazing out at the twilight sky, he recalled how Will Shakespeare had been great fun as he wrote his love stories and comedies. No one could shape sonnets or add that wry twist of humor to a lover's situation quite like Will. He still laughed to think of Titania kissing that ass-headed mortal. He'd also enjoyed helping the Grimm Brothers shape those fairy tales they collected from the old women and mothers in the hills and forests of Europe. In more recent centuries, he'd frequently found himself working with women, like Miss Jane, as he'd been instructed to call her, and Juliette.

On the rare occasion, he'd done more than inject ideas for stories into his mortals. Sometimes, he'd warmed their beds and their bodies, giving heat and passion to the stories they wrote, but he made sure to abide by Apollo's edict to keep his emotions out of the relationship. Respect and passion, yes. Love? No.

Finally, he answered Juliette's question. Then, she pestered him until he bought the Ferrari.

"I know you have the money, Nik. Look what you've done for me. And I'll help you buy it. Let's go."

He smiled, remembering how she'd grabbed her handbag, taken his arm and steered him to the front door. Once off the ferry, they'd cabbed it to a dealer who promised delivery in weeks. Pride and delight lit her face the first time he'd driven it to the cottage, and now her home stood empty.

He scanned the water, then turned from the sea to stare at the cottage perched on a small rise. Empty now of the warm cheerfulness and honest interests of Juliette. He shook his head. If his mother knew what he was feeling, if Apollo guessed how much he'd come to care for the old woman, almost like a second mother. He cut that thought off, glancing down at his watch.

Juliette's granddaughter apparently did not have her grandmother's respect for time.

Chapter 3

MJ turned on the MINI Cooper's fog lamps, relieved when she could actually see more than a few feet in front of the car's bumper.

How had she so badly lost her way? Once the ferry arrived at Block Island, she was sure she knew where she was going as she drove off it. But finding her grandmother's cottage had confused both her GPS and her. She'd spent the last hour or so driving around on dirt roads with no idea of where she was. How was that even possible on an island this size?

"In one mile, turn right onto Sweet Rose Avenue," the oh-so-calm voice of her car's navigation system instructed.

Right? Again? Hadn't the last three turns been rights? Was she going in circles? In this fog, she couldn't tell if anything looked familiar. She should have printed off the directions from the Internet and then checked them against an actual atlas. She shouldn't trust someone else's directions, even ones delivered in a smooth-talking woman's voice.

"In one hundred feet, turn left."

"Left! I haven't even turned right yet, you idiot."

"There is no need to be rude," the voice calmly said.

MJ wanted to punch the dashboard and that was what made her pull over and take a deep breath. She peered into the deepening darkness, but her tired eyes burned with fatigue and the dry heat from the car's vents. She snapped it off. Trying to peer through the murk to anticipate turns and road signs had worn her out. She leaned her head back against the head rest. If someone came along right now and offered her a room for the night and it was just twenty feet down the road, she'd take it, even if it had "Bates Motel" lit up in neon above the lobby door.

A nap tempted her, but Mr. Stefanopoulos was waiting for her. She sighed. Searching for location and directions on her phone wasn't working. No signal, and only a couple of bars to make a call. She yawned. Unless she wanted to sleep in the car and seriously annoy that man-of-affairs, she better look for a street sign or a road marker. She put the car in gear and drove further down the road. Her plan had been to get to the cottage, spend the next few days learning everything she needed to know about Gran's finances and the rest of the legacy, and then get back to work on her dissertation. If the cottage wasn't exactly comfortable, she could work at a local coffee shop or on the beach. But first she had to find the place!

"In twenty feet, make a right turn."

"Oh, shut up!" MJ switched off the navigation, just as a left turn emerged from the fog. She pulled over to the shoulder of the road, put the car in park, and climbed out after grabbing the flashlight in the glove compartment. She stood for a moment, realizing how dark and quiet it was, especially with no one around. The sound of the waves and the smell of the ocean drifted to her, but for all she knew, she was the only person on another planet. She imagined her mother's rebuke for letting her imagination run away with her. "I should never have let you spend so much time with your grandmother. She never had both feet on the ground."

Well, her feet were firmly on the road, so she flicked on the flashlight. The fog appeared to thicken. Ears pricked, she walked quietly to the turn off and, relieved to find a road sign, beamed her light up at it.

"Homer's Way," she read aloud. She snorted, "Does that make me Odysseus?"

Oh-oh, she was getting punchy. No time to waste. She hurried back to the car, sliding gratefully into its warmth and safety. She doubted she had to worry about someone attacking her, but the fog was creeping her out. Reluctantly, she picked up her phone, then pulled out the business manager's card and dialed the number.

"Hello?" Crisp, sharp even.

"Uh, Mr. Stefanopoulos, this is MJ, Marie Juliette Montague?"

"Finally! Where are you? I expected you an hour or more ago?"

She cleared her throat. "Yes, I know. I'm sorry about that. I'm lost. My car's navigation system doesn't seem to be working. I've been driving around on the island for at least an hour, and I have no idea where I am in relation to the cottage. I was wondering if you might give me directions?"

"Where are you?"

"I'm at the intersection of Beach Road and Homer's Way. Do you know where that is? Can you give me directions?"

"Just stay where you are. I'll be right there."

"But, can't you just..." He'd hung up before she could finish. *Why not just give her directions?*

She shrugged. She'd done all that she could, and now that she didn't have to worry about driving through the fog, she realized she was hungry. She'd eaten lunch hours ago, planning on being at the cottage before dinner and getting something to eat before settling in. Dragging over the insulated pouch she always took with her on trips, she turned on the overhead light, zipped open the pouch and searched through empty wrappers. A small bag of toasted almonds, packs of mixed dried fruit, and finally found a cheese stick. She started to pull it out.

Rap! Rap, rap!

She shrieked and the pouch went flying, landing on the floor, its contents scattered. Hand to her heart, checking her door locks, she looked out her window at the shadowy form of a man leaning over her car. Quickly, she pushed the car's door lock again, then she turned the key in the ignition.

Rap, rap!

"Ms. Montague," the voice yelled through the window. Even muffled by the glass, she could hear her name and the tone of irritation. *How did the man know her name? What to do? What to do?*

"Ms. Montague," he yelled again, "it's me. Nik."

Nik? As in her grandmother's Nik? Oh, thank goodness. She dragged in a breath as she lowered the window just an inch.

"Mr. Stefanopoulos? You frightened me."

"My apologies. I suppose I did suddenly loom out of the fog." She heard the smile in his voice. She felt silly. "Do you want me to drive back to the cottage. It will be easier."

"But..." She turned to look back over her shoulder. "Where is your car?"

"I was out walking when you called. I wasn't far from here."

Walking? On a night like tonight? Strange. Still, she wasn't going to cavil about his personal habits when he was rescuing her. She opened the car door and he stepped back, holding onto it with one hand, and offering his other hand to help her out, a warm, strong hand. Tingles rushed up her arm and down her spine.

What was that? She pulled away, curling her fingers into her palm. Taking a breath, she hurried around the back of her car, yanked on the passenger door handle, and almost yanked her arm out when the handle didn't budge.

"Uh, could you press the unlock button, please..."

He was staring at his hand, but he looked up, then the door lock clicked, and she slid into the passenger seat, surreptitiously brushing wrappers, and fruit packs from the seat to the floor. She'd pick them up later. Carefully, he folded himself into the driver's seat.

"Oops, sorry, I didn't think about how small the car is for someone like you."

He fiddled with the side of the seat and, finding the seat adjustment, slid it all the way back. "No problem." He winked at her, then put the car in gear.

She reached up and turned off the overhead light, plunging them back into darkness with only the blue-white glow of the dashboard to illuminate the interior, and eerily light up his profile, long elegant nose above a full mouth set in a beard-shadowed jaw. And eyelashes. Even in the dim light, they were long and dark beneath a high forehead, draped by inky, softly wavy hair. He glanced over at her and she shivered.

"What's wrong with your GPS? Wasn't it working earlier?"

"Yes." She shivered again and sat forward to adjust the car's heat. "It was fine until I drove off the ferry. Then it went crazy. After a while, I thought I might be driving in circles. Must be something on the island interfering with the signal."

"Hmmm," Nik murmured. Never mind that. How could he be so careless? He should have waited a few minutes before arriving at the car. But no, he had to appear at her car like some genie out of a bottle. Stupid, stupid, stupid. Apollo would have fried him if he'd seen him do that.

But he hadn't been thinking, he'd been worried. The MJ that Juliette had talked about was a very responsible person who, even though she might not visit her grandmother, at least wrote regularly—and called. She'd never missed her regular, though short, monthly call to her grandmother. As the minutes, then an hour and more passed and she hadn't arrived, he wondered at first if she changed her mind. He became concerned, especially as it grew dark and foggy. Oddly, the fog had dissipated.

"I don't get it," she said quietly. "Why were you out walking in the dark? How did you find me so fast?"

He shifted in the small confines of the car seat. "I was restless—and concerned. You were late. You didn't call, and I couldn't reach you, so, since I was tired of pacing your grandmother's driveway, I decided walking was better. Fortunately, I was close by when you called." Silence. Well, as they said, a good defense was offense. "Why didn't you call me sooner and let me know you were lost?"

She faced forward and crossed her arms, as the scent of roses drifted to him, and he shifted again. "I kept thinking that the cottage was just another mile, or beyond the next turn, so I kept going. I meant to call earlier but my signal was blocked most of the time, so I kept going. I'd still be driving but I could barely keep my eyes open."

More silence. "Why would you go walking in those shoes and your suit?"

Nik repressed a smile. Smart woman, just like her grandmother. And persistent, also like her grandmother. He'd have to watch himself around her. "I wasn't planning on running a marathon, Ms. Montague. I just wanted to stretch my legs."

"Please, call me MJ."

Good, since that was how he thought of her after years with Juliette. "Not Marie or Marie Juliette?"

"No!" Sharp. "Marie doesn't fit me. And Marie Juliette makes me sound like a belle from the South, too formal. Only Mother insists on calling me Marie Juliette," she sighed, "and I wish she wouldn't."

"Then why does she, if you don't like it?"

Another sigh as he turned onto the street for the cottage. "My mother loves the full name. I think she hopes if she keeps calling me that name, I'll somehow become this ladylike, graceful..."

Her words trailed off as he turned into the driveway and the motion-sensitive light for the drive and the front of the cottage came on. He'd also left one light on in the living room. It wasn't the first view he preferred she have but it would do.

He shut off the car and turned to look at her. She was staring open-mouthed.

MJ liked the word "dumbfounded." She and her grandmother had collected fun words from the very first. When she babysat, Gran never read the books her mother deemed acceptable, instead, she read myths and fairy tales, sometimes illustrated, sometimes not. Whenever a word popped up MJ didn't know, her grandmother wrote it down in a special notebook kept just for that purpose, until MJ was old enough to first print, then write in it herself.

Dumbfounded was one of those words MJ recorded herself. Looking up the definition gave her another great word to add, gobsmacked. Now, as she peered out at the dimly-lit silhouette of her grandmother's cottage, both words aptly fit her response to the view in front of her—speechless with amazement, caught off guard by something extraordinary.

"So," Nik touched her shoulder, "what do you think?"

She blinked. And remembered her mother's nose-wrinkling disdain as she said, "Really, Marie Juliette, there is absolutely no need for you to spend your summer at some ramshackle out-of-the-way beach shack on some crazy old-woman whim of your grandmother's. The place is probably overrun with vermin."

Ramshackle. Beach shack. Overrun with vermin.

Her grandmother's cottage was as much a cottage as an Adirondack camp was a camp. In other words, large, impressive, and, from what she could see from the security lights, beautiful. Yep, she was dumbfounded.

She giggled. She couldn't help it. She tilted her head back and laughed, then laughed some more. If her mother only...

"MJ?"

She held up her hand as she gasped, trying to get her laughter under control. "Oh, good grief! When my mother sees this. Well, no worries there. But, Gran? Oh, Gran..." And just like that, she was finally crying. Crying for the woman who, even in her absence, had been more of a mother than her mother. Why hadn't she ignored her mother's demands and insidious words? More tears welled even as she tried to choke back the sobs that pushed in her chest. Frantically, she popped open the glove compartment and searched for tissues, her hand shuffling through the contents since she could hardly see through her tears. Where were the tissues?

"Here."

A pristine white handkerchief was shoved into her hands. She pressed it to her eyes, catching a whiff of sun and sea as she tried to press back the grief that insisted on spilling out. He shifted and his strong warm arm wrapped around her and pulled her closer. The warmth and solidity of his chest sheltered her while she cried, and felt as though her grief was shared. Finally, she drew back, pulling in a ragged breath. Grateful for the darkness, she wiped her eyes and blew her nose.

"Okay now?" His voice was soft, concerned.

She nodded and straightened, looking out the side window, the damp handkerchief balled in her hand. "I'm sorry. I don't know why I did that. I'm tired and..." she gestured at the cottage again, smiling to think of Gran calling it that even in the will, "this was so unexpected and funny and just like her."

She swallowed back the tears that still threatened.

"Your grandmother was definitely something special."

She turned to look at him in the light and shadows of the car. She couldn't see his eyes clearly but he sounded sincere. *How close had he been to her grandmother anyway?* She looked back at the cottage, which was not a mansion by her mother's definition, but wasn't a small cottage either. Rather, it stood large and tall, bigger than her parents' home from the looks of it, with board and batten siding and a steeply pitched roof, typical of built-for-winter-snows New England homes. And welcoming, noting the porch with a light that illuminated the red front door. She couldn't help the giggle that escaped just before a hiccup.

"What's so funny?"

"Mother assumed Gran's cottage was a ramshackle ruin overrun with vermin." She looked at Nik in time to see the gleam of white teeth in a smile that seemed almost wolfish. *The better to eat you with, my dear.* She really was exhausted. Or losing her mind.

"Because of the rift between your mother and your grandmother, she kept this and everything in the cottage a secret... for you. So you'd have a place all your own to let your imagination run free from the expectations and confines of your home. Her words." He opened his door a crack but paused before the interior light came on. "Her secrets are yours to discover and explore and then decide whether or not they remain secrets. Meanwhile, shall we go in? I imagine you are exhausted."

We? "Are you staying here too?"

He hesitated, the car door slightly ajar and the sounds of ocean waves whispering in. "Of course. I always stayed here when I was working with her. What with the length of the ferry ride and such, she didn't want me wasting time going back and forth. She kept a room ready for me. And even if I wanted to stay elsewhere, it's really too late for me to do so. Is this going to be a problem?"

She barely knew this tall, dark, and yes handsome man who had lent her his clean handkerchief. Still, her grandmother was the best reference there was. *Was she really going to turn him away? What would her mother think? Really, that was her concern? How old are you, MJ? Get a grip!*

"No, of course not, Nik, certainly you can stay here. It will let us get an early start in the morning." And with that she slipped out of her car and stared up at the magical place that was hers, all hers. Her own home. From Gran. The sound of the ocean was louder and a soft night breeze lifted the hair around her face, carrying the scent of the sea.

I'm here, Gran. I'm here.

Thalassa slammed her hand into the tide pool, exploding the vision of the female mortal and that traitorous Nikos, and soaking her sisters.

"I told you to put a sleeping spell on her, Leucothia. Better she crash and die, or spend weeks in a hospital than be rescued by him."

Her sister reached out and patted her arm. Patted her! "You don't mean that, Thalassa. You can't mean that. That would be cruel."

"And being permanently banned to this island isn't? Why should I care about an insignificant mortal who will be gone in the blink of Saturn's eye? They are just tools."

Pelagia just shook her head, but Leucothia opened her mouth to protest Thalassa was sure, but she wasn't going to give her sister the chance. She shot up from her place on the rocks and strode off. Her sisters could sit staring out over the ocean waters waiting for the next ship to appear but not her. She was hungry and her mind didn't work at its best if she was hungry, so first she would eat, then, she would plan.

She hated Nikos, he of the dark eyes and broad chest, remembering the warm strength of that chest against her breasts. She'd given herself to him long ago, before...before she'd lost her wings. And he'd taken her, not once, but many times, in the fullness of spring as blossoms lost their petals and the fruit started to swell. Before she'd been cast here with her sisters like so much offal.

He'd gone his way, to serve his mother and Apollo. Now, no male entered her bed on this gods-forsaken island. The mortals that washed up on its shores pleasured her on the sand or not at all. They were not fit to enter her bed, and they had no staying power. Not like Nikos. And to see him holding that weak mortal woman while she cried! Bad enough to be the intermediary for his mother, to whisper words and ideas and visions from Erato into mortal minds, but to allow a mortal to cry on him as he held her? Thalassa threw back her head and shrieked. Leaves dropped from a nearby tree, and the ground shook beneath her.

Drawing a deep breath, she entered the stone building that sheltered them, and headed to the pantry. In one basket sat a hunk of goat's cheese beneath a linen cloth. After slicing off a wedge, and tearing off a chunk of dark bread scrounged from a recent shipwreck, Thalassa returned outside to sit beneath one of the few olive trees on the island.

The Muses thought she and her sisters were helpless here, a belief fed and reinforced by their mother. They and the rest of that arrogant pantheon were in for a surprise. Thalassa had just begun stirring the pot of trouble she was capable of.

And today's work was only the beginning.

Chapter 4

*W*hat in Hades just happened?

Nik led MJ up the path to the wide steps of Juliette's cottage as he tried to rein back his emotional stew. Do not get emotionally involved with your mortal was the primary rule he and the others had hammered into them by their mothers and Apollo. If they were to fully serve the Muses, and bring back the power and magic of creativity in the world, they could not get involved on a personal level. This was a mission, an assignment. Nothing more.

Over the centuries, he'd faithfully followed that rule. No mortal had snared his emotions. He was stunned, confused, and finally dismayed to find his own throat tight as MJ cried for Juliette. Probably just the surprise of MJ's emotional response. Other than the phone calls, she'd been relatively absent from her grandmother's life for so long, according to Juliette. He assumed the young woman was a cold-hearted, self-absorbed bitch. Sorry, Juliette. But here she was, and her response to the cottage, first the laughter then the tears? What in Hades? Even after all these centuries, he just didn't understand mortals.

He stuck the key in the cottage door lock and braced himself as he swung it open. What would she do next? He stepped back to allow MJ to enter. She brushed past him, wafting the scent of roses as her thick braid moved with her steps, its length pointing to her nicely rounded ass cupped by form-fitting jeans. He shook his head and shifted, glad for the softer fabric of his slacks.

MJ halted in the soft light from the lamp Juliette always left on. Whenever he arrived late, Juliette had the light burning for him and, on the simple dark wood table next to it, a plate with a slice of her famous chocolate cake or a few of her decadent brownies. Tonight, the table was empty of treats, and he shoved away the stab of sadness. The lamp's bronze base held a figure of a mermaid gleefully riding a dolphin leaping over a wave, the mermaid's hair curving and swirling like the sea waters. Reins of twisted seaweed curved from the dolphin's smiling mouth to the left hand of the mermaid. The shade of the lamp, made of capiz shell, curved over them in the shape of a scallop shell.

MJ stood blinking in the light. He waited for her to take in the entry hall, its plush rug in creams and blues, the lamp, and the one picture on the wall next to the lamp that greeted Juliette—and him—upon every arrival.

"Oh, Gran!" she whispered, moving to the picture and stretching out a hand to touch it.

This was not the MJ he expected after his time with Juliette. After all, except for the phone calls, cards on birthdays, and Juliette's visits to her family at Christmas, this woman had been mostly absent from her grandmother's life. But, as her fingers caressed the glass over the face of her grandmother, curiosity rose.

What had kept her from her grandmother and her life here?

MJ used Nik's handkerchief to wipe away a few lingering tears as she caressed the framed photograph. There she was, probably no more than five or six, sitting on Gran's comfortable lap, in her overstuffed armchair while she read to her. Memories of shared stories and storytelling, of warm cookies and milk before bedtime, and games of make believe.

She peered closer. Yep, the book was that collection of fairy tales that her grandmother had given her and she had rescued from the trash in her mother's kitchen and stored—hidden away, actually—first in her father's study, and now, somewhere in her condo. She recalled the beautiful illustrations of the princesses.

"My father must have taken this picture," she whispered, noting how her grandmother's head was bent over hers, their cheeks touching.

"She loved that picture and always pressed a kiss to it with her fingers when she arrived home from her errands or outings." Nik's voice was soft as he leaned against the far wall, his arms crossed.

"How would you know?" It irked her that he seemed to know so much more about her grandmother than she did.

"I spent a lot of time here. We'd go out for lunch or dinner, or to run some of her banking errands, and when we returned, she walked in the door, hung up her coat, then gave that photo a finger kiss, as if she was greeting a sacred icon. I never saw her not do it."

Grief and guilt roared up and washed over her. Too late now. When her mother stopped taking her to Gran's, she'd been too young to do more than cry. All that did was get her time alone in her room "until you can be reasonable again." But when she got older? No excuse. No damned excuse. She reached up to rub the tears and the memories from her eyes. This man who appeared to know more about her grandmother than she did, said something under his breath and then touched her arm.

"You must be exhausted. Let me show you where you can sleep. I'll give you the tour tomorrow."

She nodded, exhausted physically and emotionally. She bent to pick up her suitcase, but he grabbed it first, lifting it with ease and motioning with his head to the staircase that led from the entry.

"After you."

She grabbed the stair rail and half pulled herself up the steps, while repeatedly swallowing against the ache in her chest that kept climbing into her throat.

"The door on the left," he said behind her. She pushed open the door and fumbled for the light switch.

"Here," he reached in and flicked the light on, "it's lower than you'd expect."

A large, king-sized bed dominated the room, with four-posters, carved headboard and footboard made from a dark red wood, and decorated with a beautiful wedding ring quilt in light blues and pales greens against a white background, topped by a pile of decorator pillows. Beautiful, luxurious, and a welcome sight after her long day.

"This was your grandmother's room," Nik said softly. "I thought...well, I thought since it has its own bathroom, you'd prefer it."

She was afraid to open her mouth. Instead, she concentrated on breathing and just nodded. Part of her would have welcomed the sterile environment of a hotel room, a room empty of memories, but the other part of her... "Thank you," she managed.

He cleared his throat and moved across the room to open a door. A closet. He set her suitcase down on a bench next to it. Then he gestured to another door that stood slightly ajar.

"The bathroom."

Bleary-eyed, she watched Nik move around the room as if he was at home here. She shook her head. What was she thinking? She wasn't, that was the problem. The day had beaten her down, first with the fight with her mother, then the frustrating drive, and now a cottage that wasn't a cottage. And a man who seemed too much at home. Her eyes sought the bed. She just wanted to crawl under the covers and—

"I'll see you in the morning."

She started and looked over her shoulder. Nik stood at the bedroom door.

"I'll see you in the morning," he repeated. "You look ready to collapse. Get to bed. I'll lock up."

She opened her mouth to thank him, but he was gone, closing the door behind him before she could get the words out. She swayed. She really was exhausted. Her curiosity about the room and everything else about the surprising cottage would have to wait.

MJ stepped out of her shoes and pulled off her badly-wrinkled linen jacket. The matching skirt fell to the floor, followed by the knit top. She padded across the thick carpet to the bathroom, and didn't even bother turning on the light, finding her way to the toilet to pee and then wash her hands. After shoving the pile of decorator pillows to the other side of the bed, she turned off the light, and walked carefully back to the bed. Turning back the quilt and summer blanket, she slid in between the crisp white sheets, still in her bra and panties. She hadn't brushed her teeth, or washed her face. Her mother would be horrified.

She didn't care. The bed linens smelled of fresh air, sunshine, and some sweet spicy scent, maybe lavender, reminding her of all the times she'd stayed overnight at her grandmother's other home. If only Gran was here to read a bedtime story to her.

"Oh, Gran." MJ curled up and hugged one of the pillows to her.

Close your eyes, MJ, and tell me what you will dream about tonight? Faeries? Castles? Unicorns?

That question had been part of their bedtime ritual. Sometimes it led to wonderful dreams. Often to fun imaginings with her grandmother. Sometimes laughs and giggles.

"Fairy godmothers, Gran," MJ whispered into the empty room. "Fairy godmothers."

The smell of coffee teased her from sleep, her stomach growling as she rolled to her back and stretched her legs and arms. A seagull screeched and her eyes shot open. *Dorothy, you're not in Kansas anymore*, she thought as she sat up.

Instead of the small, north-facing window of her apartment bedroom, a row of tall windows to her left, with no curtains, just blinds that she'd been too tired to notice last night, let sunlight stream into the room. From her position on the bed, she could see clear blue sky. The seagull flew past the window, screaming at her again.

"Yeah, yeah. I'm getting up," she waved at the bird, "get off my case."

She rubbed at her eyes. If not for the manic gull, she'd probably have slept longer, especially after tossing and turning all night with unremembered dreams...except for the one of a man with dark eyes and untamed dark hair, like N— She rubbed her eyes again. *Good grief, no way*. She ran her tongue over her teeth. Ugh. She should have taken time to at least brush her teeth before succumbing to the temptation of bed. And what a bed, soft but not too soft, with crisp, fresh sheets and cloud-like pillows, a great bed for lounging in all day, but she smelled coffee.

Her stomach growled again as the delicious aroma of frying bacon joined the coffee. Was Nik cooking? He certainly seemed at home here. Whose fault was it that she'd never been here before? She threw her legs over the side of the bed. How could she resent a guy who had nothing to do with her separation from her grandmother? She was glad Gran had had someone to look out for her, someone she could rely on. MJ certainly hadn't been that, had she? She didn't deserve this cottage and what came with it. Had Gran been in her right mind when she'd done that? One more question of many she had for Nik, along with how Gran had been able to afford this place on top of upkeep for her other house? Why didn't her dad know about this place or did he?

Apparently, the gulf between her grandmother and her was wider than she thought. She rubbed her eyes. It hurt to know she'd let someone she'd treasured and loved slip away from her, becoming as foreign and insubstantial as a fairy tale. Only one way to get answers to her questions, but first, a shower. She staggered into the bathroom and halted.

The day's light revealed tiled walls up to chest-height in large squares of marbleized blues, greens, and lavenders. The same tiles cooled her feet, and lined the walls of a large walk-in shower. Although the tiles made her think of being underwater, they weren't so unusual. No, what made her wonder again how well she knew her grandmother were the prints on the wall above the tiles, and the jacuzzi tub big enough for two that sat in front of a wide picture window looking out at the ocean, allowing sunlight to fill the room.

She walked over to the tub and looked out the window that gave a view of one end of the beach. This morning, only sand and sea greeted her, along with the wheeling seagull that woke her. Hadn't Gran worried about her privacy? The tub was inviting with its jets and hand-held shower head, the basket of bath oils, sea sponges and brushes, and the several thick pillar candles at the faucet end of the tub.

The tub was shock enough, but then she looked at the prints. Wow, Gran! While her mother would have cringed, then ripped them from the walls, MJ smiled. One print hung on the wall above the tub faucet. The other three hung in a line over the towel bars. She stepped closer to the print above the tub. Framed in a simple gold frame and matted in white, the print was of a book cover with the author's name printed in a swirly font—Kathleen Woodiwiss. In what appeared to be a tropical setting, a man, naked from the waist up, sat bracing himself with one arm against a rock, while his other arm firmly held a long-haired beauty to him, his chin at her chest level. The woman, dressed in a long white dress—why would she wear something like that in the jungle?—had her near leg extended and bare. Tropical blooms in the foreground were in colors of peach, pink and lavender, as was the title, *Shanna*.

She grimaced at the next print, hanging above the towels. On this cover, the man, seen from the side, was entirely naked as he held a woman in a full-length flowing gown to him. *Tender is the Storm*? she read aloud. Indeed. The man was certainly worth exposing, but really, Gran? The other two prints were tamer, actually kind of sweet in a way. Nostalgic. But Gran never had anything like this hanging in her other house. Had she really gone off her rocker as her mother implied or was it just that MJ never had the chance to know Gran as an adult? Children always saw—and remembered—things differently.

Her stomach growled, reminding her of the bacon waiting downstairs. Hanging one of the thick fluffy white towels on the hook next to the shower, she turned on the water and seeing a shelf with more sponges and bath products, stepped into the welcome heat. Turning her back, and pulling her braid over her shoulder, she let the water ease the knots from her shoulders and neck, then decided she might as well wash her hair while she was at it. Minutes later, she toweled herself off, then drew a comb through her still wet hair before braiding it. Throwing on a pair of jean capris and a cropped top, she slid her feet into sandals, and opened her door to head downstairs, but halted at the explosion of sunlight through the floor to ceiling windows to her left. The light reflected off the white walls and spilled onto the two slipper chairs that sat in front of the windows facing the water. Another place to sit and linger, when she had time.

At the bottom of the stairs, she kept her gaze from the picture of her and Gran and followed her nose into a large living/dining area. More windows. More light. At this level, the sunlight spilled over the water like liquid gold.

"Beautiful."

MJ turned at the word. Nik stood to her left, plate in hand and gestured with it at the view. "The view. It's beautiful, isn't it. I never get tired of looking at it."

She nodded, her gaze fastening on the plate of softly scrambled eggs and bacon. "Is that for me?"

Nik nodded and set the plate down on a long rectangular table of some light wood. "You must be hungry after last night. Have a seat and I'll pour you some coffee. That is, if you drink coffee?"

"Yes, please, black."

She pulled back the chair upholstered in a sandy linen fabric and sat down. Mouth watering, she bit into the bacon, moaning at the salty flavor. Behind her, something clattered to the floor. She paid no attention, instead forking up a bite of the eggs and shoving them in. Closing her eyes she savored the taste of thyme and cheddar and the moist texture of the eggs. Just the way her grandmother used to fix them. Behind her, Nik cleared his throat.

"Should I assume you like the eggs?"

She swallowed. "Yes." Questions raced through her mind but she had priorities and eating this delicious breakfast was first, followed by a cup of coffee. Then the questions, although…

"My grandmother used to fix eggs this way." She took another bite.

"I know. She used to fix them for me when I was here. I watched her make them. I thought you might enjoy them."

She swallowed another bite, swallowing a crumb of resentment with it, then bit into the bacon again. The food perked her up. He set a mug of coffee next to her plate and she grabbed it.

"Careful, I just brewed it."

She blew across the top of the mug then carefully tested the temperature. Hot, steaming hot, but not burn-your-tongue hot. She took a swallow and almost felt normal again. Almost. Her grandmother was gone and she was having breakfast alone with a man she barely knew, and every time she turned around, she discovered more of how little she knew of her grandmother's life.

"Why are you up so early."

Nik sat down across from her with his own plate of eggs. He looked up at her and shrugged. "I'm an early riser. I often made breakfast for your grandmother so she could work for an hour or so first."

Her fork clattered to her plate, as Nik took a bite of his eggs.

"How often did you stay here? It sounds as if…as if you practically lived here."

He frowned. "Of course not, but I came frequently to update her on investments, and advise her of expenses and income. Occasionally, I helped her with her stories. She said I was a good sounding board. When I was here, I liked to make her breakfast."

"In bed?"

Nik struggled to keep from laughing. *That's what she thought? Should he feel insulted? Probably not given his work with other mortals.* He shook his head. "No, she'd usually be down here by the time I had breakfast ready." There, let her think what she will.

She took another bite of her eggs, another sip of her coffee. She didn't look at him. Fine. He took a bite of his own eggs. Perfect, even if he did say so himself. Doing simple mortal tasks like brewing coffee, making breakfast made him happy, but he wasn't going to examine the reason. He swallowed another bite of the warm, moist eggs. "What was your mother's problem the other day? She seemed angry. Why?"

MJ set her fork on the plate, took a sip of coffee, and looked out the window. "That's just my mother. For some reason her relationship with Gran was always…tense, I guess. Or stressed. I don't think she liked Gran's influence on me, considered her too flighty. Not practical."

This time, he let the laugh loose. Her gaze jerked to him. "What?"

He waved his hand at their surroundings, "She was very practical. Go on."

She frowned at him. "Something happened when I was in kindergarten that embarrassed my mother, I think, and then again a few years later. I don't remember exactly. Something to do with my tendency, at that age, to play make believe." She shrugged.

"Is that what kept you from visiting? Your grandmother wondered if it was something she did."

She shoved her plate away. "When I was younger, I'd beg my parents to let me visit Gran at the other house. We didn't know about this place. But there was never time. My mother wouldn't let me visit her on my own and she just never had time to go with me. Father offered once or twice but for some reason, Mother was always irritable with us when we got home. Once I could drive, I was busy with school, or the car wasn't available."

She rose and walked to the window, crossing her arms in front of her. "Look, none of this is your business. Can we get to the tour and...and stuff."

She was right. To a point. But there was more to Juliette's extraction of his promise to help her granddaughter than the long-term break between them. Time to work his magic.

"One of the reasons your grandmother left you this cottage, and other things, is because she wanted you to have the freedom to chase your dreams. I think the phrase was, '...go for her Happily Ever After.' What does your Happily Ever After look like, MJ?"

She turned and pointed at him. "First, again it's none of your business. And second, happily ever afters are for princesses and fairy tales. I believed in them when I was little, but not now. They're not real. My parents certainly don't have one. Gran lost hers years ago when Gramps died. Are you living your happily ever after?"

Wham! Stunned, he sat back. Damn, these Montague women knew how to make him squirm. How could any immortal live happily ever after when his ever after was forever? He remembered Juliette's delight in helping him buy his car, her desire to give him something that made him happy. Maybe, just maybe, MJ was more like her grandmother than he thought. Still, he had a job to do.

"I was happy helping your grandmother. But this is not about me. We're here because your grandmother wanted you to be happy. So, what is your dream?"

She didn't answer, just turned back to look out the window at the sea, her arms wrapped around herself. Not only had she lost her connection to her *meraki,* that creative spark that fired the passion of creativity so that something of the essence of the creator was imbued in every creation, but apparently, she'd shut down the possibility of her own HEA. Good thing he was an immortal because she was going to require patience.

He walked over to stand behind her. She was almost a head shorter than him. Her hair, still slightly damp, smelled fresh and bright, like lemons, and was tightly braided. *What would it look like, freed from the braid and flowing down her back like a luxurious mantle, with secrets and scents tangled in the tresses?* He erased the arousing image. "Your grandmother made me promise to help you achieve your dream, whether through finances or connections or—"

She half-turned, holding up a hand. "Enough. That's enough about my dream. Let's just do the tour and whatever else we need to do, shall we?"

Nik drew in a breath. That way, was it? He nodded to her. No sense pushing her at this point. First, she needed to see, to learn more about the real Juliette, so he led the way into the hall, just as chimes sounded rang out. She halted and pulled her phone from the back pocket of her capris, holding a finger up to him, then turning away. He waited.

"Hello, Mother," she said softly. "What? Why would you worry? Of course, I arrived safely. A little late because I took a wrong turn."

A wrong turn? More like many wrong turns, Nik thought. Obviously not something she was going to share with the mother, though.

"No, the cottage is fine. No, it's not a shack. Why are you calling, Mother?" her voice rising. She rubbed her forehead. "Really? You are calling to ask me that? Mother, I am fine. Nik—Mr. Stefanopoulus is here and we were about to tour the cottage... No, I didn't see it last night. I was too exhausted after the drive."

Nik shifted to lean against the wall next to the picture of Juliette and MJ. She turned to look at him. Her gaze shifted behind him and she closed her eyes, turning away again. "No, I am not coming home in a few days. No. There is no need for you to come here. You have your own work to do. Don't you have a reception scheduled in a day or two? I will. I'll get back to work on the thesis just as soon as I've done what I need to do for Gran's—Damn it!" The last was said softly.

"Problems?"

If she was a cat, her back would be arched and she'd be hissing, instead, she tossed the phone on the sofa.

"Yes—no. Just...stuff. Please, let's just do what we need to do, can we? I have to get back to work on my dissertation."

Nik bit back a remark about priorities. He didn't want to get scratched. She scanned the view of the ocean as if searching. For what? Escape. He was right there with her on that. He cleared his throat. "Let's start with a tour of the cottage, then."

She frowned and looked at the dining area and around the living area. "Haven't I already seen most of it?"

He smiled, looking forward to surprising her. "Not quite. Let me give you the full tour of the place. We'll start on this floor and work our way up. Follow me."

Without protest, she followed him out of the living area, back to the hall, to a door just before the stairway. He opened it and gestured her into a two-car garage with its metal shelves neatly stacked with tools, seeds and fertilizer, and rubber boots and gardening gloves.

She looked around. "Where's her car?"

"She didn't own one. Whenever she needed to go somewhere, she called the island taxi service or one of her friends if she needed something on the island. If she needed something off island, I usually drove her. She didn't want to pay for something she'd only use on occasion." But she'd been happy to help him buy his car just to make him happy. He stifled a smile. "As you can see, there is plenty of room here for your car, if you want to pull it in later." He led her back into the cottage past the small but well-organized laundry room and broom closet, and the powder room. She nodded and followed.

Back in the living area, he asked, "Ready to move to the second floor? You've seen everything down here on the first level."

He led her upstairs, and pointed to the door on his left. "You've seen that one, and over here..." He led her to the other side of the hallway. "Here are two additional bedrooms." He stood by the hall windows while she checked them out, then came back into the hall. She frowned and gestured to the door that was between the second bedroom she'd stepped out of and the doorway of her grandmother's—now hers—bedroom.

"Where does that lead?"

Chapter 5

Nik pulled open the door and flicked on a light that illuminated a narrow staircase. He bowed slightly, gesturing to the stairs. "After you."

She peered up. *Whatever.* Grabbing the worn wooden handrail, she climbed, conscious of Nik behind her. Her face flushed at the thought of his eyes on her hips. She swallowed. Just a few more hours and he'd leave. Wouldn't he? She reached the top of the stairs and drew in a breath, shocked and surprised. She forgot about Nik, her dissertation, everything as she took in the views through the windows in three of the four walls of the room. She stood in a tower surrounded by sea and sand and sun. Her own private aerie.

When she turned her gaze from the view, she discovered the next surprise, a writing desk centered in the row of windows facing the ocean. She crossed the bleached pine floors, reaching out to caress the polished dark wood of the closed, slanted surface that would drop open to provide a place to write. This was the same desk she used to sit and do homework at when she stayed with Gran at her other place. She rubbed her hand over its polished surface, realizing she hadn't noticed its absence at the meeting with the lawyer.

Above the writing area was a row of three shallow drawers with round, wooden pulls, and on top of those stood a lamp with a shell shade. Next to it, spread evenly across were three framed photographs, one was of her grandfather, taken when he was promoted to partner at his law firm years before he died of a heart attack. She had no real memory of him, just the photograph. She picked up the next one, the picture taken of Gran, her father, and her in cap and gown when she'd been awarded her Master's. She replaced it and picked up the third.

Nik moved up behind her, clearing his throat. "Your grandmother spent a good part of every day at this desk."

She ignored him. The other two pictures didn't surprise her, but this did. Her fingers tightened around the frame. In the photo, her grandmother, in Capris and a tunic in her favorite shade of peach, smiled up at Nik. Dressed in shorts and a fitted T-shirt, he beamed down at her. She held out a set of keys to him, probably to the Ferrari behind them.

"How long ago was this?"

He cleared his throat, again. "A few years ago."

Taking the picture from her, he set it back on the desk. Why was it there with the one of her grandfather and her? She pulled out one of the drawers, noting paper clips, rubber bands, tape, and other office detritus. "How long have you worked for my grandmother?'

He looked out the window. "A while. Your grandmother was a special lady. Her body aged, but her mind and heart didn't."

"That was her problem," MJ muttered.

Nik's gaze jerked to hers and narrowed. "What do you mean?"

She regretted her words. She shook her head. Now was not the time. But Nik moved to stand in front of her, hands on hips, bending his head until she felt his breath on her face.

"What do you mean, that was her problem?"

"She didn't act like a normal person. My mother said...she complained Gran was...what's the word? Dotty."

Nik took his turn muttering, as he turned away from her and strode across the room. "Come here."

"Do I look anything like a dog?"

"Come here, please."

She shrugged. "Okay..." She crossed to where he stood at the back wall lined with bookshelves so crammed with books that some lay sideways on top of the upright ones. They looked like her own shelves back at the condo.

"Look at these."

She scanned the shelves, tilting her head to read the titles. The topmost shelf, above her head, was filled with books on writing along with reference volumes like an Oxford dictionary, *Roget's Thesaurus*, and even the small, slim copy of *Elements of Style* Gran had used since high school and often recommended to her students. But they didn't look old enough to be from Gran's school days.

The next shelf held history books, most about the 1700 and 1800s, and included an old etiquette book, and another one that aroused her curiosity, *What Jane Austen Ate and Charles Dickens Knew*. Below that, not unexpectedly, were books on myth and fairy tales, including a worn edition of fairy tales like the one her grandmother used to read to her.

An arm shot out in front of her as she reached for the one about Jane Austen's eating habits and she drew back. For a moment, she'd forgotten Nik. He pulled out a paperback and handed it to her. "Here, look at this."

He sure was bossy all of a sudden. The cover's style was familiar. A romance, the kind of book she loved to read but seldom had time to do with her teaching and her work on her dissertation. The kind her mother would have tossed away as trash. "Not literature, Marie Juliette, don't waste your time." *The Secret Embrace* by Julie Moon.

"Oh, she is one of my favorite authors," she blurted without thinking, but what did she care what Nik thought about her less than literary reading habits? "This must be a new one."

"Look at the author's dedication page."

MJ turned back the cover where a woman in a bright blue, off-the-shoulder, multi-tiered gown looked yearningly up at the man in top hat, ascot and tails whose hand cupped her cheek and whose other hand was spread at her low back. She turned a couple of pages until she came to it.

To my dearest granddaughter. Her love of fairy tales, tea parties under the table, and her search for a happily ever after is the reason I write. For all those "what ifs?"

What? She read it through three times, her heart pounding, her cheeks heating. She flipped to look at the author's name on the cover again, then flipped back to the dedication. It didn't make sense. "I don't understand," she said, though she was afraid she did. Her grip tightened on the book. Tea parties under the table...for all the what ifs. Gran! Her other arm curled around her stomach. Gran wrote this? How could she have? Was this the only...? She dropped to her knees in front of the bookcase, her eyes searching out the author's name and the titles. *Love's True Labor, A Restless Heart, For All the Tomorrows,* and more. Her fingers slid over the tops of the books, some in paperback, some in hardcover. She sat back on her heels.

"Your grandmother..."

Her hand shot up to halt his words. *How?* This was a grandmother she didn't know. Ever since her mother stopped letting Gran babysit or spend time alone with MJ, implying something was wrong with her, something not quite right mentally, MJ worked hard to not miss her. She repeatedly pushed down the ache of missing those special times of stories and tea parties.

She'd even finally believed, as her mother implied, the reason Gran was such a great playmate was because as she'd aged, she'd become more childlike. Dotty, her mother said.

She ran her finger over the tops of the books again. These told another story altogether. Julie Moon, according to the author's page was a pen name for someone who liked their privacy. She knew from reading at night in the privacy of her bedroom, there was never an author picture, not even on the website. Nothing about pets, or trips or anything. MJ assumed it was someone who had a publicity-sensitive job. Or was a man writing as a woman, since romance was a top-selling genre. But this...

How many books? She opened the one she was holding...one she hadn't read yet.

"That's her newest book. Released two months ago," Nik told her, "It was her tenth novel."

He watched MJ. She reread the dedication, then put it on the floor next to her and pulled another one from the shelf. She opened it to the dedication page and read aloud, "For the love of my life who left me too soon, but was still my happily ever after."

She looked up at him and whispered, "Grandfather?"

He nodded, stiffening. Was she going to read every book's... She pulled a third one from the shelf. Maybe he should leave the room now.

"For my son, who gave me reasons to make up my own stories of adventure and the seemingly impossible."

She closed that one and set it on the others. Book after book, she scanned through the dedications to readers, editors, and others. He waited, anticipating a blow up when she picked up the ninth book and flipped it open.

"For Nik with love and appreciation for all of your inspiration and support. If I could have had a grandson, he would have been you," she read aloud.

His throat tightened. He'd read that when it was first published and wondered how he was supposed to ignore the emotions it aroused, emotions he wasn't supposed to feel. He needed to get out of the room. Before she blew up. He turned and walked out, closing the door quietly behind him, and headed down the stairs and out of the cottage.

Cowardly? Perhaps. But he needed some distance.

The door closed softly behind her. Good. Before she said something she'd regret. Because why shouldn't Gran dedicate a book to him just as she had to her agent and editor? But that comment about if she'd had a grandson? Jealous. She was jealous.

Sighing, she stared at the books piled around her on the floor. Gran's books. Maybe if she stared at them awhile, it would finally sink in that her grandmother had written all ten of them. She scooped them all up into her arms and bent her head over them.

"Gran, why didn't you tell me? Why?"

All this time, all these books. For years, her grandmother had been a successful, popular author of romance novels. MJ never knew, never had a clue. Why had her grandmother never told her, never hinted she was writing? She understood not sharing her new career over the rare family Sunday dinner, with MJ's mother sitting and monitoring every word and topic. But surely on one of their phone calls. Did she think MJ, like her mother, would disapprove of what she was writing?

It hurt to think Gran worried MJ felt the same way. She might be getting her doctorate in literature, but she loved well-written romance novels. She looked at the desk, the books on their shelves, the incredible view of the ocean. Her grandmother created all of this herself. Without a husband or son. Without her granddaughter. Only that distracting man-of-affairs, to whom she'd dedicated a book, to help her. Sighing, she hugged all the books to her chest, rose to her feet, and left the room. Back in her grandmother's bedroom, she made two neat stacks on the nightstand next to the bed. Although she'd read most of them before, she was going to read them again while she was here, in order, with the knowledge that Julie Moon was Juliette Montague. Gran.

In the bathroom, she looked at the posters with new understanding. Gran hadn't turned into a lecherous old lady. These were Gran's literary role models, women writing stories about finding true happiness and love with another, while also having adventures and experiencing passion. More power to them. MJ's past dating experiences lacked all of those things. And her parents' marriage? Did they still love each other? Did they ever love each other or had they only married because of the pregnancy?

She walked back into the bedroom and touched the smooth covers of the top books. They were Gran's version of fairy tales, written—and published—in the last years of her life. MJ looked out the windows at the sun shining on the ocean, sea birds swooping and diving for their meal. She scanned the room. Fairy tales or not, her grandmother managed to create an independent life for herself in a beautiful setting, doing work she loved. All that success and reasons to celebrate, and who was in Gran's life to share in the celebration? Only Nik.

So where was that irritating man-of-affairs?

Chapter 6

Shedding his sandals and t-shirt, Nik dove into the cool water, glad to be out of the cottage, away from the memories and MJ's stormy brew of emotions. He stroked under water then rose to the surface, swimming, farther from shore. *How could she believe her grandmother was—what did she call it—dotty? Even after the regular holiday visits Juliette had made to her son's home?* Stroke after stroke, he thought about what a brilliant and caring person Juliette had been. It made him angry, angry for Juliette.

The anger worried him as it signaled he cared more than he should. Number One rule for Apollo's Voices, don't get emotionally involved, especially don't fall in love. Faking it was fine to inspire or motivate mortals in their creative work, and sex was allowed, naturally, as it was a great stimulator for creative expression, but he was not to fall in love—or hate—with their mortal clients. They were to discourage any emotional attachments their mortals might feel as well.

Nik dove, rose to surface and turned to float on his back. The sky was a blue, cloudless bowl above him. He hadn't let himself admit it before, but with Juliette, he'd begun to question and resent those rules. The old woman had worn away the emotional barriers he'd successfully erected with his other clients. Although Nik was centuries older, he still had the body and energy of a man in his late twenties or thirties, and Juliette treated him like the beloved grandson she dedicated her book to. It was a unique experience for him.

She fussed over him, concerned about him driving late at night after a day of working together, and pushed delicious food at him, telling him he needed to eat more. She'd been nothing like his actual grandmother, Mnemosyne, who wouldn't know what to do in a kitchen. How did mortals phrase it? She wouldn't even know how to boil water. He laughed, his voice echoing over the waves.

"What's so funny, bro?"

Nik jerked upright, splashing his face. Spitting out the salty water, he blinked to clear it from his eyes. His friend, Alek, grinned at him.

Normally, Alek's surfer dude persona didn't bother him. His immortal cousin loved adopting mortal lingo and dress styles although he was often a decade or two behind. Most times that amused him. But not today.

"What are you doing here?"

"We were supposed to hang out, man. I asked at the barracks where you were and they said you were on assignment. Already?" He looked at the beach. "I thought your assignment died. Why are you here again?"

Nik spit out another mouthful of sea water. "After she died, Juliette made me promise to help her granddaughter."

Alek shook his head. "That sucks. You spent years with her. I'd be cool to take over for you, instead. I've spent enough time home under Apollo's watch. Wouldn't mind hangin' with a mortal for a while. Is she a looker?"

Nik turned his back on his friend to swim swam parallel to the shore. Alek shouted "Hey!" and followed. If he let Alek take over, his promise to Juliette would still be fulfilled, wouldn't it? MJ was going to be a challenge, not a quick fix. And he was so tired of, of... He stopped swimming and shook the water out of his hair. Damn Hermes!

Thalassa dropped beneath the water to quench the flare of fury when she spied that blasted immortal playboy, Alek.

Why was he here? Now, she couldn't work a little siren seduction on Nikos in her element. She flipped her tail and rose to the surface again, careful to stay near the rocks visible at low tide. The heads of the two men, one dark almost black and the other a dark blonde bobbed about, Alek's laughter riding the waves to her.

Her seduction and attack on Nikos would have to wait since she didn't want witnesses. She did not want to be responsible for revealing the sisters' secret ability to leave the island, only her mother and her one aunt knew it. They were the ones to approach Hecate and ask her to cast a spell to ameliorate the curse, which she did, just enough so that, though the island was the only dry land they were allowed to put foot, or fin, on without immediately and permanently being turned into harpies, they were able to travel anywhere in the mortal realm salt water traveled, even up into bays and estuaries. The ability gave her—and her sisters—an advantage Thalassa had no intention of losing. No one must know, but she'd make an exception for Nikos.

Though the flying would be wonderful—she missed her wings—a human-headed, bare-breasted, vulture-like harpy was not how she wanted to spend eternity. Thank the goddess she wasn't stuck on the island. She and her sisters easily rode waves of both salt waters and sound. They still had power. Suddenly, a sea turtle rose next to her, its shell covered with seaweed. It turned its head and gazed at her.

She ignored it and looked back at Nikos. She'd been so close to him, she'd seen the way his body powered through the water. A few more breaths and she could have slipped beneath him, her breasts to his chest, her belly to his. Keeping him distracted, playing with him until the moon rose, when, perhaps, the cursed mortal woman in the cottage would lose patience, get angry and leave. Or Nikos would forget about the mortal because he would be too enthralled by her skilled seduction. If the mortal left, Nikos would have no reason not to spend time with Thalassa, and she would thence sabotage another mission of Apollo and his Voices.

Male laughter echoed again. Her jaw tightened. She'd never had sex with Alek, so she had no thread of connection to him, but she'd find a way to punish him for thwarting her plans this day. No matter he had no knowledge of her presence. Perhaps she'd wait until he decided to leave— A sudden push sent her sideways. She flailed her arms and kicked her tail to keep herself upright. *What in Hades?*

She looked for the source of the push. That sea turtle's head was down, swimming in her direction. *For another push? Sea turtles didn't harass mortals or others, did they?* The turtle bumped her side so that she turned, her back to the beach. *What in Hades was wrong with this sea turtle?* Raising its head, it looked at her, eye to eye. Oh-h-h, those were not the eyes of a sea turtle. One eye was luminous green, the other a lapis blue. Only one god had those eyes. She dove into the water and swam swiftly away, from Nikos, from the sea turtle, and from trouble.

For now.

Nik tread water as Alek surfaced next to him.

He swiped droplets from his eyes, jaws clenching. In the distance, up the beach towards the cottage, he spied someone walking in their direction. He turned back to his cousin.

"Time for you to leave."

"You didn't answer my question, bro."

Alek, more brother than cousin because of their close relationship, smirked at him, his wet hair sleeked back, as dark and shiny from the water as a seal's coat. He glanced up the beach as well.

"Shut it. You should not be popping in like this. How do I explain you if someone sees you?"

"You mean like the cute bit walking towards us? Relax. I could have been swimming mostly underwater for all she—or anyone—knows. Why the concern?"

Nik shook his head and looked back up the beach. Yes, it was MJ. Already, he recognized her lithe silhouette.

"Is that her? Oh bro, let me take over for you. She looks like quite the mortal morsel." He licked his lips.

As Nik watched MJ stride down the beach, gaze on the water, the end of her braid appearing and disappearing behind her swinging hips, she might have been a sea nymph, lithe and beautiful.

"Introduce me, bro, and I'll take it from there."

Introduce him? No, he certainly would not. He wasn't sure he wanted his friend to "take it from there." The thought tightened his shoulders. No, he promised Juliette he would try to help her granddaughter. He would keep his promise. He'd take his long-needed break afterwards.

"This is not the time..."

But his cousin wasn't paying him any attention. His gaze was fixed on MJ. He whistled softly. "I can see why you'd want her all to yourself. She's not the old crone."

Nik backhanded his friend's shoulder. No one was going to talk that way about Juliette. She may have been old as a mortal, but her heart had been forever young and generous. He swept his arm through the water, sweeping up a small wave that washed over his cousin.

"She is not a mortal to be played with, trust me. Unless you want Apollo to come down on your ass?"

"Yeah, yeah," Alek tilted his head and tugged on his ear "too bad, she's a sweet piece of—"

He swept another wave of water at this cousin. "Time to go, Alek. I don't want to have to answer questions about you."

"Nik," MJ, finally reaching the part of the beach near him, cupped her hands around her mouth and yelled, "are you ever coming back to the cottage? We have work to do."

Alek snorted, "Whoa, right. Not my type at all. All work and no play."

With barely a ripple, he sank below the surface of the water and swam off. Nik dropped his shoulders, took a breath, then dove into the water, kicking toward shore. Time to get back to work.

Chapter 7

MJ paced back and forth across the deck as she waited for Nik to change. The other guy with Nik disappeared while she'd watched Nik's wet, tanned, fit—supremely fit—body emerge from the ocean, water dripping from his hair to slide down pecs that were—

She smacked her forehead, squeezing her eyes shut to banish the memory of the dark nipples separated by wiry dark hair narrowing to a line traveling all the way to the top of his swim trunks. His muscular legs and long, narrow feet as they strode to her were dusted with sand. Like an ancient god rising from the sea.

What was wrong with her? Her focus was supposed to be on Gran's legacy and then her dissertation. But watching him walk up the beach toward her make her think of those posters on Gran's bathroom wall. A large bird, not a gull, winged up and down over the water, then dove in and burst back up shrieking with a fish flailing in its beak. Kind of the way she felt when Nik turned his focus on her. Gran would likely smile and wink at her. Her mother would frown.

Had her mother ever looked at her father with desire, feeling flushed? She must have. Otherwise, MJ would never have been born, and wasn't that the problem? The one her mother warned her about all the time. "Men just lure you off your career path. I'd be president of a college or university by now if I hadn't…" She never finished that statement but MJ knew what was left unsaid. If she hadn't unexpectedly gotten pregnant.

Nik opened the French door and stepped onto the deck. His still damp hair rioted in dark, springy curls around his head like some Cupid come to life. His day-old beard shadowed his wide mouth and highlighted his eyes. He grinned. She jerked her gaze up. Ugh, she'd been staring at his mouth, enough. He gestured her inside. "Ready to work?"

She nodded and moved past him, ignoring the heat and clean scent emanating from him as she passed.

Totally ignored it. Totally.

Nik didn't miss the heat and appreciation in MJ's stare, or, unfortunately, the way it warmed his blood, even as it surprised him, just as it had at the reading of her grandmother's will. It also delighted—and tempted—him. What would she be like during sex? Playful? Passionate or prim? Probably prim given her mother. She'd be the do-it-and-get-it-over-with type. That cooled his blood. Sure it did.

"Before you show me her accounts, who is Gran's agent?"

"Me."

"Yes, you. Who are they?" she asked, hands at her hips. She glared at him now as if he were a particularly annoying little boy. He suppressed the smile tugging at his lips. Maybe she wouldn't be quite so prim. In her current stance, he imagined thigh-high boots and a whip. Oh, Aphrodite, that was not the image to have in his brain right now. He shifted his stance. "I apologize for not making myself clear. I am her literary agent."

"You! But..."

He ran his fingers through his drying hair. "If you'll take a seat, I'll show you everything you need to know about your grandmother's writing career and business. Then you may ask all your questions, yes?"

She glanced out the window as she sat down at the table facing the water. "Who was the guy you were talking to in the water?"

Skata. She must have seen him talking with Alek. "That was someone out for a morning swim—like me." He looked out at the water with her, then shrugged. "He must have swum off."

"He just disappeared."

He forced a laugh. "Maybe Scotty beamed him up." She frowned at him.

"You know...Captain Kirk? Bones? Spock? 'Beam me up, Scotty.' *Star Trek*."

"Oh, that." She shrugged. "I never watched it. I was too young and not allowed."

"Why not?" No wonder Juliette worried about her.

Her chin came up. "Mother discouraged me from watching shows like that. Too fantastical. A waste of time." She made air quotes for the last statements.

"Too bad, because much of what seemed fantastical at the time of the show became common technology, like cell phones. After all, for developments and inventions to occur, someone has to first let their creative spark, that is, their imagination wander out of this world, into areas where things seem impossible and fantastical."

"Whatever. Can we get back to business now?"

So what if she'd grown up watching almost no television.

She folded her arms on the table where she ate breakfast which now felt like days ago instead of hours. The revelation about her grandmother still had her off balance. She needed to finish this so Nik vanished from the house and her mind. He was too distracting, his words, his actions, his body. She was a PhD candidate and should have better control of her mind. This fascination with a man who was almost a stranger unsettled her.

"MJ? MJ?"

She jerked in her chair. He'd left his seat next to her and was standing on the other side of the table. Had he said something? She blinked. "What?"

He put his hands, strong hands with long fingers on the back of the chair in front of him and leaned toward her. "I asked if you want some coffee before we get down to business. I think there is some left in the pot from this morning."

"Yes." She nodded. A dark curl fell onto his forehead before he turned away, and one of Gran's little rhymes popped unbidden into her head.

"There was a little girl who had a little curl, right in the middle of her forehead. And when she was good, she was very, very good, and when she was bad, she was horrid."

Only in this case, it was a boy. A big, dark, sexy-looking... Hoo, boy! She was the one who was horrid. She must finish her business with Nik and send him on his way, otherwise, she'd never be able to focus on that damned dissertation.

He set two white mugs of steaming coffee on the table, and sat in the chair next to her. She took a quick gulp of coffee, almost spitting it back out again. *So hot. Damn!*

She swallowed, the heat almost too much for her throat. "So," she whispered past the burn in her throat, "in addition to being her financial adviser, you were also Gran's literary agent?"

He nodded. "And her intellectual property lawyer."

"Were you anything else?" she asked, only half joking.

He set his mug down with a clunk and turned his head to look into her eyes. "I'd like to think I was a good friend, too."

She was tempted to ask him if friendship was all he offered Gran, but as much as she didn't know about her in recent years, her grandmother always talked of her grandfather as the great love of her life. Still, those posters in the bathroom. She'd bet Gran wasn't immune to Nik's attractiveness. Had she modeled one of her heroes after him? Now she truly wanted to re-read all those books sitting next to her bed. First, she had to finish with this man of many talents and send him back to his office and out her life. So, Mr. Stefanopolous, financial adviser, agent, and lawyer, now that we've established that Gran wasn't, wasn't dotty..."

Chapter 8

N ik heard the sorrow and regret in her voice and looked away, reaching for his satchel on the table next to him, giving her a moment to gather herself. He was relieved that he didn't have to argue further with her about Juliette's mental capacities. She probably didn't fully realize her mother's role and manipulation, but that was an issue to deal with later.

The sooner he did his job, the sooner he could get back to Mt. Helicon. He'd give her the big picture on the finances and the level of her grandmother's success to finally put the dotty old woman story to rest. Pulling a folder from his satchel, he opened it to the listing all of Juliette's investments, accounts, and royalties. Although comfortable using a computer, she'd always preferred seeing her reports on paper. He'd do the same for MJ until she told him otherwise.

Over the centuries, Nik, in addition to keeping up with mortals' current language idiosyncrasies, he learned how markets worked, how far mortals would go to gamble their money for the possibility of more money, and, because he lived through the rise and fall of governments, civilizations, and industries, he had an eagle's eye for patterns. He'd been a responsible steward of Juliette's funds, as well as her stories. Now, he would ensure

MJ understood what he and Juliette had grown together so she could decide whether to carry on or put an end to both stories and investments. The possibility saddened him, but he pushed the feeling aside and cleared his throat.

"Most of these investments were made with monies from the royalties for her books."

Her gaze followed his pointing finger to the top sheet. She gasped, "You mean, she made all this from writing her stories?"

His shoulders relaxed. "Some investments were made from the money from her husband's life insurance but, see this number? These are her earnings from all her book sales. Of course, it took some time for her to achieve this, but once she'd built her audience..."

"How long?"

"What?"

"How long did it take her ..." she waved a hand at the spreadsheet. "...to build her readership and start making serious money."

"Well, she started writing about ten years ago. And five years ago, I began working with her as her agent and financial adviser. I was able to get her better contracts and show her how to invest her income to make it grow. I also hired someone to help her with her brand and her social media since it was something she had no interest in at first, until she discovered how easy it was, and how much fun it was to engage with her readers online. She refused to have her photo on her books or do public appearances, though."

Her head came up. "Why? I always wondered why there was never a picture of Julie Moon on her books."

"She didn't want to fray the relationship with your mom and dad any further than it already was. And she didn't want to make things harder for you."

"But…" MJ pointed to the numbers on the spreadsheet. "She was a huge success. Why would…"

"Not at first, she wasn't. At first, she was just an older woman writing love stories. And what would your mother think of that?"

She rested her forehead in her palms and closed her eyes. "That they're not worth the paper they're printed on."

"Exactly. Your grandmother knew your mother would be incensed if anyone at the university found out that her mother-in-law was a best-selling romance author." Even now, when he thought about it, put it all into words like this, his fist craved violent contact with a wall. His shoulders knotted with the anger at Juliette having to hide or defend what she did so well—write love stories so powerful that Erato, his mother, found joy in reading them. Mortals were such fools.

By the end of day with only a short break for lunch, he'd shown MJ all the accounts and explained the investments. He'd retrieved Juliette's laptop and showed MJ the software and applications her grandmother used for her work. He showed her how to access the passwords. Finally, he was done—mostly. She was too from the looks of it. Her shoulders were slumped, her head was propped up on her hand, and her eyes glazed as she stared at the laptop screen.

MJ stared at the screen, seeing the lists of investments and the amounts of money her grandmother had made, was still making. Her grandmother was Julie Moon, the popular, and obviously, from the numbers on the screen, very successful author. To think, all those books she pre-ordered to ensure she had copies as soon as they were released, were written by her grandmother. MJ rubbed her tired eyes.

"Part of your grandmother's success was because she produced a book a year." Nik straightened in his chair, his arm brushing hers before he moved away a fraction. But she'd felt the soft hair of his arms on her bare skin, and suddenly, she was aware of how close he was, and of the size of his hands as he straightened the papers, tanned, strong hands. She drew a breath, took a sip of cold coffee. The mug hadn't been refilled since lunch. Focus, MJ. *What did he say? Oh yes, a book a year. Not that much for some independent authors but for a traditionally published one? Perfect.*

"How...how amazing."

"Well, she loved the stories she wrote. What else did she have to fill all her days alone? And I didn't mean that the way it sounded. It was just reality." He rubbed his hand over his face then turned to her. "She was lonely. Sure, she spoke to neighbors and met people on the beach, but she spent most of her time here in this cottage alone, except when I came for a visit. Let's finish up here and then we can eat."

MJ nodded, all the assets and investments her grandmother built up over the years floated around in her mind. Her grandmother may not have been a billionaire, but she'd certainly created a nice nest egg for herself. The monies from those investments and the royalties were more than enough to live on for years. The interest alone—

"Most of these investment accounts will continue to grow unless your father decides to cash them in, in which case, that will be that. Your account from the royalties, however, will continue to grow as long as your grandmother's books continue to sell because all of her royalties will now pay into that account once you've met the requirements of the legacy."

"What if I don't meet the requirements? What happens to the money then? Does it go to my father, too?"

He shook his head and placed the page back in the folder. "No, all her royalties would go into a charitable trust that I administer on your grandmother's behalf, benefitting writers and other artists."

She sat back. "That's so like Gran, waving her wand like a fairy godmother, and helping others."

"If you accept the legacy, you'll be co-administrator with me of the trust. I guess that means you'll be a fairy godmother, too." Nik quirked an eyebrow at her. "Would you like that?"

She glanced at her laptop at the end of the table, silently rebuking her. Once her dissertation was completed, and she'd defended it before the committee, she hoped to become a full-time professor. Would she even have time to help manage something like this?

"Hey, it's not something you need to decide now. I'm ready to take a break and get some dinner. What about you?"

Her stomach growled in answer, he laughed and stood up. "C'mon, I know a great place on the island to get a burger and relax. Obviously, you've had enough for now. How about I take you out to dinner? There's this place I used to take your Gran after we'd been at work for most of the day."

She rubbed her eyes again. "I don't know. I'm not in the mood to get dressed up and put on makeup." She blushed, embarrassed that she hadn't bothered to put any on for him.

"I don't care if you have makeup on or not. You certainly don't need it. And the place we're going to? You won't need it. You're fine as you are. It's casual but a great place for a burger, or a lobster roll if you prefer something from the sea. Come. You need to explore the island and see something of it besides fog and the cottage."

He pulled back her chair for her. She sighed. Might as well. She had to eat anyway and she certainly wasn't in the mood to fix something.

"Let me make up for forcing you to look at numbers and contracts all day. I promise I won't get lost or drive in circles." He held out his hand.

She raised an eyebrow at him. "Funny." But she put her hand in his larger warm one, and allowed him to pull her out to his car.

On the road, MJ listened to the deep rumble of Nik's car engine and felt its vibrations through the seat and through her. She squirmed. She must really be exhausted, if this induced images of making out in this car with the man next to her. As he down-shifted around a curve, she stole a glance at him. He was intensely absorbed in driving, his eyes on the road, one hand on the gear shift, a small smile on his lips. Those lips.

She jerked her gaze away. He reached up and pushed a button, and the car roof retracted. Wind whipped through his hair, strands catching on the scruff of his beard, while her hair stayed neatly, for the most part, in her braid. Thank goodness. She couldn't imagine having to brush out the snarls. The road appeared to parallel the shore and she caught intermittent views of the ocean and its salty, fishy scents, and even glimpsed a sailboat out in the distance. Would she be able to see dolphins and whales from her grandmother's deck? She'd always wanted to see them for real, not on some television program or in an aquarium.

The car veered inland, the road lined with tall, dark green pines casting long pine-scented shadows and creating a tunnel effect. A sharp left turn led into a parking lot surrounding a rustic, cabin-like building. She stared. More tall pines stood sentinel behind the building. A few cars, mostly SUVs, and a few motorcycles were parked in the lot. Broad wooden steps led up to a landing and the door to the building, over which hung a sign from a cast iron rod with an arrow-like head pointing in the direction of the ocean. Painted on a dark green background, white foamy waves curled beneath the words, "White Horses Bar and Grill." The doors of the car rose, and suddenly Nik stood outside her door with his hand out to help her from the car. Her grandmother must have loved his old-fashioned manners.

"Why are there waves on the sign and not a white horse?" she asked him as she rose from the car.

He laughed and warmth crept from his hand to hers. "You're not a girl of the sea, are you?"

He stood there with a smile so wide she couldn't help smiling in return. His hair was wild and mussed from the ride, and his eyes sparkled. There was something so… she didn't know what but it tugged at her.

"I'm not yet, but I could be turning into one." She'd meant it as a joke because he'd laughed at her and because she felt off balance here in this wild place so far from the usual carefully tended university landscapes and colorless class rooms. But he didn't laugh, and nodded instead.

"Indeed, you might be." He let go of her hand, leaving her adrift. He clicked the car remote and the doors winged down and locked. "I'll tell you about the name once we get inside and order."

She looked around again as she followed him to the stairs, noting the differences between here and the cottage. Those dark pines. The quiet except for an occasional bird. What had Gran thought of this place? She could imagine what she'd say if they'd come here together. "What if, MJ, this place was a place of magic? What fairy tale would happen here?"

The trees behind the building seemed to go on forever. *Were there bears? Witches ready to cast a spell? Fairies flitting among the branches? Were ogres lurking, waiting for someone to enter the woods and become their dinner?* "Get real."

Nik turned to her. "What?"

She kept walking. Her mother would castigate her for letting her imagination run away with her. Gran would tell her she was a princess with magical powers and nothing in the deep dark woods could hurt her because Gran always made her feel invincible. As she climbed the steps, she heard a vehicle behind her and turned to see a dark blue SUV pull in and park next to Nik's car.

"After you." He waved her in.

As she crossed the threshold, she looked back just in time to see two tall, fit men emerge from the car next to Nik's. One had dark curly hair, the other with very short blonde hair. Both were hunky model material.

"Whew!" She stepped into the restaurant. "Is this where all the hot guys hang out?"

He halted her with a hand to her elbow. She blinked up at him as her eyes adjusted to the light. She couldn't ignore it any longer. He was hot. Dark eyes revealed nothing in the dim light, brows raised. Lips...mmm, lips tilted in a small smile. And that end-of-day beard that made her hand itch with the urge to stroke it and feel just how rough it really was. Oh yeah. Hot.

"Are you saying you think I'm hot?" He grinned at her.

Oh god, she hadn't said that out loud, had she? She pulled her elbow from his grasp and turned away, pretending to look for a host or hostess. She was not going answer his question. Nope. Not a good idea. She had too much on the line to be distracted by a guy, sexy as sin though he was in his shorts and tight t-shirt.

Chapter 9

Nik stifled a laugh when she pulled her elbow away. Hot. She thought he was hot. Guess he was making an impression, after all. He put his hand to her back. She stiffened, but he kept it there as he led her into the restaurant, signaling to any Voices present—and mortals, too—that she was his.

Well, not "his" exactly, but under his... Not under, but... Now he was hot. Was the restaurant's air conditioning working? As they entered the dining area, she stepped away from his reach and turned. "Do we sit at the bar or at a table?"

"How many for dinner? Two?" Hermes again. This time, dressed like a hard-working blue-collar mortal in jeans and plaid flannel shirt. Was he spending all his time here lately?

"Two. A table, please," Nik gritted out. Ever the trickster, what was Hermes up to now?

He led them to a corner table with a window that looked out into the shadowed woods. Setting down the menus, he pulled out a chair for MJ, smirking at Nik over her head. "Your server will be right with you." He smiled down at MJ. "If you need anything...you just let me know." MJ smiled at him up at him, a full-on, teeth-bright, flirty smile. *Hades take it!* She had yet to smile at him like that. Still, she hadn't denied the "hot" comment. He tapped his menu on the table. "Please send our server over immediately. We're hungry."

Hermes clicked his heels and bowed his head. "Right away, sir." He winked at MJ and sauntered off. MJ turned her head to watch him walk away, and he caught her mumble, "Another hottie."

"What?"

"Nothing." She turned back to him. "Why were you so rude?"

Nik looked at the menu. "What are you talking about? I said please. And we are hungry."

"I haven't even had time to read the menu."

"Get the burger. It's out of this world, here."

Silence. Nik looked up. She stared at him, one brow raised. "What?"

"Are you one of those?"

"One of what?"

"One of those men who like to tell a woman what to eat, what to wear, and..."

"No, I am not. It was a recommendation, not an order."

She went back to reading the menu. *Good. No argument. Where was the server?* He looked around, seeing at least half a dozen Voices at the bar, all of whom studiously ignored him. None had a mortal with him.

A young woman with an apron around her waist, and order pad in hand, hustled over to the table. "Sorry to keep you waiting. What can I get for you?"

MJ said, "I'll have the..." She glanced at him. "...burger. Medium rare. And may I have a house salad with that instead of the fries?"

The waitress nodded, took Nik's order, also a burger but with the fries, and hurried off. MJ folded her arms and leaned forward on the table. "You promised me a story about the White Horses."

Juliette asked him the same question the first time he brought her here. Smart, observant women must run in the family. Juliette, however, had also asked about all the men in the place, and if Nik noticed that the bartender, Hermes again, had eyes of two different colors. She soaked it all in and he had wondered how long it would be before some or all of it turned up in one of her books.

He never found out.

MJ waited patiently for Nik to explain.

Smiling, he said, "As I told your grandmother, in Greek myth, Poseidon is the god of the sea."

MJ nodded. Gran had loved the Greek myths.

"He created the horse, the animal of power, speed, and virility." Nik continued. "The white horse has other specific associations but the reason this tavern is called White Horses is because it is located close to the ocean."

"What does that have to do with it?" *Was he going to make her play Twenty Questions?* Guys were supposed to be so straightforward. They were anything but, in her experience. He folded his arms and, like her, leaned on the table putting himself closer to her, and suddenly she smelled sea wind and pine. *Was that his after shave?*

"Are you familiar with Greek mythology?"

"You're kidding? You remember who my grandmother was, right?"

His eyes lit up. "Right. So, you know the story of Pegasus? How he is the son of Poseidon, god of the sea?"

"Yes, Pegasus, the winged white horse."

"Well, as I said, Poseidon is the creator of horses. He was challenged to make a beautiful land animal, so looking at the motion of breaking waves, their curls, their sound, he created horses, especially white horses, known to be a symbol of royalty, freedom and..." he coughed a word, picked up a glass and swallowed the remaining beer. MJ gaze followed the movement of his throat.

"What?"

He looked away. "Sexuality and fertility." He hurried on. "The next time you are outside here and it is windy, look at the breaking waves, the way they curl and froth. The waves look like the manes of white horses racing toward the shore. And the thunder of the surf is the sound of their hooves."

MJ looked out the window next to them. The darkening woods were the screen for the images in her mind. A herd of white horses, heads thrusting forward, ears back, muscles bunching in shoulders and hindquarters, and their manes twisting and, yes, frothing in the wind. Oh, the power and beauty. Her blood was doing the thundering now. The image made her long for— She blinked her eyes open to see Nik's dark eyes on her. Dark eyes. Sea wind and pine drifted to her again.

"Which way are the restrooms," she asked, shooting up out of her chair. He pointed and she hurried in that direction. *This is what happens when you let your imagination—or white horses—run away with you, MJ.* She shouldn't feel attracted to him. He was an uptight, financial adviser attached to his spreadsheets and numbers and dollar signs. Just because he'd been a knight in shining armor for her grandmother didn't mean she'd accept him in that role. It was the twenty-first century and women rescued themselves, after all.

But something about him unsettled her. In more ways than one.

As she walked away, the soft knit capris cupping her ass, her long braid bouncing just above it as if to ensure Nik kept his eyes there, he was uncertain whether he wanted to finish this assignment as quickly as he originally thought. He narrowed his gaze at Alek who also watched MJ as she moved past him. He turned and smiled at Nik, raising his mug of beer at him. Nik's grip on his own mug tightened. He knew Alek was purposely aggravating him, but he couldn't help the clutch of possessiveness that grabbed at him.

Certain that MJ was a spoiled, modern woman who didn't have time for anyone or anything but her career and friends, he was surprised that, instead, she reminded him of women from decades ago, uncertain, a little naive, and too easily swayed by the expectations of others. Her uncertainty, her desire to please, and her sorrow over the loss of her Gran pulled at him.

Alek turned back to the bar, laughing at something Hermes said as he dried glasses. Nik risked bringing MJ here because they both needed to get out of the cottage and away from all the emotions embedded in the walls, hanging in the air. And here he was with his kind. Still, no telling what mischief Hermes and the others might try if they thought it would make him a little crazy.

MJ walked back, chin up, eyes on their table, seemingly unaware of all the looks from the men. Or did she pretend to be oblivious? In his centuries of experience, most women had internal sensors alerting them to the presence and awareness of males around her. Most loved the attention, but she didn't look at anyone, put an extra swing in her hips, or do anything but walk back and sit down, just as the waitress arrived with their orders. The smells of juicy hamburger and freshly fried potatoes made his mouth water. He lifted his burger and took a bite, savoring the flavors of beef and cheese and tomato.

"Mmmhh..."

Hearing it, Nik looked up to see MJ with her eyes closed as she chewed. Licking her lips, she opened her mouth to take another bite and Nik watched, mesmerized and waiting.

"Mmmmmhhh..."

Another lick of the lips. Mmmm was right. He wanted to lick her lips. He shifted in his seat. If she kept doing that... "Told you they were the best burgers you'd ever eat," he said, hoping to avert disaster. She opened her eyes and smiled. A genuine, delighted smile, her eyes wide and happy. It was the first he'd seen it and his heart stopped. All this for a burger. Had Hermes doctored hers?

"Yes, you did say that. They are delicious. Fit for the gods."

He nearly spat out the bite he'd just taken. Was she hinting? No, she swirled one of his fries in ketchup then ate it small bite by small bite. White teeth and red lips. A spot of ketchup clung to her lower lip and he had the sudden urge to lick it off, probably tasting salt as well as ketchup. He glanced around the bar to see if anyone was paying attention. Alek nodded at him and mouthed a silent "Whew!" Seeing Alek's action, Hermes looked over and smiled at Nik with sharp white teeth. If Hermes was messing with him, with MJ...

Hades! Next time, he'd take her somewhere else. Somewhere only mortal men hung out, men easily intimidated by his glare.

"Mmmmhhh."

Blast. He finished his burger, trying to ignore her murmurs and purrs over her food. His mother would love how she enjoyed and savored her food, but the little sounds were making him twitchy. She tucked the last bite of burger—thank the gods—into her mouth, chewed, swallowed and, yes, of course, licked her lips. Nik swallowed, too, even though he had nothing in his mouth.

"You've proved you're a good financial manager. And you obviously know a good burger, but that's almost all I know about you."

Oh, Hades, he knew where this was going. "Do you want dessert?" he asked quickly, hoping to derail her train of thought.

She frowned and stuck her fork into her salad. "I haven't finished, but, no, I'm full." She took another bite, then laid fork and knife neatly across her plate, took a sip of her drink and dabbed at those moist lips with her napkin.

"So?" She placed the napkin neatly next to her plate.

Watching her mouth frame the 'o' he wondered if those lips were as soft and plump.

"Earth to Nik."

His gaze shot to hers. "What?"

She frowned again. "Tell me something about yourself. For instance, do you have any siblings?"

He picked up a cold fry, shoved it into his mouth and sat chewing. Anything to stall while his mind figured out what to say. Then he shrugged. He'd play the strong silent type.

"Yes."

She pressed her lips together. "Okay... Well, if you don't want to talk about your family, what about your work. Do you like what you do?"

Nik felt like a character in that movie where the mortals' heads exploded in colors throughout a banquet hall. No one, not his mother or Apollo or Alek or even Hermes, had ever asked him that. No one, with the exception of Juliette, had ever cared enough to ask it. All those mortals, all those centuries of inspiring and collaborating and advising, and he'd only ever been a business partner, at best, or a servant. Gods, he used to like what he did, but he was so damn tired of it. What would it be like to be a mortal, to fall in love, have a family? He shook his head. Thinking like that was an exercise in frustration.

"No? If you don't like it, why are you doing it?"

He realized she misinterpreted. Or had she? He saw the waitress and signaled for the check. She sat silent while they waited. He shrugged but kept his eyes on the view out the window. He paid the check, telling her, "It's a business expense. Don't worry about it." Then he rose, pulled out her chair and followed her out through the restaurant. She was already through the door when he reached Hermes, who stood looking after her." What's she uptight about all of sudden?"

"She's asking questions I can't, won't answer."

Hermes nodded, then put a hand on Nik's shoulder, leaning closer. "Be careful. Something is in the wind. Feel it?"

Nik shook his head. He'd been too caught up in MJ, but he'd pay better attention.

Chapter 10

S tanding by the car, arms folded around herself, and staring off into the woods, she looked lost. Lonely. Nik walked up to her and placed his hands on her arms. She gasped and he gently moved her back from the car.

"Sorry, but I can't open the doors with you standing so close to it." He clicked the remote and the doors rose. "Your carriage awaits my lady." Ignoring him, she looked toward the ocean, although they couldn't see it from there.

"Do you think there are white horses now?"

"We can certainly find out, if m'lady will have a seat."

She frowned but took his hand and slid into the car. After he pressed the ignition button, she sighed loudly enough to be heard over the rumble of the engine.

"We should just go back. I have work to do."

Shifting the car into gear, he tore out of the parking lot. *Why did she fight him on everything?* If it hadn't been for her "hot" comment, he'd think he'd lost his touch. Most of the creative women he worked with in the past were easily charmed into following his suggestions and guidance, even Juliette. Oh, from the others, there'd been arguments and tantrums at times, but they'd been brief and led to productive moments, sexually and creatively. Not with Juliette, regardless of what her grand-daughter wondered.

MJ showed no signs of being charmed or capitulating to his guidance. He shifted again, and the car flew down the road. She clutched the door handle, and he lifted his foot slightly from the gas pedal. No sense scaring her to death, especially since he had yet to bring up Juliette's unfinished manuscript. If he convinced her to finish her grandmother's novel, it would be easier to charm her into writing her own. Her grandmother insisted MJ was a natural storyteller, with books, like horses at the starting gate, just waiting for the signal to run.

He looked over at her. She was leaning back, silently staring at the passing view. Lowering the windows slightly on either side of the car, the sea air whipped in. Her eyes closed. No questions, no empty chatter. Just the sound of the wind and the car's engine. He could ride with her like this all night, if only he could. If only he was mortal, driving down this road with nothing more important on his mind than taking this woman home to bed. Instead, he blew out a breath as they pulled into the driveway of the cottage. She reached for the door, but he hit the button and the doors rose. Wind whirled around them. Not a summer zephyr but a storm bringer.

White horses.

She was startled to feel the wind rush through the car and tease strands of hair from her braid. The car's speed and the darken-ing twilight had made her feel contained in another world, one with just her and Nik. She sighed as she exited the car. Playtime was over. In fact, she shouldn't have been playing at all, she should have eaten here at the table while she worked, like she did most of the time. Still, glancing at her watch, she had a few hours to work before giving in to sleep after an exhausting—and emotional—day, as long as Nik stayed out of her space and mind.

He followed her to the door and reached for the knob. The knob didn't twist in his hand, and he looked at her in the light of the porch, waiting. She stepped past, slid her key in the lock, and pushed open the door, catching a faint scent reminiscent of her grandmother. She swallowed, and ignored the framed photograph as she walked into the dining area and dropped her purse on the table. *Time to get to work. Where was her computer? Oh, yes, over on the sideboard.* She retrieved it and her bookbag and set them on the table.

A breeze brushed against her neck. Looking up, she discovered Nik at the open French doors. The wind ruffled his hair, and she heard the waves tumbling onto the beach. "Perfect!"

"What's perfect?" She dug her pad and pen out of the bookbag.

"Conditions for seeing the white horses. Let's go look."

What? He stood at the door with his hand out to her. *Really? Didn't he get it? She had work to do.*

"Don't you want to see the myth in action? You know, the white horses."

"I have work to do. I told you."

"You did tell me, and I respect that, but ten minutes isn't going to keep you from your work for long, and you wanted to see the white horses. Come. Let us see them before the storm rolls in."

He opened the door wider and beckoned to her. Was she tempted by the white horses, or by the good-looking guy holding out his hand to her? Or was she just looking for an excuse to avoid the damned dis—

His smiled disappeared. "Fine. I'll go myself. The fresh sea air would be good for you, wake you up. But, go ahead. Work."

"Wait!"

Did her mouth utter that command? Fresh air would be good for her. She hurried to him and followed him out the door and down the steps to the beach.

"Just for a few minutes," she said.

He took her hand, its warmth radiating up her arm. His fingers were long, firm, and she sensed the strength in them, as he led her to the shoreline, her hand feeling at home in his. She pulled away and bent over, using the removal of her sandals as a reason. No handholding. He was her financial advisor, not her boyfriend. Not even her friend. Too soon for either.

He, too, slipped his shoes off and strode toward the water. "Do you see them?" he yelled back at her over the sound of the waves and gestured at the water.

The sand was still warm under her feet from the day's sun. She wiggled her toes, sinking her feet into the sand. *When was the last time she was at a beach? Maybe one time with Gran, when she was a child? Had they come here, to this beach?* She walked over to Nik at the water's edge. The foaming roll of waves on the beach thundered in her ears. The wind blew against her, ironing her blouse to her skin. There was just enough light left to discern ocean from sky but it wasn't about the view now. It was about the wind and the waves.

She certainly was awake now, and more. Exhilarated. Another word to add to that list of magical words.

"Do you see them?" Nik yelled, leaning towards her to make himself heard, and pointing at the water. Wave after wave rose further out and hurled itself at the shore, frothing and foaming whitely before falling to the beach and sending ripples up to swirl and dance around her feet.

"Yes. Yes, I can see them!" She smiled at him, and clapped her hands, as if she was ten again, as she watched more waves roll in, thundering like many hooves. Her heartbeat quickened, doing its own thundering in her chest and she took a step closer to the water and the white horses. The water rose around her feet as she stepped further into it, breathing in the air. She spread her arms, wondering if she could take flight in the wind. She took another step, the horses stampeding past her. Magical, like out of a story. She heard Nik yell to her, but she ignored him. The horses wanted her to join them. To play with them.

Just a little farther. Come just a little farther.

Thalassa watched the stupid mortal respond to the spell she cast, walking deeper and deeper into the water.

Nikos called to the mortal, but Thalassa waved her hand, deflecting the sound waves. Too bad for the woman that he was behind her. Too far behind. Too bad for him that he had no idea she waited here in deep water.

Waited. And waited. And...

Now!

Why was MJ ignoring him? It wasn't safe to go so far into this rough water. He pushed through the water towards her. Suddenly, her legs went out from under her and she disappeared below the water. When she didn't emerge after a few seconds, he dove into the water and swam in her direction. *Where was she? What had happened?* He reached where she'd been standing and stood up, looking for her. One breath. Two.

The water pushed at him as if to separate them. *Shit!* He dove again, deeper this time, trying to peer through the gloom of the water, reaching and searching with his hands. *Where was she?* "Poseidon, help me," he prayed to the god of the sea. This was his fault for insisting she come look at the white horses. He swam in even larger circles from where she'd disappeared. She had to be here somewhere. He stood, the water almost up to his chin.

"MJ!" he yelled, his voice echoed back. He was about to dive again, when a giant sea turtle with two differently colored eyes rose in front of him, MJ draped across his back, unmoving.

"Hermes, thank the gods. Thank you." He lifted MJ from the turtle's back and braced her head, face up, on his shoulder.

"I told you to watch out, be careful. Are you paying attention now?" Hermes as turtle said.

"Did you do this?" Nik asked, knowing the answer even as he asked it.

"Don't be insulting, Nikos. Poseidon alerted me earlier so I made sure to be here. In case."

"Alerted you to what? Did he know this would happen?"

"Suspected. Go. Take care of your mortal. Now is not the time..."

The turtle sank below the water and was gone.

Nik gripped MJ tightly and swam to shore as fast as he could. Carrying her up onto the sand, he lay her down, and breathed into her mouth repeatedly until she gasped. Turning her on her side, he held her up by the shoulders as she retched up the sea. When she stopped, he scooped her up and ran the short distance to the cottage. Her long braid swung heavily, lashing against his side as if to rebuke him for insisting she come outside to see the white horses. If he'd left her alone to do her work... He'd almost lost her.

He tightened his hold on her as he ascended the steps to the deck. Light from the cottage spilled onto them and he looked down at her face. Her skin was dusted with sand, her lashes wet and clumped, her lips pale. Without thinking, he bent and brushed his lips against hers. Only to warm them. If he'd lost her, he'd have failed Juliette and his duty as a Voice.

Managing to twist the handle of the French door, he pulled it open with the hand under her knee. Without pausing, he rushed through the cottage to the stairs and climbed them to Juliette's, no, MJ's bedroom and into the bathroom. Dropping to sit on the side of the jacuzzi tub, he maintained his hold around her shoulders and used his other hand to turn on taps.

Finally, she stirred. "What are you doing?" she asked, her voice weak.

"I'm running you a hot bath. You're shivering from shock and cold, and it's the fastest way to warm you up."

"Okay." She sighed against his neck, her breath warm. He was as wet as she was, the two of them dripping sea water all over the floor. He had to get her out of her wet things and get her warm. Himself, too. He tested the water again. Hot but not too hot.

Standing, he carefully set her on the closed toilet and stepped slowly back. She sighed and dropped her head but stayed seated. He grabbed one of the towels and draped it over her shoulders. She huddled into it.

Turning, he shut off the water, then yanked off his shirt and shorts, left on his boxers though he wasn't sure it made a difference. They were soaked and stuck to him like paint on a canvas. Grabbing another towel, he rubbed some of the moisture from his hair, then draped the towel around his waist. Now for her.

First, her hair. He pulled the braid free of the towel and managed to pull the hair band off the end. Then, he pulled apart the three strands of the braid and continued to unwrap them from each other. The strands were thick and sticky with sand

and salt. They seemed to grab and hold his fingers as he kept unraveling the braid.

"What are you doing?" She straightened, lifting her head and blinking her eyes open. Her eyes widened as she saw her unbraided hair and she swatted at his hands. "Stop that. Leave it braided."

"Can't." He gently pushed her hands away, and continued unbraiding her hair. "If we leave it braided, the sand and sea water will make it a sticky mess impossible to deal with once it dries." Besides, he'd been waiting and wanting to see her hair undone ever since he met her that day for the reading of the will, since he'd followed her up the stairs the night he brought her to the cottage for the first time and he'd watched the braid swing back and forth in front of him like a mad hypnotist at work. He had to see what it looked like unrestrained.

He wanted to linger over the task, but she shivered, so he quickly finished freeing the strands and ran his fingers through them to loosen the hair. She sighed and leaned her head against his thigh. He froze. And reminded himself that this mortal woman was not trying to seduce him, had no idea what she'd made stir beneath his towel.

And she would not welcome any attempt on his part to seduce her. Not yet.

Chapter 11

MJ was freezing. And confused, and, if she was truthful, frightened. *What happened out there?*

Safe in the bathroom, warming up from the steam from the tub and the heat Nik was giving off, she still shivered. The speed of the night's events shocked her. *If he hadn't been there...* He stepped away and she missed the warmth of his body. Fear crept in. What happened out there was too weird. As if something or someone—

No, she wasn't going to dwell on it. The active imagination her mother accused her of could scare her spitless. *What in the water could grab at her ankles, or pull her by her braid, and not let her go? What made her walk into the water at all?* She shivered again. Focus on the rising warmth of the room, the steamy water filling the tub. She'd be deliciously warm once she was in the tub, after Nik got her clothes off.

She blinked and realized Nik's head was bowed above her, his hair as wet as hers, dripping on her legs, as his fingers slipped first one button then another through their buttonholes on her shirt.

Whoa!

"Stop that," she said weakly, batting his hands away from her.

"You need to get into the tub. You're shivering with shock and cold."

"Yes, thank you, I realize that, believe me, but I can undress myself. You're wet, too. Go shower, I can do this."

His gaze stayed on hers, as if measuring the truth of her declaration. He nodded. "Take your time. I'll shower and dress and then check on you."

She shook her head. "There's no need. I'll see you downstairs."

"Fine." He stopped at the door and looked back, his eyes darkening. "Let me know if you need help brushing your hair."

Nik blew out a breath as he headed to his room, pulling the towel from his waist to rub the dampness from his hair so he didn't leave drops of water on Juliette's carpet and floor. The air on his damp boxers would chill the ardor of the last few minutes with MJ.

In his bathroom, he turned on the shower's cold water tap. Gods, the feel of her long hair sliding through his fingers, the soft swell of her breasts revealed as he unbuttoned her blouse, and the warmth of her breath against his thigh as she'd leaned against him. He wanted more, to pull her close and wrap himself around her, feeling her warm softness. He wanted...

Not yet.

Maybe never.

He stepped into the shower, muscles tightening against the shock of the cold water. According to Juliette's knowledge of her granddaughter, MJ hadn't had many short- or long-term relationships. Not like other mortal clients who easily fell into and out of bed with him, too wrapped up in themselves or their work to let sexual pleasure evolve into attachment or love. She probably wasn't a woman to indulge in meaningless sexual play. He recalled the way she walked back to their table at the tavern, totally oblivious to the male attention she attracted. If he had sex with her, she might well interpret it to mean more than it should...or could.

Thoroughly chilled, he turned on the hot water and reached for the soap. What happened to her out there? From where he stood in the water, he hadn't felt any pull from a current or sea weed. After he dove in to find her, there was nothing to fight against. It was weird. Poseidon had warned Hermes who had warned him, but about what? Hermes must have known the threat was serious enough to warrant him getting there fast. Poseidon usually didn't bother with mortal affairs unless his seas or the creatures thereof were threatened. He would ask Hermes, and thank the god for saving MJ.

His biggest concern now was how this incident would affect his relationship with her. He cranked off the water and stepped out of the shower, muscles relaxed. He dried off, pulled on a t-shirt and a worn pair of sweat pants, and headed downstairs to the kitchen. She was probably still cold, and, according to Juliette, a mug of hot chocolate was a favorite treat for MJ. The milk in it would help her relax and fall asleep. Passing the dining table on his way into the kitchen, her laptop and books rebuked him. No way was she going to be in any shape to work on her dissertation now. Guilt rose, if he'd let her work, she wouldn't have almost drowned. Damn it! Nothing of this assignment was easy, and he was beginning to think not only that he'd lost his touch, but perhaps it was time to stop being a Voice.

But for that white streak in his mother's hair which wouldn't be there if mortals weren't abdicating their creative powers left and right. Erato needed him to do his job, he had a responsibility to his mother and aunts. He sighed and turned off the heat beneath the cocoa. Pouring it into a mug he'd given to Juliette that said, "Only the strongest women become writers," he climbed the steps up to her room and tapped lightly on the door.

"MJ? I brought you some hot cocoa."

No answer. He tapped again, a little louder, titling his head and listening. Still nothing. What was she doing? Was she still in the tub? Surely the water had grown cold by now. Quietly, he turned the knob and eased the door open, prepared to step back if he was invading her privacy. He whispered, "MJ?"

The lights were out, so he pushed the door open wider. Moonlight spilled through the windows and onto the bed where MJ lay soundly sleeping. He eased closer. Though her hair was still wrapped in a towel, her arms were bare atop the covers. He set the mug on the dresser and padded over to the bed; his bare feet silent on the plush rug. Shorts and T-shirt lay on the bed. She'd obviously intended to meet him downstairs, but the experience and adrenaline rush must have worn her out. Good thing she hadn't fallen asleep in the tub, otherwise, he'd have had to lift a warm, naked, if wet, woman out of the tub, dried her off and tucked her into bed.

And now he needed another cold shower. *Should he pull the towel from around her hair? What if he woke her?* She shivered, though, so keeping his eyes on her face, he pulled the covers out from under her arm and up over her shoulders. Picking up the mug, he took one last look at her sleeping peacefully in the moonlight, and tiptoed from the room, pulling the door closed behind him. Drawn by the moonlight shining through the hallway windows between MJ's room and his, he walked over to look out at the ocean.

The almost full moon gave everything a shadowy yet magical aura, and painted a silken path upon the water. For who? Or what? What happened to the threatening storm? Not a cloud was in sight now. The almost-full moon reminded him this phase was prime time to use one of the tools sometimes available to a Voice, the ability to walk in dreams. After the day's events and the revelations about her grandmother's books and finances, how was she going to respond to the idea of completing her grandmother's unfinished manuscript? In order to persuade her to do it and thereby open the gates to her own creativity, a walk in MJ's dreams might be needed.

He was about to turn from the window to take the mug back to the kitchen, when something broke the surface of the ocean. He stepped closer to the glass. Was someone swimming at this time of night? Wasn't that when sea predators hunted? The form bobbed in place for a few minutes as if looking back at him. Suddenly, a high-pitched sound rang in his ears, vibrating against the glass. Just as quickly, it stopped. The form sank beneath the water, out of the moonlight, and was gone.

He waited, scanning back and forth. When nothing or no one emerged, he released the breath he was holding. *Had that been...?*

Impossible.

Nevertheless, he'd tell Hermes about it the next time he saw him.

MJ cracked her eyes open to peer at the bedside clock. *Holy guac!* She hadn't slept in this late in forever. Sunlight streamed through the windows and the noisy clamor of the gulls threatened to break the glass.

A damp towel lay spread on the pillow beneath her head. As she pulled it away, every part of her body twinged and complained, especially her neck and shoulders where her hair lay tangled. A shower. She needed a hot shower. Flinging back the covers, she eased from the bed and stumbled into the bathroom. She turned on the water to let it heat up and realized she wasn't in her pjs. *Had she even put them on?* When the water was warm enough, she stepped into the shower. And sighed. *Oh, the bliss. The utter bliss.*

She remembered Nik unbuttoning a few buttons but she'd ordered him from the bathroom, so he definitely hadn't seen her naked. She moved her head from side to side, letting the hot water soothe the aches in her neck and shoulders, warming the muscles and tendons beneath. As they warmed, her shoulders dropped, the aches eased. Grabbing the mesh shower pouf, she poured some honey coconut body wash on it and lathered up her body. She'd feel more relaxed if it wasn't for what she remembered—or didn't—from the previous night.

She had followed Nik out to the water's edge to see the white horses for herself, but how had she been swept under the water, unable to pull herself to the surface? She shivered and cranked up the hot water a notch. Had she ever been so frightened, certain she was going to drown? More scary was not remembering how she hadn't. Nik must have rescued her because she did remember his strong arms around her as he carried her into the cottage. He surprised her with his gentle care, how carefully he unbraided her hair, moving his fingers slowly, carefully through it.

She shivered again but not from cold or fear. He wasn't as cocky and unsympathetic as she'd thought. His fingers had been warm against her skin as he began unbuttoning her blouse. She yanked her mind from the memory, rinsing the last stiff vestiges of salt from her hair. Quickly, she dried off, wrapped her hair up in the towel, then grabbed the same scented body lotion. After rubbing the excess moisture from her hair, she pulled the thick length of it over her shoulder. Once again, the time it took to braid made her wonder if she ought to cut it.

Dressed, she opened the bedroom door and smelled the reviving aroma of coffee.

Her stomach growled and she hurried down the stairs into the living and dining area, halting as she caught the view out the French doors. Sunlight cast diamonds on the water as seagulls swooped and dove from a cerulean blue sky. How could something so breathtakingly beautiful be so dangerous and deadly? No white horses this morning. The ocean appeared peaceful.

A glint of light from glasses set out on the deck's table caught her eye. She opened the French doors and stepped out, smiling at the pink roses from the front flower bed in a fat, round vase sitting on the glass-topped table. White plates under plain white cereal bowls sat on multi-colored placemats. White linen napkins guarded the cutlery, and teacups and a teapot stood ready. Her vision blurred. Not quite a tea party under the dining table but still. If she looked hard enough, would Gran be there, waiting to pour tea for her?

"You must be hungry after last night's events."

The spell evaporated at the sound of the voice behind her. If only she could tell Gran she was sorry, that she loved her. Surreptitiously, she wiped the moisture from her eyes.

"I'm starving."

Chapter 12

Nik tried not to look at MJ as he set the bowls of fruit and granola on the table in the shade of the large pink umbrella. He wasn't sure what her mood was going to be after last night's harrowing episode. *Would she blame him or want to leave?*

"I'll bring out the yogurt. Do you want any juice?"

"No, thank you." Her voice was quiet, subdued. Maybe she was still tired.

He fetched the yogurt and braced himself for whatever was coming. He hoped the meal would lift her spirits after last night. He sat down across from her, both of them sideways to the ocean. He gazed out over the sparkling water and took a deep breath of the morning air. At home, the sky and water would be bluer, but this would certainly do, for him, anyway. Finally, he looked at her. Her gaze was out to sea as well, then down at her bowl. He waited. She dished out some granola and berries, then sat staring at her bowl. Surely granola and berries weren't that fascinating?

He picked up the bowl of yogurt and held it out to her. "Yogurt? Or do you want cream?"

She shook her head and took the yogurt. Sunlight shone on her hair. The strands were golden in the light but back to being restrained in the tight braid. Her face was bare of makeup which only made her appear younger and more vulnerable. His gaze sharpened on her cheeks. Were there traces of tears? He stood up.

"Are you in pain? Should I have taken you to a hospital last night?"

She shook her head. "Sit down. I'm not in pain. It's just that…"

"What?"

She didn't look at him. She glanced at the water and then down at her bowl.

"MJ?"

"I feel as if I've stepped out of my normal life," she said quietly, "out of the real world, into some strange land where nothing is as it appears. Where I don't know what to do, who I am, who you are. It's like a bad fairy tale, all strange. And unreal." She paused, then whispered, "And frightening."

Wow, this was not the MJ he was used to, vulnerable, scared. All his protective instincts rose to the surface. He remembered diving repeatedly into the darkening waters to search for her, not finding her. Frightening? More like terrifying. "After your experience last night, I think feeling frightened is expected. I was too."

Her gaze jerked up to his. "Really? You?"

He nodded. He was immortal, but she didn't know that. Why would she think he wouldn't be at least a little scared? "I'm sorry I put you through that. Thank you for rescuing me." She looked down at the bowl and fiddled with the spoon.

"MJ?" He waited for her gaze to meet his again, then he leaned across the table to her. "It was my fault. If I hadn't insisted on going out there, if I had let you work, it never would have happened."

She pulled her braid over her shoulder and sat back in her chair. "True," she brushed the end of the braid across her palm, "but I shouldn't have walked into the water. I don't know why I did. It was almost as if…"

"As if what?"

She shrugged and threw the braid back. "Nothing. It was just…strange. I don't think I'll venture back into the water for a while."

"At least not without someone who can swim well and rescue you if necessary."

She stared at him for a moment, her eyes dropping to his mouth and he held his breath.

"Yes, well." She picked up the teapot, poured herself a cup and then moved the pot to his cup, raising her brows at him.

"Please," he said, but what he really thought was yes, come over here and let me kiss you, and run my fingers through your hair like I did last night. When she had leaned against his thigh and he'd felt her warm breath. He shifted in his seat. *Damn.* She picked up her spoon and began eating, not looking at him. At least they were done with the subject of her scare. He ate, too, determined to give her space to think, to be silent if she wanted to.

She took a final bite, then put her bowl on the tray he'd used to carry everything out. Grabbing her mug of tea, she stood. "Thank you for fixing breakfast. Again. Since I didn't work last night, I need to get to work now. I'm falling behind."

He stood. "We aren't done yet, you know."

She eyed the tray of empty dishes and frowned. "What do you mean?" Then she smiled at him. "Are you hiding pastries somewhere? Chocolate croissants, perhaps?"

A breeze off the water stirred the strands of hair that had come free from her braid. She was like a delicious wood nymph. Slowly, he reached up and tucked a strand behind her ear. Her hair was so soft. He heard the slight inhalation and, realizing what he was doing, dropped his hand, and put his own bowl on the tray along with the yogurt and napkins, then picked up the tray.

"Sadly, I have no croissants hiding anywhere though I know a good place to get some."

She opened the French door and he walked inside, setting the tray down next to the sink. Teacup in hand, she drifted to the table and picked up a sheet of paper and began reading it.

"MJ?"

"Hmmm?"

"There is more I need to talk about with you regarding your grandmother's legacy."

Her head shot up. "Now?" she asked frowning, "Can't it wait. I really need to get some work done, in case mother calls."

He bit back what he thought about her mother. Instead, her shoulders slumped and he remembered what she'd said out on the deck. He didn't want this experience to be like a bad fairy tale. Juliette would never forgive him, and seeing as how he was going to see her tonight, he'd better help MJ, not make her feel worse.

"Of course. I'm sorry. I don't mean to make things harder on you. Why don't you work on your dissertation this morning, and then, after lunch, we'll go over your grandmother's publishing contracts."

She nodded, but she'd already settled into a chair and was organizing index cards. Nik knew that, as far as she was concerned, he'd disappeared.

So, maybe he would. For a while.

Nik strode into the Voices' bar. Unlike the White Horses, this place was an odd mixture of ancient building and modern mortals' toys. The pool table, for example. Alek and another Voice stood next to it, cue sticks in one hand, drinks in the other. Other Voices sat, elbows on tables, while they laughed and drank. Although it was midmorning at the cottage, here it was late afternoon and time for winding down. Or winding up, depending on whether the Voice had an assignment or not.

"Dude!" Alek called to him, "Wanna play me after I beat this guy?"

He shook his head and took a seat at the bar, but froze when he saw Apollo standing behind it. *Skata!* He was going to have explain himself. What was the god doing there in the first place, tending bar?

"He lost a bet," someone whispered in his ear. He turned. Hermes stood behind him, dressed in jeans, sneakers with that swoosh symbol, and a troubadour shirt in a sparkling black fabric. His long brown hair was tied back. *What was he dressed for—scaling castle walls?*

"What bet?" He avoided looking at the god's eyes which were unnerving with their two different colors. The god smirked, sticking his hands in the back pockets of his jeans.

"Let's just say it had to do with a shepherdess and her sheep. He lost, so he had to bar tend today. How's MJ?"

Nik glanced at Apollo, then quietly answered the trickster, "Seems fine, back at work on her dissertation."

Hermes nodded then drifted over to where Kristos sat strumming on a guitar. Hermes picked up his lyre and joined him. Apollo raised an eyebrow. "What'll it be? Ambrosia?"

Nik couldn't get his brain to work. Apollo as bartender. He shook his head.

"Is that a no?"

"No, I'll have a drink, but of one of the mortals' finest bourbons."

Apollo pulled two glasses out from under the bar, then turned and scanned the shelf of liquors behind him. He pulled a bottle of Pappy out, opened it, and poured several fingers into each glass. It was a good thing Nik's metabolism didn't react to liquor the way a mortal's would, since his body was operating on mortal time. Now if that was ambrosia...

He set Nik's glass in front of him and picked up the other. "What are you doing here, Nikos? Why aren't you with your mortal?"

Nik swallowed back a third of his drink, relishing its burn on the way down. The drink slightly soothed his impatience with MJ, and his concerns. He took another swallow. "I had to leave her alone for a bit. She insisted on working on her dissertation." He emptied his glass, licking the last drops from his lips. Why did the gods make such a fuss about ambrosia when the bourbon was warming and smooth? Mortals had so many delicious intoxicating beverages. No wonder many of them stayed intoxicated.

"How are things going?" Apollo swirled the bourbon in his glass.

"She's overwhelmed. And frightened. Something happened last night. Did Hermes tell you?"

He nodded. "I don't like it. I'll be talking with Poseidon to find out what he knows."

"You don't think it could be, well..."

"Spit it out, Voice, it's not like you to be reticent."

"After MJ was safely asleep in bed, I saw something out on the water." Nik picked up his now empty glass. With a sigh, the god poured them both another shot. "Thank you, sire." Nik sipped then dared to say what was on his mind. "I heard a loud sound, similar to a scream or a screech and I wondered if it was one of the sirens, and they tried to drown MJ."

Apollo crossed his arms and frowned. "I don't see how they could. They are banished to their island. More, why would they? What would be the point? Still." He straightened and looked around the room. "Hermes!"

Hermes twanged a last chord then, placing the lyre on top of the stool he'd sat on, crossed to the bar. "You bellowed?"

"Nikos wonders if one of the sirens is hanging about his mortal's cottage. Could she have been the cause of the mortal almost drowning?"

Hermes looked at Nik. "I told you to be careful."

"You didn't tell me what to be careful of."

Apollo put his fists to his hips. "What is going on, brother?"

He shrugged. "I will not speak of what I know. There is no need as long as you do what you are meant to do, Nikos. Just as I will do what I am meant to do."

With that, he disappeared.

"Hermes!" Apollo roared. The room darkened. The glasses behind the bar vibrated. Kristo and the other Voices silently left the bar. Nik held his ground, just as angry as Apollo. *Was his mortal in danger? From a Siren?*

"I will speak with your aunt, their mother. This will not be allowed."

Nik said nothing. What was there to say? But if it was a Siren?

He would guard MJ with every measure of power that was his.

After spending the afternoon going over publishing contracts with MJ, Nik told her he had a meeting that evening and encouraged her not to work too late and reminded her he had a key.

He made no effort to muffle his footsteps as he approached the cave, since he didn't want to start off on the wrong foot with the god whose permission he needed. His idea to walk in MJ's dreams solidified that afternoon with MJ's concerns about managing her grandmother's legacy. Not once had she mentioned wanting to be a writer like her grandmother, and that worried him. Was she so entrenched in self-doubt from her mother's dismissal of her imagination that the idea of ever writing her own novel, was buried too deep to be resurrected?

If so, then anything he said to her about finishing her grandmother's manuscript or writing her own story was going to be discounted and argued about. He needed a different approach, one the Voices resorted to...often because it was the easiest way to communicate with mortals when their defenses were down. He needed permission, though, since he wanted someone not a Voice to walk in the dream with him. Fortunately, he'd discovered an almost full bottle of poppy seeds in Juliette's spice cabinet, a necessary tribute to Morpheus, and something he was sure MJ wouldn't miss. He stopped in front of the god's cave where a dream runner stood guard before a wide oaken door.

Nik nodded at him. "Requesting permission to speak with the Dream Lord." He held up the bottle. "I bring tribute."

"Name?"

"Nikos, one of Apollo's Voices."

"Wait here."

The runner entered the cave, and Nik gazed up at the night sky, finding the constellation the mortals called Orion the Hunter. Being in his own world again, he was tempted to drop in on his mother but there wasn't time. Even an immortal needed sleep, especially when he was working in the mortal realm.

The door of the cave swung open again. "Follow me," the runner ordered.

Inside, the walls of the carved stone tunnel were dimly lit but even in the lackluster, flickering light of the torches set on sconces along the tunnel, the dream runner's trews and sleeveless tunic sparkled, as if he'd run under a waterfall. It wasn't water, Nik knew, it was stardust, stardust on a dark netted fabric perfect for nightwork.

After several turns, they entered a large grotto, one filled with activity that was more hive than cave. Dream runners, most dressed like his guide, dashed about, some running to the center of the cave, grabbing slips of paper, and then streaking out of the cave. Others ran into the cave from different tunnel openings than the one he entered through. They gathered around two winged figures who floated a foot or two above the milling runners and made notes as the incoming runners shouted at them.

At the center of it all, stood a massive, carved pulpit of dream crystal, patterned with inclusions of pink lithium, green prehnite, and yellow-green epidote. It would have financed the building of a skyscraper in the mortal realm as the crystal was rare and costly, and the pulpit was big enough for several people to stand in comfortably, even three huge men such as stood there now, Morpheus and his two brothers, Phantas and Phobetor.

Morpheus, dressed in a black leather jacket over black t-shirt and jeans, ripped a slip of paper off a fat tablet sitting in the pulpit wall in front of him. He handed it to a runner and then turned and spoke into Phantas' ear. Laughing, Phantas clapped his brother on the back.

"This way," the runner said, "and stay close. You don't want to interrupt the flow."

Flow? It appeared more like turbulence, but he stayed on the dream runner's heels and quickly arrived at the pulpit. And Morpheus.

Nik put his right fist over his heart and bowed. "Lord."

He kept his bow until Morpheus said, "Remind me. Who are you?"

Nik straightened and looked up at him and his brothers standing on either side. Phantas grinned, his blonde hair falling over the right side of his face, and Phobetor, his silver hair caught back and tied, stared back at him with his lips pressed in a straight line. Phantas said something to Morpheus, handing him a slip of paper which he handed off again to a runner.

"Lord, I am Nikos, Voice of Lord Apollo, and son of Muse Erato."

He nodded. "And you are here because..."

"I respectfully request permission to walk in the dreams of a mortal, and while doing so, bring the shade of the mortal's grandmother to visit her in her dreams."

Scanning the activity in the grotto, Morpheus dropped his gaze back to him. "I should grant this request for what reason?"

Nikos spoke carefully, "I believe, Lord, that the mortal, Marie Juliette Montague has buried her *merika* so deeply that even with my encouragement and her own desires, she refuses to give herself permission to do what she longs to do."

Another runner ran up, accepted another slip of paper from Morpheus and ran off again.

"Why is this mortal's *merika* so important? There are thousands of mortals out there who have yet to claim theirs."

"She's a storyteller, Lord. Or she has the ability to be one, one as popular and widely read as her grandmother, Juliette

Montague, given support and encouragement. One as favored by my mother as her grandmother."

"Thus, the visit from her grandmother's shade?" He nodded, then leaned over to speak to Phobetor who hadn't stopped frowning at Nik. Phobetor nodded and disappeared.

"He has gone to alert Hades to your mission and the need for the Montague woman to visit her granddaughter. Now, what did you bring in tribute?"

Looking over at the mountain of poppyseeds resting against the cave wall, Nik held up his small bottle of seeds, embarrassed. Morpheus took it, ran his other hand below the pulpit wall and pulled up a smaller dark bottle. While pouring a few seeds from the tribute bottle into the smaller one, he whispered words too soft to hear. Then he set it down and, taking a tiny cork from behind the pulpit the Dream Lord tapped it into the dark bottle and offered it to Nik.

"When you wish to walk in her dreams, put a few drops on your tongue and a few drops on the shade's eyelids." He raised a finger and a runner came up. "See this one out."

Nik bent low at the waist, "Thank you, my lord."

Over his head, Morpheus said, "Give my greetings to your esteemed mother when next you speak with her."

He stifled the impulse to look up, nodding instead. It wouldn't do to let the Dream Lord see the smirk on his face. What had his mother been up to? He turned and followed the sparks like stars—or fireflies—of the runner's garment through the tunnel and out into the night.

Taking a relieved breath to be out of the cave, he gripped the small bottle tightly in his hand, and headed back to the cottage.

Chapter 13

MJ sat back and stretched her arms over her head, trying to get the kinks out of her neck and back. *How long had she been working, anyway?* A glance at the computer clock showed her it was one o'clock. Except for a few bathroom breaks, and a refill on her coffee, she'd been sitting at the table working on her dissertation for hours. Stiff though she might be, she was pleased with the morning's work. A dozen new pages were in the document, and a dozen index cards had joined the completed pile.

But her stomach complained loudly. The fridge wasn't empty but it certainly wasn't full with only greens, cheeses, eggs, yogurt, two jars of jam, one grape and one raspberry, butter, half and half, and that was it. She definitely needed to find a grocery store.

A search of the cupboards revealed peanut butter, rice, pasta, and crackers. She checked the bread box next to the fridge and found a loaf of sourdough bread. Hadn't she seen...? She opened the cupboard with the peanut butter and yes, on the shelf above it, a can of tomato soup. Oh Gran. Even when she wasn't here, she was making sure MJ had comfort food. Quickly, she put the soup to heat in a small pot on the stove, then cut slices from two of the cheeses she pulled from the fridge, an aged cheddar, and a Monterey Jack.

A knock sounded at the front door. *Who in the world?*

She adjusted the flame under the soup to low and hurried to the door. When she opened it, Nik stood on the doorstep, hands in his shorts' pockets, hair windblown, and a broad smile on his face. Her heart picked up its pace, pounding in her chest. *Whew!* He was—she didn't know what he was, but he dumbfounded her. Or rather, her reaction to him did. His smile disappeared. "May I come in?"

Embarrassed, she shut her mouth which had drifted open while she stared at him, and stepped back, gesturing him in. "I'm sorry. I guess I expected you to let yourself in so I was surprised to see you standing there."

His smile reappeared. "It's your place, not mine. I'm a guest. I didn't want to startle you or catch you unawares."

She nodded and he brushed past her, enveloping her in a scent of spice and sun. She closed her eyes and drew a deep breath. *Acck! What was she doing?* She shut the door and sped back to the kitchen.

"I'm fixing soup and grilled cheese sandwiches for myself. Want some?"

"Ah, a Juliette specialty. I'd love some."

The twinge of jealousy that she felt about his time with her grandmother faded more quickly than before. He wasn't to blame. It was kind of nice to have someone who had appreciated her grandmother as she had.

And now it was her turn to cook for him.

Nik took a last bite of his delicious sandwich. As much as he had been enjoying the quiet meal, it was time to get back to work. After setting their dishes on the counter, he retrieved his satchel.

"That was delicious. Thank you. We have one more matter we need to talk about in relation to your grandmother's legacy. Want to go sit out on the deck?"

She looked at her laptop and papers, still spread out on most of the table except where they'd been eating, sighed, and followed him out to the deck. Once seated, he pulled a stack of pages held together with a wide binder clip from his satchel, and placed it in front of her. "This is the last book your grandmother was working on."

"Oh," MJ said softly and laid her hand on the cover. "*From the Depths,* by Julie Moon. How wonderful."

"Yes, well, there's just one problem. It isn't finished."

"Oh, no!" She rifled through the pages.

"And it will remain unfinished unless..." He'd begun to lose her. She was reading the first page of the manuscript. "MJ?"

She jerked her head up. "What?"

"It will remain unfinished unless you finish it."

She laughed and bent her head back to the manuscript. "MJ, I'm serious."

She shook her head and turned back to the manuscript.

"MJ, look at me." He waited patiently as she read a few more lines then looked up, reluctance plain on her face. "She's written more than half of the book, so you'll have an idea of the story line and the characters. She made copious notes about directions for the story which are at the back of the manuscript and include the plot points and such."

MJ shook her head again. "You are nuts. I've never written a romance, let alone finished one in someone else's voice."

"Maybe not, but you've read enough romance novels, including your grandmother's, right? You know her voice and style."

"That doesn't mean I can write them. I'm not a novelist. I'm a teacher."

Momentarily speechless, he sat back. Juliette certainly had reason to be concerned for her granddaughter, and frustrated with her daughter-in-law. Here was a prime example of why mortals lost their *merika*, that inner spark of imagination and creativity. Someone along the way, usually in childhood, suffocated it intentionally or not, often to "protect" the child, sibling, spouse, or student. "Who says you're not a novelist? Have you ever tried to write one?"

"Well, yes, but..." She chewed on her lip.

"Ahhh. Where is it? Did you finish it?'

"Yes, but it's a silly story I wrote for myself and stashed away."

"Why?"

She shrugged. "I don't know. I didn't have time to work on it. I was busy with my studies. Besides..." She trailed off but he wouldn't push her on it now.

"If that's true, how do you know you aren't a novelist? If you haven't tried to submit or write another story, how do you know what you're capable of? Your grandmother told me that you used to write stories all the time with her. Aren't you getting your degree in women's literature?"

"Again, because I've studied other women's writing doesn't mean I can do it myself. Besides that's literature not..." She waved her hand over the manuscript.

"Not what?" He leaned toward her, jaw clenched. "You weren't about to call your grandmother's books trash, were you?"

"No, of course not." She gave a nervous laugh. "That's what my mother calls them, a panacea for the uneducated and sentimental. When I lived at home, I kept those books hidden from her."

He shook his head. How had she survived all those years living with a woman who denied her daughter's imagination and heart? Silence filled the space between them, broken only by the ever-present susurration of the ocean's waves. "Your grandmother shared many stories with me about the two of you under the dining table, in bed before sleep, and elsewhere, telling each other stories, playing the what-if game."

"Just because I made up stories with Gran as a child, doesn't mean I can write a book now for adults. That's ridiculous."

"Why? If you were a mathematics or science teacher, I might believe that, but you are on your way to becoming a full professor in American and Women's Literature."

She rubbed at her forehead. *Had he pushed her too far, too fast?*

"Look, before you make a decision, why don't you at least read the manuscript and her notes. Take time to get into the story, and once you do, I'm sure you'll sense where the story is heading, especially with her written notes to guide you. You can do this, MJ, for your grandmother. Please."

He sure knew how to work the guilt angle, as if she didn't already feel guilty enough. She glanced down at the manuscript. She'd be the first to read the story, and how wonderful was that! But finish it?

She'd dreamed of writing more novels someday, ones she wouldn't leave ignored on her computer. After she received her Ph.D. Some summer when she wasn't teaching and grading papers and her students' writing. She rubbed at the spot between her eyes. Looking up, she found Nik's gaze still intently on her.

"Just read it, okay?"

She nodded. Anyway, who was she kidding. Try and stop her.

He jumped up from his chair. "Great! I'll get you something to drink, shall I and then I have some errands to run. Would you like pizza for dinner? I can pick some up while I'm out?"

She removed the binder clip and turned over the title page to the page she'd been sneaking peeks at during their discussion. It read, "Chapter One. Overboard."

"MJ?"

"Hmmm?"

"Pizza? Toppings?"

Without looking up from the page, she said, "Yes, onions, mushrooms, and olives. Now go away and leave me alone so I can read."

A glass of iced tea appeared on the table above the manuscript. Quiet returned. It was only her and her grandmother's manuscript. Many pages later, MJ read, "...and Jolene dove into the sea. Maybe she'd sink into the depths and stay there, give it all up. Because if he didn't come to save her, if he didn't search for her, or return to her, why go on?"

They were the last sentences on the last manuscript page. Surely Gran wouldn't have the heroine waiting for the hero to rescue her. Women had agency now, they rescued themselves. MJ wanted to know what happened next but there were no more pages, only story notes. She flipped slowly through them. Yes, Gran did know what she was doing and now MJ had a sense of what might happen. Still, it wasn't the same as experiencing events with the heroine. Darn.

Frustrated, she imagined how she might finish the story. It was maddening to not be able to read the end, but finishing it? Nik walked past her into the kitchen carrying a pizza box, the scent of tomato sauce and cheese wafting to her. She hadn't heard him come in. Apparently, he hadn't knocked this time. She rose and gathered the manuscript and story notes.

She'd think about it tomorrow.

Chapter 14

"Remember, Juliette, the mission tonight is to encourage MJ to finish your manuscript. Remind her of her ability to tell a good story. Urge her to trust me to help her with it and with building a successful career for her as an author if she wants."

Nik took Juliette's hand and helped her step up onto the moving walkway out of the Underworld. She patted his arm after taking her place next to him. She looked lovely in flowing pants and tunic in a pale shade of lilac.

"I know, dear boy, I know. I am so grateful for this chance to let her know I love her and she has no reason to feel guilty."

A little guilt, in his opinion, was a not a bad thing, considering MJ had neglected her grandmother for too long, but that was between the two of them. "And, Juliette, remember, do not tell her who and what I am. I'm sure you will be tempted but—"

She balked as they walked off the walkway and toward a door. "What? Why not? If I vouch for you not just as some financial whiz but as someone special, she is sure to—"

"No, Juliette, you mustn't reveal my secret. You can vouch for me as someone who knows what they are doing but don't tell her what I am. It's against the rules of the Voices."

Crossing her arms, she glared up at him. Now he knew where MJ got it. Juliette's hair, still silver but darkening to a soft grey that would soon turn into her original hair color, was a soft nimbus around her face. Her eyes, a sharper blue and clearer than he'd ever seen them in the time he worked with her, were leveled on him. Her chin was lifted, determined. He sighed. He'd missed this surrogate grandmother, and wished their time together wasn't measured and directed to one purpose.

"I should tell her, Nik, otherwise she probably won't listen. There is too much of her mother's influence in her." Her chin trembled.

Hades. Sighing again, he tilted his head back. Mortals and their emotions. But he wasn't going to give in to her. He couldn't. Wouldn't. He put an arm around her shoulder, and she uncrossed her arms as he turned them toward the door. "Juliette, as much as I'd love to say yes, I'm telling you no. This isn't one of your books where you can write a happy ending. This isn't just your story. It's MJ's and it's mine. Swear to me you will not reveal my secret or we turn around and I take you back to the Underworld."

Her shoulders slumped and he hugged her to him. Was she truly surrendering or planning her next strategy? She could be wily and he'd have to be on his guard.

"You do know you already look twenty years younger, right? And you're certainly not weak and helpless, so don't play the sad old lady card with me, Juliette."

She elbowed him in the ribs. "Tsk, tsk, Nik. Is that any way to talk your elders?"

"Technically, I'm your elder, Juliette. A fact you are not going to share with your granddaughter, correct?"

She nodded.

"Swear to me."

Pulling away from him, she turned, hands on her hips. If looks could kill. Well, they could, but not looks from mortals. She closed her eyes and took a breath.

"Okay, I swear."

"Thank you. Then let us enter MJ's dream."

Leading her to the door, he stopped and pulled out the small bottle Morpheus had given him. After dinner with MJ and waiting hours for her to go to bed, read one of her grandmother's books, and finally fall asleep, he'd dropped a few silken drops from the bottle onto MJ's eyelids.

"What's that?"

"Morpheus's permission for you to walk in MJ's dream." He tilted the bottle upside down and let a couple of drops land on his tongue and his finger, and swiped his finger lightly across Juliette's eyelids. Capping the bottle and dropping it back into his pants pocket, he grasped the doorknob in his hand, turned it and opened the door, waving Juliette through. Not sure where MJ's dream was going to land them, he was surprised when they stepped out onto a familiar-looking beach at night. If asked, he would have sworn this was the last place she would be dreaming of, unless Morpheus' brother, Phobetor, was supplying the dream. Gods help them if he was.

Juliette took his arm and silently walked arm-in-arm with him along the shore but he sensed the tension in her, the way her body leaned forward as if to hurry their steps. They spied MJ, sitting alone on a large chunk of driftwood. Her hair was down and spread around her like a cloak. Her chin was propped on her hands, elbows on knees. She gazed out over the water as if searching for something. Or someone.

Juliette dropped his arm.

"Remember your promise, Juliette," he whispered to her.

Nodding, she stepped toward her granddaughter and waved her hand over her head. "MJ," she called out, "MJ!"

She straightened and looked toward them. Scrubbing at her eyes, she looked again.

"Gran?"

He brought his gaze back to Juliette, discovering she no longer wore the flowing slacks and tunic. Instead, as she dashed towards MJ, a dress like something out of a British television production about Queen Victoria rustled around her. The gown was sewn with multiple layers of frothy fabric that sparkled even in the light of the moon, as if she'd sewn the fabric from one of Morpheus's runners' outfits. Doubtful, but she did seem to run almost as fast toward her granddaughter. He stepped back into the shadows.

"MJ, my darling girl."

"Gran? Oh, Gran!"

Gran is here! She's alive!

MJ jumped up from her driftwood seat and ran up the beach toward her grandmother dressed like a fairy godmother ready for another tea party. Not under the dining table but on the beach. At night. How fun.

Even as she ran, though, she sensed something was different, odd, but she didn't care. Gran was here and it wasn't too late to tell her how much she loved her. And she was sorry.

She rushed into her grandmother's out-flung arms and buried her face in the woman's neck as her arms wrapped around her. She smelled like MJ remembered, of roses with something else added, something fresh and bright. Tears welled but she didn't care.

Her grandmother released her, but set her hands on MJ's shoulders. "Here, let me look at you.," She gently wiped the tears from MJ's cheeks. "Now, none of this, sweet girl."

"Gran, I'm so sorry. I've missed you so much. I didn't know..."

"Hush, child. I understand. It's not your fault."

"But it is." MJ swiped at her tears and straightened. She owed this wonderful, magical woman an apology and she was going to give it.

"I should not have let all that time pass without a visit, or more phone calls. It was careless and selfish and..."

"Oh, pish-tosh." MJ almost giggled. It was something Gran would say to her whenever she thought little MJ was being silly. "Do you think I was such a wobbly-minded, weak old woman I couldn't have figured out a way to see you or invite you here to my cottage if I wanted to?"

MJ blinked. "But, you... But Mother said..."

Her grandmother took MJ's chin between her thumb and forefinger, and she was five again, waiting for Gran to tell her something she thought MJ needed to pay attention to. "No buts. I never pushed the issue with you, not when you were small nor when you were grown. I didn't want to make things harder for you or for your father."

Gran released her and looked out over the ocean. From the corner of her eye, MJ thought she saw Nik but when she turned to look for him, she saw only shadows. She turned back to her grandmother.

"Your legacy of storytelling—and you can tell stories, by the way, if you'd stop choking it—didn't leapfrog from me to you. It passed from me to your father to you."

What? What was she talking about?

"Dad doesn't write stories. He writes, but articles and papers about other authors for academic publications."

Gran's shoulders dropped. "Your father used to write wonderful stories. All the time. Everywhere. He was never without a pencil and paper, or pen and notebook. We didn't have tea parties under the dining table but he would climb into the old apple tree—remember, in the back yard at the old place?"

MJ nodded. The old tree was the best for climbing and hiding in.

Her grandmother turned to the dark sea. "He would climb up into that tree and scribble away. Stories of dragons and knights, space ships and aliens, boys who could wield magic. When I'd call him in for dinner and he didn't come, I'd send your grandfather out to find him. He was usually lost in his own world, writing."

MJ's chest tightened. Thinking of her father as a small boy writing stories. She would never have imagined it.

"In college, I remember, he had several stories published in one of their magazines. One even won a prize. I had visions of him one day being a well-known author."

MJ could swear she heard a break in her grandmother's voice. Her own throat ached. What had happened? Her father never talked about writing a novel. Or a short story. She imagined him in his study, surrounded by books.

"It might be too late for him, though I hope not." Gran turned back to her. "But it's not too late for you. You have stories to tell, my darling girl. Do it."

MJ jerked upright in the bed and rubbed her eyes. Gran! The dream felt so real.

But she was in her bed in the cottage, sunshine again streaming through the windows. She climbed out and crossed to the window, pressing her face to the warm glass to look up the beach as far as she could.

Of course, Gran wasn't there. No magic wand or wishing on a star would bring her back. Except in dreams. Now she wished she hadn't wakened, had stayed in the dream with Gran, at least a little while longer. How wonderful and heartbreaking it was to hug her grandmother again, and catch the scent of her powder, and feel the crinkly texture of her dress. MJ smiled. The twinkly, star-dusted dress was so typical of her grandmother when they played dress-up. But in the dream, they didn't have time for dress up or tea. Instead, Gran uttered those words...

It's probably too late for your father. But not for you, MJ. Not for you.

He wrote stories? How did she not know that? She wished they'd talked longer. She had so many questions, like why her mother thought Gran was losing it? Because her grandmother wasn't a loopy old woman out of touch with reality, but a smart, money-wise, creative, popular author. A woman with a career, just like her mother was always going on about, an independent woman, successful in her own right.

Turning around, she scanned the room. The soft, coordinated colors, the patterns of the fabrics, the luxurious depth of the rug, the paintings on the walls, all spoke of a creative vision, of organization and implementation. The room was welcoming and warm, like Gran. So how had she bought into the idea of a batty old lady? And how had she never seen her father as anything but the cliche of the absent-minded professor, elbow patches on his sweater, and all?

She dropped onto the window seat. Her perspective had been so off kilter. Was she only seeing things, people, her father and grandmother, the way her mother wanted her to see them? Did her mother truly believe Gran was "dotty" or was that just a story to keep MJ from spending time with her? For most of her life, MJ went along to get along. But her dad? She knew her father loved her mother. She'd seen it in his eyes and in the things he did for her mother regularly. But had he sacrificed his creative dreams for her mother's career and expectations?

She gripped the seat cushion. Why did Gran say she hadn't wanted to create stress for MJ's dad or her?

Nik stepped out onto the deck below and set bowls and spoons on the table, then returned inside. By buying this cottage and spending most of her time here, Gran set her stake in the sand, away from MJ's mother and father. She'd given herself the place and time to do what she wanted to do—write books.

It might be too late for your father. But it's not too late for you.

Wasn't it? Sure, she'd written her own stories since elementary school, writing them out on tablet paper, then in notebooks in high school when she was supposed to be taking class notes, then on her laptop in college, actually finishing the first draft of a novel inspired by, she knew now, one of her Gran's books. But she'd never entered her writing in any contests because her stories had shifters, and gods and goddesses, and fairies, and owls who could talk. She never wanted her mother to find out about them or hear what she would say about MJ's fantasy-filled stories. For years, she didn't have time for writing because she'd taken a full load of classical literature courses, literary crit classes, and women's studies, all requiring paper after paper on what she discovered and thought about someone else's writing. For her bachelor's, then her master's and now her doctorate in Women's Literature. What irony.

Had her father given up on his writing because of mother? She was tempted to call him and ask but how would she explain her question? "I had dream about Gran, Dad, and she said you used to write stories."

And then what? It was just a dream. Probably all made up in her mind for some reason. Could she find out if it was true without directly asking her father? Below, Nik walked down the steps of the deck, coffee cup in hand, and headed up the beach. His dark hair blew about his face in the breeze off the water. His shorts stopped just above his knees but showed off the muscular calves that flexed as he walked barefoot on the sand. He worked with Gran for years. Was it possible she had talked about her father with him? If so, he could tell her if her dream was true.

But did she want to know?

MJ was awake. Nik had heard her steps overhead as he fixed coffee in the kitchen. The question now was whether she'd mention the dream or would he have to? He took a sip of his coffee.

He needed her to work on Juliette's manuscript. It was the only way to seduce her into writing her own stories. And he didn't know how much time he had before her mother showed up and threw all his plans out the window with MJ's dreams. She'd have her daughter on the ferry back home to finish her dissertation before he could recite the names of his mother and eight aunts.

He took a few more steps up the beach. For the sake of the mission, he didn't want that for MJ. She wouldn't be happy long term if her mother did that to her. From everything Juliette told him about MJ, not writing her own stories was going to dim her light, stifle her *merika,* the creative spark that was her special gift. Juliette would also be unhappy. So would his mother, Erato.

He winced thinking how displeased Apollo would be if a Voice failed in their mission. He wouldn't be happy either, to see MJ lose such an important, beautiful part of herself, but, in the long run, his feelings about the situation didn't matter. He was in service to the Voices and the Muses, there to follow orders, like a good soldier. He scuffed through the sand, then turned to face the water, automatically scanning for anything unusual after the other night's episode, remembering Hermes' warning. Taking another swallow of coffee, he almost choked on it when he heard her shout, "Nik! Wait up."

She ran toward him, her hair in its braid swinging like a clock's pendulum, back and forth behind her, and her perfect breasts bouncing every time a foot hit the sand. He might be a Voice but he was male and yes, he noticed and was mesmerized by the motion that counterbalanced the movement of her hips. He yanked his gaze upward to see her brows were drawn together. Uh oh. What now?

Panting, she halted in front of him, breasts rising and falling. Wisps of hair had escaped her braid and without thinking, he reached out and tucked a strand behind her ear so it wasn't blowing in her eyes. Her panting stopped and her eyes widened. One beat. Two. She took a step back and Nik dropped his gaze, sipping his coffee, trying to ignore the sudden tightness at the front of his shorts. He tossed the dregs of the coffee into the water.

"How are you this morning? Sleep well?"

She grabbed her elbows with her hands and looked away. "Yes. No. Well... I had a dream."

"I'm not surprised." He watched her eyes widen again. "It was a full moon last night. I've heard people tend to dream more or remember their dreams around a full moon." He turned to walk back to the cottage, not wanting to appear too invested in what she had to say.

"I suppose that's true. Sounds like something Gran would have said."

He hummed an agreement and kept walking. She stopped and he paused, looking back. She was gazing up the beach in the direction of where the dream had taken place.

"I wish she was here."

Nik barely caught the words over the sound of the waves, but he could hear the pain. He wanted to put an arm around her and hold her as he had when she'd broken down in the car that first night. Instead, he tightened his grip on the coffee cup and stuck his other hand in his back pocket.

Why was he so tempted by her? It didn't make sense. Not after centuries of all the women he'd helped—and had sex with. Why was he so drawn to this one? Maybe he'd gone too long without. Casual sex with this mortal wouldn't be casual at all on her side. Not if what her grandmother shared with him about her was any indication. He didn't dare risk it. Juliette would kill him—if she could but she couldn't—for messing with her granddaughter's heart.

"I dreamed about Gran last night."

"Also normal, according to what I've heard, to have dreams of the dead."

She flinched and he wanted to hit himself over the head with his coffee cup. *Where was smooth-talking immortal Nik when he wanted him? Why had bumble-brained Nik shown up instead?*

"I'm sorry. I didn't mean to be so blunt. Want to tell me about the dream?"

Please tell me about the dream. She shook her head. Well, what did he expect after that comment. He turned to walk back to the cottage.

"Did you talk to Gran about...about me, about my family, about my father?"

He halted and released a breath. Maybe they were going to get somewhere after all. Looking over his shoulder, he said, "Such as?"

"Did she ever tell stories about my dad, when he was younger? Before he married my mother?"

He rubbed his forehead. Still not going to talk about finishing the manuscript or her grandmother's words about it not being too late for her? No, she was going to ask about her father. She had avoidance polished to a fine sheen. Shrugging, he turned back to her.

"I suppose she did. I think she was worried about him."

"Why?"

"I don't know for sure." Oh, he knew. He just wasn't going to tell her. "I think she believed he was unhappy about something. But she was more concerned about you."

"Because I didn't come to visit? I'll always regret that."

Polished to a fine sheen. "No, my impression was she worried you were pursuing an academic career to make your mother happy, at the expense of your own happiness. I think she believed you were stifling your creative dreams and desires out of a need for your mother's approval."

She crossed her arms and looked away. Yeah, she didn't want to hear that.

"That's why she left you the cottage and money, so whatever else happened, you had a place that was yours. A place to explore your dreams." He paused, trying to decide whether to throw the last words at her that might jar her from her go-along path.

"I think she left them to you because she hoped it wasn't too late for you."

Chapter 15

"What did you say?" she gasped.

He hadn't said that, had he?

"I said, she hoped it wasn't too late for you. Too late to recapture the storyteller in you, to step back into your imagination and—"

"Stop! Just stop!"

Her chest hurt. *Why was it hard to breathe?* She hadn't run far. Nik watched her, eyes alert, strands of his dark hair lifted by the breeze. He was so damn good looking. And he made her so damn mad. And hurt, like she couldn't breathe. Like an elephant sat on her chest. An elephant of guilt, grief, and frustration. She tried to drag in a breath. Suddenly, his hands were on her arms.

"Relax, MJ, it's okay. It's okay."

Okay for him, maybe, not for her. Gran was gone. She'd been so close in her dream. But it was only a dream. His thumb gently moved against her cheek. "Don't cry," he whispered to her.

His eyes. Amazing eyes, so dark they were mesmerizing. Finally, she dragged in a breath as another tear escaped. He gently wiped it away too, while his other hand still held her arm, firmly but gently. His touch heated her skin and made her heart pound.

Was the sun brighter? Hotter?

Nervous, she licked her lips. His gaze dropped to them and the air thickened between them. Slowly, he bent toward her. His lips brushed hers. Once. Twice. She rose to her toes. Her arms lifted without thought and circled his neck. The mug he held thumped on the sand as he cupped her face.

When he licked along the seam of lips, she opened her mouth. He dove in, his tongue stroking hers. *Holy moly!* Everything from her mouth down lit up, blazed brighter than the sun as he wrapped his arms tight around her so their bodies touched everywhere. He explored her mouth, nibbling, stroking. A wave tickled her toes, the cool water grounding her.

Unbelievably, he was kissing her and he tasted, umm, delicious. Of coffee and something spicey, salty, and she remembered the description of a kiss from *Princess Bride,* "Since the invention of the kiss there have been five kisses that were rated the most passionate, the most pure. This one left them all behind." Not that she had much experience in that arena but still. Then she tasted honey and she slit open her eyes to look at the giver of this magical kiss. His eyes were closed, his dark hair curling over his forehead and behind him—

She blinked again. Behind him rose a temple out of myth. Bells tinkled softly accompanied by the cooing of doves. She pulled away, turning her head back and forth from the temple to the water. Nik relaxed his arms, to lean back and look at her. He must have seen her shock in her face because he looked in the direction of her wide-eyed stare.

Skata! she thought she heard him hiss.

"Close your eyes and kiss me, MJ." He pressed his lips to hers. Dazed, she blinked but closed her eyes and gave herself up to another passionate embrace, while his hands cupped her face. Again, she tasted honey. *What had she seen?* She jerked back from him and spun around, eyes wide, expecting to see the temple. No, they still stood on the beach.

She put trembling fingers to her lips. *What just happened? Had her imagination finally run away with her sanity?*

Nik licked his lips, catching the lingering sweetness of honey.

"Did you have some honey before you came out here?" Nik asked her. She stared at him, shaking her head. *Well, what in Hades just happened? Why did he see a temple like the one on Mount Helicon? Did she see it too?* He wiped his hand across his mouth. *Why did he still taste honey? Was that why he so badly wanted to kiss her again?* No, not wanted, needed. He wanted to wrap her in his arms and lower them to the soft sand.

Obviously, she wasn't feeling the same compulsion. Her eyes scanned the beach as she spun around in a quick circle, then shook her head. He didn't know what to say to her. As a mortal, he should be freaked out. He was freaked out. As an immortal, in all his years as a Voice, with all the mortal women he'd bedded, this had never happened.

"Did you see it?" Her voice trembled. She wrapped her arms around herself and kept scanning around them.

He wanted to shelter her with his arms, his body, to make her feel safe as he had the night he carried her from the water, but he didn't dare. He didn't trust himself. He needed answers to why they'd had a mutual hallucination. Hermes or his mother should know. Apollo, probably did, but he wasn't asking him. The god didn't like surprises, which was why Hermes irritated him so often. So, until he had answers...

"See what?"

She rubbed her forehead. "Never mind. It must be the air here." She looked at him, confusion in her eyes.

He didn't blame her, adrenaline pumped madly through his body. She licked her lips again. Like him, she must still taste the honey of their kiss, but why?

She looked around the beach. "Ever since I arrived here, one strange thing after another has happened to me." She looked at him as if expecting him to doubt her. He waited. "First, the GPS in my car went crazy and I got lost for hours. On an island!"

He frowned. He'd forgotten about that.

"Then I was attacked by the sea." He'd argue with her but what was the use. Something strange happened that night or Hermes wouldn't have shown up in time to rescue her.

"And then the dream..."

At last.

"What dream?"

She looked up the beach to where she'd sat in the dream. "Last night, I dreamed Gran met me here on the beach. I was so happy, to see her, to feel her hug me again." She smiled then looked down when a wave washed over their feet. Bending, she picked up something between her feet and held out to him.

"Sea glass."

"Oh." She brought it close to examine it. It was a brilliant blue, polished smooth and frosted by the friction of water and sand.

He smiled. "The sea gave you a gift. Maybe it's an apology for scaring you."

"Scaring me? It almost drowned me. Some apology." She turned toward the water and he held his breath, waiting to see if she'd throw it back. *Don't do it. Don't.*

She swung her arm back, paused, looked at it again, and shrugged, stuffing it into the shallow pocket at the front of her capris. He released his breath, then caught it again when she said, "And you kissed me."

He nodded, "Yes, but why was that strange? And what was strange about the dream?"

MJ rubbed her hands up and down her arms. "Nothing, except you said the same thing to me a minute ago that Gran said to me in the dream. She hoped it wasn't too late for me. It's weird you'd say it now. And the kiss..." She put her fingers to her lips and looked behind him. He turned, worried, but nothing was there.

He intended to shake her up a little by repeating what her grandmother said in the dream, so that wasn't weird. But the kiss, the kiss had shaken him as well as her. The taste of honey lingered and he still desperately wanted to kiss her again. "I mentioned it was not too late because it was something your grandmother often said to me. She hoped it wasn't too late for you to reclaim your ability to tell stories. She worried your mother had suffocated your imagination and creativity, erasing all the magic and joy in your life. She was afraid you were turning into a copy of your mother."

Her arms dropped and her hands curled into fists. Her chin came up again and she glared at him. "First of all, so what if I was. My mother is a respected professor at the university, on her way to becoming dean, and maybe even president. Second of all, she hasn't suffocated all my—" She broke off and turned away. Nik waited. Maybe if he confronted her on this now, she would forget about the honeyed kiss and the temple.

"Why are you getting your doctorate in English?"

"What do you mean? I'm getting my doctorate in English because I love literature."

"But why are you getting your doctorate?"

"Because I want to teach."

"Do you? Where? At the same university as your mother?"

"Yes, and again, so what? I like the town and the university. Mother said—"

Nik shook his head. *I give up, Juliette, I don't think I'm going to get through to her.* "Never mind," he said, noting the flush of anger in her cheeks. "Anything else strange happen to you since you arrived on the island?" *Might as well return to that. When she laid all the events out, they did sound strange.*

"Isn't that enough? I've only been here a short while and I've been lost, attacked by the sea, had a strange dream, you kissed me and, and..."

"You kissed me back," he said, trying to distract her—or him. She kissed him with total focus, and sent him into a spin. He seriously had to get out of there, leave her to her work while he talked to someone about the kiss and the honey. Maybe he should kiss her again to see if it happened again. He took a step forward, his gaze focused on her mouth, but she stepped back, her hand up.

"No!"

"Don't!"

The last thing MJ wanted was a repeat of what happened. Well, she'd love a repeat if she was being honest, but she didn't want to see a temple, or hear bells, and have her insanity confirmed. Better to remove temptation.

"I think you should leave."

Nik froze and frowned at her. "What do you mean? Leave the beach?"

"No, I think you should go home. I need some space. Maybe your absence will put an end to all the strange happenings, and

I can get back to work on my dissertation. Aren't we done, anyway?"

"No. For one, there's the issue of your grandmother's unfinished manuscript. She told me what a natural storyteller you are, and—"

"I can't think about that right now, understand? It's all been too much too fast." She rubbed her forehead where a headache had taken up residence. "I need time to work, to think, to be here without expectations and pressures from you, from my mother, from—"

"Your Gran?"

She bit her lip. "I know that sounds terrible after our time apart but yes, even from Gran. I feel like, like I'm out there." She waved toward the water. "I'm drowning again, and I can't breathe." She drew in a deep breath, then released it, lips pressed together.

He reached a hand out but withdrew it when she stepped back.

"As you wish. I'll pack a few things and take off for a couple of days so you don't feel crowded and pressured. When I come back, we'll talk about your decision on the manuscript and take it from there with the legal and financial paperwork."

She nodded. "Thank you."

He walked past her, but threw back over his shoulder, "Your grandmother talked about you all the time, the little-girl-you and the big-girl-you. The little girl wasn't afraid of her imagination and gifts. But the big girl?"

He walked away, and after a few moments of staring at her sand-coated feet, she turned to see he was down the beach, almost to the cottage. She drew another deep breath and dug her toes into the sand. Part of her felt free and floating for the first time since the meeting with the lawyer after Gran's funeral. The other part of her wanted to chase after him, tell him she didn't mean it, she wanted him to stay, to kiss her again. So what if she ended up outside a temple with bells ringing. She hadn't been kissed in a long while, not so passionately. *Would another kiss lead to other things? What would he expect of her then?*

It was as if she'd stepped into one of Gran's fairy tales, one MJ wasn't familiar with. But would this one have a happily ever after ending? She picked up a handful of sand and shells and threw them as hard as she could into the water. She did it again. And again.

It didn't relieve the pressure around her heart or her eyes.

Chapter 16

Nik didn't know whether to swear at himself, MJ, or Juliette. That kiss.

Everything was going fine, well, no, not fine. Usually, he didn't have to try so hard to get his mortals to follow directions. He'd figured MJ would either immediately reject the legacy because she was too busy being her mother's daughter, or be so grateful to her grandmother—and him—for the legacy and opportunity to do her own thing that she'd quickly fall in line and finish the manuscript.

There would have been no time for attraction or water rescues. Or kisses. Out of respect for Juliette, he hadn't wanted to cross that line with MJ no matter how sexy or sweetly appealing she was. He ran his fingers through his hair and looked around his bedroom. The results of their kiss were surprising and unsettling, but she needed time to feel safe and work, and he needed answers. He'd give her time for the dissertation and to ponder on her dream, the bequest, and what she wanted for herself.

Perhaps more kisses. Perhaps more than kisses. He shook his head. He couldn't let the kiss change everything. Right now, only one person might understand the strange kiss and have answers for him. He packed shorts, swimsuit, long pants, a button shirt, a couple of T-shirts, underwear, and his kit into his duffle because that was what mortal Nik would do, and then walked out of the cottage to the car, anxious to be gone before MJ returned. Otherwise, well, he'd feel compelled to stay and—

Skata! He clicked the key fob so the door rose and threw the duffle into the passenger seat, then slid behind the wheel. Pushing the Start button, he revved the engine, hoping the sound would carry and MJ would know he was in truth leaving. Putting it in gear, he roared down the street, letting the car express some of the frustration he felt. He turned toward the White Horses, needing some time with other Voices before anything else, and to wash away the taste of honey lingering on his tongue.

And figure out why he—and MJ—tasted it.

Thalassa, head barely above water, smiled as she watched Nik stalk up the beach while the cursed mortal stared after him. She almost choked on the sea water when the woman started throwing handfuls of sand and beach detritus into the water.

Voices weren't supposed to get attached to their mortals, and she seldom worried about most of the ones Nikos worked with, especially not the last one, but this one, attractive and with long hair... This one could be trouble. Although she didn't want him to succeed, she didn't want him in trouble with Apollo either. Too well she knew what havoc an angry god could wreak on a lesser immortal. Still, if he failed, Erato would weaken. That was what they wanted, she and her sisters.

Over the sound of the surf, she heard the rumble of Nikos' car as he revved away from the cottage. The mortal stopped throwing sand and, after a few minutes, hurried back to the cottage. Too late. Thalassa sank below the water to return home to her sisters. The mortal was safe.

For now.

When the roar of the Ferrari's engine fade away, MJ stopped throwing sand and other bits into the water. Nik was gone.

But what had she expected? She'd asked him to leave, to give her some space and, like a gentleman, he had. *Damn!* She wanted to be alone and now she was. Waves washed up over her feet, cool and refreshing. A gull cried far off in the distance. She was alone, without her mother, without colleagues and students. No one waited for her to do something, take care of something, or make a mistake. She was alone.

She asked for solitude, so why wasn't she happy? She was familiar with it since her few friends also had schedules filled with teaching, grading papers, and research. Finally, she could work, and that's why she asked Nik to leave. Fear of everything in her life changing in dramatic ways had nothing to do with her request. She just needed to focus on the dissertation. Kicking at the sand, she trotted back to the cottage.

When she opened the French door, absolute silence greeted her, only the ticking of the old-fashioned clock on the dining area wall broke it. She sank into a chair at the table, propped up an elbow on its surface and listened to it. Minutes passed. She should open her laptop and get to work. Like a good student, a good girl. Except, she was tired. Tired of being the good girl. The good student. The good daughter. Not such a good grand-daughter, though.

But she wasn't here because she'd been a good granddaughter. She was here because her grandmother loved her, without reservation or judgement. Unlike her mother. Sometimes the harder MJ tried to please her, to make her mother happy, the more likely she was to fail. But it wasn't MJ's fault her mother became pregnant with her and had to interrupt her climb up the academic career ladder. Thankfully, after years of working and waiting, her mother finally had a chance at the newly-opened position of department chair.

She looked around the cottage and out the windows to the beach. Although the place wasn't a beach shack, her mother wouldn't like it here. It was too unpredictable and too far away, since she was always busy with departmental meetings, committee meetings, supervising graduate students, and writing articles. MJ sighed and watched the waves roll in and out. Now Nik was out of her hair, there was nothing to distract her. She licked her lips. She could still taste him—or the honey. She jumped up. The first thing she was going to do was make herself a cup of Assam tea, nice and hot and strong.

While she waited for the water to boil, she arranged her laptop, research notes, and index cards on the table. When the tea was done brewing, she ignored the honey on the counter, carried the mug over to the table and sat down. Taking a few sips, she bent her head to her work and didn't look up until her eyes were dry. Blinking, she tilted her head back and forth to release the tension in her neck and saw on the kitchen clock two hours had passed. Her tea was cold and she needed more index cards to make notes. Yes, she was old-fashioned that way but she liked the ability to easily move ideas and such around on a surface larger than a small screen. She searched in her computer bag for more, but found none. Maybe Gran had some somewhere.

Climbing up to her grandmother's writing aerie, she sat down at the desk and ignoring the unfinished manuscript Nik left sitting on the desktop, she searched through the drawers. She found paperclips, rubber bands, pens, sticky notes, and legal pads but no index cards. Weren't those a given for writers? Where else might she have them? She went down the stairs and into her grandmother's bedroom, checking the nightstands on either side of the bed. Nothing there except a small jar of hand cream. MJ smiled and unscrewed the lid and took a sniff. Lavender. Of course. She returned the jar and closed the drawer then turned to look around the room. If she were her grandmother, where might she store the cards?

The only other piece of furniture besides the bed and nightstands was the antique dresser that used to be in the other house. Two narrow drawers sat on either side of a piece of flat marble atop three wide drawers. When, as a child, she asked her grandmother about them, Gran told her they were glove drawers, used when a lady never left the house without wearing a pair of gloves.

She slid the right-hand drawer open. A few scarves lay neatly folded on top of several pairs of gloves, white and black. She smiled and closed the drawer, then pulled the other one open, curious. She blinked at the contents. "Oh, Gran." She lifted out the little book, a pamphlet really, but MJ's first book, written when she was eight and printed on pages of typewriter paper, cut in half, folded and stapled to create a fairy tale her grandmother helped her write about a little girl who wanted to fly. She'd drawn the little girl on the cover and given her butterfly wings covered in multicolored glitter. MJ left the book with her grandmother for safety's sake, but she couldn't believe her grandmother still had it and kept it close. Flipping through it, smiling at her little girl illustrations, she discovered, between the pages, an envelope with her name written on the back.

Heart thudding, she sat down on the bed and opened the envelope, pulling out the thin stationery pages covered in Gran's handwriting.

Dearest MJ...

After stowing his car in a heavily shadowed spot behind White Horses so it couldn't be easily seen, Nik walked around the pub where he'd already spoken with Hermes, and crossed the road, following a path invisible to mortals, leading to the beach. His conversation with Hermes inside the pub gave him no answers just more questions. "Ask Apollo. Better yet, ask the Muse of love poetry. I can't tell you a thing."

Because of Hermes' trickster reputation, Nik wasn't sure he believed him, but when he tried to push for more, the god shook his head and disappeared. Frustrated, Nik decided the only thing to do to get answers to the kiss and the temple was to take Hermes' advice and return to Mt. Helicon to talk with his mother. Shucking his sandals, he followed the line of water and sand, focusing in his mind on the image of the temple. A few steps through the ocean foam, he crossed the threshold between mortal and immortal realm, and was walking barefoot through the grove of olive trees below the temple.

The olives were still small, barely visible among the silver-green leaves this early in the season. He paused to put his hand to the rough bark of a tree and sensed the energy of sun, wind, and rain running through it. He enjoyed the mortal realm—most of the time, appreciating the mortals' energy, their inventions, their curiosity, and their ability to imagine the impossible. But there were times when he was grateful to return to Mt. Helicon, where the air was clear and time moved more slowly.

Nik stepped into the temple, smelling the familiar scents of bay laurel and frankincense. Breathing deeply, he let his mind and heart slow before walking to the altar where his mother and aunts were gathered, hands joined, voices softly chanting. His mother noticed him when he took up position opposite her, and nodded to him. When the chant finished, she stepped back from the circle, linking the hands of Clio on one side of her, with the hands of Euterpe on the other. Softly, she walked from the temple with Nik trailing behind her.

Once they descended the steps, she threw her arms around him. "Nikos! What a wonderful surprise on a beautiful afternoon." She kissed both of his cheeks, then leaned back, holding onto his arms. "How are you? How goes your mission? I did not expect to see you so soon."

Nik embraced her in return then looked into her eyes. "Something happened between my mortal and me, Mitera, and I thought you might be able to explain it to me."

Smiling, she said, "I am, as always, delighted to help you, my son. Come, let us walk through the gardens as we converse."

He offered his arm and turned to amble with her through the beds of roses and larkspur, anemones, and dianthus, he in his t-shirt and jeans, she in her traditional peplos, woven of untraditional light cotton, that floated around her.

"Something happened today that has never happened to me before," he said, "and it not only unsettled me but it truly upset my mortal, MJ, as well."

His mother bent and pinched a pink rose from its stem and, after sniffing it, tucked it into her hair above her left ear, calling attention to the strand of white running through it. Had it widened?

"Tell me, my son.," She straightened and resumed their walk. Tell her? Right. "Well, I kissed MJ."

She laughed. "Surely, after all this time and all those mortal women, you don't need any advice from me about that."

He sighed. Mothers! "Thank you, *Mitera*, but no. I don't need advice on kissing. It's what happened during the kiss that concerns me."

"Are you sure this isn't something you should be talking about with your friends—"

"Please! Just listen."

She turned, laced her fingers together at her waist, and looked at him.

"When I kissed her, when we kissed... This has never happened to me before, in all these centuries." He ran his hand through his hair. She stood waiting. He'd talk to someone else but his mother was Erato, the Muse of love poetry. Who else would he talk to?

His mother reached out and laid a hand on his arm. "Just tell me, my son."

"When we kissed, it was as if we stood there," he pointed back at the temple, "not on the beach outside her grandmother's cottage. There." He stabbed the air with his finger. "And though neither of us had any to eat, we tasted honey in the kiss. Strongly."

His mother paled, her eyes widening. The hand on his arm tightened. "Honey? You tasted honey? Truly?"

"And when we opened our eyes during the kiss, we saw the temple."

"Oh!" she breathed. She put a hand to her forehead "Oh!"

That didn't reassure him. "What? What is wrong? What do you know about this?"

His mother reached up to cup his face with her hands. "Nikos, I am concerned for you. I wish I could be happy, too, but I am too concerned." She brushed a curl from his forehead. "You have been so steadfast in your service to the Voices and Apollo, to your aunts and I over the centuries, never asking for anything for yourself."

He was proud of his service but it was lonely, too. "Thank you. I do my best, though..." He trailed off, unwilling to speak aloud his loneliness and soul fatigue in his service.

His mother smiled sweetly at him. "This I know, my son. Do you think I do not sense what you will not speak of? This is what concerns me. Duty and responsibility are not enough to sustain life, immortal or not. You need something, you need love to give them more significance than labels or medals."

What? What did love have to do with duty and responsibility?

"Nikos, why did you join the Voices?"

He shrugged. "You know, because I wanted to something that was important, that made a difference." He paused. "And because it was important to help you."

She smiled again and stepped back from him. "Precisely, because it was important to me whom you love. And now? Why do you continue in your service?"

"How can you ask," He reached up to touch the silver streak in her hair, "when this gets wider with every turn of the Wheel?"

"So, you serve out of fear and love?"

He straightened. He hadn't thought of it quite that way. Fear? Yes, for her and his aunts, but also for his world as well as the mortals'. "How does one love and not fear, Mitera, when the ones you love are vulnerable?"

His mother, still young in appearance, even with the streak of silver hair, tilted her head back and laughed. "Now you sound mortal. But yes, that is a true question. Do you not understand, my Nikos, fear is one of the spices in love's dish? Fear of death, of loss, of separation? Of illness and pain? All those fears are what makes love, true love special, valuable, and worthy of the fight—and the risk."

"But what does this have to do with our kiss?"

"Ah yes, the kiss. We better go see your Aunt Clio for your answer. Come with me."

Chapter 17

D*earest MJ,*

I've been blessed to have you as my granddaughter. I loved every moment of our time together, whether we were reading fairy tales, or having tea parties, or making frosted cookies. I loved you from the moment I first saw you, when I came to visit you just after they brought you home from the hospital. I'd forgotten that wonderful baby smell of powder and new life when I held you.

I remember your father's joy with his new daughter, how gently he held you, the pride on his face when he handed you to me. I buried my nose in your down-soft hair and kissed you all over your head and face while you blinked curiously up at me. You made me smile. You still do.

I'm glad you found this letter. I hoped you would discover it. By now, my sweet financial advisor, Nik, will have revealed my secret life to you, my secret identity. I hoped to share this with you before my death, but apparently the Fates decided otherwise.

MJ sniffed then smiled. Gran couldn't write or speak without a bit of the fabulous sneaking into her words.

Since I began my writing career, I knew I must work under a spell of silence, for your sake. For your father's sake, too, because your mother wouldn't appreciate word getting out that her moth-er-in-law wrote those "bodice rippers." I hoped after you received your PhD and were safely ensconced in your ivory tower, the spell of silence could be broken and I could reach out to you. Perhaps then we could have renewed our special bond.

Oh, Gran. Regret washed over her.

Once your mother refused to let me care for you, in case I might influence you in some unacceptable way, I decided to follow a dream I'd had for many years. I set it aside in order to be wife, mother, and even grandmother. I loved being all those roles, but reading to you when you were small, and making up stories together, reminded me of the long-buried desire to write novels.

Although I worried about my storytelling ability, I delightedly discovered I could do more than make up stories for a five-year-old. I wrote story after story, book after book. I did it even though I didn't know if they would sell, if anyone would want to read them. I wrote the books to honor my Muse and myself. Surprise—they sold, which delighted my agent and editor—and my Muse.

Writing made me happy, too, because I knew that someday I could share my stories with you again, over real tea cups and pastries, perhaps sitting side by side on the wicker sofa on the cottage porch. The sales made me smile because they gave me enough money to help others as I wished, and to leave a legacy for you.

Remember how we played the game of "I dream that I..."? One of the things I always dreamed of was a home on the beach. I bought this place before I was making the income I am now but after the sale of the first book. I believed enough in myself to take the risk. I spent many joy-filled and contented hours here. I hope you will too.

Nik promised me that he will help you settle things with the cottage and my estate. Trust him, MJ. He has a good heart, though he hides it well.

She looked out at the beach and the water. Trust him? With money, maybe. She touched her lips, remembering the power of his kiss and the taste of honey. But with her heart? He wasn't like the graduate students or associate professors she dated in the past. They were comfortable, easily distracted by whatever new idea was running through their minds. Most of them lit no sparks within her body or her mind. Nik did both and he certainly wasn't comfortable. Irritating, challenging, and distracting, yes. She continued reading.

I wish I could be with you as you read and discover my books. Or have you already? I received so many wonderful letters from readers, from fans, but I always wished...

I'm sorry, my darling girl, that I surrendered my time with you too easily. I should have made more of a fuss, taken a stand, insisted that we have our private time together again. But I didn't want to come between you and your parents, or you and your mother. My dearest granddaughter, know that you were always a gift and a light to my heart.

I wish we could have one more tea party beneath the table.

All my love,

Gran

PS: I hope you won't wait as long as I did to trust your heart and your dreams. Please, my dearest, follow your dreams. Don't let anyone suffocate your imagination, MJ, not even your... Well, not anyone. Once upon a time, dear granddaughter, still has power and magic. Once upon a time...

She read the letter again, her throat aching as she tried to swallow the grief. Sentimental drivel, her mother would say. More evidence of the woman's overactive imagination and love of drama and...*it's not too late for you.*

Grief welled up in a wave larger than she'd ever experienced, rising from her toes, up through her legs, getting bigger as it rose from her belly, still rising. MJ ran to the bathroom and leaned over the commode. Certain she was going to spew her breakfast, she stood, one arm wrapped around her stomach, the hand of her other arm holding her braid out of the way, while she panted and swallowed and waited. When nothing happened, she straightened, freeing her braid to wipe her hand over her forehead.

She swallowed again and blinked back the tears that lingered. She wished she lived in a magic land where she could wave a wand and bring her grandmother back. Maybe then she could make up for time lost, time she should have spent here with her grandmother. But there was no magic. She didn't live in once-upon-a-time land, and no matter how hard she wished for it, she would never spend time with her grandmother again. Except, perhaps, in dreams.

She realized she was still holding Gran's letter and, behind that, her little book. Tears welled again, and she tried unsuccessfully to blink them back. Gran had saved her book. She'd always respected MJ's stories, regardless of how fanciful they were. She'd listened and asked questions, and then repeated back parts she especially liked. She'd helped MJ record her stories in little books like this one or draw pictures to illustrate her stories, and then hung them on her refrigerator. She always respected MJ as a storyteller whether she was four or eight. Always.

But MJ believed her mother when she admonished her for reading fairy tales or fantasy, stressing that she should read "good" books. When MJ tried to write her own stories, full of magic and make believe, as she had with Gran, her mother pressed her lips together and shook her head. "Isn't it time to grow up? If you want to write something, write an essay about your favorite teacher, or what you saw on our trip to the museum. See if you can make that interesting without telling lies."

She choked back another sob. Her grief now wasn't solely for the loss of her grandmother. It was for the loss of her imagination, of herself. The girl who made up fairy tales and tried to live them every day. What happened to her?

She laid the small booklet and letter gently on the shelf over the toilet. At the sink, she turned on the cool water to wash the tears from her face. Cupping water in her hands, she splashed her face, grabbed the hand towel to blot it dry, then looked up and stared in the mirror. Look at her with her braid. When she was young, she'd wanted long hair because it was what princesses had, part of dress up and make believe with Gran. She'd thrown a fit the first time her mother took her to a salon to have it cut. And the next time, and the next, until her mother gave up—sort of. Instead, she diminished the fun of princess hair by insisting if MJ was going to wear it long, then she was going to keep it neat in a tight braid, instead of loose and flowing like a princess.

So why still wear it this way? What prince would need to climb her rope of hair and rescue her from the clutches of the wicked witch? She shivered, imagining some guy pulling on her hair and climbing it to reach her. The weight of her braid pulled on her neck enough. Raising her chin, she opened the medicine cabinet and found a pair of scissors. Not sure if they could do the job, she brought the braid forward anyway. At the very least, she was going to free her hair.

Snip. It was a weight she didn't want to carry anymore.

Snip. Snip. The scissors obviously weren't meant to cut hair as thick as her braid, so she cut through it chunks at a time. Finally, the braid pulled free and she dropped it to the floor where it coiled like a thick rope. Blinking, she turned her head from side to side, feeling light, even light-headed. She cut more to even out some of the strands, then shook her head and watched her hair flex into curls that feathered around her face and stopped at her shoulders. She took a deep breath and smiled at herself.

Ta-da! It's magic, Gran.

She shook her head again, watching the curls bounce as though alive and remembered another of her grandmother's maxims.

Magic doesn't just happen... you have to help it along.

Picking up booklet and letter, she ran up the stairs to her grandmother's writing aerie. The unfinished manuscript sat on the desk. Opening the middle drawer, she found the scene list and laid that on the manuscript pages along with the letter and booklet. She looked around, chewing her lip. No, she wasn't ready to write in Gran's special place yet.

Hugging everything to her chest, she returned downstairs to the dining table. Pushing her research notebook and papers out of the way, she spread the manuscript and scene list on either side of the laptop. She propped the booklet against the stack of research books in order to see it when she looked up from her screen. In the kitchen, she switched on the fire under the teapot. While the water heated, she hummed as she made toast, spreading it with butter and honey. Setting toast and tea near the laptop, she crossed to the window on the other side of the table and opened it to the sound of the waves, the thunder of the white horses.

"Okay, Gran. I'm here. I'll try. You've asked me to finish your story, and I'll be grateful for any help you can give me."

Instead of entering the temple from the front, Nik's mother led him to the posticum at the back, a doorway he had never used. Was she trying to avoid being seen? Through the doorway, she led him down one flight of stairs to a landing with another door, then continued down yet another flight of stairs, this one longer, narrower, the stone treads worn.

At the bottom, they walked into a large cavernous space filled with row upon row of bookshelves laden with books. One bookcase on the far left was divided as if to hold wine bottles on their sides, but instead held scrolls. Sconces, lining the walls and running in rows across the cavern ceiling, were lit not with flame but with large crystals.

Nik was struck dumb by the sight. He'd forgotten this was here and he'd been a fool to never even set foot in the space once in centuries past. What could he have learned here? He had access to books in the mortal realm, but he bet there were books and scrolls here that the librarians of Alexandria would lust after. As for the librarian, he spied his Aunt Cleo behind an amethyst-carved counter talking to his cousin. He hadn't seen the cousin in ages, since they were both Voices kept busy with assignments. She wore a straight skirt that hit just below the knee and a white buttoned blouse. Large, round glasses perched on her nose. Glasses she didn't need. He smiled. This was going to be fun.

"Greetings, Diana Prince," he called to her. She hated being called that by other Voices, even though she purposely presented herself in that look-alike form when in the mortal realm. She turned to him with a frown, whipping off the glasses.

"What are you doing here?" She tilted her nose up. "I thought you were on assignment."

"Diantha, where are your manners?" his aunt asked her.

"He started it."

His aunt sighed, looking at his mother, who shrugged. "Nikos, it is good to see you. Your mother has missed you."

His mother smiled and patted is arm. "Yes, I miss him. He works too hard."

Diantha snorted but when Cleo glared at her, she bent her head and moved some books onto a cart.

"What brings you both to my realm," Cleo asked.

"Nikos has a question about—"

Nik interrupted, "I have a question about something that has to do with my assignment. *Mitera* thought you would be able to help us find an answer."

"Of course," she waved her hands at the rows of bookcases before her, "if I don't know the answer, I know where to find it. What is the questions?"

Before his mother could say anything, Nik said, "Perhaps we should return at another time. I don't want to interrupt your visit with Diana."

"Diantha," she almost growled at him. He raised a brow at her. She shook her head. "I was just helping mama with some cataloguing and shelving. I'll leave you to your private matter and return later." She leaned over the counter to embrace her mother then beat a tattoo, hurrying past him and his mother, and up the stairs. When the echo of her steps faded, his mother turned to her sister.

"We apologize for upsetting your daughter, don't we Nikos?" He nodded and managed to hold back a smile.

Cleo waved away the apology. "Sister, she knows you are entitled to privacy. She just doesn't like being left in the dark about things. It's in her nature as it is in mine to want to know everything about everything and everyone, even as we also know that is impossible. Now, tell me what you have a question about, and I'll help you if I can."

When she looked at him expectantly, he cleared his throat. *How embarrassing was it to have to talk to his aunt about kissing a mortal? But, better her than Apollo.* "I need to know why, when I kissed my mortal—"

"Do I really want to hear this, Erato?"

His mother gripped her sister's hand across the counter. "Cleo, you *need* to hear this, because I think you are the only one who can help my son."

Cleo searched her sister's face, then turned to face him. "Continue."

He inhaled, then told her of the kiss, of seeing the temple while still on the beach, and of the lingering taste of honey in the kiss.

She nodded. "Has this ever happened to you before?"

"No, and my mortal experienced it first, seeing the temple, that is. I was not paying attention, but she stiffened in my arms in the middle of the kiss. And we both tasted honey."

"You were right to bring him here, sister. Have you told anyone else of this?"

Nikos shook his head. "Only Hermes."

Her eyes widened. "Well, if you are lucky, he won't tell anyone else yet. But, in that case..." She reached out and picked up a silver bell from her blotter and rang it. Its musical note echoed and re-echoed through the cavern. Through several breaths, they stood waiting, though for what, Nik was curious to see.

He heard the sound of soft-soled running feet head towards them from one of the long aisles between bookshelves. Dressed in doublet and hose, with a hat adorned with another long, brightly-colored feather, fleet-footed Hermes arrived before them. He swept his hat from his head and bowed first to his mother and then to his aunt. Ever the dramatist.

"At your service, beautiful Muses." He placed the hat back on his head at a jaunty slant. Cleo handed him a slip of paper she'd written on once they heard his steps. He looked at it, then at her, and then at Nik, nodding. "Ah." Lines creased his forehead.

"Do you know where to find it, Searcher?"

He nodded slowly. "Are you sure?"

"Some secrets cannot be kept forever," his aunt said. Hermes ran from them, across the cavern to the wall of scrolls, then through the wall. Nik jerked. He knew he shouldn't be surprised when it came to Hermes but he was. Probably came from spending too much time in the mortal realm. What now? Did they stand here waiting? Come back? He'd expected Cleo to just give him an answer, simply relay something that would solve the kiss mystery, not send the trickster god on a search.

His mother stood motionless next to him, making him more nervous since she and her sister obviously knew something he didn't. Why not just tell him? Finally, when he'd had enough of waiting and mysteries, Hermes popped back through the wall carrying a scroll that looked older than Earth. As he approached, Nik saw the scroll was sealed with wax. Even closer, the lightning bolt on the seal raised the hair on his neck. Zeus's mark?

Hermes handed Cleo the scroll with another flourish and then, clapping Nik on the back with the words, "Fates be with you. You'll need them." He turned and ran off down an aisle.

Hades! Now what?

Chapter 18

MJ typed away as the story unfolded in her mind, hearing her grandmother's voice telling her story. She was so familiar with the way her grandmother told a story, whether to a little girl or to her adult romance novel readers. Once again, they were creating a story together, playing their "what if?" game.

She'd loved that game as a child. Gran would start off the story, "Once upon a time, there lived a little girl whose home was a hollow tree." After several lines of description, MJ would pipe in with, "What if...?" Then she would take over the story for several more lines before Gran took her turn at "What if...?" Before long, they were either laughing until their sides hurt because they got so silly with the what ifs, or their eyes would get bigger and their voices softer as the story took them to some magical place.

She sighed and leaned back in her chair, stretching her arms above her. She checked the scene list which helped her stay on track but mostly she kept writing. It was time to take a break, maybe go for a walk on the beach... Her cell phone vibrated across the table like an angry bee.

"Hello?"

"Ms. Montague?"

She straightened in the chair, catching a glimpse of the time on her grandmother's old wall clock.

"Yes, Professor Gibbons. How are you?"

He cleared his throat. "Fine, thank you. but I'm a little concerned. I saw your mother on campus earlier today. She asked if you'd been in touch with me about your dissertation. Apparently, you are spending the summer at the beach? Your deadline is looming, Ms. Montague."

MJ closed her eyes and took a deep breath. Of course, her mother would take action the moment MJ set foot outside her mother's domain. "Professor, surely Mother told you my grandmother died? I am spending time at my grandmother's place on Block Island because I have to be here to settle part of her estate. And I worked on the dissertation this morning, in fact."

She looked at her laptop and Gran's scene list and notes on the table, and grimaced. Well, she had worked on her dissertation, just not in the last couple of hours. "One of the terms of the legacy is I must live here for the summer while taking care of estate matters in order to inherit the cottage and settlement."

He was silent for a moment, then cleared his throat. "I apologize for jumping to conclusions. Your mother—"

"I'm sure mother didn't mean to mislead you." Of course she did. Her mother didn't want her here. It didn't fit in with the plans she'd laid out for MJ. "You know how mother's worry."

She looked down at the scenes notes in front of her. What if—

"Yes, well, are you going to be able to meet your next deadline?"

What if she didn't?

"I'm doing my best, Professor. Do you think it would be possible to get an extension? After all, a death in the family and estate requirements were not something I planned on."

"I don't know about an extension, Ms. Montague. I understand your predicament but you must understand mine and do your best to finish the dissertation. In the meantime, I'll speak to the committee and see what they say."

"Thank you, Professor. And sir?"

"Yes?"

"This is my dissertation, not my mother's. Please don't discuss this conversation with her."

He cleared his throat again. "Of course not. Good bye, Ms. Montague."

"Goodbye, Professor."

She swiped the phone, ending the call, and placed it gently back on the table. Were all mothers like hers? She doubted it. She'd read books, seen movies with mothers who were loving and nurturing, who wanted their children to live their dreams. But she had to admit she'd also read of or seen mothers like hers, controlling, demanding, and withholding. Of course, most of those were stepmothers in fairy tales. MJ had waited most of her life for her mother to hug her, and whisper to her how much she loved her, how proud she was of her daughter. She was still waiting.

Was that why she had loved being with Gran so much, because she always made her feel loved and accepted, like a fairy godmother? She smiled. "Well, Gran, I guess I'm going to have to be my own fairy godmother now."

The letter and booklet lay on the table just beyond the computer. She picked it up and read through it again.

I'm sorry, my darling girl, that I surrendered my time with you too easily. I should have made more of a fuss, taken a stand, insisted we have our private time together again. But I didn't want to come between you and your parents, or you and your mother.

For the first time, MJ realized she wasn't just grieving over Gran's loss. She was mad, angry at being abandoned by the two central women in her life. Women who should have had her best interests at heart. Gran had—when she'd been allowed to. But not long enough.

The letter crinkled in her hand. Sighing, she smoothed it out and put it back on top of the booklet. Her mother was undeniably a force to be reckoned with. Look at how her professor had responded. Her mother always seemed to know what she wanted and how to get it, except, of course, when she became pregnant with MJ. She also knew how to make everyone fall in line with her plans. How did her father stand it? Could she be angry with Gran when she herself seldom stood up to her mother?

Papers covered the table in piles and pages. The screen of her laptop was blank now, having gone to sleep while she talked with the professor. Too bad she couldn't have done the same thing. The computer stared at her. She'd been having so much fun working on her grandmother's story, something she hadn't done since she was a teen.

The notes and books for her dissertation lay on the far end of the table. Gran's notes and index cards sat next to the computer on one side. Her first "book" sat beyond the laptop. She and Gran had worked on it on one of the last stay-overs. They'd played the "what if" game, Gran repeatedly asking what-if until MJ had a complete story about a young girl who had no friends because she had wings and could fly. Gran helped her print the story out, draw a few simple pictures for the cover and the inside, and then they'd cut and folded and stapled the pages. Gran even helped her glue a little glitter onto the girl's wings on the cover. They sparkled now in the light from the beach-facing windows.

She picked it up and touched a finger to the glitter. She used to imagine she could feel the wings flutter when she did that. Did they still? After all these years? She smiled to think how she might react if they did. She sighed, put the little book down, with the wrinkled letter and other books, and moved them and the scene list behind the computer where she couldn't see them. Pulling the dissertation notes—she still didn't have any index cards—to her, she clicked on the keypad, waking the computer, and minimizing the novel manuscript, then maximized the dissertation file.

She'd spent enough time in her imagination. Time to get back to reality. As she looked at her list of famous women novelists, she wondered about all the women who wrote but never published. Because—it wasn't done, it was a silly hobby, women didn't write serious literature. Just because they were women.

Sighing, she put fingers to keyboard. Without an extension, her deadline loomed.

"Come. We will leave you to read this alone," Clio said. She winked at Nik and led him to one of the tables lining the walls. "That way, we cannot be accused of telling you this, only aiding you in your own discoveries."

Nodding at him to take a seat, she gently laid the scroll down in front of him. Slowly, carefully, she the rubbed the seal until it disappeared, then unrolled a portion of it, took two smoothed and polished chunks of amethyst from a pouch at her waist and wedged them into place in front of the rolls of papyrus so the scrolls wouldn't roll shut. She glanced up at the sconces and hummed a little, making the light brighten on it.

"Sometimes," she said, "it is necessary for secrets to come to light. Perhaps it is this one's time."

She tapped the wide panel of papyrus with its inked symbols and words. "Whatever you read here, Nikos, may not be the whole story or the only way of seeing the story. Remember that." She stepped away, beckoning to his mother. "Come, Erato. Let's go for a walk in the fresh air. I need it."

His mother looked at him, raising a brow. He nodded. He was, after all, a grown man, one thousand plus years. He could handle what was here. She turned and linked her arm with Clio's, and the two of them walked away, heads bent to each other, murmuring softly.

He waited until they climbed the stairs and closed the door at the top behind them. Wasn't this unduly dramatic for a mere kiss, even a honeyed one? He glanced around the library. No one was there. No one watched him, so why did he feel uneasy? He could choose not to look at what lay before him, but what good would that do? He sighed. Plus, he wasn't the only one this issue concerned. MJ was involved, too, very much involved, whether she knew it or not. For her, for Juliette, and yes, for himself, he must read what lay before him.

He blew out a breath and lowered his gaze to the scroll.

It is decreed...

Doggedly, MJ sat at her laptop, adding word after word to her dissertation document. As she wrote, she couldn't help but feel sympathy for the women writers of the 19th century, the subject of her dissertation. Many of them had used a pen name, often a man's name, to hide their identity from a society that frowned on women writing fiction, especially those stories where women fell in love or, thinking of Colette, had sex.

But weren't they really the lucky ones? How many other women who longed to tell stories and see them in print, never put words to paper? Or put them on paper but hid them? How many denied their own desires to create in order to not anger husbands or families or social groups? Honestly, the thought put knots in her stomach, and if it did that to her what had the reality done to those women? For the ones that persisted, they must have fit their writing in and around their roles as wives, mother, and even daughters.

Her fingers typed harder on the laptop keys. Perhaps their careers, like Gran's, had been delayed, or their budding careers smothered in conception, or at the conception of children. She reeled back in her seat. The phrase triggered a painful childhood memory. A heated discussion between her parents, late one night when she was supposed to be in bed asleep.

She'd been buried under the covers reading with a flashlight a couple of hours after she should have been asleep. She hadn't intended to read long but the story was so good, about a magic tree house. She'd borrowed it from the school library and snuck it up to her room before her mother saw it and condemned it as fantastical and not worth reading. She had just turned off the flashlight and stowed it and the book back in their hiding place when she heard the yelling from her parents' bedroom down the hall. She slipped from her bed and cracked open her door, seeing the door to her parent's room slightly ajar.

"You have to stop expecting her to be like you, Martha, especially at this age. She's a kid. Let her be a kid."

"What claptrap, Frank. You sound like your mother."

"Oh, and of course, that's a terrible thing."

MJ dared a few steps out into the hall, staying close to the opposite wall where they couldn't see her, her heart pounding. "It is when it keeps her from living in the real world. Life is not fairy godmothers and flowers and happily ever afters. Marie Juliette is smart and I won't let her waste her mind on nonsense."

MJ's breath caught in her chest. *Her mother thought she was smart? She'd never told her that.* She smiled and waited to hear what else her mother had to say.

"She lives too much in her imagination. You remember what happened with a boy at her school when she was in first grade. She embarrassed me with the school and with the boy's parents."

MJ stopped smiling and bit her lip. She hadn't meant to make the boy wet his pants. How was she to know he'd believe her story about the monster that lived in the school toilet?

"Oh, for crying out loud. Are you never going to let that go? She was six. It was a couple of years ago."

"It doesn't matter how long ago it was. People have long memories around here. I won't let her or her imagination keep me from the dean's chair. I've waited too long to get back to where I was before...before we had her. I'm not waiting any longer."

Her father sighed. "Are you going to hold that against me—and her—forever?"

She should go back to bed. Her father sounded sad. She didn't like it.

"I don't hold it against you," her mother's voice was quieter. MJ took another step closer. "It took two of us to make me pregnant." Her mother paused. "You knew I never wanted children—at least not until—"

MJ clapped her hands over her ears, and ran back to her bedroom. She dove under the covers and swept her velvet rabbit to her chest where it hurt. The rabbit was a gift from her father after he'd read "The Velveteen Rabbit" to her about twenty times. She grabbed one of the ears and rubbed its soft, velvety tip back and forth, back and forth, against her cheek. She tried not to remember the words but they repeated over and over. "I never wanted children...I never wanted children...I never wanted children." *Did that mean her mother didn't want her?*

MJ straightened in her chair and watched the cursor blink at her from the last word she'd typed. A long time had passed since she last thought of that night. She cried herself to sleep, and then next day acted as if she hadn't heard a thing. Weeks passed before she stopped wondering every time her mother kissed her hello or goodbye or good night, if she loved her. Now, as an adult, she understood the dismay her mother must have felt at finding herself pregnant just when she was ready to take the next step in her academic career. Still...

She closed her eyes and willed the memory back into the closet it had sprung from. She was a kid then who probably heard things wrong or misunderstood them. Probably her imagination at fault—again. She put fingers to keyboard but her brain rebelled. She couldn't think and didn't want to.

When her stomach growled, she realized she needed to eat and rose to search the refrigerator and cupboards. Nothing looked appetizing, so, from a drawer, she pulled a couple of menus that promised to deliver hot and fresh. Not pizza. Not Chinese. She needed something more satisfying, like a burger.

The White Horses. A delicious burger, plenty of people around and a beautiful drive along the shore. And since Nik was away, she wouldn't have to worry about running into him. She touched her fingers to her lips, remembering the feel and taste of him, as well as the scene of a temple she couldn't have seen. She jerked her fingers from her mouth. No, she didn't need that temptation, nor did she need to give her imagination more fuel. After closing the lid on her laptop, grabbing her purse and keys, she locked the door and climbed into her Mini. She was pretty sure she remembered the way.

And at least it was still light with no fog.

Chapter 19

Nik put his finger close to, but not touching, the manuscript, and moved it along the lines of Greek. He jerked it back when images and sounds like a movie unrolled with the movement of his finger, stopping when he removed his finger. He glanced around the library, but only the books kept him company. He put his finger to the scroll again, watching and listening as the movement revealed a scene.

"Read it!" Hera ordered, leaning from her throne toward a scribe who stood before her holding a scroll the height of his arm from elbow to fingertip.

Zeus sat next to his royal wife, erect on his throne, hands curled over the carved ends of the throne's arms. Apollo—a younger Apollo than Nik knew—stood next to his father. His sister, Artemis, stood on the other side of Hera.

Zeus was plainly not happy, his brow furrowed, his jaw clenched if the jut of his beard was any indication. What was happening? Nik moved his finger further along the lines.

The scribe cleared his throat and looked to Zeus who only glared at some point past him.

Hera hissed, "I said, read it."

The scribe bobbed his head and read, "It is decreed that to ensure the security and health of the immortal realm and to protect the mortal realm, there will be no further matings between immortal and mortal, the term to be understood as a pairing between immortal and mortal who love each other. The risk to the immortal realm of semi-immortals populating and disrupting the balance between mortal and immortal realm is too great. For those immortals engaged in mortal activity who wish to plow a mortal field, they will use the power of withholding seed, only possible when love is not present. The ability to withhold seed is made null, and mortal means of protection are also made ineffective when the partners love each other."

Zeus rose, hands fisted. The scribe paused to roll up one side of the scroll and unroll the other. It trembled in his hands.

"Continue!" Hera ordered.

"Lest there be confusion, the test for the presence of love shall be immediately apparent in the kiss when the partners experience the taste of honey, and hear and see…"

Nik shot up from his chair, "*ma Heran!*" No, he wasn't falling in love with MJ. He'd lived for a thousand years and never, ever fallen before. Impossible. He wasn't in love with her. She certainly wasn't in love with him. She found him bossy and annoying, after all, and she was the one who asked him to leave her alone. He paced past the rows of shelves, then back to the table. He hovered his finger over the scroll. Should he continue reading? Perhaps, but he knew what he needed to know, didn't he? Gods knew what he'd see if he "read" more. He had to get out of there. The stone walls and rows of books were closing in on him, so he ran for the stairs.

As he raced, his steps echoing, through the temple to the side door, he recalled how his mother put her hand to her head and looked worried. No wonder. If he actually fell in love with MJ, he would break both rules of the Voices, rules pounded into him before and after his initiation into Apollo's select cadre. Don't fall in love. Don't reveal what you are. The second rule had been easy until now. The first—he'd never had problems with the first before. Affection was all he'd felt, for all his previous mortals. Affection and lust. Totally allowable according to the scene from the scroll.

But love? Love meant breaking one of the rules. Which probably meant expulsion from the Voices. He wouldn't mind so much as he was soul-weary of being the creative intermediary for his mother, but what would happen to his mother then? Would the strand of grey in her hair grow wider? Would she weaken? He ran from the temple as if Cerberus were after him, then halted. Where was he going to go now?

One thing for sure. He wasn't sticking around and risk running into Apollo.

Thalassa popped to the surface, swirling her tail back and forth to keep above darkening cool water as she eyed the mortal's cottage. She smiled, smug about the situation between Nikos and that woman. He still hadn't returned.

When he'd kissed the woman, she'd worried that this might be the one time a kiss tasted as it shouldn't. Of course, she'd worried about it every time Nikos had a young, attractive female mortal as his mission. She wasn't supposed to know about Hera's edict, but her mother knew about it and had shared the knowledge with her daughters. The Voices didn't know because the gods were idiots who thought they could control everyone and everything, and as a way to test the commitment and loyalty of those who served. Another test, like the one she and her sisters had been put through.

Every time he had another assignment, Thalassa worried. But every time, he followed the rules, except for the old woman, of course. But she hadn't worried one fish scale about her. He might not come to Thalassa's bed any longer, but he certainly wasn't the immortal to sleep with anyone, unlike Zeus. Not many of the Voices were like the errant god, which was why Hera's edict was stupid. And arrogant. She breathed through her fury. Screeching wasn't a good idea right now.

Thankfully, Nikos still hadn't returned, and now the mortal was driving off, too. Mess with the guidance system again? She laughed, no point in wasting her energy. Nikos was gone. The woman was off to gods knew where. If Thalassa was mortal and could set foot on the beach, she'd dance about as the woman had done, she was just that pleased. He was safe. For now.

But she wouldn't give up her vigil yet. He might yet need her to save him from himself.

Parking the car in front of the pub, MJ tilted her head to look through the windshield at the dark pines towering over the pub's roof and thought again of fairy tales like Goldilocks and Hansel and Gretel. Surely, three bears would appear at any moment. Or, perhaps if she walked behind the building and stepped beneath the branches of sharp smelling pine needles, she'd find a trail of breadcrumbs?

The sunlight fought a losing battle with the pines and broad-leafed trees, finding only small patches to creep through and illuminate spaces between the deep shade, mysteriously beckoning and foreboding at the same time. She pulled the keys from the ignition, shaking her head. Wow, her imagination had really taken off, it was a stand of trees, a forest. Nothing more.

Her stomach growled at her to get moving, so she got out of the car, locked it, and walked quickly to the door of the pub. As she reached for the handle, the door swung outward.

She stepped back as the most beautiful—no, not the right word. Gorgeous. The most gorgeous guy she'd ever seen stepped out. His blonde hair shone in the sun, his bright blue eyes froze her in place. What was the song about something so bright "I gotta wear shades"?

"Excuse me, miss." The man tipped his head to her. So-o-o courtly.

She couldn't help smiling at him. "No worries. You just startled me. Did you enjoy your meal? Did you have the hamburger? It's delicious. I had one, my first, the other night. Gourmet good."

What was she doing? She shut her mouth. She needed shades, and a muzzle, with this guy, apparently. He was so tall, and his skin looked like he spent hours out in the sun, like a surfer guy, but this was Rhode Island not California. Smiling down at her, he closed the door, shutting out the competing noises of dinnerware and voices.

"You like the hamburger?"

"Um, yes." She'd love to be biting into one now but he was in the way. She wasn't getting past those broad chest and shoulders. She looked up at him to ask him to move and paused. The sun was low enough in the sky to light up his hair. It dazzled her for a minute but he bent his head a little and the effect disappeared.

"I'm glad to know you like the hamburgers. I don't cook them myself, but I was smart enough to hire the chef."

"Oh, are you the manager?"

"Manager and owner."

"Well, I'm new on the island and I had my first burger the other evening when I was here with my financial advisor."

His gaze sharpened on her. "Are you Ms. Montague?"

She took a step back. *How did he know her name?* He held a hand up. "Do not worry. I know Niko...Nik. He's mentioned he was working here with a new client."

MJ relaxed. He wasn't some weird, sex-starved guy who was going to drag her off to the woods.

His smile grew wider. "I won't drag you off somewhere. In fact, I'm—"

Did he read her mind? Maybe she should go back to the cottage. The pub door swung open again and the pub host from the other night stuck his head out.

"Oh good, you're still here. I just returned from the t..."

The blond god turned sideways, revealing her to the host.

"Er, excuse me. I was so focused on him, I didn't see you," the host said to her.

"This is Ms. Montague," the blond said, "Nik's client. I told her Nik has mentioned her a few times when he's been here. She says she had her first burger here and loved it, so I'd like you to comp her meal here this evening. It's on me."

Wow! How nice of him but... "You don't need to do that. It isn't necessary, thank you."

He turned to her, his brows drawn together, his eyes boring into her. Her body warmed.

"You would refuse a gift from the g—" the host cleared his throat, "—from the owner?"

How embarrassing! "Uh, no, sorry, thank you. I shall enjoy my meal."

He nodded. "It's always wise to gratefully accept a gift when freely given." He turned. "Anything I need to know now?" The host shook his head and looked at her. "Very well. I leave you in charge." He turned and walked down the steps, the sunlight seeming to follow him. *Weird.*

"Please come this way, Ms. Montague."

She followed him, or rather his white shirt, into the pub, almost blind in the dimmer indoor lighting. "Call me MJ. No need to be so formal. Speaking of which, the owner never introduced himself. What's his name?"

The host paused and she almost ran into him before he resumed striding past the bar into the dining area. "We call him Sunny. It's a nickname."

"What's yours?" she asked, as he pulled out a chair for her at the same small table she and Nik had sat at a couple of nights ago. He handed her a menu. "Your waitress will be right with you." He strode off to seat another couple.

Without answering her questions.

Nik stood beyond the temple wondering where to go.

He didn't want to return to the cottage. Well, he did but that held danger at the moment, until he sorted out his feelings for MJ and that kiss. Until then, he couldn't be within a mile of her, let alone in the cottage with no one else around. He'd be constantly tempted to kiss her again, and again.

Hades! He ran his hand through his hair. Who was he kidding? If he kissed her, he wasn't going to stop there. The memory of her warm, soft lips, the scent of her skin made him think of trailing kisses from beneath her ear lobe down across her collar bone, between her breasts to her belly— He blew out a breath. He definitely wasn't going back there yet. Or the pub. The Voices barracks? He could hide himself there as long as Apollo didn't come looking for one of them. If the sun god showed up, it might be difficult to keep his knowledge off his face and he didn't want the god to question him. Surely Clio and his mother wouldn't have said anything. Where to go? Then it hit him.

He had no home. Not the mortal sense of home, a space that sheltered and protected you and those you loved. A place you were happy to return to when you were tired, sad, alone. All he had was his quarters in the Voices' barracks. It was all he'd ever had since he joined the cadre. It had never bothered him until now. Because of his work in the mortal realm, he had an apartment with an address, of course. The location changed with each client, so he seldom slept there and certainly didn't keep anything personal there. It was an address to maintain the appearance of being mortal. He often lived out of a suitcase, because it was what a mortal did, not because he needed it, since he could always cross into the immortal realm if he needed something. Or he bought what he needed when he needed it. Money was never an issue.

Sometimes, he lived with the mortal he was working with, like Juliette, and truthfully, that was the closest he'd come to a place that felt like home. But MJ was there now. It was her home, not his—if she fulfilled the conditions of the legacy. Too, she had her condo, and even her parents' place. Plenty of places to seek shelter and protection and comfort with family and even friends. It was one of the aspects of being a mortal.

He walked into the olive grove next to the temple to seek out a hint of shade. He wasn't a mortal, but he spent so much time in the mortal realm. If he suddenly disappeared from there, would anyone miss him? Like MJ. Was she missing him now? Pacing between the trees, he realized it was a ridiculous question for him to ask. Why should he care if she missed him or not? Better she didn't. Better he didn't miss her, either. He stopped and listened to the silence of sunlight and the gentle murmur of life in the trees. Taking a deep breath, he appreciated this rare moment of solitude, increasingly difficult to find in the mortal realm. He'd enjoyed spending time with Juliette because she didn't need entertained. She enjoyed talking with him, but more often, the two of them would sit on her deck and work and listen to the sea birds. In those moments, he felt no division between mortal and immortal worlds. And he had belonged.

Now? For now, maybe forever, the barracks were his home. He'd go to the barracks and workout in the gymnasium, maybe sweat out his edginess after his time in the library. Maybe spend some time on the bag. Punching something would feel good, right now.

If he could avoid Apollo, he'd be fine.

Chapter 20

MJ left the pub grateful for the delicious meal, glad she hadn't had to eat alone. Well, technically she ate alone at her table, but others ate and drank in the bar, too, including some hunky guys.

Who, darn it, reminded her of Nik, and her last trip here in the Ferrari. Yeah, she was missing the thrill of riding through the dark in that sporty car. She opened the door to her Mini Cooper, belted herself in, and as she backed out, looked up at the night sky, bright with the last rays of the setting sun. She sighed. Face it, she was missing Nik, too. Damn that kiss!

Up until the kiss, she successfully ignored those dark eyes focused on her that seemed to see her more deeply than anyone other than Gran. She ignored the tingles in her body when his fingers brushed hers, when the scent of his aftershave drifted to her, or when she saw his muscles flex—anywhere. Whether in a suit or in swim trunks, his physique, was all sleek, restrained power. Whew! And now she needed a cold drink. Good thing she had cold drinks back home—back at the cottage. Darkness was falling and she didn't want to spend hours circling the island again without Nik here to rescue her.

Irritated at herself for putting him and rescue together in the same thought, she floored it and sent the little car shooting up the highway. She turned on her headlights when she reached the section of the road where the ocean was a dark if noisy presence on her left, and a line of trees loomed over the road on her right. Periodically, the trees broke rank for a lighted house or two. Quiet. Peaceful. Creepy in some primitive way. She swallowed and used the controls on the steering wheel to dial her cell phone which was always linked to the car.

"Hello?"

"Hi, Neri. It's MJ."

Switching to high beams to pierce the now full dark of night, she caught Neri up with her past few days, even though it felt as if she'd been on the island longer.

"Wow! Not quite the quick and easy legal process you were expecting, is it? And why does your voice change when you mention the financial advisor, Nik, right?"

MJ shook her head. "No reason." She sighed. "Well, except he kissed me."

"Oooh. And?"

"And what?"

"C'mon, girlfriend. You share more details about a dead author than you do about a kiss. Which you haven't had in a while. Did you like it? Did you kiss him back?"

She made the turn into the cottage drive, put the car in park and turned off the car. There was no way Neri would settle for the bare facts.

"I did kiss him back—"

"I knew it!"

She sighed and thunked her head back against the car's headrest. "Neri, I could really use a friend here right now. Nik isn't here for the time being. Please, can't you come for a short visit, a couple of nights. I'll pay for the gas. Please."

"Don't be silly. You aren't paying for my gas." She was silent. "Okay. I'll come. I could use a few days off. This past week has been brutal with all the students finishing up exams and letting loose after. Buck owes me for overtime. I'll give him a call when I get off here. Text me the address and I'll drive over tomorrow."

MJ smiled, her shoulders dropping in relief. "You're a gem, Neri. I can't wait to see you. Oh, by the way, if your GPS goes crazy and doesn't work once you drive off the ferry, call me and I'll come find you."

"Don't worry. I'm sure it will be fine. See you tomorrow."

Smiling, MJ texted the address and the link for the ferry schedule to Neri, then stared out the car window at the so-called cottage, hers if she could stick it out for the summer. If she could get her dissertation completed and defended. If she got a job at the university that let her pay for the upkeep and maintenance of this place, even if she only made use of it on weekends and in the summer because it was too far from the university to commute.

If she didn't let her mother didn't talk her into selling it.

Smiling at the turtle knocker as she unlocked the front door, she stepped inside and locked the door behind her. Walking toward the living area, she paused to put her fingers to her lips and then to the photograph of Gran reading to her child self.

"Love you, too," she whispered to the photo, remembering the intense, real-feeling dream of Gran. She looked at the table covered with research notes, index cards, her e-reader, and her laptop. Her shoulders slumped and she sighed. Instead of being motivated to get to work on her dissertation, she was overwhelmingly tired. Those crisp cotton sheets on Gran's bed called to her to come get a good night's sleep. She had hours to work in the morning before Neri arrived. She turned off the shell lamp. In the morning, she'd be better prepared to get back to her work. No distractions, especially of the hunky kind, demanding she finish Gran's manuscript. In the bedroom, with only moonlight to guide her, she turned on the bedside lamp and realized what a contrast it made to the darkness peering in at her.

This was her first night alone in the house. No Nik. Everything was locked up, right? Tempted to go back downstairs and check, she chastised herself. "You are being silly. There is nothing to worry about. You are perfectly safe. After all Gran lived here by herself for years." Nevertheless, she dropped the blinds on the windows before going into the bathroom for her nightly routine. Afterwards, she pulled on her short pajama bottoms and cami top, and crawled into bed, sighing into the comfort of the cool sheets. Reaching to turn off the light, her gaze landed on the stack of paperback books written by Gran. She picked up the top book, realized it was one she either hadn't read or had read so long ago, she didn't remember. Reading a little before going to sleep would help her unwind from the day, so she stuffed another pillow behind her back and opened the book to Chapter One.

Nik shifted uncomfortably. This was ridiculous! He was an immortal. What in Hades was he doing, trying to sleep in his not-so-very-comfortable-for-sleeping sports car like a homeless mortal?

After beating a punching bag until sweat dripped down his head onto his back in the cadre's gymnasium, followed by a shower, and dressed in jeans and t-shirt, he decided to avoid the barracks. Knowing something that affected all of them, he wasn't in the mood for hanging with other Voices. He didn't want to talk about MJ, and he certainly didn't want to talk about that kiss. Nor was he ready to face Apollo. Or his mother. Or MJ.

He'd called a couple of the island hotels like the Beach House, but it was the summer season and nothing was available. He didn't have the patience for more calls, he was an immortal, after all, which made sleeping in his car a ridiculous situation. He snorted, the sound filling the silent car. Equally ridiculous was that no homeless mortal would sleep in a Ferrari. They'd sell it and sleep in comfort for months if not years. He wasn't homeless. He wasn't. He was just a coward, and could imagine Hermes taunting him. He just needed time to think—and adjust.

He shifted again, lowering the seat back a little more. Where did he truly belong? Here, with whatever challenged creative mortal he was assigned to? With MJ? Or back on Mount Helicon with his mother, aunts, Apollo and the other Voices?

Lowering the window next to him, the wind whispered through the branches of the pines he was parked beneath, hidden behind White Horses. One advantage to his current location—no one would think to look for him here. Not Apollo or Erato or even Hermes. He could have a few hours of quiet. Time to think. And plan. The light of the waning moon flickered and danced through the trees and caught the silhouette of an owl as it swooped in front of the car from one tree to another. An owl. Nothing more. The quiet darkness surrounded him and he relaxed. There were times when the mortal realm was as beautiful and magical in its own way as the immortal realm. Sometimes more so. He stretched out a leg as far as it could go. And there were other times...

He wanted to sleep, but every time he closed his eyes, he saw MJ's eyes rounded in shock, the O of her luscious lips, pink and moist from their kiss. Damn, how was he supposed to sleep with blood pulsing through his body. He adjusted his jeans. With strands of her hair escaping from her braid to dance in the ocean breeze, she'd looked like a fairytale princess from that story...What was it? Oh yes, *Rapunzel*. And he was just the prince to rescue her. But from what? Her dragon of a mother? From herself?

Or from him?

He sighed. He was never going to get any sleep if he didn't stop thinking so hard. Too bad the pub was closed now. Maybe a beer would help him drift off. All his thinking and worrying was an open invitation to Phobetor the Frightener to enter his dreams and turn them into nightmares. After reading that scroll, he didn't need those. He sighed, sat up, adjusted the seat back and started the car. He couldn't stand it. He needed to check on MJ. Make sure she was okay. He shifted into gear. Make sure she didn't need him. He shifted back into park.

She didn't need him, she needed space. She'd basically told him to leave. But what if something happened like that first night? Hermes was still being close-lipped about it but Nik wondered if perhaps... He shifted back into gear and tore out of the parking lot. He wouldn't even go in.

Mile after mile streaked by, the car lights often the only thing to break the dark night, until he reached the neighborhood near the cottage. Occasional house lights broke the darkness and broke up the dark. He stopped a short distance from the cottage and got out. Looking around, most of the houses were dark since it was after midnight. Quickly, he strode down the road until he reached the cottage. The lights in the front rooms, upper and lower were off. He decided to check the back, just to be sure.

At the back corner, soft light illuminated the flower border along the side of the house. He looked up. A light was on in MJ's room. Probably the lamp on the nightstand. *Why was it on so late? She couldn't still be working on her dissertation, or the novel, could she? Nah, she preferred the dining table where she had plenty of room to spread out with all her papers and notebooks as well as her computer.*

What was she doing up there? Reading probably. Maybe she'd fallen asleep with the light on. He sighed. He wanted to be in that bed with her. Her warm, soft body curled into his. He rubbed his face. How much torture could one man, mortal or immortal, take? Enough. Time to leave before he did something they'd both regret. Or would they? The question made him halt. Would he regret breaking the rules of the Voices if it meant he could be with MJ? Have a life with MJ? A home?

He shook his head. Not something to decide tonight. But soon.

MJ yawned wide as she tucked sheets and blanket under the mattress of the guest bed and considered falling onto it and catching a nap. She shouldn't have stayed up so late reading. Instead, she straightened and grabbed the comforter from the small wingback chair in the corner and threw it on the bed. She grabbed the decorator pillows and centered them carefully against the sleeping pillows, then stood back, hands on hips and surveyed the room.

The walls were painted a soft grey, and the trim a bright white. Several framed seascapes hung on the walls, probably to make up for the lack of windows facing the ocean. One double window faced the street and was softened by silky grey drapes. She thought about putting Neri in the bedroom that Nik used so her friend would have a view of the ocean, but since she wasn't certain when he'd return, she put her friend in this room so she wouldn't have to worry about shuffling them around should he show up unexpectedly.

Another yawn. She was going to pay for reading more than one or two chapters of Gran's book last night, but she couldn't stop turning pages, which would have delighted Gran. Not every author could do that, so how did Nik expect her to finish her grandmother's manuscript with that same magic?

She leaned over and smoothed out a wrinkle in the comforter, and with a last critical glance at the room, headed down the stairs. She hoped Neri wasn't lost. Since it was mid-afternoon and the sun was out that seemed unlikely. Still, she kept her cell phone in her back pocket, just in case. Her phone vibrated against her butt. She pulled it out and swiped to answer without looking at the number of the caller.

"Hey there. Are you lost?"

"Marie Juliette? What are you talking about? Of course I'm not lost."

MJ suppressed a groan and collapsed onto the stairs. "Sorry, Mother, I was expecting a call from Neri."

"Neri? That artist friend of yours?"

"Yes, she's coming for a visit for a couple of days and I told her to call me if she can't find her way here."

"How are you going to work on your dissertation if your friend is there? Is that financial advisor for your grandmother gone, then? Did he give you the name of a reliable real estate agent?"

Let's see, bash her head against the wall or run screaming into the ocean? But no, Neri was coming. She unclenched her jaw, took a deep breath, and said, "No, Nik and I are not done, but he had some other things to do so he took off for a few days." Liar, liar, but she was not telling her mother the real reason he wasn't there. "I convinced Neri to come stay for a few nights because she's been working so hard. We both need a break."

A big sigh. "You can't. Bad enough you're there, but you need to finish that dissertation. It won't look good if you don't meet your deadline. What will people think if the next dean of Women's Studies has a daughter who can't get her priorities straight enough to turn her dissertation in on time? Why don't you come home?"

MJ opened her mouth to explain yet again why she was where she was when she heard the light tooting of a horn out front.

"Oops, have to go, Mother. Neri just arrived. Give my love to Dad. Bye." She swiped her phone to end the call before her mother could protest, and shoved the phone back into her jeans pocket. Running to the front door, she unlocked it and threw it open.

Neri's well-loved and well-used lime green VW Bug sat parked off the road in front of the cottage. Her friend stood half in and half out of the driver's side.

"Neri!" MJ shouted, happy and relieved to see her friend. "Perfect timing!" She ran out and grabbed her friend in a huge hug.

"I'm so glad you're here. So very glad."

As his car doors winged up, Nik brought his seat back into driving position. Had he really spent the night here? He stepped out of the car and groaned as he straightened. Yes, he had. Well, at least half of the night. Never again.

He was being ridiculous. Only three people knew that he'd seen the scroll and why. All he had to do was act as if everything was normal, that he hadn't kissed a mortal and tasted honey. He wasn't in love. How could he be? Barely a week had passed since she arrived at the cottage, and for an immortal, that was no time at all. True, she wasn't the heartless, self-centered bitch he assumed she was, but she wasn't his type, definitely not. She was mortal, that alone made her not his type.

So why, after all these centuries of working with mortals, of serving Apollo and his mother and aunts, was this happening now? He shoved his hands into his pockets and strode across the parking lot and the road, to get to the beach where he kicked off his shoes. Glancing back at the pub, he was grateful it was too early for the pub to be open. He didn't want to be seen or questioned, even though he should probably talk to Hermes. The god had to have some idea of what was in the scroll he'd fetched for Clio. But he wasn't ready to be poked and prodded by the god who often found humor in others' discomfort.

First, he needed a clear plan for getting himself out of this situation. If he left MJ and didn't help her re-discover her imagination and ability to tell stories, he'd break his promise to Juliette. If he stayed with MJ, he might find himself kissing her again. Hades take it. No might about it. He would kiss her again, and more, breaking his promise as a Voice, to not fall in love, to not reveal what he was.

He kicked at the sand.

Love between mortal and immortal was impossible, wasn't it? Yet, what would it be like to commit long-term to one woman? To love and cherish 'til death do you part, as the mortal ceremony said? He gazed out over the water. Something larger than a fish moved quickly through the water just below the surface several yards out. A dolphin?

Was long-term commitment to one woman much different from the one he made to his clients as a Voice? Sometimes, like marriage, that ran until death did part, as it had with Juliette. His mortal clients received his devoted attention and time, his every effort to help them dive deep into their creative wells, recapture their *merika,* and emerge renewed, and, in the end, successful in their literary pursuits.

What did he receive in return? No family of his own, certainly no children, as he ensured that sex with mortals never resulted in that form of creation. No home to call his own, and no one to share the gifts and challenges of the day with, other than other Voices. He could screw any one, any time, without love, but after all this time, while the act was temporarily satisfying, afterwards all he felt was angry—at the client, the cadre, Apollo.

Huh. He unclenched his fists. Hadn't quite thought about it that way before. He could imagine telling the other guys, "Nah, I don't like screwing any more. It just makes me mad." They'd laugh him out of the cadre. Perhaps he'd watched too many films, helped inspire screenplays, where love conquered all and everyone lived happily ever after, in couples and families who shared deep bonds that strengthened through the ups and downs of being mortal.

Love. Blast and damn! He was going to have to talk to the only expert on the subject whom he trusted.

His mother.

Chapter 21

"What's this?" MJ asked Neri as they grabbed her bag and other stuff from the back seat of her car. Something in a white bag smelled of cinnamon. "Did you bring your own food in case you got stranded or something?"

Her friend laughed as she flung her backpack over her shoulder and pulled up the handle on her small suitcase. "Well, yes and no. I brought leftovers from the pub. I thought that way you wouldn't have to cook tonight, and we could just hang out and enjoy."

"I like how you think," MJ said as they ambled back toward the cottage.

Neri looked around. "Wow, this isn't anything like what I expected. It's not really a cottage, is it?"

"No, it's nothing like what I imagined," she said, opening the door and leading her friend inside. "It's a beautiful place. Set your stuff down and follow me. I'll give you the quick tour of the downstairs and put this food away. Wait until you see the view."

She smiled when Neri gasped as they entered the living area. "MJ, this is... It's breathtaking. Inside and out."

MJ nodded, looking at the sunlight sparking off the water as the gulls wheeled back and forth over the water searching for their meal. "It's a magical place, really. C'mon. Let's put your cold stuff in the fridge, and then I'll show you your room."

After storing stuff in the fridge, she grabbed her friend's suitcase while Neri took her backpack, and they climbed the stairs. When she showed her friend into the guest room, she wished she'd dared to put her in "Nik's" room. "I'm sorry you don't have a room with an ocean view but the only other bedroom is the one Nik uses and since I don't know when he'll be back—"

"Don't worry about it, MJ. I'm just so glad to have a chance to see you and your new place."

"Mother is pushing me to sell it."

Neri turned from setting her suitcase on bench at the foot of the bed. "Why?"

MJ shrugged. "She thinks it's a beach shack and assumes there is no reason for me to keep it, especially if I get the position as associate professor once I have my PhD."

"Well, if it were me, I'd hang on to it. People dream of owning a place like this, even if they only enjoy it on weekends and a few weeks out of the year. You could rent it out."

"Yeah, well, never mind that for now. Are you hungry after your trip? Ready for some lunch?"

Neri rubbed her stomach. "Am I ever. You know me. I can always eat."

In the kitchen, MJ pulled out the cheese and tapenade Neri brought, and added a jar of cornichons from the fridge. She put those on a wooden cutting board with a cheese knife and added Parmesan crackers, and the leftover slices of a baguette.

"Wine?" She held up a bottle of white wine. Neri nodded, then MJ with her bounty led the way out onto the deck. Once they settled into chairs on the deck and served themselves, Neri stared at the ocean and sighed. "You're right, this is magical.

How do you get anything done? I'd sit here and gaze at the ocean all day."

"It is kind of mesmerizing but I have a dissertation to write, remember?"

Her friend smiled. "I'm so grateful you invited me. I confess I was about to call you because I have a favor to ask."

MJ waited while Neri took a bite of cheese and cracker and followed it with a sip of wine. She set her glass down. "Buck told me yesterday some of his student employees are leaving to head home for the summer break. Although he is cutting back on hours a bit, he's asked me to work more hours to cover gaps."

"That's great! You'll have money saved up for your Europe trip in no time."

Neri shook her head. "The problem is that in order to work those hours, I have to take fewer credits. If I take fewer credits, I don't qualify for graduate student housing. I have to find somewhere else to live."

"Oh, no!"

"Oh, yes. I looked at apartment rentals but I'm not finding anything affordable or rentable for a few months so I wondered if, until I can find something, I could sublet your apartment while you're here?"

MJ sat back, surprised. "I hadn't really thought about my place being empty for the summer, but of course it will be." She tapped her fingernails against her wine glass. It made perfect sense to have someone use the space while she was here. "Okay," she said slowly, "It's probably better to have someone there keeping an eye on things."

Neri squealed and clapped her hands, then grabbed MJ's. "Thank you, thank you. You are the best. I didn't want to get into a year's lease or sublet, since I only need a place for the summer. I should be back to a full semester and student housing in the fall."

"You're welcome. Glad to help." She spread more tapenade on a cracker.

Neri did the same. "Yum," she said after a bite. "And speaking of yum, tell me more about the yummy financial advisor. Will I get to meet him?"

MJ swallowed the last of her cracker. "Let's clean up and go for a walk on the beach before it gets any warmer."

Her friend smiled and stood. "I know avoidance when I hear it, but okay. You're not off the hook, though. I want more details."

Details? She was trying to forget those details.

MJ bent to pick up a small pink piece of sea glass, dusted it off and handed it to Neri.

"Oh, I love the pink. What do you think it was? So feminine." Of course, her painter friend appreciated the color and its association. Once they'd admired it, Neri safely tucked it in her pocket. "So, spill. No more stalling. What's up with that hunky financial adviser?"

Oh, if only he was solely her advisor, someone in his forties who had a paunch. If only he hadn't kissed her and turned her world upside down. She wanted to tell Neri all about it but would she think MJ was crazy? Only one way to find out.

She shrugged. "Well, he's obviously successful at what he does, if his hot red Ferrari is any indication, but that's not the only sign he knows what he is doing. He helped Gran become successful as an author, as well." She turned and gestured back to the cottage. "With his help as agent and adviser, her books sold enough to enable her buy the cottage and furnish it." She took off her sandals and resumed walking up the beach. The sand was warm under her feet, and shifted beneath them.

"Wow! An author. How wonderful! And it's going to belong to you by the end of the summer? Have you corrected your mother's misconception about the place?"

MJ shook her head. "I'm not ready to share it with her. For the first time, I have something completely mine and out of her…"

"Control?" Neri asked.

She sighed and nodded. *Was that it? This cottage, the legacy was something her mother didn't control?* She nudged her friend to a wide flat rock jutting into the water, then shifted to dip her toes in the small waves edging the rock. "She probably assumes once I start teaching as a full-time professor, I'll be too busy to make the trek out here."

"You're certain you'll have a job at the university once you get your PhD?"

MJ shrugged, "Mother keeps hinting about conversations she's had with the dean and others. Of course, I'd start out as a lowly associate until I publish more articles and papers."

"You don't sound enthusiastic."

She sat down next to Neri, put her feet in the water, and shook her head. "I like teaching. I don't like academic politics. I've seen and heard too much about it from Mother. Worse than teenage girls fighting for a place on the cheerleading squad."

"Do you need to teach? I mean if your grandmother left you this place and her money?"

MJ's gaze jerked to Neri who seemed absorbed in creating small waves with her feet. Did she? Did she want to teach? Her mind whirled. Gran's inheritance changed all that.

"I don't know. What would I do if I didn't teach?"

Her friend shrugged. "I'm sure you'd think of something, like be an author like your gran. What did she write?"

"Remember those romance novels by Julie Moon I loaned you?" Her friend nodded. "Gran wrote them."

Neri grabbed her arm and shook it. "Are you kidding me? But that wasn't your Gran's name, was it?"

MJ smiled. Gran fooled everyone. Her son, her granddaughter. Her daughter-in-law. "She used a pen name. Altogether she published ten books. She was working on another one when she died."

"Oh, too bad. Maybe you can hire someone to finish it. You know, a ghostwriter, like the celebrities use."

MJ caught her breath. It was a good idea but it made her chest tighten. The story was Gran's. The idea of some stranger taking it... "Nik suggested I finish it."

Neri twisted on the rock to face her, eyes wide. "Oh, brilliant! I've read your writing. Remember the short story you shared with me that you wrote for a class? Even your essays show how good you are at evoking emotion in the reader. Isn't that what storytelling is all about? Oh, do it, MJ. It's a perfect idea. You are going to do it, aren't you?"

"You're kidding, right? I've never written—"

"Stop right there. I know what you're going to say, but don't bother. You may never have written a full-length novel but you wrote short stories as an undergrad that won contests. And you said several professors praised your writing in those creative writing classes you took for your BA."

MJ gazed at the water. True, she'd won contests with her writing, but Neri didn't understand. How could she? "Would you feel qualified to finish a painting by Wyeth or Hockney just because your landscapes won awards?"

"Probably. After I spent a little time studying their techniques, looking at their past work so I was familiar with the tone and palette. C'mon, MJ, that's what forgers do. And they paint the whole canvas. Sounds like you only have to 'forge'..." she made air quotes "...part of the canvas, not the whole thing. Did she have any notes or an outline of the story?"

MJ stared at her friend dumbfounded—that word. She was right. Art forgeries abounded. So did ghost writers. She'd read all of her grandmother's books. In fact, several of them, she'd read more than once. She did have a sense of Gran's voice as a writer, her rhythms, language choice, and the other elements that made her work unique to her. As a teen, as those stories of hers Gran had kept upstairs in the drawer proved, she did know how to imitate other writers. She bit her lip. So why did she believe she couldn't finish the manuscript. Or was it more she shouldn't? She frowned.

"MJ? I'm sorry if I insulted you or your Gran. I didn't mean..."

MJ shook her head than leaned forward to give Neri a grateful hug. "You are a brilliant, wonderful, insightful friend and I adore you."

Neri preened. "I am, aren't I? But why?"

A sudden brisk breeze whipped strands of MJ's hair into her face and she looked up. Dark clouds were gathering and she hadn't noticed. It was going to rain any moment. She rose and tugged at her friend's arm. "We better get back, because the heavens are going to open up any moment and being on the beach in the rain is...well, better to be inside. Race you back!" She grabbed her sandals and sprinted away.

"Wait for me," Neri yelled, "No fair getting a head start."

Soon, Neri ran in step with her as they raced up the beach, their feet pounding on the damp sand until they reached the cottage and ran up the steps to stand panting and laughing. The wind was blowing steadily and rain drops blew into her face. MJ threw open the French doors and they hurried inside, dropping their sandals on the throw rug by the door.

Neri, dark curls wet around her face, said, "Well, that was invigorating."

"Yes. I'm ready for a cup of tea. You?" When Neri nodded, MJ listed off the choices. Neri chose Earl Grey, and MJ set out a mug, a tea ball for the loose leaf, the only kind to use according to Gran, and the tin of tea. She moved aside tins until she found the one that brought back other rainy afternoons spent with Gran at her other house. She opened the lid and breathed in the aroma of chocolate. When they had tea parties, Gran brewed this tea then poured in a dollop of half and half. Delicious. She didn't need the cream or sugar now but she put them out for Neri, and found another tea ball and filled it with the aromatic leaves of her choice. When the water came almost to a boil, MJ poured and the scent of chocolate floated through the kitchen. She put some shortbread cookies on a plate and said, "Let's go sit in the living area."

They carried their mugs into the other room, taking opposite ends of the sofa. MJ put the cookies on the coffee table in front of them, curled her hands around the mug and took a sip. So satisfying. And nice to share the moment with her friend. No pressure to do something, be someone. She turned to Neri who raised an eyebrow at her. "What?"

"Ever since I arrived, you've avoided talking about Nik. Yeah, see, right there. Your body language is all avoidance. Time to spill it. Something is going on. Time to spill the tea." She giggled and took a sip of her own.

Outside the rain spattered windows, the wind whipped the waves into a froth. MJ straightened her shoulders. "I'm afraid to tell you. Afraid you'll think I'm going crazy, or that my imagination has run away with me, just as Mother warns me about."

Neri snorted. "You are as sane and unlikely to let your imagination run away with you as anyone I know. Besides, remember what Einstein said?"

Now it was her turn to raise a brow. Neri smirked. "'Imagination is more important than knowledge. For knowledge is limited, whereas imagination embraces the world.'"

Imagination embraces the world... MJ took a deep breath. Wasn't that part of the reason she loved those fairy tales of Gran's? The game of What If? That in the stories and the possibilities, the world was a bigger place she was free to explore and discover. While the university world of her mother was so...so linear and insular, above it all, for all its research and big ideas. Constraining. MJ took another sip from her mug.

But if that was true, where did she fit in?

Chapter 22

S hould he head back to the cottage or what? Nik knew what he wanted to do. His body and heart pulled him in the direction of the cottage, the place that felt like home. He wanted to find MJ, run his fingers through her curls, kiss her until they both lost their breaths. But then what? If that bonded them more to each other? Or made them crave each other more? Did he care if it did?

Skata! Right there was the problem. He wasn't sure he cared about the consequences. If Alek knew of his quandary, he'd laugh himself breathless and tell Nik to go find a willing acolyte of Aphrodite. Or spend an evening with his comrades, drinking mead and throwing dice. Sex wasn't what he needed, though. Well, not exactly. What he needed was sex with MJ. He dropped his head. He was an immortal, and this is what he was thinking? Yeah, Alek would laugh. He pushed his fingers into his hair and tugged. He had his duty as a Voice which meant he needed to check in on MJ. But he didn't need to do it in person, or, rather, he didn't need to do it the mortal way.

Which was why he now stood in front of the door to Morpheus' cave. Again. This time, at least, he had a bag of poppy seeds courtesy of the island co-op. Would Morpheus be irritated with him for showing up again so soon? He didn't have a choice. He needed to check up on MJ without being physically present, without taking their attraction (which was all it was, certainly) farther.

"Are you going in or not?" The guard standing next to the cave entrance frowned.

"What?"

"You've been standing there staring at the door for many breaths. The moon will set and rise again at this rate."

Nik shook his head. Time to get back in the game. "My apologies. May I enter?"

"I thought you'd never ask," the guard grumbled, raised the bar, and shoved the massive door open. "Wait here for a runner. Shouldn't be long."

In the darkness, a pale light moved side to side, growing larger until a runner stood before him. Though not the same one as the last time, this one was dressed in the same fluttering garment lit with stardust, brightening the tunnel as Nik followed him back. As they stepped from the tunnel into the cavern, he braced himself for the chaos that reigned here last time. Instead, movement back and forth to the podium was more harmonic, a little slower and easier to follow, even a little quieter.

The runner cleared his throat. "Something amiss?"

"No, I'm surprised by the lack of, well, noise. And chaos."

"Oh. Yes, well, we're generally only that way at the full and new moon. Activity slows down between them. Come. I have other things to do."

He followed the runner until he stood again in the middle of the huge cavern, below Morpheus' black podium. The god stood reading something on a clipboard, so he cleared his throat. Morpheus turned his head slightly and side-eyed him.

"Back so soon?" He set the clipboard down and turned to give Nik his full attention. As he gazed at Nik, the god's dark eyes swirled as if they held a star-spangled night sky. It was dizzying and though Nik wanted to look away, he dared not. He was a Voice after all.

The god leaned forward a little more from his elevated podium. "Did you deliver my message to your esteemed, enticing mother?"

He suddenly sympathized with Eros. To have to constantly be running love messages and arrows between immortals, when mortals were bad enough. He cleared his throat, remembering the title and phrase from a mortal rock song, "*The Things We Do for Love.*" Gods, yes, but in this case for his mother.

"Yes, lord. She said if I saw you again to tell you she'd be happy to meet with you again in the same place." He refused to use the term his mother had used, Dream Man. It was too cliched and sappy. Nevertheless, was color rising in the god's face? Had he read Nik's mind? Better make his request now while Morpheus was distracted by thoughts of his mother.

"Lord, I am here to ask permission to walk in the mortal's dreams again—"

"With the grandmother?" He picked up the clipboard and resumed scanning it.

"No, lord. Just myself."

The clipboard dropped to the podium and the god leaned over him. Damn! Once again, he had to meet the infinite gaze.

"Like that, is it?"

Blast! Why was everyone so perceptive all of a sudden? Most of the time the Voices were practically invisible, ignored. "Like what, Lord?"

"Don't play stupid with me. You do remember what happens in dream reality still affects waking reality in the mortal realm," he paused and leaned further over Nik, "and the immortal one, too? Don't be stupid."

Nik swallowed, unsure how to respond. What was Morpheus saying, exactly?

"I'm saying, son of Erato, be careful." He reached back beneath the podium then held out his hand. When he held his out palm up, the god opened his and dropped a token in it. "You still have the oil?" At his nod, the god continued talking while taking a slip of paper from a runner, stamping it, and handing it back, "Your delicious mother would not be happy with me if something dire befell you while in my realm, understand?"

No, he didn't. Why would something dire happen? And what would that be? Morpheus wiped his hand across his mouth and scanned the cave. "I will say no more. You have your token and your warning. Now go."

He didn't like this. Why did he feel others knew things he didn't. He shouldn't have left the library in such a rush. But obviously, he wasn't going to get any more info from this god, so he put his fist to his chest and bowed. When he straightened, Morpheus's back was turned to him, and he was talking with a runner. He knew a dismissal when he saw one, so he retraced his steps through the dark back to the door of the cave. MJ would soon be asleep.

Eagerly, he left the cave and headed toward a portal.

Rain continued to fall as darkness descended on the evening. MJ shivered. The ocean was not a friendly place.

"Are you sure you weren't hearing bells and seeing stars, too?"

She shook her head and turned back to her friend. "Not funny, Neri. I was scared. I thought all my mother's predictions about my imagination running away with my sanity had finally come true. I saw a temple...at least for a moment." She paused, biting her lip. "But how could I? We were out there." She pointed out the window. "On the beach. Not in Greece. There's no temple out there. You walked the beach with me. Did you see anything?"

"No, but I was more focused on the sand and water then inland. Did you have too much to drink? Eat any funny mushrooms?" She straightened in her place on the sofa. "Who gets your money if something happens to you or you don't accept the terms of the legacy."

MJ swiped her hand through the air. "Now who's letting their imagination run away with them? Certain charities get the money. Not Nik. He has plenty of his own, is my impression. After all, he's the one who helped Gran make hers." She paused, remembering the picture upstairs. "I also think he loved her as a grandson."

Jealousy still zipped through her at the thought, but it was silly. He wasn't to blame. Gran was lovable. Her faded relationship with her grandmother was her own fault. At least in the last few years. She shoved away the guilt and resumed her seat on the other end of the sofa, curling her legs beneath her, and pulling a knitted throw from the back onto her lap.

Neri took a sip of her tea and leaned toward her. "I know what you should do. You should kiss him again, several times—"

MJ shook her head but Neri ignored her, her gaze off to the side as if watching a scene. "Even better, you should seduce him. Have sex. After all, if you are going to lose your sanity, you might as well enjoy the process."

MJ groaned and dropped her face into her hands.

"Seriously, when was the last time you had sex? Or made out with a guy? All you ever do is study and teach and grade papers. I don't remember the last time you dated."

She threw off the throw and jumped up to return to stand gazing out the window.

"It's been a long time, hasn't it?" Neri persisted.

Her shoulders sagged and she leaned her forehead against the glass. Between her busy schedule, her concerns about being distracted from her work, and her mother's intense cross examination of every male she showed an interest in, she wasn't eager for lust—or love. The last male she dated, a professor hoping for a full professorship, was interested in her, it turned out, only because she was a way to get close to her mother, gain points and the position. Thankfully, they'd never made it to the bedroom because she'd felt no chemistry. Plus, he'd pushed too hard on spending time with her mother instead of her.

Neri said nothing behind her.

MJ stared at the roiling ocean. Nik had saved her from sure drowning only nights ago. Where was he now? Out wining and dining some other female client? Why had she let her fear push him away? He'd done nothing but help and support her with Gran's legacy. How long before he returned.?

"MJ? MJ?"

She turned from the window.

"Are you okay? I'll drop the sex talk if it makes you unhappy. And I apologize if I hit a sore spot."

She shook her head. "It's not you. It's me." She rubbed two fingers between her brows. "Gran died and everything changed somehow. Too much too fast."

Neri nodded. "Okay. How about a change of topic—sort of?"

MJ smiled at the friend who was willing to come support her when she asked. "What topic did you have in mind?"

"Are any of your grandmother's books here? I'd love to read one. With the rain outside, it's a good evening for it."

"Oh, yes. I have lots. Let me get one for you." She raced up the stairs to her bedroom and randomly grabbed a book from the pile on the nightstand. She paused, tempted to grab the one she'd started as well. But, no, she had a dissertation to write and while Neri read, she could work on it and not feel guilty.

"Thanks," Neri said, taking the book MJ handed her, and settling back into the sofa, pillows stuffed behind her back, feet up, knees bent.

"Want a fresh cup of tea?"

"Oh, that would be great. And grab the box of truffles I left sitting on the counter. A little chocolate with tea and a good book can never go amiss."

MJ smiled. Amiss. Sounded like Gran talking. After fixing the two fresh cups of tea and handing Neri her mug and the box of truffles, she sat down at the dining table, opened her laptop, and booted it up. Seeing the stack of index cards and the legal pad of notes for her dissertation, she sighed. Gran's unfinished manuscript peeked from behind the laptop. Another temptation, like Gran's books. She straightened her shoulders and put her fingers to the keyboard. She was strong. She could resist temptation.

Where was Nik?

Where would he find MJ when he entered her dream this time? Dining with some unkempt poetry professor (sorry, Mitera)? With her parents, apologizing for wanting something other in her life than her mother's career path?

As long as she wasn't dreaming of making love with him—or kissing him—he'd deal. Otherwise, he'd walk right back out of her dream. There was only so much temptation a guy could be expected to resist, even an immortal. Especially an immortal. Braced for anything, he stepped across the threshold, surprised but grateful to be on the beach outside the cottage. Looking toward the cottage, he saw MJ standing on the deck and staring out to sea as the waves churned only yards away from her. Given her previous experience with the white horses why did her dreams occur here?

Her face lifted into the wind off the ocean. She wore a knee-length dress he hadn't seen her in nor expected she would ever wear in waking life, since the fabric was light and flowing, billowing about her in the wind, and pressing against her and highlighting every curve. Her hair, cut short and unrestrained, ruffled around her face in a soft nimbus.

His heart pounded and yearned. Hades! Every part of him yearned for her, to hold her, drop her to the sand, carefully reveal the beauty beneath her dress, and finally make her his. *Whoa, whoa, whoa!* He ground his teeth together, tightening and releasing his fists. He couldn't go there. Even in the dream. *"...son of Erato, be careful!"* Was this what Morpheus warned him about?

She turned in his direction, discovering him, and probably because she was dreaming, she ran down the steps of the deck, across the sand, and flung herself into him, hands caressing his face, her fingers running through his hair.

"Nik, where have you been. I've missed you."

He circled her with his arms, holding her tightly to him, her body touching his in all the right—wrong, wrong places, from her cheek against his chest down to her feet wedged between his, her softness making a welcome nest for his hardness. Morpheus' warnings weren't enough. He couldn't fight his feelings for her, so he held her, absorbing the blissful, dreamy moment, a moment where he was content and happy and home. Gloom quickly replaced the light. He was not here for this. Slowly, he dropped his arms and stepped back. She gazed up at him, first into his eyes then at his mouth, her lips parting.

Unh-unh. Don't touch. No, don't get anywhere close. Not a good idea. He had a job to do. "Nik, I missed you. Why don't you say something? Better yet," she licked her lips, "why don't you kiss me?"

He groaned. Screw the job. And the warning. He swept her back into his arms, lowered his head and kissed her as if they were stranded on his mother's island and were never going to be rescued. Her kiss was like a spring of healing water, after the parching saltiness of the ocean. As he explored her mouth, and she his, he heard the tolling of a bell, like the sound of a buoy out in a channel. He pulled from the kiss, his thirst for her barely quenched, and they blinked at each other. She turned her head from side to side.

"Not again! No, no, no!"

He gathered her to him. "All is well, MJ. All is well. It's only a dream, *glikia mu*."

She shuddered, her forehead resting on his chest, her eyes tightly closed. "Are you sure?"

"Yes. Look, to prove it, I'll transport us back to the beach." He snapped his fingers. This better work. He snapped three times, waiting for the effect of the kiss to wear off.

"Are we there yet?"

He smiled. At least she still had a sense of humor. "Not quite. I think I need to snap a few more times."

"I can click my heels if you think that would help and repeat, 'There's no place like the cottage.'"

Praying to his mother, Apollo, and Morpheus that the effect would disappear sooner rather than later, he snapped a few more times and finally, they were surrounded again by sea and sand.

"We are back. You can look now."

"This is a just a dream, right? It didn't really happen."

"Just a dream, MJ" he said, though it had happened. Perhaps walking in her dream wasn't such a good idea after all, "and in dreams, magic can happen, right?"

She looked around and nodded. "You mean like talking with Gran and being here with you?"

"And like believing, knowing you can write the rest of your Gran's story—if you want to. Do you?"

She glanced out to sea, stepping out of his arms, leaving them empty. "Until Gran died, I thought I wanted to be a professor."

"Was what your dream? Or your mother's?"

He braced for her irritation but she frowned. "I thought it was mine. I like reading and research. I like teaching. Sort of."

"Sort of?"

She walked a few steps toward the water. Why was she drawn to it? He shadowed her. Dream or not, he wasn't risking her safety again.

"The teaching and everything that goes with it, like prepping for class, grading papers, and my own research, means I never have time for anything I might want to do."

"Like writing?" *Subtle, Nik, real subtle.*

She spun towards him, hands on her hips. "Maybe. Maybe. Why do you keep pushing that?" She spun back to face the water. "I've always wanted to write but..." She sighed. "I don't want to write literary stuff like everyone in the department is so enamored of. I don't want to. I won't write unhappy endings." She laughed, wrapping her arms around herself. "Mother would say Gran ruined me for the real world, for serious subjects, but love and loss, happiness, happily ever afters are serious subjects. They are."

Nik swallowed and resisted drawing her to him. "That's why I loved your grandmother's stories. They honored love, love that was courageous and endured." Something his mother and her mortals exalted in their poetry and literature but he saw too little of both in the mortal, and immortal, realm. "I—it's why I think she wanted you to finish her manuscript, to remind you of the importance of love. It's her legacy to you in more ways than one."

Beyond MJ, the sky darkened over the ocean and the wind blew stronger. The waves rolled in higher, almost at MJ's feet.

"You *can* finish her manuscript," he shouted into the wind. "You can."

Instinct made him glance at the water. A wave rolled toward them, high and wide. Hades! Where had it come from?

"Wake up, MJ." Nik shouted urgently at her. "Wake up. Now!"

Chapter 23

MJ shot up in bed, gasping, her heart in her throat. Dark. She was in her bed in her room at the cottage and it was dark. No wave, no wind. No Nik.

Wake up now! She still heard his shout, the urgency in the command, and she also heard the waves. She hugged her knees to her. What a crazy dream. She missed him, yes, but the temple after the kiss, and the big wave? She bowed her head to her knees. If she was going to dream about him, why couldn't it have been as sexy and wonderful as it was at first, without the temple, or the threatening wave, or his urging to finish Gran's manuscript.

Why not more wonderful, sexy kisses leading to more sexy doings on the beach? Maybe even a few orgasms? She recalled Neri's words, "You should seduce him. Have sex. After all, if you are going to lose your sanity, you might as well enjoy the process." Why not that in the dream, instead of temples and big waves? Frustrated, she rose from the bed and walked over to the window. The waves continued to hiss at her. What was her subconscious trying to tell her? Why did a temple appear the two times she kissed Nik? Okay, once was in a dream where what happened didn't have to make sense, but still. Nik's reaction was strange. If he didn't see what she saw, why didn't he tell her she was imagining things? It's what her mother would do, only she would follow it with a shake of her head and a tightening of her lips.

MJ wrapped her arms around herself. She could accept Nik's response in the dream. Anything was possible in a dream, even moving between locations with a vehicle or objects appearing and disappearing. But that first kiss? She touched her fingers to her lips. When she opened her eyes and thought she saw a temple, he cursed, then kissed her again. *Had he seen it, too?*

But why a temple? It looked like a Greek temple, all Doric columns and shining marble. She rubbed her forehead. She was going to make herself crazy if she didn't let this go. She had no answers, maybe Nik did. Until he returned though, she needed to put all this out of her mind and sleep. Wishing for the comforting arms of her grandmother, she pulled open dresser drawers, one after the other until she found what she was looking for, one of Gran's nighties, silky, blue, and smelling of the lavender scent she'd loved. She curled up in bed, tucking the nightgown beneath her chin so the scent drifted to her as she breathed. Closing her eyes, she imagined Gran singing to her as she'd done when she stayed with her as a child. She sighed, relaxing into the bed her grandmother slept in. Gran, close to her now.

"Gran, what should I do?" she whispered into the darkness.

The sound of the waves beyond the windows were the only answer.

Nik patrolled the other side of the dream portal, his muscles tense with desire to rush back in and make sure MJ was safe.

Was he on this side of the dream because she'd wakened when he ordered her to?

What the hell happened? One minute, they were kissing, the next he was trying to convince her she could write the book, and suddenly a wave loomed over them. Sure, dreams were unpredictable, but they also carried messages from the gods, the Muses, or other spiritual entities, usually using the dreamer's own symbols and lexicon. So, what was going on in MJ's mind? And why did the wave threaten her? Was it her mother? Her dissertation? Juliette's manuscript? Surely, it wasn't him. He wasn't frightening or overwhelming her, was he?

Was it a threat, more of what almost drowned her in waking reality, or gotten her lost in her car? Both Hermes and Morpheus warned him, but of what? Something more was going on than the kiss and the threat of him breaking one of the rules of the Voices. He had suspicions he should probably share with Hermes and Apollo, but not now. Now, he wanted to sweep MJ away to his mother's special island where he could keep her safe, except then she would definitely believe she'd lost her mind. And he'd break all the rules. Had he ever had so little success with a client? This one fought him every step of the way.

He forced himself to walk away from the portal. Why did she fight him? Other clients were delighted to receive his help and guidance—and lovemaking. Most appreciated it when he was more directive and guiding, though he tried not to do it often. He didn't want them becoming dependent on him. Not a good thing for either mortal or Voice. Why, then, didn't beautiful, sexy, smart MJ want nothing to do with his suggestions or support?

Maybe he should admit defeat and tell Apollo she was a lost cause. He rubbed his chest. What then? He'd be reassigned and never see her again. He stopped walking. He looked around at the dark shapes of the olive trees. He could smell the scent of the fruit warmed by the day's sun. Who was he kidding? He loved it here on Mount Helicon, but he didn't want to leave MJ, he wanted to keep working with her. He'd promised Juliette and he was determined to honor it. How to free her from her mother's expectations? He took a deep breath. He wanted more time with her, a long time. If he never worked with another mortal but her, he'd be happy.

Happy? Huh, the emotion had never been a measure for what he should or shouldn't do. Apollo would—how did mortals put it? Apollo would freak if he found out what Nik was thinking. He walked slowly through the trees. Although one was never sure if the answers Hermes gave to questions were to be trusted or not, he was the only person Nik could think of to talk to right now. He hoped the god would take pity on him. He needed answers for MJ's sake.

And his.

When MJ finally dragged herself out of bed, and stumbled downstairs to make her first cup of coffee, she happily discovered a pot already made and still hot with an empty mug sitting next to it. Friends who knew your habits were wonderful.

Pouring a full cup, she picked it up and took a first sip, closing her eyes to savor the warmth as she swallowed. Ahhh, everything was right in her world, almost. Opening her eyes to the view through the windows, her gaze fell on Neri, sitting at the table on the deck, feet tucked up on the chair, knees bent and a paperback propped up on them. A steaming mug sat on the table next to her. Smiling, MJ pulled one of her grandmother's hand-painted trays from a low cupboard, and stacked small plates on it with a couple of jars of jam, butter, and a few knives.

She opened the bread box and pulled out the bag of scones Neri brought with her. Such a good friend. Putting her mug on the tray, she carried it out to the deck and set it down on the table.

"Good morning, early bird, did you sleep okay?" She sat down across from Neri and looked out to sea, squinting at the bright sunlight that bounced and sparked on the water. Her friend snapped the paperback shut, marking her place with a finger, and lowered her feet to the deck. She held the book, cover out to MJ. "I almost didn't. I read and read, thinking I'd read only one more chapter until I finally fell asleep over the book. Your grandmother sure knew how to write a page-turner, and it's not even a suspense novel."

Neri took one of the scones on the plate MJ held out to her, and the jar of strawberry-rhubarb jam from the tray. Not ready to eat yet, MJ set down the plate without taking a scone.

"Which is why I worry about trying to finish her latest manuscript."

Neri nodded. "Didn't you tell me you've already written several scenes? How did it go?"

MJ sipped her coffee, remembering the excitement of working on it the other day. The luscious feeling of slipping into another world, one of her grandmother's creation. She'd been deep in it until that phone call from her advisor. She set the mug down. "Honestly, it was... magical. I was totally immersed in the story. Then my advisor called and brought me crashing back to the reality of my dissertation deadline." She rubbed at her eyes. "Writing takes time, whether it's a novel or a dissertation. I'm not sure I have enough time to do both, or, at least, to do both well."

"Which do you want to write?"

"What kind of question is that? What does it matter which one I want to write? I need to get my dissertation done."

"What do you want to write?"

"The manuscript, but—" She stopped talking, surprised.

Neri smiled and pointed a finger at her. "Just as I thought."

MJ sat back. "Remind me why I invited you here, Miss Smarty Pants."

"Because I'm your very good friend and I care about you. Because I won't let you lie to yourself. Can't you get an extension on the deadline so you can finish the manuscript first?"

"I've asked about an extension because of Gran's death and having to settle the estate, but my advisor didn't sound enthusiastic about the idea. Besides, my mother's already campaigning with the department head for a teaching position for me. She'd have a kitten if I put off the dissertation any longer."

"Do you hear yourself? How old are you anyway?"

MJ shook her head. "I sometimes wonder that myself." Her stomach growled so she gave in and helped herself to a scone, split it and spread butter and some of the lemon curd on it, then picked up a half and took a large bite. The tang of the lemon blended with the saltiness of the butter and the slight sweetness of the scone.

"Mmm," she murmured, eyes closed as she savored the flavor, and opened them to see Neri watching her. "What?"

She shook her head, took a bite of her scone, and looked out at the water. Dabbing at her mouth. "I know you need to work—on one project or the other," she smirked at MJ, "and I'm happy to put my feet up and spend the day enjoying the sunshine while reading all these marvelous books, but how about another quick walk after we eat, to clear the nighttime cobwebs?"

MJ took another big bite of her scone, giving herself a moment to think about her answer. She looked at the water. All small waves and swells today, so no big waves to worry about. She should get straight to work, except Neri was here and a little exercise would be good for them both.

As long as they didn't get too close to the water.

Thalassa peered at Nik's mortal and the other woman from the surface of the water. The two of them sat there laughing and eating.

What would it be like to sit and laugh with a friend?

What did she care? She was an immortal. They were pitiful mortals doomed to die in a few decades. Or sooner.

As long as Nik didn't return to the cottage. If he stayed away, the mortal could live her pitiful life for however many years it lasted.

As long as Nik didn't return.

Chapter 24

Tap tap. Ratta-tat-tat.

Nik froze, pen in hand, for the third time in as many minutes. Minutes should mean nothing to him, an immortal. A minute ought to be the blink of his eye. Instead, each was heavy with impatience and indecision. But tapping his pen on his desk wasn't alleviating them. Immortals did things to change the world. They did not drum pens on desks out of frustration or ...

Hades. Out of frustration and anger. Anger at the situation he was in. Frustration because Hermes had been ducking him just when he needed answers, and because he wanted to be with MJ and—face it—in her. He threw the pen at the wall. Fortunately, he wasn't aiming or it might have become a missile with the energy he put into it. Kissing her should be no big deal. He'd kissed plenty of women in the past centuries. Too many to remember. So why this woman? He'd kissed her, felt the soft curves of her body yielding to the hard planes of his, sensed the desire in her kiss. Had delighted to find she was fully as sexy as she was smart and imaginative and responsible. She had moaned when he pressed her more firmly to his chest, her breasts molded against him.

Nik scrubbed his hand over his face, time to stop torturing himself. His eyes scanned the desktop. There must be calls to other clients he needed to make, or contracts to sign—or something, before he went crazy trying not to think about how much he wanted to return to the cottage and the danger waiting there. He picked up one of the messages his part-time secretary had stacked under the handcrafted glass paperweight a client gave him decades ago.

The message said his client, Giles, a musician, and composer who wrote popular ballads, had signed the new contract and should he mail it to the office or would Nik like to join him and his wife for dinner that evening and get it then. He'd been assigned to this musician at the request of Erato because of the romantic nature of his music, and with Nik's help and guidance, Giles career, and income writing and leasing his music for television and film had boomed. Now, Nik acted as any other agent, advising on contracts, and insuring royalties arrived on time.

Thank the gods, a distraction. Quickly, he texted his acceptance of the invitation, then grabbing his suit jacket from the back of his chair, left the silent office. Thirty minutes later, he stood, wine bottle in hand, waiting for someone to answer the doorbell. High-pitched voices yelled and shouted beyond the door. Should he ring again? As he reached for the bell, the door flew open and Sarra, Giles' wife, stood smiling at him, a toddler on her hip. What MJ would look like with a toddler on her hip? Of course, for her a child meant a husband. His gut knotted and he blinked. Sarra was still smiling at him.

"Are you coming in or do the little ones frighten you?" she asked winking.

Nik laughed and stepped across the threshold into a small entryway that opened into a living area chaotic with those plastic building blocks that had helped spark more than one creative, a few stuffed animals, and a blue bear beneath an upturned laundry basket. A little boy rushed into the room.

"Mommy, Mommy. I have to rescue Fweddy. Where is my sord?"

Fweddy? Sord?

"You left the sword on the deck when you were out there with your dad. And I bet Mister Nik can help you rescue Freddy without the sword. Can't you Mister Nik?"

He looked from the little boy to the bear to Sarra. "Uh…" He lifted the bottle of wine.

"Oh, right. Well, here take Meli while I put this in the kitchen. I'm sure you can hold her and free Freddy at the same time. We know you're a guy who works magic." What? He threw her a look, but she was already striding off, many pounds lighter, bottle in hand.

"Dawlly." A six-inch bundle of rags with a stitched face was thrust in front of him and waggled.

"Help, Mister Nik, help," the little boy said, jumping up and down. "Fweddy is scared and wants to be fwee."

"I know how he feels," Nik muttered, wondering how an immortal managed to find himself in these situations. A little hand patted his face. "Hep," the little girl said.

He cleared his throat. "Here's what we're going to do," he said, moving closer to the basket and slipping the toe of his shoe under the curved handle. "You—what's your name?"

"Luke."

"Okay, Luke. I'm going to say the magic word and you are going to point at the basket, er, prison, and together we'll free Fwed—Freddy. Right?" The little boy, eyes round, nodded.

"So, point your finger." He pointed with both hands. Nik bit back a smile. "Ready? On the count of three. One." Luke stood taller, arms straight out. "Two. Three!"

He waved and pointed frantically and Nik shouted, "Shazam!" and gave a quick jerk to his foot and the basket flipped over.

"Yay! Fweddy is fwee," Luke yelled happily. Grabbing up Freddy, he turned and hugged Nik's leg with his other arm. "Thank you, Mister Nik."

He reached down and ruffled the kid's curls. "You're welcome, Luke."

One little hand patted his face, then a wet kiss was planted on his cheek. "Tank oo."

The boy dashed off toward what Nik assumed was the kitchen. "Mommy, Mommy, Mister Nik and me fweed Fweddy!" He followed, hoping her mommy was ready to take little Meli from him now. Sarra stood at the sink washing her hands. She turned as Luke pulled on her arm. "Look, Mommy."

She smiled down at her son, her face beaming with love and delight. "Wonderful. Did you thank Mister Nik?"

As he nodded, Nik said, "He did indeed. And so did Meli."

Sarra dried her hands, threw the towel on the counter, and held out her arms. "Here, let me take her. She probably needs a diaper change before we sit down to dinner. Thank you for holding her. Go on out to the deck. Giles is out there grilling steaks and burgers and veggies." Meli waved at him over her mother's shoulder as they headed down the hall and he grinned at her and waved back.

"C'mon, Mister Nik, I'll take you to Daddy." Luke reached up to grab his hand and pulled him through the kitchen to a screen door leading onto the deck. Nik opened the door and Luke dropped his hand to rush onto the deck. "Daddy, look. Mister Nik is here."

Giles, with tongs in hand and dressed in an apron, stood next to an open grill. He turned at Luke's announcement. "Nik." He smiled and reached out for a handshake, "About time you came and met the family."

He lifted his nose to the scent of grilled beef, and heard the sizzle and pop of the fat hitting the flames. "Those smell great." He gestured to the printing on the apron front reading, "Musicians know how to heat things up."

"The grill or something else?"

"My wife gave it to me so what do you think?" Giles winked and turned back, saying over his shoulder, "Grab a soda from the cooler and have a seat."

Nik spied the cooler on the other side of Giles at the edge of the deck. Before he could raise the lid, Luke lifted and waved his hand over the cans nestled in ice. "Do you want cola, or woot beer, or this other? I like woot beer."

"Well, I'll have a root beer, too." The boy grabbed a can and held it up to him. "Here you go."

"Thanks." Taking the soda, he headed to a glass and metal table shaded by a brightly striped umbrella, surrounded by metal chairs with plump, matching seat cushions. Sitting, he watched the boy head down the steps into the fenced yard where he kicked around a soccer-sized ball. Minutes later, Sarra emerged from the house carrying Meli, whom she settled into a high chair, strapping her in. While Giles moved the steaks, burgers, and vegetables onto platters, she carried out a tray with small cups obviously meant for the kids, a basket of bread, a small plate of butter, and a dish of baby carrots.

Nik watched the meal unfold in a kind of chaotic harmony. Giles broke a burger into bits and piled them on Meli's tray while Sarra helped Luke squeeze ketchup on his burger without a bun. She cut it up and Luke stabbed a chunk with his fork and stuffed it in his mouth. When he caught Nik watching him, he smiled, and Nik got a view of ketchup-coated teeth. He turned to say something to Giles and caught him looking at his wife. Nik tightened the grip on his fork and knife and dropped his eyes to his plate. Love, adoration, and a touch of humor filled the look.

Immortals usually didn't envy mortals. More often they pitied the short-lived beings. But now? In this moment, he was jealous. Of the obvious love between parents and children. Of the laughter and humor and play. Of the enjoyment of simple pleasures like ketchupy bites of burger. He looked around at the house and yard and back at the family. Was it weird for him to want what Giles had? He dabbed a spot of ketchup from Luke's chin and smiled at Nik. "Ah, the joys of fatherhood. Nothing like it."

Sarra smiled at her husband. "Of parenthood. Nothing like it." He nodded in agreement. "Especially when you have a terrific partner to parent with," Giles said, taking her hand and squeezing it. Their son rolled his eyes and stuffed another chunk of beef into his mouth.

Nik blinked. On such small gestures, worlds changed and shifted.

"The End," MJ typed, and leaned back against her chair, stretching her arms over her head.

She'd typed madly since she and Neri had returned from their walk on the beach. A few breaks for iced tea and to use the bathroom, but otherwise, both of them had been deeply engrossed all afternoon and into the early evening. Her bottom was sore, her shoulders ached, and her eyes were tired, but she did it. She did it! Her grandmother's manuscript was finished with only a few changes from her Gran's notes, including more action on the part of the heroine to rescue herself. Also, a few changes in language so it more accurately reflected current use, but other than that, she'd done her best to stay in Gran's voice. She was uncertain about the quality of her work but at least she had fulfilled the request. From Gran, and from Nik. She couldn't believe it.

And that dratted financial advisor wasn't here to congratulate her. She looked over at Neri curled up on the sofa still, book in hand. Had she even moved in the last hour? She looked back at the screen, then at her printer with its stack of paper. Should she? She hit the keys, the portable printer whirred to life, and page after page slid forth.

Smiling as she watched the pages pile up, she remembered to hit "Save". She jumped up from her chair and crossed to fling open the French doors. Stepping out onto the deck, she threw her arms up and yelled, "I did it!"

"What? What did you do?" Neri came up beside her.

MJ hugged her friend. "I finished Gran's manuscript. It's done. Thank you so much for encouraging me."

Neri shrieked, almost as loudly as one of the seagulls circling overhead, and clapped her hands, jumping up and down.

MJ laughed and scurried down the steps to the edge of the water. Splashing into it, she stomped and kicked up water. Her friend was right beside her.

"When can I read it?"

She halted and looked at her friend. Right. A finished manuscript meant eventually someone would read it. Her stomach flipped. Someone like Nik...and Neri. Oh, geez, this wasn't like turning in a thesis or dissertation where any criticisms of the work had more to do with research and thought processes than with creativity. Maybe what she'd written was utter trash and the only good parts were those written by Gran. How had her grandmother done this book after book after book? How had she dealt with the uncertainty and self-doubt as it passed from agent to editor to reader?

"MJ? Are you okay?"

She realized she hadn't moved, hadn't answered Neri's question. She closed her eyes. This was what it meant to be a writer. She was going to have to brave up. And better her first reader was her friend than some stranger, or Nik. Opening her eyes, she smiled at her friend. "Trying to get up my nerve to let you read it."

"MJ." Neri put her hands on her hips and leaned toward her. "I'm sure it will be great. Don't worry." She dropped her hands. "And I can't wait to read it. Let's head back so I can get started. And you don't have to worry until I'm more than halfway through the book anyways since you didn't write that part, right?"

"Right." She hadn't thought of that. She could relax for a couple of hours, until her friend was about three-quarters of the way through the manuscript. "Okay, let's head back and while you start reading, I'll work on my dissertation for a bit and whip up something for dinner."

Back at the table and her computer, she wondered if she was cut out to be a novelist. At least now, she could get back to work on her dissertation without distractions. Except, she discovered, it was hard to concentrate while someone was reading your writing or, at least, waiting for her to get to your writing. Would Neri like it? If she did, then what? She sorted and re-sorted the note cards filled with sources, ideas, and points she needed to include. She looked up at her document open on the screen. She moved the cursor backwards for several lines. Finally, she put her fingers to the keys. She glanced at Neri, who didn't look up, didn't take her eyes from the page.

MJ sighed and typed more lines. The word count so far for this time period was 289. She looked at another index card, tapped her lips with her finger, typed a few more sentences. She heard the rustle of fabric and shot her gaze to where her friend sat on the couch. Still reading. Not looking at MJ. Forget trying to write original ideas and perspectives. That was a lost cause. She saved her work, then got up quietly from her chair and went into the kitchen to search the fridge and cupboards for dinner ideas. It would definitely be easier. And in the kitchen, she couldn't see the couch so she wouldn't be looking up every five minutes.

Hmmm, peering into the fridge, she found bacon, eggs, half and half, a wedge of Parm and baby spinach. She could make a spaghetti carbonara and add the steamed baby spinach in at the last minute. She opened a few cupboard doors before finding the spaghetti. Grabbing a large pot, she filled it with water and put it onto boil, and slipped several slices of bacon into a pan.

Half an hour later, she was ready to plate the meal. She still hadn't heard a word out of Neri. Walking softly out of the kitchen, she discovered her standing in front of the window, hands on hips. Looking over at the coffee table, she saw the manuscript neatly stacked next to her coffee mug. Had she finished reading it?

"Neri?" MJ said softly. Her friend turned to her, tears on her face. Oh no, had it been that bad? Had she ruined Gran's story? Her friend walked over to her and hugged her.

"Stop it. Stop worrying. I'm a little teary-eyed because I am so happy for you. So happy you broke free enough to finish this. It's wonderful!"

She froze, her brain trying to process Neri's words. Wonderful? "You mean the whole book is wonderful or just Gran's part?"

"I don't know where her part ends and yours begins. The whole book is like her other book I read here. And what a treat it is, to sit and read and escape."

Wonderful! She couldn't tell where Gran's writing ended and hers began? She swallowed back the six-year-old scream of delight wanting to escape. "I have to edit and do some revisions, of course..."

"Not much. Your grandmother must have planned the story well or she was revising as she wrote because it is in good shape."

MJ smiled. Actually, her whole body smiled. "I'll do that after you leave tomorrow. For now, let's celebrate. I don't have any champagne but the meal is ready and after dinner we'll see if we can find a good rom-com on television."

"Sounds like a plan." They moved into the kitchen and she dished up the spaghetti carbonara, its enticing aroma of bacon and cheese filling the kitchen. Her friend carried the plates over to the table. MJ found a bottle of chardonnay in the fridge, and pulled out the buttered bread she had warming in the oven, then carried them over to the table. As she opened her napkin and placed it on her lap, she realized she was still grinning broadly.

"MJ?"

She looked up. "What?"

"Promise me as soon as you are done with the few edits or revisions you'll send it to Nik right away."

She blinked at her friend. Right. An editor was waiting for it. She couldn't keep it.

"Don't try to make it perfect."

She laughed. "Neri, you know me too well. Okay, I promise I'll send it out a day or two after you leave. I have to, for Gran's sake."

Her friend frowned. "For your sake too."

Maybe, because sending Nik the manuscript could throw her world into utter chaos.

Nik stood at the rail of the ferry that would take him and his car back to the island. Sky and water met at some unseen horizon, the only break in the late-night darkness were the lights receding from the aft end of the ferry. He looked down into the dark waters and thought about the evening he'd spent with Giles and his family.

He'd lived long enough to know what he experienced in their home was not what happened in the homes of every couple and family. He'd witnessed too many clients beaten physically or emotionally by partners or others who did not appreciate their creativity or work. In fact, it was a primary challenge for a Voice. Parents, partners, children often didn't like it when someone revealed a passion and ability to create something from their imagination, especially if they weren't well-paid for it, as they often weren't. Until he started working with them. It was why many had a hard time believing their stories or poems or song lyrics had any importance, made any contribution. It was difficult to convince them otherwise.

Like MJ. Apparently, though, she'd broken through enough to finish Juliette's manuscript. It arrived in his email box, but at first, he was so excited to see he had a communication from her he didn't notice the attachment. Scanning her email, hoping she was missing him even a little, he was surprised—and disappointed—to read nothing more than a formal, "Please find attached the complete manuscript for *His Captured Treasure* as requested. Best, Marie Juliette Montague." He was shocked and delighted that she'd finished it, and spent the next few hours reading the manuscript.

"I knew it!" he shouted and his part-time secretary came to the office door to see if he called for her. Apologizing for disturbing her, he wrote a quick email to Juliette's editor stating the manuscript was finished, attached the file, and said to let him know if there was anything else he or his client's granddaughter needed to do. Proudly, he hit "Send." Then, he sent MJ a quick response saying congratulations, and once he heard back from the editor, he would be in touch.

He breathed deeply, relieved that she'd pushed past her fears and her mother's demands to do something for herself and her grandmother. If only this breakthrough led to the bigger one, writing her own stories. He gazed toward the island, knowing she was there—somewhere, and wished he could drive straight to the cottage to see her. But he didn't dare, not yet, even though he missed her. For now, he'd admit it to no one but himself.

He missed the way she tilted her head up to the sky, eyes closed, a smile on her face, as if the sky was whispering a secret to her. He missed the sparkle and passion in her eyes whether she was biting into a delicious burger or expressing what she thought of his bossy, interfering ways. He missed those full lips that tasted... Oh, gods. He was doomed. Whatever happened from here on out, the gods had made it impossible for him to have his ambrosia and imbibe it, too.

After he reached the pub, he was going to head straight to Mt. Helicon and have a conversation with his mother. And perhaps Hermes, if he could find him, about what to do. *What do you want, Nik? What would make you happy?*

He heard Juliette's questions in his mind. He knew what would make him happy. But how others would feel? He shook his head and headed back to his car.

The Fates knew.

Chapter 25

After waving goodbye to Neri, MJ closed the door and walked back into the living area.

While her note cards, research papers, books, and laptop were spread out on the dining table, the rest of the cottage was clean, empty of any sign of Neri's visit with two exceptions. The two books by Gran that Neri read were stacked next to the printed manuscript of Gran's last book on the coffee table. The one she, MJ, completed.

She smiled as she picked up the thick stack of pages, added the two paperbacks on top, and carried her armload up the two flights of stairs to the writing aerie. The two paperbacks went back into their places on the shelves of Gran's books, then she ceremoniously placed the manuscript on the center of the small desk. "I did it, Gran. We did it." She patted the manuscript and looked around. Her mother would think she was nuts but she swore she felt her grandmother's presence here. She wished they could have a tea party to celebrate.

She sighed. It wasn't to be, but she touched her fingers to her lips and then to the picture sitting on top of the desk of her with Gran. "Love you."

Back downstairs, she sat down at the table. Time to get back to working on her dissertation, no more dreaming or writing anything other than her paper. She opened the file and got to work. As she typed, she noticed how quiet it was without Neri. Or Nik. The clock ticked in the kitchen, and the keys clicked as she typed. Under it all, was the soft susurrus of the sea, tempting her to close her eyes and sleep, or walk along the beach. Either was hard to resist after an hour at the computer.

She looked up from the screen. The waves were tame today, the sky above almost cloudless. Sea gulls whirled, screaming and circling above the water and beach, ever searching for sustenance worth stealing. If she moved her work out to the table on the deck, would she work? Probably not. The desire to close her laptop and stroll down to the sand—She jerked her gaze back to her computer screen where it belonged. Where was she? Reading back over the last few paragraphs, she recaptured her thoughts and began typing once again.

Writing about 19th century Ellen Price and how she supported her family with her writing after her husband's business failed, MJ thought about how long women writers, either under their own name, or a male pen name, had been doing that. Just like Gran.

She glanced around the living and dining area. How much had Gran paid for this place? She should have asked Nik. Her mother would have asked so she'd know what to ask for the cottage when she put it up for sale. But why sell? She liked seeing the ocean just beyond the windows as she worked. She enjoyed being able to step out the French doors and walk on the beach. She couldn't bring herself to spend much time in Gran's writing aerie yet but she could imagine what it would be like to sit up there and write in bad weather. Or to sit out on the deck with only the waves and the sea gulls to keep her company.

What would it be like to support yourself by writing as Gran and those Victorian writers had? What would it feel like to get up each morning and, instead of dressing to teach at the university, she slipped on yoga pants and a cami, and sat on the deck, drinking tea and writing? To revise and edit her own stories instead of grading too many stories eating up too much of her time?

Do you even need to teach? I mean if your grandmother left you this place and her money...

She closed her eyes. If she didn't teach, though, what would she do?

The second most magic words are "What if?" With those magic words, almost anything is possible...

What if she didn't teach? What if she wrote and published? Could she? There were a lot of wannabe writers out there. Was she one of them? Just because she finished Gran's story didn't mean she could write a novel. If she could write, what would she write? Novels, of course. Novels with happy endings because the world was filled with unhappy endings. She and Gran had believed in the magic of stories that ended happily. They encouraged and inspired and nurtured hope.

So, novels with happy endings. But which genre was right for her? Oh, who was she kidding? She loved Gran's stories. Long ago, before she knew what her grandmother wrote, and before her mother began herding her in the direction she'd taken for her studies, as a teen, she'd secretly read romances borrowed from the library and hidden at home. Inspired by them, she wrote her own happily ever afters. Boy meets girl, rescues her from one bad situation or another, or realizes she is the girl he'd been dreaming of. In spite of the betrayal of friends, or the rules and disapproval of parents, the two would ride off on the horse, or in the sports car, or on the plane, to their happily ever after. Of course, in those stories, because she was a teen, supporting herself and having a career never got in the way of the happy ending. Did her father still have those stories hidden in one of his file cabinets for her?

The idea of riding happily off into the sunset with someone you love and who loved you was still magical, still made her yearn for her own happily ever after. With someone like Nik. She smacked her forehead. *Stop that!* She looked back at her computer screen and typed a few more sentences about Ellen Price. *How did she squeeze writing novels into her life?* MJ lifted her head. What if she wrote a story about a heroine who had to write her stories in secret? What would be the reason for the secrecy? She smirked. A mother who wanted her to be practical? Well, the advice was write what you know.

She pulled a few empty index cards to her and started jotting down story questions. After she filled two with notes, she grabbed more and wrote scene ideas on one after the other. She opened a new file in her word processor and started typing the questions in there. The name for her character popped into her mind. She tapped her chin with her pen. Who would the love interest be? She typed more notes. Added more character ideas. Filled out more scene cards.

Feeling a tightness in her shoulders, she sat back, straightening and rolling her shoulders. She looked at the time on the screen. *Holy heck! She'd been working on the novel for two hours! How had that happened?* Enough. She had serious work to do. She saved the document and closed it. Time to get back to the dissertation.

What would be a good title for the novel? She smiled, re-focused on the screen. Back to Ellen Price and friends.

As Nik drove off the ferry, he struggled to ignore the strong temptation to drive straight to the cottage and MJ. He checked the dash clock. Ten o'clock. She might still be up, working on her dissertation, or she might be snuggled in bed, reading. All soft and warm.

He shifted into fourth gear and pushed the image away. No, he was not going there in any way, shape, or form, not even in her dreams. He'd head to the pub and use the portal to Mt. Helicon. Maybe talk with Alek or Hermes. Or his mother, lame as that sounded, as mortals termed it. But she was the Muse of love songs and erotic poetry and more. Who better to offer advice than her? He sped through the dark, keeping one eye on the speedometer. It wouldn't do to get stopped by a cop.

Pulling into the parking lot of White Horses, he drove to the back and parked in the farthest corner again, away from lights, where no one would notice how long the car was there. He didn't have to worry about anyone trying to break into the car and steal it. Apollo had safeguards and spells around the building, the parking lot, and partway into the trees. Security cameras installed in and around the pub reassured the mortals and provided information to police should any altercations or other problems arise. The immortals knew the cameras were there and were careful to behave when in view of them.

He ran up the steps and pulled open the door, catching the scent of the burgers and onions and beer. A young woman stood behind the bar, shaking a cocktail shaker with all the vigor of a gambler shaking dice. She nodded at him, letting him know she was aware of him, then opened the shaker and poured the pale, frothy cocktail into a waiting martini glass which she placed on a tray. Next to it, she set a bottle of imported beer Nik recognized, and a small dish of mixed nuts. She tapped the call bell, yelling, "Drinks up."

She turned to him to ask what he wanted to drink as Hermes came through the door that led to the kitchen. "I've got this, Jenna, thanks," he said, smiling at her. She nodded, grabbed a towel, and began drying glasses.

Turning to Nik, he said, "I see you are back from your retreat."

He frowned. "What are you talking about? I didn't go on a retreat."

"No, but you did retreat, didn't you."

The trickster god set another imported beer in front of Nik after prying off the cap. This beer, Mythos, was made in Greece and not usually available beyond the country's borders. He took the first swig and swallowed, appreciating the taste of home and ignoring his irritation with Herme's question.

Setting the bottle down, he said, "I made a strategic decision to give her the space and time she needed to decide what she wants to do and do it. My job is not to force anyone into anything. Arguing with her about finishing her grandmother's manuscript was not getting me anywhere."

"So, you retreated."

The god could be so very annoying. Nik stared at him. Hermes shrugged. "I didn't retreat. I left at her request. Honoring her wishes worked. She finished the manuscript, sent it to me, and I read it, and it was good. The entire manuscript. I sent it on to Juliette's editor and I'm waiting to hear back from him. Besides, you weren't exactly available either, were you?"

Hermes tilted his head and stared off over Nik's shoulder. Nik looked over his shoulder but saw nothing unusual. He turned back to see the god grinning at him. What was he up to? "Have you checked your emails recently?"

He squinted at the god. "What do you know?"

Hermes smiled and gestured at the beer bottle. "Have another swallow. And check your email." Then he walked away, back through the door to the kitchen. The god was enough to drive any immortal mad. But he followed instructions, taking another swallow of the delicious beer, then pulled out his phone and opened his email app. Shaking his head when he saw the note from the editor, he tapped the icon to open and read it. Smiling, he raised the bottle and swallowed down the last of the beer. Not a bad way to celebrate. Now to report this to Apollo and his mother.

And still he hadn't questioned Hermes.

MJ lifted her head to stare out the window at the sea. Clouds blocked the morning sun, making the water look cold and unfriendly. She shivered remembering the terror of being dragged beneath the waves, grateful Nik had been there.

Of course, if not for him and his fairy tale—okay, myth—she would never have ventured into the water in the first place. Truly, it appeared the hunky adviser could tempt her into doing many things she wouldn't otherwise. Trying to view the white horses. Gran's manuscript. Writing her own novel. Kissing.

Kissing. Back to that. She shook her head and looked at the notes scattered on the table around her laptop. Better to keep thoughts of kissing to her story. She checked the word count and discovered she'd not only written three chapters but just under eight thousand words. She smiled. She was doing it. Maybe she only had a rough outline of the story but her hero and heroine were fleshed out with their back stories and wounds and such. She knew the conflict between them and the sparks that would ignite the romance.

Sighing, she gazed out the window. She was supposed to be working on her dissertation. She worked on it yesterday after typing up the initial ideas for the novel, and meant to keep working on it but her mind kept straying to the story until finally she'd given up the battle and written those first chapters. Gran was right. MJ needed a break. From school, from her dissertation. From her mother. She needed to give herself the chance to write her own stories. That little bit of praise from Neri gave her the courage to start this new story.

What had Gran said in the dream? *You have stories to tell, my darling. Do it!*

"I am, Gran, I am." She did have stories to tell, like fairy tales, with happy endings and characters and situations you wouldn't find walking the sidewalks of the university. This story would probably be categorized as paranormal or speculative fiction. Whatever it was, it was her story, and she was going to let herself enjoy the magic of writing it from her imagination. Her fingers rested lightly on the keyboard as she read the last few lines on the screen. Ah, yes, the heroine was about to kick the—

Knock, knock, knock!

She jerked in her chair, jarred by the interruption of the cottage's silence. Was Nik back? Silly of him to knock but... Happily, she saved her work, then rushed into the hall. Stopping to check her hair in the mirror, and pull the delighted look from her face, she flung open the door. Her mother stood on the threshold, eyes moving back and forth, up and down the façade of the cottage. Her gaze dropped to MJ. "So, this is the right place. I was sure you'd given me the wrong house number or address."

Her hold on the door tightened. Why was her mother here? She took a breath. "Hello, Mother. This is the place."

Her mother turned in a circle, taking in the neighbors and neighborhood. She looked as though she'd driven there from a faculty meeting, dressed in beige linen slacks, a pale green silk blouse, a blazer that matched the slacks, and the Hermès scarf her father had given her on her fortieth birthday. MJ cleared her throat. "As you can see, it's not exactly a shack on the beach."

Her mother turned back to her and tilted her jaw up. "I can see that, Marie Juliette. Now, are you going to leave me standing here or invite me in?"

She took a quick step backwards into the hall. "Sorry, Mother. Of course, come in."

Her mother walked in, moving past her into the hall, glancing right and left as she moved further in until her gaze fell on the large photo of Gran reading to MJ. Turning her back on the photo, she walked into the living-dining area and stood looking around. Why was she here? Why hadn't she called before coming all this way? MJ repressed a sigh. There went her lovely afternoon, not to mention the next several days her mother was probably planning to stay. Now she was grateful Nik wasn't here. It wasn't difficult to imagine her mother's outrage and words if she discovered Nik comfortably ensconced. Well, nothing to do but deal.

"Would you like a tour, Mother? We can do that and afterwards I'll fetch your luggage."

Her mother walked over to the French doors and waved away MJ's suggestion.

"I'm not staying here," she said, "I'm staying at the Three Dolphins BnB up the road. I didn't think I'd be comfortable here."

Ah yes, this was supposed to be a shack with—insert shudder here—vermin. MJ almost snickered but coughed instead. She hadn't corrected her mother's assumption the few times they'd talked on the phone. She hadn't seen the point. Her mother had ideas about the way things were, and MJ learned early on not to waste energy trying to change them. "Would you like that tour? Then I'll fix some coffee. You must be tired after the trip."

Her mother turned from the doors, nodding. "Yes, let me see what it's like. You should be able to get a lot more for it than I originally thought. How did she pay for this place?"

MJ didn't answer, just led her mother up the stairs to the bedrooms. Bad enough she hadn't kept up with Gran the last few years, but her mother? How long had she and her father been married? Almost thirty years. Yet her mother knew so little about her mother-in-law. Had Gran kept it all secret for her father's sake—and hers? Everyone was entitled to some secrets, weren't they? But secrets also undermined relationships. She looked back at her mother who followed MJ up the stairs. What secrets did her mother have? Truth be told, MJ had a few of her own, and a few of Gran's she was going to keep as well.

She moved to the door of Gran's bedroom, gesturing with her arm into the room. "This was Gran's bedroom. It's mine now. It has a bathroom and walk-in closet." Her mother stuck her head in the door and looked about. MJ crossed her fingers. Don't look in the bathroom. Don't look in the bathroom. She wasn't prepared to listen to a harangue about the "trashy" posters hanging there. She enjoyed them, imagining what it was like to be those swooning heroines in the strong arms of those hunky heroes, dressed and undressed.

Her mother sniffed and turned back into the hallway, noting the windows. "How did she stand it out here alone. It's depressing."

MJ followed her gaze. "It feels that way today because the skies and the sea are grey and overcast. When the sun is out and the water sparkles, it's cheery. Happy."

Her mother shook her head, waving her hand back and forth gesturing to the windows. "There's no privacy with all these windows. Anyone can see in."

MJ bit her tongue. Why couldn't her mother appreciate the beauty of the place? "Let me show you the other two bedrooms." She crossed the hall and opened the door to what she thought of as Nik's bedroom. "Each room has access to a small shared bathroom with shower."

Her mother's examination of that room and the other guest room were perfunctory, and she turned to head back down the stairs but stopped and pointed to the door between the bedroom doors.

"Is that a closet?"

To show her Gran's aerie or not? Part of her wanted her mother to see the full extent of what Gran created with her stories and imagination both in the room and with her books. But the other part of her, the part that hadn't been able to claim the space and write there yet, didn't want to share it with anyone.

"It's the door to the attic. We can go up there if you—"

"No, of course not," her mother predictably replied. "I don't need to get dust and cobwebs all over me."

MJ nodded agreement and followed her mother back down the stairs to the first floor, grateful to keep Gran's aerie a secret. When she was ready to return to the space and claim it, she wanted it to be solely hers and Gran's without any tainted comments her mother might make.

"I'll take that cup of coffee now," her mother said.

"Why don't you sit out on the deck and I'll bring the coffee out there. The skies are clearing and you can enjoy the view." She headed into the kitchen.

"I can enjoy the view from here without getting my hair messed or smelling fish." Her mother sat at the table. "Oh, I see you've been working. Good girl. Tempus fugits, you know."

About to reach for the coffee beans sitting on the shelf in the fridge, MJ froze. Crap! All her notes for her story, scene cards and such, were scattered over the table, on top of her research and notes for her dissertation. Why didn't she think to stack them all and put them away? Because she'd thought it was Nik at the door, damn him. And now...

"Marie Juliette, who are you researching with these quotes? 'Mariel spies the small creature peering at her from beneath the fern fronds.' Well, nice alliteration but how odd. And this one. "Cristos watches her afraid to reveal himself, what he is. Afraid to frighten her.' Really, who wrote about this? It almost sounds like one of those trite fantasy or romance novels."

MJ pulled the beans from the refrigerator and closed the door. To lie or not to lie? She set the beans on the counter, pulled the coffee grinder to her, measured them, and turned it on. Thankfully, the loud clatter of them in the grinder gave her a moment to think. If only she could grind the entire bag. The grinder stopped and silence fell, except for the pounding of her heart loud in her ears. She poured the ground beans into the coffee maker, added water, and pushed the button.

"These can't possibly be notes for your dissertation, can they?" Her mother shoved them away from her, and one slid across the table to the floor. "They read like some of that commercial junk you find on a drugstore rack."

For a moment, MJ wondered how her mother knew what those books on a drugstore rack were like? Had she ever read one or was she judging a book by its cover? "They're mine."

The coffee burbled and dripped into the carafe.

"Well, I know they are yours. Who else would they belong to? But I thought you were researching women authors who—"

"No."

Her mother looked at her, frowning. "No, what?"

MJ took a deep breath and poured the fresh coffee into a proper cup and saucer, then carried it over to set it next to her mother. Quickly, she swept up her note cards and papers, picked up the card on the floor, and placed the materials on the counter behind her.

Clasping her hands together, she said, "No, they aren't quotes from one of the authors I've been researching. They are ideas for..." She swallowed. *Gran give me some of your bravery.* "They are ideas for my book."

"You are already working on a book from your dissertation? Do you have interest already? Who from? That's wonderful! Wait until your committee hears about that. I'm so p—"

MJ held up her hand, even though she wanted to hear, just once, her mother say those words. Her mother paused and MJ said quickly, "They are ideas for a novel I am writing. Not a book related to the dissertation, although I've been working on that, too."

Her mother rose, clutching the back of the chair, her jaw clenched, her brow furrowed. It was the look. The look her mother got on her face when MJ did something to make her mother angry.

"Are you saying you're done with your dissertation? Because, surely, you aren't working on a frivolous novel when you have a dissertation to finish."

"I had some story ideas I needed to—"

"Are you insane?"

Chapter 26

Nik strode through the olive grove. He had worked out at the gymnasium with Alek and a few of the other Voices, lifting weights, wrestling, hitting the bag. He and Alek hiked Mt. Helicon, although Nik had to tell his friend to "shut it" when he kept talking about his "hubba hubba mortal" as he called her. He'd gone to the White Horses and in the employee parking lot, washed and waxed his car like any other car-mad mortal would. He'd sweated and panted and steamed, but not in the way he preferred. MJ was haunting him. Drinking at the bar back on Mt. Helicon with other Voices should have distracted him. It didn't. He couldn't empty his mind of images of her, of the scent of her hair fresh out of the shower, and of the taste of that kiss. Damn!

Restlessness rode him. Insanity wasn't far behind if he didn't soon get back to the cottage. Growling, he flung himself down on the ground beneath an olive tree. It's wide, low canopy shaded him from the sun. He tucked an arm under his head and gazed up through the leaves. After centuries of service to Apollo and the Muses, why was he no longer content to simply do his duty? While he'd lusted after some of his previous mortals, he never risked his job or immortality before. Why now?

Why now, when everyone on Mt. Helicon was aware *meri-ka*, the creative spark all mortals were gifted with at birth, was weakening, thereby endangering the Muses, evidenced by the white streak in his mother's hair along with other signs in his aunts? Doing his job wasn't just about his commitment to the Voices but, more importantly, about the continued strength and vitality of his mother and her sisters. He closed his eyes beneath the canopy of the tree protected and valued by mortals and gods alike. Though the olives were young on the branches, he caught their fruity scent, mixed with the scents of grass, basil, thyme, and other herbs growing amongst the trees.

Long ago in immortal time, a debate raged among the Olympian royals about whether to cut off energies and connections between the mortal and immortal realms, meaning inspiration and creative support from the Muses and the Voices would cease. Zeus roared with anger at the idea because he knew who was behind it, knew it was another attempt to corral his sexual forays with mortal women. After divisive and heated arguments back and forth, Apollo's oracle was consulted. Even she could not foresee what would happen if the realms were set asunder, whether each realm would thrive or one or both would wither and fade away.

Nik knew other pantheons believed that without mortal worship, beliefs and services, the gods, not the mortals, would weaken and die, so none of the immortals were willing to risk it. Of course, if they had been separated, he wouldn't be on the very uncomfortable horns of his dilemma. He still didn't comprehend why, knowing of Hera's long-ago proclamation, someone (Apollo?) had the bright idea to send unsuspecting, uninformed Voices off into the mortal realm with only the vow not to fall in love. As if that was something anyone—even the gods—could control. Was it Hera's idea in order to sabotage the

Voices and thereby eventually eliminate the Muses and destroy any power mortals had because of their creative abilities?

He plucked a blade of the grass and stuck it between his teeth, tasting sunshine and the rich soil of the mountain. Mount Helicon had been his home—at least the barracks had—for most of his immortal life, always here. Unchanging. Like him. He sat up, spitting out the grass and crossing his bent legs. Was he meant to live year after century after eon always the reliable, responsible, loyal Voice? In the past, that satisfied him. The clients changed and sometimes what they needed from him and his mother, the Muse of love and love poetry changed, but his role—and his life—stayed the same. Which was fine. Until...

He shot to his feet and kicked at the ground. And, here he was, restless. Again. He shoved his hands in his pockets and sighed. Only one thing to do.

He stepped out into the sunlight.

"Has the ocean air infected your brain and taken away your common sense? This is why I separated you from your grandmother years ago. To stop these airy-fairy notions of a world where you get to do what you want to do and everything will magically go your way. You have a deadline, Marie Juliette, which you seem determined to ignore. For what?"

Her mother reached over to the notes she had stacked on the counter. With swift movements, she held them sideways between her hands and ripped them in half, then let them fall to the floor.

"For a bunch of nonsensical trash, and imagining you can be a published novelist too just because your grandmother wrote a few trashy books."

MJ stared, shocked, at the pieces of cards scattered at her feet. Maybe it was crazy to think she could write an entire novel. Afterall, finishing Gran's manuscript had been more a matter of following her outline and notes. Not difficult for someone who could string words into a sentence and had been reading the author's novels for years. But why tear up her notes?

What if... What if those characters and those scenes already existed in a story only she could tell, waited for her to tell it? What if writing stories was what she was meant to do all along, listening to her own yearnings and dreams instead of feeling obligated to follow her mother's? What if her mother was wrong about her and her stories just as she was wrong about Gran and her books? What if she finally stood up to her mother at the ripe old age of twenty-four? If only her mother loved her as herself.

What if... Okay, Gran.

She unclasped her hands and stooped to gather the pieces of cards scattered on the floor, blinking away tears. A few pieces had skittered under the table. She'd get those later.

Standing, she opened a book on the stack of papers and placed the bits inside.

"Those books Gran wrote," she said softly, closing the book and looking out at the sea, "made her money. Enough to buy this cottage and maintain it. Enough money, I won't have to work for a long time if I don't want to. Enough money, I could do nothing but write."

She bit her lip. Did she really say that? She looked at her mother, who shook her head, brow furrowed, mouth pursed. "Just what the world needs. More trashy books fit for people with no taste. After all I've done for you, you want to waste your mind and your life writing books like that? So you can live in a fantasy world believing someday your prince will come and you'll live happily ever after? You don't need a prince. They only get in the way."

Was that how she felt about her father?

"If you aren't careful, before you know it, you'll be pregnant and you can forget your career and professional dreams."

Still throwing that in her face? After the papers written, the degrees with honors, about to earn a PhD, her mother still expected her to make up for her own lost dreams? Why couldn't she be a successful novelist? Her mother stepped closer, her breath warm on MJ's face as she hissed, "Is. Your. Dissertation. Done?"

This was the mother who scared her.

After leaving the olive grove, Nik discovered his mother and aunts gathered around the scrying pool. Well, this was going to be problematic. He couldn't ask his mother to look into it for him or try to do it himself, with all the aunts gathered around it. He shouldn't be surprised to find them there, though. They used that pool like mortals used television, only the reality shows from the pool were genuine and unscripted.

His mother looked up, finding him. Her face was troubled and was that a tear on her cheek? Concerned, he hurried to her and she rose from her place to greet him. His aunts appeared captivated by the images in the water, but they slid glances at him as he approached. Whatever was happening must be important, but why his mother's tears? As he walked within viewing range, his mother stepped in front of him.

"Nikos," she said, touching his chest above his heart and pushing at him until he took a step back. He reached up and wiped the tear from her face.

"Mitera, what grieves you?" He glanced at his aunts, seeing traces of tears on one or two other faces. "And my aunts?"

She patted his chest. "We watch one who battles fear and loss for the right to create—and is wounded in the battle." Sighing, she shook her head. "Why do mortals not respect each other's right to create? It is as important as the right to love. Why do they seek entertainment but abdicate the joys of creating? How have we failed to help them nurture their creative sparks?"

Another tear traced its way down her face. He swallowed. His mother was usually so joyful, so ready to see potential and possibility in every moment. Then he remembered the "one" who battled and was wounded. No!

"Mitera," he bent his knees to look into her eyes, "who battles and is wounded?"

She reached up and patted his cheek this time. "Your mortal, Marie Juliette."

He started to push past her but she grabbed his arms. "My son, before you look into the pool, you must vow to observe only and not interfere."

Gently, he took his mother by the arms and moved her aside, hurrying to look into the pool.

"Wait, my son."

Wavering in the pool's surface was MJ's face, chin up, her beautiful eyes welling with tears she blinked back. Her hair as he'd seen it in her dream. To the left of her, her mother's face, taut with anger, brows drawn together, lips tight. He looked back over his shoulder at his mother.

"Why should I wait, Mitera. MJ is hurting. I should—"

"No, Nikos, you should not. She must fight this battle on her own. This has been a long time coming. She must do it now for herself or the victory will not last beyond your time with her."

The words bunched his shoulder muscles. He didn't like the reminder, although he usually stayed with a client until they dismissed him or died, like Juliette. He turned back to the pool but his aunt, Euterpe, Muse of music and lyrical poetry, slowly swirled her hand in the water. The image of MJ was gone.

Frustrated, he turned back to his mother. "Why would I leave?"

His mother patted his chest again and sighed. "Only you know the answer to that question, my son."

She moved past him to kneel by the pool, then waved her hand over it, stilling the waters. Nik curled his fists as she leaned forward with her sisters once again. Suddenly, his mother reached back to him.

"Though you may not interfere," she turned a fierce gaze on him, "I think you should see this so you better understand the battle your mortal has waged for years. If not her entire life."

He took his mother's hand and looked over her shoulder. MJ stood facing her mother who leaned into her, fists curled, jaw clenched. Pride filled him as she stood with shoulders back, chin up even as tears sparkled in her eyes. She was a warrior, one without any weapon but her courage. She would do Athena proud.

Chapter 27

Her mother never encouraged her in anything other than her academic work and even then, stories she'd written in junior high and high school were dismissed as "that's nice but you can do better". If she brought mystery or romance books home from the school library instead of the classics, her mother made her return them the next day, unless she was able to smuggle them in and hide them first.

That inner little girl still trembled before her mother's fury. If the magic wand she'd made with Gran worked, she would have waved it and turned her mother's fury into sympathy and understanding. She'd only ever wanted to crawl into motherly arms that rocked her while whispering, "There, there." But no, her mother expected abject apologies, and, after she deigned to briefly hug her daughter, she would tell Marie Juliette she hoped her daughter had learned a lesson and wouldn't do *that* again.

Staring into her mother's angry eyes, she realized she couldn't give up writing her story just to receive a brief hug that wasn't compassionate or understanding. Besides, how much had she already given up? All her time with Gran. The bits of torn note cards still lying beneath the dining table looked as sad as she felt. Her jaw tightened and she blinked back tears. Not sad tears.

Mad tears. Tears for letting her mother push her away from what she wanted in her life, away from her creative dreams, away from her fairy tales and happily-ever-afters. Away from Gran.

Her mother nodded, answering her own question. "It's not done, is it? Well, it's a good thing I arrived today." She picked up her handbag. "I'm going to check into my room at the inn. While I'm gone, you can get back to work on your dissertation." She headed into the hallway, and MJ followed. "While you do, I'll make some call to realtors and set some appointments to have them come look at this place and give us an idea of the market value."

Had her mother always been like this...this tyrant? And she never noticed because she always went along? Poor Gran. No wonder she hadn't made an issue of MJ spending more time with her. She shook her head as she walked past the picture of her grandmother reading to her. *Sorry, Gran.* "Don't bother, Mother. I'm not selling," she said, the words spilling from her mouth. She loved this place, Gran's place, and she wasn't going to give it up.

Her mother halted her march to the door and MJ almost walked into her. "MJ, don't be wearisome. It doesn't make sense to hold onto this property for which you'll be paying high property taxes from the look of it, when you'll only use it in the summer and a few weekends during the year."

Teaching full-time would mean her presence at the university most weekdays, especially when you added in office hours for the students, and faculty meetings. In winter, it would be even more difficult to get out to the island because of weather. "You're right, Mother."

"Of course I am," she said smugly, opening her purse and pulling out her car keys. "Good to see you haven't lost all common sense." Anger flared again. She was not a little girl any more. Her mother did not have the power to push her in a direction she didn't want to go. "So, I am going to live here full-time."

Her mother whirled back to face her. "You can't mean to commute. That's impractical."

Of course she couldn't commute from here. But, the heck with it. "No, I mean I won't teach. I'm going to put my dissertation on hold until I decide if teaching is what I want to do, now or in the future."

Her mother stared at her open-mouthed as if she had just grown a second head. "You aren't serious."

Why not? She stood in her own house, or what would be her own house at the end of the summer. She now had money and investments, and, if the book she'd finished for Gran published, she'd have royalties from her work as well as Gran's. And if she wrote? Well, she wouldn't count on that yet but, "Yes, I'm serious. I want to write. I don't want to spend all my time grading everyone else's writing. "

Her mother pointed at her with her car key. "I knew you coming here was a mistake, a huge mistake." She snapped her purse shut. "Well, you chose to come here. You've chosen to stay. Your dissertation committee will not approve. I had a terrific position lined up for you in the English department, teaching women's fiction, but that won't happen now...or ever."

"Thank you, Mother, that's okay. I'll be writing women's fiction, instead." She swallowed the ache in her throat. Her mother pointed back at the dining room. "You mean that, that maudlin, cliched..."

MJ yanked open the door. "Yes, romance fiction. Happily ever after stories. Like Gran."

Her mother walked through the doorway, then turned back. "I'm finished, Marie Juliette. I've done everything I could to help guide you into a career you can succeed at and be proud of as a woman. You're on your own now. And please, if you ever publish, use a pen name so my colleagues will never know I have a daughter who could have been a respected professor but chose to write trash instead."

MJ bit her lip as she watched her mother get into her car and drive off. She refused to cry. No tears. Absolutely no tears. She closed the door as tears rained down her cheeks. Hurrying back into the dining area, she swiped at them before kneeling to pick up the few remaining pieces of note cards under the table. Standing, she looked around at the empty rooms and at the ocean beyond the windows. Alone. Truly alone now. Her heart still pounded and her throat still ached, but she took a deep breath and sat down at the table. Laying out the torn pieces, she matched them to each other. She'd find tape later. The last pieced-together card was the one about her hero. Her lips tilted as she realized she'd made her hero look like Nik.

She missed him. Something had started to grow between them, hadn't it? He'd been gone a while and hadn't been in touch since she sent him the manuscript of Gran's last book.

Where was he?

"Ah-h-h," his mother breathed softly, "Look at her, Nikos.'

Look at her? He couldn't look away from her image in the scrying pool, watching her settle into her chair, seeing the traces of tears on her face. His fists curled. She was beautiful and brave and...His mother watched him expectantly.

"Juliette will be so proud of her for breaking down the walls her mother built around her."

"And you?" his mother asked. "How do you feel about her?"

"I..." What did it matter given the rules? Her brows were raised as she waited for him to answer her question. He looked away only to notice his aunts were all staring him, also waiting for his answer.

"Well," he said, clearing his throat, "I am proud of her, too. She is a beautiful and strong warrior for her creative dreams."

His mother put her hand to her hip and tilted her head.

"What? What's wrong?" he asked.

She waved away her sisters who rose and left the scrying pool, heading to the temple. But Clio approached him. "Surely," she said, "you will not let fear and an overblown sense of duty rule your heart? Listen to your mother." She patted him on the shoulder as if he were a small boy, then joined her other sisters at the temple steps.

Now he was the one to cock his head at his mother. "Overblown?"

She nodded. "Overblown. Your very admirable sense of duty has served you—and my sisters and me—very well, making you one of the best of Lord Apollo's Voices, my son. Do not think, however, I haven't noticed how you have grown weary of your service."

Her hand shot up when he opened his mouth to respond, so he closed it. "Do not think to deny it. A mother knows these things, especially an immortal mother."

What was he to say? It was true. He was weary of it, wanted something different. Something more for himself. Was it selfish? Perhaps. After centuries of service, was that so bad? So, he said nothing, and crossed his arms.

His mother tugged on them. "Do not close yourself off to protect yourself from what I have to say. After all, isn't that why you are here?"

He dropped his arms and looked over at the pool of still water. Nothing showed on its surface. She was right. He was here to ask for her insight and guidance. Why deny it? "I do want something more, yes. But... I worry. About you and your sisters.

About the increasing loss of creativity in the world and what it might do to you. How can I ask for something for myself if it means I abandon you and my aunts?"

She pulled him to sit on one of the marble benches near the pool, where a small oak cast some shade. "Tell me, Nikos, I know we are immortal but isn't it a bit arrogant to assume only you can save the Muses from extinction? Are you the only Voice?"

"No, but I am your only child who is a Voice. I don't want to see the white streak in your hair grow any wider. "

His mother smiled and took his hand. "My Nikos, I appreciate your care, your commitment. As you want me to be happy and well, I want the same for you," her chin quivered, but she raised it and said, "And I know what will make your heart sing. The question is, do you? And if you do, what are you willing to do about it?" She leaned over to kiss him on the cheek. "Don't use me as an excuse, my son, to avoid what might be fearful or uncomfortable. It is time to reach for what you truly want, even if it changes your life completely."

She rose and turned to walk toward the temple, but turned back. "Whatever you decide, whatever happens, you have my love and support, Nikos." With those disconcerting words, she walked away, while he sat trying to figure out what his mother and his Aunt Clio, were encouraging him to do. He thought he knew. He sighed. Better report to Apollo, then he'd return to the cottage. To MJ.

To give her the good news about the book, of course.

MJ stepped onto the deck, closing the French door behind her. Inhaling, she stretched her arms up and back, trying to work out the kinks from sitting so long at her laptop working on her story. Not her dissertation. Her story. She couldn't believe how happy that made her feel in spite of everything else. In spite of the phone call this morning from her dissertation committee chair telling her the committee had turned down her request for an extension. In spite of the bad dream about her mother. It figured she'd dream about her after the emotional scene they'd had. Before going to bed last night, she'd been tempted to call her father but, like Gran, she didn't want to make things difficult for him.

She strode down the beach, thinking about the other disturbing dream of last night. Not of her mother or Gran but of Nik. It wasn't a frightening dream. Oh, no. On the contrary. What disturbed her were the feelings—emotional and physical—the dream aroused in her, even upon waking. In the dream, they were on the beach, embracing like they did weeks ago. The kiss sparked desire and made her ache. Nik bore her down to the soft warm sand, pressing his body against hers so she was warmed both back and front, the heat from Nik's body greater than the sand. His kiss was sweet, not like the kiss of honey, nor did she glimpse the temple, but it was sweet and assured and arousing. He stroked a hand down her body, from cheek to neck to shoulder to breast. As his hand moved lower and her hips instinctually tilted toward his, she awakened.

Aroused and irritated it had been a dream. An unfinished dream. She'd thrown herself from the bed into the shower where she tried to replace the heat of the dream with the heat of the water. She'd never been this aroused or haunted by a guy. Why him? Damn it, where was he? Two weeks since she'd sent him away. Now, she kicked at the sand. Was he ever coming back? He had to. Papers needed signed. Wasn't he supposed to let her know about the editor's response to Gran's manuscript? She wanted to show him the first chapters of her own novel.

After all, he suggested he would act as agent for her as he had for Gran. So, where was he?

Why did she care? Because, dreams aside, kisses aside, he was an agent, that's all. But care she did, too much. More than she'd been prepared for. Damn! That dream, the sexy, luscious, over-too-soon dream, was not because she thought of him as her agent. She'd been honest with her mother, wasn't it time to be honest with herself? She'd fallen for the guy. For the way he made her feel smart and capable of living her dreams. Because he made her feel desirable.

Walking to the water's edge, she scanned the horizon. A wave broke and washed around her ankles. The water was cooling but not cold. No way was she going any deeper. She shivered, looking up and down the beach. Why was she the only one around today? Usually, a few people were out enjoying the sun or running with their dog. Looking over the water, she thought she saw a head bob up in the distance. Was someone swimming that far out? Were they okay? The head disappeared into the water. She waited. Maybe she should call for help. Looking around at the empty beach, she wondered who would hear.

Or, perhaps, given the past weeks, she imagined something out there, as she had imagined seeing the temple. What was it about this place? Hands on her hips, she scanned the water. She wasn't a strong swimmer, had little experience of swimming in the ocean. If someone out there was in trouble, she wasn't sure she had the ability to do anything but drown herself. She took a few more steps into the water. A head popped up only a few yards away from her and asked in a smooth voice, "Looking for me?"

MJ stumbled back and blinked at the woman in the water only yards in front of her, wet hair dark and sleek against her head, dark arched brows, and wide eyes above high cheekbones. Her mouth was full and red and curled in a smirk.

MJ said loudly so the woman could hear her. "I wanted to make sure you were okay. I almost drowned out there a—"

"Yes, you did." The woman's voice carried easily over the water.

MJ frowned. "What?"

"You did almost drown."

MJ closed her eyes and shook her head. How did she know about that night? Maybe she should head back to the cottage. She stepped back.

"Where are you going, mortal?" This time the woman's voice was louder and sharper? But mortal? Who called someone that? "You would dare walk away from me?"

MJ stopped, hands on hips, and looked at the woman, then scanned the beach. If this woman did something crazy, no one was around to help. Turning her gaze back to the woman, she asked, "What are you talking about? And why are you calling me mortal? You are too."

"No, I am not."

MJ took two more steps back, certain she was awake. But the woman was intimidating and confusing and seemed to know things. *There are more things in Heaven and Earth, Horatio, than are dreamt of in your philosophy.* She remembered Gran saying the quote to her numerous times, and she often thought it herself when her mother tried to insist fairies and gods and goddesses were nonsense. But this? Was the woman on drugs? Drunk? She moved forward in the water which sank below her shoulders so MJ saw the slopes of her full breasts. No straps broke the expanse of skin. Was she skinny dipping? Was it allowed on a public beach? Good thing Nik wasn't here to see this.

"I am not mortal. And yes, you almost drowned. You were lucky. If Nikos and the turtle hadn't been there, Hades take them, you—"

"A turtle? A turtle saved me?" MJ shouted. This woman had her beat at fabricating stories out of thin air. If only she'd brought her phone with her, she could call 911 and get them to send someone to help her get the woman from the water. Obviously, she wasn't thinking clearly. Or was she someone who delighted in confusing others, in yanking their chains? MJ took a few more steps back so the breaking waves only reached her toes.

Frowning, the woman slapped her hand against the water's surface, then sank beneath it. MJ stepped forward until the water once again swirled above her ankles, but stopped there, hesitant to go any further. The woman's head broke the surface again, rising far enough this time to reveal breasts and chest covered with a tattoo of feathers.

"What are you afraid of? Why don't you join me in the water? The temperature is wonderful and there are so many amazing things to see beneath the surface."

Imagine how many amazing things were in the water, magical things she'd never seen—she took a step forward. She took another step when a wave broke, wetting her calves. She jerked back. What was she doing? Another step back.

"Stupid mortal. Are you so stuck in your belief of what is real, that you discount what is in front of you? This is my world. And Nikos'," she said, beckoning to MJ.

She blinked. What was she doing? She felt pulled toward the woman, like the last time. Like the last time. Straining, as if against invisible ropes, she took one step back, then another, and another until the water no longer reached her and suddenly, it was as if the ropes were abruptly cut, and she fell to the sand. The woman frowned at her.

"You are fortunate, mortal."

"Stop calling me that. Who are you?"

The woman moved closer and MJ held her breath. Would she leave the water? The tattoo of feathers seemed to flutter as she moved. "But I know of you, mortal. Chosen by the Muses to regain your creative spark. Bah! What a waste of time for Nikos. How can the son of Erato desire to embrace such a passionless being."

MJ's head was hurting. The more this woman talked the more confused she became. "Who is Nikos? Are you talking about Nik, my Gran's financial adviser?"

The woman bared her teeth, then tilted her head back, opened her mouth and a sound filled the air that was neither yell nor scream, shatteringly loud, and piercingly inhuman. MJ bent over her knees, hands clasped to her ears, eyes tightly shut as the sound echoed and reechoed. It stopped as suddenly as it started. Hesitantly, she lifted her hands from her ears and looked up. The woman was erect in the water waist-deep for her, her arms crossed, her brows drawn together.

"Of course, Nikos, Nik," she said the last name as though sucking on a lemon. "You endanger his life in your ignorance and give nothing back to him because of your fears and rules. You tempt him to forget his vows for nothing. To sacrifice for nothing!"

The woman's anger was almost as palpable as the scream had been, as the word "sacrifice" was. "How do you know..." she almost said Nik, but didn't want to upset the woman further, "Nikos?"

The woman smiled slyly at her. "He is a cousin. And I have taken him into my bed and into my body. He is a wonderful lover, vigorous and..."

MJ clapped her hands over her ears again. Nik and this woman had been intimate? When? Not during those days when they worked together, when he'd kissed her. He'd been with her almost constantly. Cousins? The more she heard the more convinced she became the woman was on something. And messing with her as a result. Still, how did she know Nik? She dropped her hands.

"Who are you?" MJ demanded.

Chapter 28

Thalassa stared at this poor excuse for a woman who had enamored her Nikos. What was it about this woman whom he had not even yet taken to his bed? It made no sense, and it enraged her that, according to her mother, every time he helped a young mortal woman, he risked his immortal life. Did he not know this? Why did none of the Voices know this? Typical Hera manipulation. She wanted to scream again. She shouldn't have done it the first time but she was so furious at the woman, at Nik, at the Muses, at Hera.

Still, should she give the woman her name? What if her aunts or Apollo or one of the others found out she was able to leave the island? The desire to taunt the woman, make Nikos worry, was too much. Besides, she knew how to do this and have none of the gods any wiser, especially Hera. She wanted them to keep believing she and her sisters were confined to the island and its waters. The woman rubbed her eyes. If only Thalassa could tempt her to walk further into the water, but the woman pulled out of her spell. She grit her teeth. Getting rid of her would relieve Nik of his responsibility as Voice, and would lessen any danger of his breaking of his vow.

"You can call me Tally." She cringed at the name but it would do for her purpose.

"Nice to meet you, Tally," the woman said. "Come out of the water, and we can go to my cottage where you can warm up. I'll fix you a cup of tea." Typical mortal. Offer a beverage as if it will cure everything. "We can get someone to come pick you up."

Thalassa shook her head. "Keep your tea. Did you not hear what I said? I am not a mortal. I am not in need of yours or anyone's help." Though it would have been useful to have it centuries ago when her wings were torn from her. "Why do you not believe what I spoke to you? Bah! I don't know why Apollo continues to send his Voices to help you mortals. It is not as if working with a few of you at a time will make a difference, especially now, when each of you is distracted by your technology. You are such a waste of Nikos' time and efforts. You threaten his life."

"His life?" The mortal stepped closer. Oh, so that was the way to get her to come to her.

"Yes, his life. If you want to know more, ask him what he risks if he, if he..." Suddenly, she couldn't get the words out. Her throat tightened. She moved back in the water, looking about. She tried again, "Ask him what happens if..." No words emerged. Panicked, she grabbed her throat and looked around. Who was doing this to her? She couldn't lose her voice. She'd lost so much. Frightened, she whirled her tail so she turned in a circle. Seeing nothing, she looked back at the woman who stood with her head tilted to the side.

"Are you okay?" she yelled at her.

No. No, she was not. She dove into the water, slapping the surface with her tail in frustration and anger. Damn the gods. Damn Hera. Most especially, damn the Muses.

MJ's heart beat a mad rhythm in her ears and chest. Was that a fish tail she saw smack the water? No. How could it be? Where had the woman—or whatever—gone? She scanned the water but didn't see the woman's head emerge. What if she drowned? Should she call emergency services? To tell them what, exactly? The woman had been totally comfortable in the water. Arrogant, too. Besides, by the time she got back to the cottage for her phone, the woman would be gone or dead.

She dropped to the sand. Or maybe the whole thing hadn't happened. She pinched herself, then looked up and down the beach and saw a woman walking a dog. She'd observed them on the beach before. She ran her fingers through her hair. So, she wasn't imagining the fish woman. How could she? She wasn't like anything MJ had experienced or read about or imagined. She talked as if everything she said was totally true. Immortality?

Her mind kept insisting what she'd seen was impossible. Unreal. Believing it real was a path to insanity. But she saw the woman, heard the woman, and maybe seen... No. She shivered. Her world was coming apart and all she wanted was to get back to the cottage, shower, and get something to eat. Giving the water one last scan, she rose and turned to slog through the sand back to the cottage.

If she wasn't dreaming, then was someone playing a nasty trick on her? Who would do that? The only person who knew about her nasty adventure in the water—other than Nik—was Neri. And neither of them were likely to do something like this. Surely, it couldn't be real. If it was? Then he was keeping something from her. Something important. How was she risking his life? She'd been so happy before she'd come out to walk the beach. Sure, the fight with her mother had left her sad and angry by turns. But she was writing! And Nik would return eventually. Wouldn't he? Now, she wasn't sure. And if he did? Tell him what she'd heard and seen? Ignore it? Confront him?

She walked back into the cottage feeling as if she was seeing it with new eyes, as if she was a new person. Someone who needed the comforting presence of her Gran and the escape into make-believe. She picked up her laptop and note cards and climbed the two flights of stairs to Gran's writing aerie. Setting the laptop on the small desk, she sat down in the chair. Looking up, she smiled at the picture of her and her grandmother, then turned down the picture of Nik and Gran with his new car. She didn't want to think about him now, or the woman in the water. She just wanted to think about her story.

"I'm here, Gran. I hope you'll help me," she whispered before setting fingers to the keyboard. *Once upon a time...*

She swallowed back the pressure building in her throat.

Nik walked into the barracks filled with other Voices, hanging out reading, throwing darts or shooting pool while music played through the speakers on the wall. Not mortal music, though. He thought he recognized something by one of the other Voices, played on a lute. Very mainstream immortal.

Normally, he would make himself comfortable and take part in the conversations—heated discussions—about the best way to deal with a recalcitrant client. Or the bets being laid about Zeus's latest paramour. But the urge to make his report and finally return to MJ, especially after what he'd seen in the scrying pool, pulsed through him. Since Apollo wasn't in the temple or here in the barracks, perhaps he was in his office. He strode through the barracks to a door opening into a hallway. Slipping through it, he walked to the end and the finely polished and carved wooden door. It had an inlaid solid gold Sun big enough to act as a shield for his chest should he be able to pry it from the wood. Should he be so bold or stupid, the god of sun and light, of prophecy and healing, would incinerate him.

He dragged in a deep, bracing breath and raised his hand to knock but before knuckles touched wood...

"Come!" boomed through the door.

Hades take it, he hated when Apollo anticipated him. If the god could do that, why did he need to report to him? He probably knew everything Nik was going to say. Throwing back his shoulders, he pushed the door open. After centuries of service, he wouldn't shirk his duty now. Blinking against the piercing bright light emanating from Apollo, he paused to let his eyes adjust, scanning the god's so-called office that in no way resembled a mortal one. No roof, for one thing. After all, why would a sun god need a roof? The walls were not some cheap composite material either, but marble, as were the floor and columns. The columns were decorative rather than functional. The marble floor was warm because, well, sun god.

On either side of Nik, crystal tables held the latest in modern technology, the best money could and did buy. Apollo's aides sat in leather chairs at large-screen monitors, sun glasses and headphones in place while their fingers clicked and clacked at keyboards or hands waved at screens just as his aunts had waved over the scrying pool water.

As the light dimmed slightly and Nik's eyes adjusted, he turned his gaze to Apollo who sat on his throne of shaped and etched gold. He was leaning forward, elbows resting on the throne arms, on which were carved ravens. A reminder to not anger the god who stared at him with brow raised. "Well?"

Oh, yes, his report. "Lord, my client, Marie Juliette Montague, finished her grandmother's manuscript, submitted it, and it was approved by the editor for publication next year.

And," he let pride fill his voice as he straightened further, "she has begun work on her own novel, in spite of pressure from her mother."

The god leaned back. "Does this mean you consider yourself to have met the promise you made to the client's grandmother and you'd like to be re-assigned?"

Re-assigned? *Skata*, no.

"Uh, no, Lord." Usually, he worked with a client until they were well established in their creative careers. Afterwards, he took on a more professional and distanced role, only seeing the client a couple of times a year, like the musician, Giles. Communication with them about contracts, finances, and other business-related concerns was usually by phone or text or emails. MJ wasn't ready for that. She hadn't even finished her first book. But if he backed off from the relationship, the constant temptation to risk breaking the rules of the Voices, would no longer be a concern.

"So, the mortal still needs your help and your presence?"

Did she? He'd watched her stand up to her mother but that was only once and her mother was persistent, according to Juliette. The mother was still a threat. She probably assumed MJ would cave after she had time to think about her mother's final ultimatum. Was MJ strong enough to dare to live her dreams and not her mother's? Yes, if it was what she really wanted. She only needed reminding of those dreams and her ability to reach for them. As for the money and writing contracts, he didn't need to be with her to provide that kind of support.

His shoulders fell as he shook his head. "She needs my help, Lord, but not my presence."

"Are you confident about that?"

Nik jerked his head up to look at the god. He wasn't used to tricky questions from Apollo. Hermes, yes. Apollo, no. The god had propped his chin in his hand and once again raised a brow at Nik while he waited for a response.

"You appear uncertain, Voice. Shall I have my oracle show you your client's future? Then you will be able to see if you are necessary to her—success—or not."

Part of him did want to see MJ's future, to see she was happy writing her books, doing book signings, and enjoying her life on the island, but not if "happy" included another man and their children, no. And if there was no happy life, if her mother got her way, if MJ became a professor, lonely and unhappy in her ivory academic tower, grading students' writings but never writing her own stories? No, he didn't want to see that either, to see he might have failed her and her grandmother. His jaw tightened. He didn't want her happy with some mortal man, but he didn't want her lonely and alone, either. Gods! What a coil his brain was in.

"Nikos, you have not answered me."

"No, no oracle, no future, Lord." No future was right. He had none with MJ. His fists tightened. Apollo narrowed his eyes, watching Nik like the falcon watched the sparrow, waiting for the right moment to stoop to its prey. What did the god of prophecy know about his feelings for MJ or hers for him? *Do not let fear and an overblown sense of duty rule your heart.* His Aunt Clio's words rose to his mind. He dropped to one knee, placing his right fist over his heart and dropping his head.

"Lord, I ask to be relieved of my duty and service as a Voice." He heard the rustle of cloth and the slap of leather on marble as the god strode to where he kneeled. He steeled himself.

"Caught your heart, did she?" Apollo asked.

Nik closed his eyes and nodded. Why deny it? After all these centuries of service, all the women he'd bedded, why MJ captured his heart was, at first, a mystery. As he spent time with her, her love for Juliette, her efforts to prove herself to her mother,

her imagination and belief in the possibility of happily ever after had drawn him in, made him want to support her, protect her, and be part of her happy ending. Was that possible?

"Are you fully aware of the sacrifices you will make?" the god asked, his voice soft and somber.

"I know I must leave the Voices."

The god's hand fell heavily on his shoulder. "It is more than that, Nikos." His voice lowered and he bent to speak to Nik's bowed head. "If you give in to love, you will lose your immortality."

"What!" Nik's head jerked up, and his mouth fell open.

Apollo straightened. "Did you not read all of that scroll Hermes fetched for you?"

How did he know about that? Nik shook his head. "I only read as far as tasting honey and seeing the temple because..." He stopped.

He heard Apollo sigh above him, then return to his throne. He looked up. "I will lose my immortality? Become as any mortal."

"Not just your immortality, Nikos, but your ability to walk in this world."

He shot to his feet. "Do you mean I will never return here? Never see my friends or my mother or aunts?"

The god shook his head, his light dimming slightly. "How could you be one of them and still be one of us?"

Nik looked up at the piercingly blue sky. Never return to Mount Helicon? Never smell the olives ripening in the grove or the incense burning in the temple? He would miss his friends in the Voices, and his aunts and cousins, but surely, he would be able to see his mother. He did not want her to grieve or add to that grey streak in her hair. Somehow, he would find a way to...

"Are you determined, Nikos? She could reject you, now or in the future. She could take ill and die. So could you."

The words echoed and re-echoed. Could die. Actually, would die. Sooner or later. Fates will that it would be later. He wanted many years of loving MJ. Of being her husband and being a father...

"Lord, will I able to give her children?"

Apollo threw back his head and laughed, his laughter resounding off the marble walls and up into the sky. He smiled broadly at him. "That's up to you, Nikos. Neither I nor anyone else will have anything to do with that."

Thank the gods. Truly. "Is there anything I must do to well, make the transition?"

"Do you love her, Nikos? Love her with your heart and mind and soul as well as your body?"

Nik nodded. That was what made the experience so new and urgent to him.

"So be it. Because of your service, I will give you one dispensation. You may return here to Mt. Helicon every summer solstice. On that day only and no other. Do you understand?"

"I do, Lord, and I thank you."

"Just make sure you and your mother don't tell my mother."

"Yes, Lord. I've never spoken to Hera. I'm sure I never will."

"Good. Then, let us walk in the orchard and I will tell you what you need to know about your new life as a mortal."

Chapter 29

T he clock began striking the hour. MJ raised her eyes from the screen and saw dusk had turned to night outside the windows. As the clock kept striking, she looked down at the corner of the screen and realized it was midnight. Had she eaten?

She looked at her word count. Two thousand in the last however many hours. Words that let her forget those of the strange woman. Words that let her forget about Nik, her mother, and everything else. But now, it was time to stop. Sleep beckoned her tired eyes and mind, although she hoped the dreams would not bother her tonight. She had no defense against them. Had she imagined what had happened out on the beach? Had her mother been right all along to worry about her daughter's imagination and propensity for making up stories?

She shook her head. The woman had been real. But was what she said true? Was she in some way putting Nik at risk? She put her laptop to sleep and pushed out of the chair. Time for a cup of hot chocolate to take up to bed. It would help her sleep, perchance to not dream.

As she poured the milk into the pan and turned the burner on, she thought again about the woman's words. They made no sense. Nik was her financial advisor, not a bodyguard protecting her from a murderer. Yes, they kissed, and she had to admit, she would enjoy kissing him again—very much. But a kiss from her wasn't the kiss of death. Other guys had kissed her and survived.

The milk simmered and she stirred in some powdered cocoa, poured the cocoa into a mug, and turned off the burner. Walking through the dining area into the hall, she turned off lights and climbed the stairs. Reaching the top of the stairs, she headed to her room but, squaring her shoulders, she stopped to look out the windows. The waning moon cast a lit path on the water. Scanning back and forth, she saw only the rolling waves and the moonlight sparkling on them. What did she expect?

She was not imagining things. She wasn't. And Gran definitely had not been crazy, nor even a little loopy. Imaginative, yes, a magical storyteller, definitely. Also practical. MJ took another sip of her cocoa and scanned the ocean again. You couldn't be crazy or delusional and write books that sold and sold. Or create this life with Nik's...

Nik. MJ blinked and took another sip. Where was he? Why hadn't he returned? Then she could tell him about her weird experience and they could laugh together about it and maybe he'd kiss her again. And more. But no, not if he was involved with the strange woman.

Her heart clenched. He'd stopped being just her financial advisor when he rescued her. She remembered how strong his arms had been, how warm his body, how safe she felt when he carried her up to the cottage. She raised her hand to her hair, recalling the intimacy as he unbraided her hair and ran her bath, his touch gentle yet strong. Patient, caring. Nothing like her mother's impatient ministrations.

He felt something for her, didn't he? He'd kissed her after all, but what did she know? Dating experiences were limited, mostly to guys she'd met while in college or, more recently, while teaching at the university, and they were always intimidated by her mother, either because of her demeanor or position at the school. The ones who stayed despite being intimidated did so because of academic ambitions and MJ's connection to her mother, so she'd break with them. She didn't need someone in her life more interested in making her mother happy than her.

She smiled thinking her father hadn't scared her dates at all, except when the porch light blinked on and off to let her and the guy she was with know the time they'd been parked in the driveway had been long enough. No, it was her mother who grilled them about their majors and future plans, asked them what their grade average was and more.

MJ entered her room and set the mug down on the nightstand. She didn't want to think about her mother and her fiercely angry remarks before she walked out the cottage door. She didn't want to think about the weird woman in the water telling her that she was risking Nik's life, either. After tending to her evening ablutions, she crawled into bed. If she was going to dream, she hoped it was about Gran again. Or Nik. Even if dreaming about him was frustrating. If only he returned tomorrow. She'd confront him about what was happening, with her writing and the legacy.

And with them. She had a right to know, didn't she?

Nik turned off the car and breathed in the sudden night silence. Venus, the morning star twinkled brightly at him. He'd been so anxious to get back here, to walk through the door and be with MJ. So anxious to talk to her about how she was feeling, about how he was feeling. To see if the future he hadn't wanted Apollo to show him was what he envisioned it to be.

But he sat, listening to the engine click as it cooled. For the first time in his immortal life, he was uncertain about how a mortal woman would respond to him, how she felt about him. Gods, how did mortal men deal with it? He was on the precipice of losing his immortality. After centuries of watching mortals fall in and out of love, he knew there were no certainties, no guarantees, at least not in this century. A century or two ago, a man married a woman and that was the end of that, whether they continued to love each other or not, whether they honored their vows or not. Of course, falling in and out of love was no different with immortals but at least they had plenty of time to recover, to figure things out, and to fall again—for a while—because when you lived forever it was harder to love forever. Zeus being the perfect case in point.

Once he made love to MJ, there were no centuries ahead to figure things out or to fall again. He would love her forever...for a mortal's forever at least. He sighed. He was stalling. It was time for action, not this uncharacteristic dithering and reflection. Alek would laugh his head off if he saw him now, although, the conversation he'd had with him before heading here certainly had not made his buddy laugh.

"Did you drink too much ambrosia? Are you messing with me? You can't leave the Voices. Apollo will fry you?"

Yeah, Alek wasn't happy, but his friend didn't know the rest of it. He would. Nik shook his head, raised his door, and climbed out of the car. This hour of the early morning, he didn't expect to find lights on in the cottage, but some faint light filtered through the window above the door. He raised his hand to the turtle knocker and paused.

What was he thinking? Asleep or awake, he'd scare MJ witless if he knocked on the door this early. Shifting on his feet, he pulled out his key and considered sneaking in. No, also not a good idea, especially if he didn't want her calling the cops. Okay, he wasn't knocking, he wasn't sneaking in. What was he going to do? The sound of the ocean reminded him he could sit on the deck and wait for her to come down for breakfast. Glancing around to ensure no one was watching, he walked around the house. He'd sit, watch the sun rise, wait for her to wake up, and hope she was as happy to see him as he was to see her.

He climbed the steps to the deck and noticed soft light filtering through the windows and French doors, dimly illuminating the deck's table and chairs. Had she left a light on, worried by the large, empty house, or had she forgotten to turn one off when she went to bed? He walked over and peered in the window.

No! No, no, no. Not again. He stuffed his hand in his pants pocket, searching for his keys. Hades! He wasn't going through this again. Juliette was sad enough, but MJ... Just when he thought he was finally going to have someone to love and love him.

He slipped the key into the lock and barged into the house, locking on MJ, slumped over the dining room table, laptop and notes spread around her. It couldn't happen again. Atropos, the damned Fate, would not do that to him, or was this some bitter punishment Apollo was meting out?

"MJ!" he said, grabbing her shoulders and shaking her. She moaned. She was warm. Nik locked his knees. Thank the gods. He drew a deep breath and stepped back. Sleeping. She'd only been sleeping.

She sighed, straightened in the chair, and rubbed at her eyes. Catching sight of him, she jerked back. "Nik, what are you doing here? How did you get in?" She rubbed her eyes again and looked around. "What time is it?"

He wanted to grab her and hold her while his breathing slowed. "It's six in the morning. Why are you asleep at the table instead of up in your bed?"

"I woke up at five and had an idea for my story, so I got up to work on it," she croaked, then rose from the chair and picked up her mug of what must now be ice-cold coffee. "You're a fine one to talk. What are you doing up at this hour? And what are you doing here?" She shoved him aside and headed into the kitchen, tugging the worn pink t-shirt down over her knit shorts that stopped mid-thigh on her long legs. They disappeared from view as she walked behind the counter to the sink.

"Nik? Why are you here?"

Why did she keep asking him that. "Why wouldn't I be here?"

The mug thumped onto the countertop and her hands went to her hips. "Because you've been gone for weeks. You've barely communicated with me. I figured you weren't coming back since you accomplished your mission. I finished the manuscript and I'm staying here through the summer."

She shrugged, yawned, and blinked at him. She wore no make-up and her freed hair stuck up in places making her look bed-rumpled and sexy. He wanted to haul her across the counter into his arms so he could kiss her until both their ears rang with bells. She blinked at him again and tilted her head to the side.

"Or maybe this is another one of my crazy dreams..."

"Dreams aren't crazy. They're messages, important...Wait. You've dreamed of me?" He leaned toward her but she moved away and walked around to stand looking out the picture window. The early morning sunlight sparked across the water.

She whispered, "I dream of you, and Gran, and..." She paused and he stepped softly closer. She continued, "It must have been a dream. She couldn't be real."

"She?"

MJ nodded and put her hands over her eyes. "I thought it was real. It felt real. I swear I was awake but—" She whirled, her eyes large, fear in them. "But if it wasn't a dream, maybe I'm going crazy like my mother always thought I might."

Now he did grab her arms. "Stop it, MJ. You aren't crazy. There is nothing wrong with your mind or your imagination. Now what did you dream? Or see?"

She dropped her forehead to his chest. "She said things I don't understand."

He kissed the top of head, and wrapped his arms around her and squeezed her gently. "Tell me."

"I went for a walk on the beach. At least, I thought I did. And I saw something in the water."

His heart began to pound. "You didn't go into the water, did you?"

She shivered. "After last time? No, I started to because, for a moment, it was as if I was compelled to, like the last time. But this strange woman appeared and she had a feathered tattoo here," she gestured to her chest, "and she was naked. At least from the waist up."

It couldn't be. Was she the reason MJ almost drowned? He clenched his jaw. Surely, the tattoo was a coincidence. Lots of women had tattoos. But swimming naked?

MJ stopped. What to say next? How to describe her experience? Describe the reality of the woman? How would Nik...

"Is your full name Nikos?" She looked up at him.

His eyes were intent on her, his brows drawn together. "Yes, why?"

She looked back out at the water, shimmering in the slowly increasing light. "She called you Nikos, said that was your name."

"MJ, what is it? It's obvious something upset you while I was gone."

Something? More like some things—or some people. First, her mother. A few days later the woman in the water. In some ways, she wished it had been a dream.

"MJ?" Nik gripped her shoulder. "What happened with the strange woman? Did she do something to hurt you?"

She leaned her head against his chest. This wasn't how she wanted his return to go. She didn't want to feel frightened of what she might learn in the next moments either. Dragging in a breath, she reminded herself she had, after all, faced down her dragon of a mother. She could tell Nik.

"She kept calling me 'mortal' as if she wasn't." She watched his face, saw his jaw drop, and his eyes move to the window so he no longer looked at her.

She gathered her courage. "She's probably not well mentally. I mean there is no such thing as an immortal, right?"

He shook his head, and asked, "What... Why would you ask? What makes you—"

Her hand flew up to stop his words. "I know, I know. It sounds crazy to me, too, but that woman, whatever she is, she knew your name. She told me she'd had sex with you." She gave a short laugh. "Actually, she said she had taken you into her body, which was such a strange way to talk about having sex. She said I am a threat to your life," her words caught on a sob, but she swallowed it back. She didn't want to cry. "She was so disdainful of me. Why? She doesn't know me. But she knows you. How? Are you dating someone?" She pushed out of his arms. "Afterall, I'm just a lowly mortal."

"MJ, stop!" Nik reached out to clasp her arm.

"She said I was lucky because she tried to drown me that night after the White Horses and if it hadn't been for the turtle..." she giggled, covering her mouth as she attempted to wrest back control of her emotions.

Nik opened his mouth to speak but she shook her head at him and continued. "The really weird, bizarre part, the part making me think it was a dream, because, after all, you are hunky enough to be an immortal, was she..." MJ shivered, "she was telling me to ask you about something but it seemed like something was wrong with her throat and when she turned to swim away, I could have sworn..." she covered her mouth and shook her head. After a minute, she dropped her hand and said, "I could have sworn when she swam away from me, she...she slapped the water with her tail. Isn't that crazy?"

She dragged in a breath. There, she'd told him. If she was being silly or crazy, he could say so and be gone. Or maybe he'd call her mother. Confirm her mother's diagnosis and ask her to come get her hallucinating daughter. A tear slipped down her cheek and angrily, she swiped it away. "She was rude and mad at me because of you. And I didn't think you had a girlfriend, or I would never have kissed you." Finally, she ran out of words and breath. Nik still held her arm but looked down at the floor. His jaw was clenched. Was he mad at her? Did he think she was making this all up?

Please no. The confrontation with her mother had been bad enough. She wasn't sure her mother would ever forgive her for not being what her mother wanted her to be. Perhaps her attempts to win her mother's love had been doomed from birth. But she thought she and Nik had something promising. Had she ruined everything with her—what? Story, experience, dream?

"Nik, talk to me. Did I imagine her? Am I...am I going mad? I know you're not immortal, but—"

"But I am."

Chapter 30

"**I** am an immortal," Nik said through clenched teeth. He didn't break his vow. Some fish-tailed cousin did that from the sounds of it, and there would be payback, but he didn't tell MJ, only confirmed what she'd heard. A fine line but the gods were great at drawing fine lines. And in light of what Apollo said would happen to him once he confessed his love for MJ? No big f-ing deal.

She frowned at him and he wanted to take her in his arms and kiss the frown away.

"Are you laughing at me? Because it's not funny." Wrapping her arms around herself, she walked away from him into the living area.

Hades take it. Nothing about what started out as a somewhat simple assignment had been easy since the day he walked into Juliette's old house for the reading of her will. He followed the woman he now knew he loved to where she stood at the other window, gazing out to sea like some long-ago wife of a sea captain waiting for his return. But he was right here. With her. Why weren't they wrapped in each other's arms?

"I would never mock you, MJ. Why would I?"

Turning, she flung an arm out, palm up as she waved it back and forth in front of him. "Because look at you. You're a successful, hunky, hot shot city guy who's probably traveled the world and slept with hundreds of women. And look at me." She brought her hand back to sweep it down her body. "I'm just another typical, boring, timid, naive academic taking up your precious time. Truthfully, I'm surprised you came back. I haven't made your job easy, and I apologize. Please, please don't make fun of me."

He dropped his head and rubbed his eyes. "I swear on all that is divine I am not making fun of you. Look, one of the reasons I'm here is to tell you the editor loved your grandmother's book with your final chapters. They are going to publish it."

He waited for a squeal of delight. For her to turn to him and throw herself in his arms. Instead, she sighed and said, "Thank you. I am so glad for Gran's sake and for her readers." Another sigh. "I'm grateful to you for coming all the way out here to tell me. I started my own novel while you were away. Do you think you'd be interested in seeing it? Seeing if you want to…"

"The editor loved your writing and wants you send them a few chapters and a synopsis of what you are working on now." Surely now, she'd fling herself at him. She did turn to him, a smile on her face that quickly disappeared.

"Thank you, Nik. I appreciate it. Especially since my mother and I had a falling out. I don't know whether to return to the university after the summer or to stay here." She looked everywhere around the room but at him. "I know you need to get back to the city and your life…"

Did she not care for him—at all? "Is that what you want, for me to leave?"

"What does it matter? Obviously, you have other women in your life. Although, I have to say, some of them are a bit, no, a lot, weird." She put her hand over her mouth and swallowed. He watched her, every particle of his body yearning for her, waiting for her to give him some signal, some sign she wanted him the way he wanted her.

"Do you really believe the weird woman, as you call her, is someone I care about? Someone I would choose over you?"

Shaking her head, she finally looked at him, eyes brimming with tears. "I don't know," she whispered, "I don't know what is real any more, including how you feel about me, and I don't want you to risk your well-being, to sacrifice your life in the city and whatever else."

That did it. He hauled her into his arms and lowered his mouth to hers, knowing there was only one way to show her how he felt about her. With a gasp, she opened to him and he swept into the warmth of her mouth with his tongue. He licked and sucked and explored. By slow degrees, her body softened into his, her breasts pressing against his chest so closely he felt her heartbeat. Her lips were warm and soft. He dropped a hand to the round firmness of her ass and pressed her even more firmly against him so she would feel his arousal, his desire for her. Moaning, her arms curved around his neck, one hand tangling in his hair.

Heart beating faster, he kissed her and kissed her, captivated by her sweet taste. Honey. Just as he tasted it, she jerked back, her eyes wide, her head turning back and forth, looking for the source of the sound of bells he also heard.

Damn! As she pushed and twisted in his arms for release, he did the smart thing.

He called for his mother.

MJ blinked. And blinked again.

She was still pressed against Nik's very hard, very warm body. No problem there. She turned her head right and left, her hair catching on the morning scruff of his beard as she did so, her mouth falling open at what she saw.

They weren't standing in Gran's cottage any more. They weren't even standing on the beach outside her cottage. She didn't recognize this beach with its tall palms and soft white sands. She didn't see a temple either, so maybe she fainted during their kiss and Nik had carried her outside and along the shore. But palms?

"MJ?" He gently shook her.

"Where are we?" she dared to ask, trying to stay calm. Was she still dreaming and in a moment, she'd wake up in her bed at the cottage and he would be shaking her? She closed her eyes and commanded herself to wake up.

"MJ, look at me."

Okay, she wasn't asleep. She could hear Nik's voice, feels his hands on her arms. So why was she standing instead of lying in her bed. "I'm dreaming. You're not here. I'm going to wake up now."

"You're already awake, child," said a woman from behind her, "keeping your eyes closed won't change anything."

Maybe not but if she pretended a little longer. *There are times to pretend, MJ, and times to not pretend.* She imagined Gran leaning over her saying that after she fell trying to fly off her bed. Still...

"Please open your eyes so I can talk about this," Nik whispered in her ear. Chills shot down her body and heat shot up. She nestled into him and his arms tightened around her.

"You're not a dream?"

He gave a short laugh. "Well, I hope you think I am—how is it said—dreamy? But no. I'm here and if you open your eyes, we can talk and I'll introduce you to my mother."

His mother! She blinked in the bright sunlight. Nik smiled down at her and she reached up to rub at his beard, watching his eyes darken as she did so. Nope, not a dream, but yes, dreamy. He cleared his throat and she remembered the mother. He released his hold on her, pulling her to his side so she saw the woman who stood behind her. Oddly, she didn't look much older than Nik, with long almost black hair pulled over one shoulder, crowned with a silver circlet of leaves highlighting the narrow strip of silver hair running through the dark strands. Calm, warm brown eyes, like Nik's, looked back at her. This couldn't be his mother. She was too young. A sister?

"Who is this? Where are we? How did we get here?"

He looked over at the woman and MJ caught her sweet, amused smile at him. A twinge of jealousy niggled at her and she shoved it back.

"I am Nikos' mother. I am Erato."

Erato? "Wait, Erato?" The woman was nodding. "Like the Muse of love poetry?"

The woman smiled brightly. "Not like. I am. And it's lovely to meet you. I've brought you to my island for star-crossed lovers."

MJ laughed. "You mean like the island for misfit toys?" She looked pointedly around. "Isn't it a little warm for them and Rudolph?" Laugh or cry? This was all too much and if she didn't get a grip on herself and the situation, she'd find herself sedated and carried off to a mental ward. She looked around and up. No, no drone. No cameras, so it wasn't some new, weird reality show she'd been pulled into.

What was all this, then? She swallowed back the frustration and tears. Was this some strange set up by her mother to convince her she couldn't discern reality from imagination? Nik wouldn't do that. What was he doing? Her confusion made her angry.

She pushed away from Nik and turned on her heel to stomp away from "mother" and son. Whatever they were up to, she was not going to be at the mercy of other people's agendas anymore. She veered toward the darker, wetter sand that was easier to walk on—or stomp on.

He could go find some other gullible woman.

She blinked back tears.

Nik watched her sweet form without its mesmerizing braid stride angrily away from him and he took a step to follow her but his mother's arm shot out to stop him.

"No, my son. Give her time. She must work this out for herself."

Fear, such an unusual feeling for him, made him take another step as his mother's grip on his arm tightened. He wanted to go to her, convince her he was speaking truth, and, that he loved her. He loved her.

He broke away from his mother, turning to her. "But isn't it my duty to help her see the truth?" What good were his powers as an immortal if he could do nothing? Her tone was gentle when she said, "As a Voice, yes, it is your duty. But, are you responding as a Voice or as a lover?"

He searched the beach where MJ had been moments ago. Here on this island, she would be safe, right?

"Nikos, my son, if she will not open to other realities, if she will not believe in you the way you believe in her..." she trailed off. If she didn't? Was this a test for her or for him? To see if he was able to set aside previous attitudes and abilities in order to respect MJ's independence and right to make choices for herself?

He scrubbed at his face. Why was this so difficult? Still, after centuries of serving as a Voice among mortals, he'd watched too many flail and struggle at relationships. He snorted. And when was anything ever simple when the gods were involved?

"Breathe, my son, and trust. Trust she cares enough, loves enough to return to you. To listen to what you have to say and to accept your gift of life and love." His mother patted his arm. He turned to her and she shrugged. "After all, there is nowhere else for her to go, is there?" Beaming at him, she waved her arm to her right.

He followed her gesture and discovered two important items settled into the sand. A small, round table of driftwood and glass set with two covered plates, and a decanter of something amber with a hint of pink. He was sure it contained his mother's special ambrosia. Not far from the table was another item of furniture, this one a bed with four posters twisted up like wind-blown cypress and supporting a canopy of bleached linen. More linen hung down, held back by ties on the posters. The bed was covered in more bleached linen and silks, and a bounty of pillows. He raised a brow at his mother.

"Trust, Nikos. And be certain you are both, how do the mortals phrase it—ah yes, very appropriate in this case—make certain you are both on the same page before you are both on the same bed." She raised herself on tiptoe and kissed his forehead, then she disappeared.

With a sigh, he settled himself onto the sand to wait. And wait he would. After all, he'd waited many lifetimes in mortal terms to find someone to love. But would she find him? Would she return and listen to his heart? Would she dare to listen to her own?

He dared to hope but never had he felt so powerless.
Never.

Chapter 31

MJ stomped along the firm, wet sand, away from Nik and his supposed mother. She kept stomping until the anger dissipated enough for her to feel a little ridiculous. Was she five?

No, but she was confused, angry, and hurt. Her throat ached with tears she refused to cry because heaven and all its angels including Gran knew she'd cried plenty of tears since her death. Enough to fill her own ocean or at least a bathtub. She lengthened her strides to a brisk walk as if out here for the exercise. She deepened her breathing and swung her arms. Sooner or later, she'd figure out where she was or come upon some other people and ask them.

Tall trees with a conical shape that might be cypress, mixed with shorter ones with wider canopies and grew a ways back from the beach. They didn't look like the trees growing around Gran's place. The sand was crystalline white and the water beneath a bright sun was turquoise. She refused to believe she was anywhere but on Gran's island, so she kept walking. What else could she do? She wasn't going back to Nik so he could continue to mock her. She picked up her pace, trotting along the wet sand.

She'd been so delighted to wake up this morning to find he'd returned. When he hadn't answered her emails or texts with more than a few short words, she wondered if the connection she felt was in her imagination. Like the crazy bells and taste of honey that accompanied those kisses they shared. What she was feeling was so new and different. Had she jumped to conclusions about what he felt for her? Was she just another client for him? Ouch! That thought slowed her steps. Was he using the other woman, his "mother" to create some distance between them? Was it the same with the strange woman in the water? Stop! That was a bit convoluted even for her.

Fast running out of breath, she pushed forward until she spied a couple, near the tree line, entangled with each other. When the guy moved over the woman and MJ realized he was naked, she turned her gaze out to the water, and kept walking. Obviously, she couldn't ask them for information. What would it be like to make love on the beach? To be so enthralled, so caught up in each other you didn't care who happened by?

Struggling for breath, she halted, checking back over her shoulder to make sure she was out of sight of the lovers. Looking ahead, she saw nothing but more beach, water, and sky. Moving up to dry sand, she dropped down and gazed out.

Now what?

Nik swore. He was going to tread a trench in the sand with his pacing but he couldn't help himself. He couldn't sit still while wondering if she'd return.

Where was she? What if she didn't come back to him? What if she couldn't break through her indoctrination to believe there was possibly more to the world, and more worlds, than mortal science had yet revealed? He searched the beach in the direction she'd stomped off. No. Finally, he started in her direction but after covering a short distance, he noted how the incoming tide was quickly erasing her footprints, and remembered his mother's advice.

The irony. Her mother had created the problem, and he wanted MJ to ignore her mother's viewpoints and advice while he worked to follow his mother's. Because if the Muse of love poetry didn't understand the human heart and the dynamics of love, who did? But oh, he yearned to run after MJ. To catch her up and kiss her, and keep kissing her until she listened to him. Temple visions and bells be damned. Immortality be damned. He turned to look at the incongruity of bed and table sitting in the sand as if blown there by some strange wind, but a potential place of lovemaking and shared joy.

If only she returned.

With a growl, her threw himself down on the sand, scooping up fistfuls and throwing them into the water. Hades take it! He'd sit here until the sun set and rose again if he had to. He'd sit longer than that, it wouldn't be easy, but he'd do it. Because he still had all the time in the worlds. And he loved her.

If only she returned.

Gradually, MJ recovered her breath as she watched the waves roll in and out.

How did she arrive here? Not here here—wherever here was—but here in this position, in this time and place? It began, once upon a time, with Gran dying. With the conditions of her will. With meeting Nik, Nik of the dark hair and eyes, of intelligence and caring. She'd never met a man who exuded the confidence and power the way he did and yet didn't use it to lord it over her. Mostly.

He was nothing like her professors or advisors who relished their superior status over grad students, especially female ones, a little too much. Of course, the male students weren't much better, talking for hours on end about their specialty but seldom asking more than one or two questions about hers, whether in a group sharing coffee or on a date.

Nik constantly asked about her work, what she was thinking, did she want to write, and more. Unlike the professors and grad students, he talked so little about himself. What little she knew, she dragged out of him, but didn't notice how little she knew about him until he left and had no way of contacting him. Or knowing where he was while he was away except through his office email and phone number. Maybe he was telling her something by telling her nothing.

But those kisses!

She bit her lip. There was something between them because those kisses, they made her heart beat faster just thinking of them. She scooped up a handful of sand and let it run through her fingers until there was nothing left but a tiny shell. Smiling, she examined it and discovered its white lacey pattern—like a fossilized doily. Or a decoration for a fairy house. Something so tiny, yet so beautiful, and it could have gone unnoticed and unappreciated. Sighing, she tucked the delicate shell into the pocket of her shorts.

"Okay, Gran, what am I not noticing or appreciating."

She watched the waves come in and go out, and thought about recent events, the strange happenings since she arrived at the cottage. Holding out a hand, she tapped the pointer finger. "Ever since I met Nik, your hunky man of affairs, Gran, nothing has been normal. My life has been turned upside down."

A soft breeze ruffled her hair. She tapped the next finger. "I almost drowned that second night. I shouldn't have gone out to the water. Even if hunky Nik enticed me out see the White Horses, I should have worked on my dissertation."

She remembered how he carried her back and cared for her until she was safely in bed. What gave her the chills was the vague, odd memory of hands on her ankles pulling her under. And of a large turtle. Like that strange woman mentioned— She shook her head and tapped her ring finger.

"Third, Gran, my dreams are so vivid and feel so real, especially the one about you and what you said about Father."

And the ones of Nik were, well, luscious and stirring, but mostly frustrating. She grabbed her pinkie, then rubbed at her head. That strange vision of a temple and the sound of bells when they kissed. She'd heard of stars and fireworks, after all. But a temple and bells? Weirdest of all? The strange, angry woman in the water who made impossible statements. With a growl, MJ shot to her feet and stepped closer to the water. What had happened to turn her life and her world upside down? Gran's death.

If Gran hadn't died, MJ would be back at her apartment or at the university library doing research, writing her dissertation, sheltered by stacks of books, surrounded by index cards and post-its, her laptop open in front of her, typing away until her eyes burned, her back ached and her head pounded. Or she'd be meeting with Neri for coffee and sharing her worries about defending her dissertation. Or listening to her mother harangue her about doing more research, writing more, preparing for her orals. Listening to her mother go on about how finally she was going to get the department head position, and how MJ—no, Marie Juliette—should get her doctorate and accept the position her mother had wangled for her. Never considering MJ might want to teach elsewhere. Or do anything else.

She rubbed her eyes, then took a deep breath. A breeze off the water caressed her face and tousled her hair as if to carry that stressful image away. What should she do? Her mother would order her to get back to the cottage, pack, and drive home. Beg her advisory committee to let her extend her deadline and complete her dissertation. Give up Gran's place and the income from her stories.

Or, she could wait until the required time had passed and then return. She'd work on her dissertation and present it for consideration the following semester—maybe. Her mother wouldn't be thrilled with that. Or... It would be great to have a pen and paper so she could write all these options and facts down. One more option. Or two. Maybe. She could break off things with Nik personally...if there was any "thing"... Stay at the cottage, live off of Gran's royalties, at least while she explored writing her own stories, and once she established herself, find a new agent.

None of those options made her heart lift with joy and possibility. The one that did?

Nik. She wanted Nik in her life, in her cottage and yes, in her bed. She loved him. Was it possible to fall so fast? Her mother would say she wasn't living in a fairy tale. Another breeze. She lifted her head.

What if... What if life was a fairy tale? With ogres and trolls, with fairies and fairy godmothers. With princes who searched through thorns and brambles, past dragons and ogres, to find the princess. She laughed and shook her head. But...

What if being a princess meant being brave enough to believe in, to work for her happily ever after? To search for the prince of her heart?

What if...

She turned and looked back up the beach. How far? She was so tired after her frustrated trek away from Nik. The wind was picking up and the sun winked out behind fat heavy clouds. Great. She was going to be soaking wet by the time she reached him. If he was still there. Waves slapped at her feet and she stepped away. But they seemed to follow her, drawing closer, growing larger. She looked out at the sea. A bank of water rose and rushed toward shore. She scurried back, remembering the bad dream and not wanting a repeat of that night of the white horses. Not now, when she was ready to reach for her happy ending. For Nik.

Spellbound, she watched the waves rise higher, white, and frothy as they raced for shore, the sound thundering in her ears, her heart echoing the sound. As they reached the shoreline, two huge, muscled horses emerged, pulling a small golden chariot behind them. Just when she thought they would run her over, they veered aside and halted, one horse looking back over its shoulder at her. A pair of white horses.

Talk about gobsmacked! Glancing back at sea, she saw the water had settled, the clouds were breaking, and sunlight cast rays onto horses and chariot. She closed her mouth. Was this another trick? Tentatively, she stretched out a hand. The chariot's metal was warm and wet. Either she was a really good dreamer who fallen asleep while walking or...

"Toto, I don't think we're in Kansas," MJ whispered. If things like this kept up, she was going to run out of fingers for listing strange events. The horses shook their heads, the one on her left glancing back again and rolling its eyes, then snorting, as if to say, "Let's get on with it, shall we?"

She gripped the very real rail of the chariot. Wasn't it time to reject her mother's limited and limiting view of the world, of imagination and fairy tales and Gran? And MJ?

She took a deep breath and smiled. It was now or never. Time to put on the crown and be the princess she was meant to be. She climbed into the chariot, spread her feet, and grabbed the front rim with both hands. The reins hung down inside the chariot and she started to reach for them, then shrugged. *What if* she trusted the horses to know where to go? She smiled. This was going to be way better than any amusement park ride.

"Giyyup!"

Chapter 32

Nik sat watching the tide roll in and out, his forearms resting on his bent knees. He clenched his jaw. Waiting was killing him.

Killing him. Like a mortal. If she returned, if he carried her to the bed behind him and made love to her there, death became a real possibility at any moment, an ever-present threat. How did mortals live with that? How did they move through the uncertainty of each day without being immobilized by the fear of unexpected death? After centuries of service as a Voice, he still didn't get it—but he would.

More of a mystery, though, was how did they manage the fear of imminent death for loved ones? If he made love to MJ today, she could die in an accident tomorrow. His stomach knotted. Childbirth could claim her, in spite of medical advances. He'd watched it happen before. They could have children and they could die of disease, or accident, or war.

Scrubbing the thoughts from his head with quick fingers, he focused on something more hopeful and bright. Did she want children? His lips curved. One? Two? A boy and a girl. Two girls. Two boys. Children he could love and raise and encourage in their creativity, even if they followed other career paths.

Children who could break his heart through loss or rejection, or grey his hair with worry and concern.

Children. But to have them, sex, making love, came first. Rising from the sand, he turned to the empty bed meant for seduction and love-making. The wind gusted, ruffling the curtains and lifting the linens slightly. An image rose of MJ stretched out naked on it, her body all lithe curves from her shorn hair to her toes. Open to him, welcoming him so two became one. His heart beat stronger, blood pulsing.

If she returned.

As he turned from the bed, a joyful laugh drifted to him on the wind. Her laugh? He drew a deep breath. Next, he heard the deep rumble of hooves on wet sand. Hands on his hips, he stood, hoping, waiting. She wasn't, was she? She didn't believe... But, what if... He dropped his hands and ran toward the sound until finally he saw something coming at him with speed, and halted. Closer and closer, and— His mouth dropped open at the surprising and awe-inducing sight, more magical, and more beautiful than any myth or fairy tale.

Two white horses, stallions, galloped at him, heads outstretched, pulling a chariot behind them. Standing in the chariot tall and proud like a goddess or a warrior princess, MJ. Her smile stretched across and lit her face, while her eyes, bright with delight, focused on him. Her hair ruffled in the breeze from the chariot's momentum, and the light top she wore molded to her breasts. She looked like who she was, a woman of magic, mystery, and power.

Oh, Juliette, look at her! She'd returned.

To him.

The closer the white horses galloped to Nik, the more MJ worried they would run him over. Looking down, she realized the reins had disappeared. What to do?

Desperate and with full authority in her talking-to-students voice she said, "Stop now!" Instantly, they slowed their pace, pulling up next to Nik before halting. She grinned. They'd listened. These beautiful, powerful, magical animals listened to her. Tilting her head back, she whooped.

"I take it you're glad to see me."

Oh, that voice. The sound of it thrummed in her ears and vibrated right down through the center of her body. She lowered her head to look at him and sighed. He stood holding the head of the inland side horse, rubbing its nose, reaching up to scratch its ears.

Those hands. She wanted to nicker for her turn of petting and rubbing. Instead, she climbed down from the chariot. Whoa! Her legs were a little shaky after bracing herself for the mad dash up the beach. Slowly, she walked to Nik. He turned to her, a smile lighting his face.

"You came back."

She smiled. "I did."

The horses snorted as if to disparage their less than scintillating conversation and with a whinny, they headed to the water. Startled, she took a step but Nik caught her arm.

"Let them go. They did what they intended to do. Their presence must be a gift from Poseidon. I'll have to make sure to thank him." As the horses entered the water, waves rose up, closing over them. They were gone. She shook her head.

"What?" he asked.

"Wonderful and magical and I don't know if I'll ever get used to it."

"You won't have to."

What did he mean? That he didn't love her after all? She shivered in her clothes, damp from the spray kicked up by the horses. He wrapped an arm around her but she held herself stiffly. He reached up and ran his fingers through her hair. Warmth, heat radiated from him like a welcoming fire after a long day.

He said, "I love how your hair has a life of its own, how it curls around my fingers as if to hold onto them."

"You're going to talk about my hair after you just said I won't have to get used to the magical? Really? What did you mean?"

He sighed, pulling her closer and kissing her forehead. "There are things I need to tell you, to explain. Before I do, I want you to agree to listen and not leave me again. Ask questions, but please, don't walk away again. Please?"

What additional crazy magic would make her walk away? Her world was already turned upside down. What she thought of as fact and truth was only one small part of the world. Gran and she had hoped for and sometimes believed in impossible things when she was young. But her mother force fed her reality, or at least reality as her mother imagined it to be.

She needed more information before making any important decisions. He squeezed her to him when she nodded, and dropped a light kiss on her mouth, before leading her from the water to where the sand was dry and the tide didn't reach. Then he gently pulled her down to sit next to him, holding her hand. He gazed at the water, and she admired his profile with his strong jaw, straight nose, and dark hair and brows, those long lashes. Why did guys always have the best lashes? Broad shoulders filled out his shirt, as his biceps filled the short sleeves. He bent his legs, digging his feet into the sand. He was totally swoon-worthy but she wasn't doing any swooning until she knew what was going through his mind.

"I know all of this, everything that has happened today—and before—is a big shock."

She snorted. "You think?"

He turned to her, one brow raised. He squeezed her hand gently with his larger one enclosing hers, making her feel protected, cared for, at home.

"I'll explain this the best I can." He looked at their entwined hands, raising them to place a kiss on the back of hers. Her heart beat faster. The kiss was sweet and tender.

"You aren't supposed to be aware of this world, or what I am. The magic, if you will."

What? She pulled her hand from his and wrapped her arms around herself and turned her gaze out to sea, away from him. "So why..."

"Because you are an assignment that's gone wrong."

She lurched to her feet, but Nik grabbed her wrist before she stepped away. "You agreed to listen," he said, shaking her arm gently, "and not walk away. Please. I need you to listen to it all. Even if what I say I say wrong, or if it is something you don't want to hear, otherwise you'll never know the truth, or understand who I am and what I feel about you. If you want a future together..."

Together? The two of them together? Slowly, she sat down, nodding. "You're right. I'm sorry. Please. Tell me."

He told her. Of his service as a Voice, his commander Apollo (she shook her head), about his mother and aunts. She reminded herself to take deep breaths, and to keep listening no matter how unbelievable it all sounded. Afterall, she'd ridden in a chariot pulled by white horses from the ocean. Much of what he shared were ideas and elements she and Gran had talked about, imagined, but they were always imaginings. Her mother talked about them as if they were the ideas of a primitive people from centuries ago.

Centuries? "Wait, how old are you?" she burst out.

He smiled at her, a glint in his eyes. "Old enough to know how to make you feel very good, very happy." He glanced back over his shoulder and when she followed the direction of his glance, she saw the bed. "But not too old to enjoy the process...for days."

Now she almost did swoon. Days in bed with him, his hands on her body, his— No, he was trying to distract her. And it almost worked. "How old?" she insisted.

He shrugged. "Centuries in mortal terms, but as an immortal?" He shrugged again. "A little older than you."

Centuries. He'd been alive before cars were invented, before the telephone and electricity and the internet. She couldn't quite grasp it. He scooped up some sand with his free hand and as it trickled through his fingers, he said, "As a Voice, I have two strict rules to abide by. Breaking them is cause for expulsion and possible punishment. The first is not to tell any mortal what I am, because doing so would lead to chaos among mortals, and between mortals and immortals."

That made sense. "Why risk it? Why interact with us at all instead of staying happily in your realm of clouds or islands or whatever?"

He sighed and scooped up another handful of sand. 'As short as your lives are, your creative spark, your *merika* as we call it, not only moves your world forward but empowers ours as well. It's the magic that powers our magic, that keeps my mother and aunts from aging the way you do. Another piece of information that would create chaos and problems should it be known among mortals. The problem is, your world has been so enchanted by your technology and your sources of entertainment that you give less and less of yourselves and your time to creativity."

"But aren't the gods and goddesses creative? Didn't they create this?" She waved at the beach and the ocean.

"Their creativity is slow and measured, happening over aeons of time, just like the length of time it took for the sea to grind down shells and stone to this sand." He released her hand to brush his hands together. "You mortals have the ability for unending creativity in a much smaller measure of time."

"I still don't understand what it has to do with you and the Voices."

He crossed his arms and rested them on his knees. "There are and probably always will be those who need help breaking free of the bonds keeping them from creatively expressing themselves."

"Like me," she said, suddenly understanding why she was an "assignment." Her shoulders slumped.

"Yes, like you but do not feel badly. Often, the bonds that imprison the *merika* are caused by outside influences—parents, teachers or mentors, spouses, or partners. The *merika* is buried and almost snuffed out under those influences. Then, one of the Voices step in to help the mortal reignite their creative spark, to give their imagination free rein."

Free rein. Oh yes, the exhilaration of letting the horses run as fast as they wished while pulling her in the chariot behind them, trusting they would take her where she wanted to go, much as the story she was working on often pulled her quickly behind it.

"Because mortals' *merika* burns less and less brightly, the creative energy empowering my world and contributing to the well-being of my mother and aunts wanes."

She put her head on his shoulder. "How awful for you!" she said, thinking of how she felt about losing Gran. How hard it would be to lose someone who was part of your life for centuries.

"Why did you help Gran?"

He smiled at her. "Your grandmother, Juliette, was something else. Her *merika* lay dormant because of the demands of family and other expectations. She just needed someone to fan the flame, is all. Besides, I loved helping her, and my mother loved her stories."

"You became a Voice to help your mother?"

He nodded. Of course he did.

"What is the second rule?"

Hades! Nik knew he needed to tell her but he hoped for a few more minutes of sitting with her, sharing his thoughts and his story. Her immediate understanding of why he'd volunteered for the Voices touched him. His mother was the only other person who appreciated the heartfelt reason behind his service and commitment.

Making love to her and sealing his fate to become a mortal would not be honest of him if he didn't share with her what was going to happen. To tell her after it happened—no, he couldn't do that. He would not take the power to participate away from her. She hadn't had that choice with her mother. He took her hand again, prepared to hold tightly to her if she tried to bolt again before he made her understand why he wanted to do this, what she meant to him.

She shook his hand impatiently. "What's the second rule?"

He turned and took hold of her other hand as well, looking into her beautiful, sea-deep eyes.

"Never fall in love with your mortal."

She didn't bolt. Instead, she closed her eyes, the light fading from her face, her lips trembling. She tried to pull her hands from his.

"No, MJ, I'm not letting you go. Not yet. Not until I explain. You agreed."

She stopped pulling, her shoulders slumping. Turning her head, she blinked.

"MJ," he said softly, "I broke the rule."

Slowly, she turned back to him, hope now brimming with the tears. "You have? How? I mean, with me?"

He wanted to sweep her up in her arms and kiss her until the tears disappeared but if he did, he wouldn't be able to stop at kissing her. Instead, he kissed the back of first one hand, then the other. "How can you ask me that? Yes, you."

"How? After you were gone for all that time? After a strange woman shows up and tells me you were her lover. Did you sleep with that woman?"

He took a breath to explain, then clamped his lips shut. He had no business telling her more about his world than she needed to know. That would not help her or him and it would just anger his aunts, Apollo, and his mother. On the other hand, they needed to be informed that one of his cousins, a Siren had revealed herself to a mortal in a place she shouldn't have been.

"I have lived centuries, MJ, and not as a monk. What happened with that woman happened a long, long time ago. I broke the rule with you, only you."

Her eyes brightened and she started to smile. His heart pounded. He longed to say the words to her, but first...

He cleared his throat. "I want you to know what happens when I break the rule, which I haven't completely. Yet. But if we..." He straightened his shoulders and nodded toward the bed.

"If I take you to that bed and make you mine, just as I become yours, the rule will be irredeemably broken."

Chapter 33

He was willing to break rules for her? Because he loved her? She wanted to throw herself into his arms. But wait.

"What happens when you break the rule?" She didn't want him sent to the equivalent of a military prison, somewhere she'd never see him again. Or brough up before some tribunal and shot. Could an immortal die from a gunshot? She was being silly. Being immortal meant no death sentence, didn't it? But he continued to look at her with wary eyes and his lips pressed together in a straight line. Whatever the consequences for him, they were serious and she needed to brave up.

She gathered her courage and asked, "What is the punishment for breaking the rules of the Voices?"

He gripped her hands tighter. His gaze lowered, and his voice was rough when he said, "I become mortal. Like you, I will age and die."

Her hands would have jerked away but he clung to them. She wanted to kick at sand, scream at the wind. She was so angry. Furious. Not at him, not this time. This time, she was furious *for* him. She shook her head. "Why would they do that to you? After all these years, no, centuries of service. Why wouldn't they simply give you an honorable discharge and let you go?"

He laughed and shook his head. "This isn't the mortal military, MJ." Sighing, he tugged her closer and wrapped his arms around her. "It's a long story from long ago—"

Like one of her fairy tales only not so happily-ever-after.

"—and it's one I can't tell you or explain. I only just learned about the consequences after the first time we kissed, when you saw the temple and we heard the bells. It never happened to me before—"

"Me either," she broke in.

He gave another short laugh and hugged her tighter, and her whole body lit with the joy of being held by him. She tilted her head back to look into his eyes. "How can I be the first woman in all these centuries you've ever broken the rules with?"

He shrugged and kissed her temple, whispering in her ear, making her shiver. "I never felt about anyone the way I feel about you." He pulled back. "To be honest, I came close a couple of times but was strongly reminded of the rules, and because I had not yet become entangled, I pulled back. Otherwise, I did what I was expected to do and kept myself emotionally distant."

"How lonely," she said, thinking of all those years and years and years without someone to love who loved you back.

He nodded and smiled. "Your Gran started to change that for me."

What? She raised a brow.

"No, no. Not that way." He shook his head, still smiling. "But she kept doing things for me instead of the other way around. She kept asking what would make me happy, like you did. She kept asking me why I hadn't found someone to love and marry." He raised his hand and brushed his thumb over her cheek. "I kept putting her off, telling her I hadn't found the right woman yet. I was right."

She turned her head to kiss his palm. She wanted to cry. To have found this, found him, and have it taken away. But she couldn't be selfish. She couldn't let him make this sacrifice for her. Someday, when old age weakened them and she was, well, like Gran, wouldn't he regret his mortality? She shoved out of his arms.

"I can't let you break the rule all the way. I don't want you to have to become mortal, grow old, die…"

"You mean like you will?" he asked.

"Death is what you always expect when you are born a mortal." She wrapped her arms around herself. "I can't let you lose your immortality because of me. Your whole life…"

She tilted her head back, looking up at the happy blue sky. "Your whole life will change. I can't let you make that sacrifice."

Her last words were whispered, then she closed her eyes and dropped her head.

Careful. He had to approach his answer to her so carefully.

"Sweet love, may I remind you I'm an immortal—for now—and you can't prevent me from doing what I want to do." He held his hand up as she opened her mouth to protest.

"MJ, do you know what a sacrifice is? A true sacrifice?" This was the key, he knew, after watching her interactions with her mother and Juliette's occasional comments about her daughter-in-law.

MJ tightened her jaw, her eyes bright with tears before she turned away from him. "Of course I do. I've known the word sacrifice since I was old enough to spell. Because my mother's reminded me of hers from forever." She put her hand to her chest and looked down as if talking to someone smaller than her. "Do you know what I've given up for you? How long it has taken me to get my career back on track? The least you can do is..." she paused and waved her hand back and forth in the air, "...fill in the blank. Do your homework. Stop playing pretend all the time. Take your studies seriously. Think about your career. Don't waste your time on drivel. Don't—"

She broke off and it was a good thing because she was breaking his heart. How could a parent do that to a child, especially a mortal one? She rose and stood gazing out over the water. He waited to see if she would turn back to him but she didn't.

"That's not a sacrifice, MJ. That's resentment and payback."

She whirled on him, eyes wide. He continued before she could protest. "A sacrifice, in the ancient understanding and in the contemporary one, is giving up something one holds to be meaningful or significant as an act of love or adoration, because, in turn, the one sacrificing receives something more significant, more important."

She clasped her hands together, watching him, waiting.

"Long ago, the shepherd sacrificed his best and purest lamb to the gods in order that they might bless him with a fertile flock. A mother bear fights to the death to protect her cubs. Mortal parents sacrifice personal dreams for the well-being of their children. MJ, they do it out of love for their children not out of obligation or with resentment. Understand?"

She closed her eyes and he held his breath, praying to his mother. MJ nodded, and opened her eyes, pinning him with her gaze. "What is your sacrifice for, Nik? What could I possibly give you that would be better than immortality?"

He released his breath. Women! She understood his loneliness but not how she filled the emptiness? No wonder his mother needed this island for star-crossed lovers. He stood and put his hands to his hips.

"Have you not listened to anything I told you?" He stalked forward and took her into his arms once again, raising a hand to cup her cheek, tilting her head back so her lips were only a breath from his.

"What I get," he breathed softly to her, "is a woman I fell in love with the moment I saw her trying to be so prim and proper at the table in her Gran's old house, the woman who looks like a fairy tale princess come to life, who loved her Gran, and who believes in magic and fairy tales and happily ever after."

He kissed each cheek and tapped her lips with a finger. "I get the woman who is smart and brave and strong and so very, very creative. And..." He tugged her closer. "...if she loves me and shares my dream of a home together with our children, then I get my happily ever after, one I never thought I'd have."

The hope and joy and love in her eyes nearly undid him. "I get *you*, MJ," he forced the words through his suddenly tight throat. "I get you."

He dropped his mouth to hers and kissed her with all the longing and hope and love bottled up inside for so long. She kissed him back, wrapping her arms tightly around his neck, molding her body to his, and desire and joy rocketed through him. So enraptured and caught up in the moment was he that he didn't hear the bells at first, not until MJ pulled from the kiss, eyes wide.

Bells pealed loudly.

Bells. Bells rang loud and clear as Nik kissed her into a warm puddle of butter.

Bells! Oh, no. She pushed back from his embrace and when he tried to press forward to keep kissing her, she took his face in both hands.

"Wait. The bells. Are you sure, Nik? I couldn't bear it if..." her voice wobbled and though she tried to blink them back, tears escaped down her cheeks. "I love you. I love you with all my heart. I don't want to lose you but I will understand if you—"

"Hush, sweetling. I—"

She shook her head. "No, I won't hush. I don't want you to hate or resent me in a few years, or in twenty when your body isn't young and strong any more. When I'm not sexy—"

He placed his palm over her mouth. "Do you think I will mind that when we are watching our children grow and go out into the world and maybe have children of their own? When I can have you with me always even—how do you mortals say it—even until death do us part?"

He kissed her again and this time she surrendered to him completely, to him and to the bells, to the stripping away of his immortality. If that was what he truly desired, then what kind of fairy tale princess would deny her prince the chance for his own happily ever after?

He tightened his arms around her and she sighed into the kiss, her arms once more around his neck, her fingers tangling in his hair. Growling, he lifted her into his arms and carried her across the sand to the bed that waited for them. Her heart beat with joy, her body heated with desire. Finally, not the dream but the reality.

He placed her gently on the bed, then moved from bedpost to bedpost, untying the cords that held back the bed curtains, providing them with a modicum of privacy. Not that anyone was there to see them. She reached for him as he stretched out beside her, but he shook his head, taking both of her hands in one of his and stretching them above her head.

"Too long have I waited," he murmured in her ear, "for this moment. I will not be rushed."

Her heart beat faster and her body lifted toward him of its own accord. "Please," she whispered, "I've waited, too. Don't make me wait any longer."

His mouth took hers, demanding, seeking, invading. Hers responded, opening to him, caressing his tongue with hers, moaning when he nipped her lower lip. Her body sought his, and she raised her leg and curled it over him, pulling him to her.

Another growl, but this time he pulled away from her and left the bed. Before she could protest, he'd pulled his shirt over his head and shucked his shorts and underwear, kicking off his sandals with the shorts. Hands on his hips, he stared at her, heat in his eyes, and his body aroused and ready.

She swallowed. He was built like a Greek god, all sleek, defined muscle. Not bulky but powerful nonetheless. She gave herself a mental slap. He was a Greek god, for crying out loud. But not for much longer. Would that change him in any way? She hoped not.

He looked better than any marble sculpture she'd ever seen, but she discovered when he lowered his body over hers that he was incredibly warmer, hotter than any marble carving. She felt his warmth even through her clothing as his chest covered hers and he nestled between her legs, his erection hard and hot against her belly.

Oh, gods, why did she still have clothes on? She shifted beneath him and heard his sharp intake of breath.

"Hold still," he gritted out. *Hmmm, not so in charge as he thought he was, huh?* She batted her lashes at him. "Are you sure you don't want to rush things?"

His eyes darkened and he nipped at her ear lobe, then moved to nip at her throat. Okay-y-y. Much more and she wasn't going to be melted butter, she was going to be sizzling melted butter right on this pretty bed. But first, she needed her clothes off.

"It's not fair!"

He raised his head, eyes intense. "What's not fair?"

She sighed. "This," she said, waving her hand back and forth between them. "You are naked. I'm not."

He smiled wickedly. "I think I can help you with that."

"I wish you would," she whispered, and lay waiting to see just how he would help her.

His smile was wicked and made her tingle all over. Reaching for the hem of her t-shirt, he slowly rolled it up, taking his time, kissing the skin of her belly, over her ribs until, yes, she was sizzling.

Chapter 34

He rolled the shirt up over her breasts, his heart pounding as he unveiled the beauty of her soft pink nipples pearling as the air touched them. As he blew gently on them, they budded even tighter.

"So beautiful," he said, and lowered his head to the first one, sucking it into his mouth, his tongue swirling around it, making her lift to him. He heard her panting and his cock swelled more with the sound. Releasing that nipple, he moved to the other one to give it the attention its pertness demand. He released it with a pop.

"Nik, clothes!"

Smiling at her response, he looked down at their bodies, captured by the contrast between his slightly darker skin and her pale one, between his angles and her soft curves. But there was more clothing to remove. He lowered his head again and proceeded to kiss his way down her body, stopping to tongue her navel.

Finally, he was going to taste her, claim her, make her his. Deftly, he unsnapped and unzipped her shorts, pulled those and her underwear—something pink but who cared at this point—off in one motion, then bent to kiss her inner thigh, this time kissing his way up.

"Nik!"

He held her in place as he explored with tongue and lips, tasting and teasing her, until she was panting and her fingers gripped his hair.

"Let go, MJ, let go, sweetling."

She tumbled into climax with a shout, her body bowing. Laying his head on her belly, he waited for her to come back to earth. Slowly, she relaxed, sinking back into the bed. He tilted his head to look up her body, now flushed. Her nipples beckoned him, so he rose and covered her body with his, once again suckling at her breasts.

"Oh, Nik." She stroked his face, her hand gentle and soft. He kissed the palm, watching her eyes, wide and loving as he rose up and entered her. Her eyes widened more as he pressed home. Home? Yes, exactly. A homecoming to the one place and one person where he belonged. Love and a deep sense of well-being filled him, love for this imaginative, enchanting woman who welcomed him into her body. Joy surged through him as he moved faster, pressing into her harder, deeper.

She was his. He was hers. The joy was reflected back to him in her eyes, in the beautiful smile that lit her face.

"Nik!" she cried, as she arched her head back, her climax triggering his own so powerfully and intense that darkness followed.

MJ sighed and snuggled in bed, warm and relaxed. As she moved, she encountered another warm body curled next to her.

Her eyes flew open as memory flooded back, of being on Erato's island, of her ride in the chariot, and best of all, of making love with Nik. But she wasn't in the bed on the island, instead she was in her bed in the cottage. She blinked. Had she dreamed it all? No, she couldn't have because the warm body next to hers was Nik, proof it was no dream. But how had they ended up back here? She had no memory of it. Rose petals, she discovered, were strewn over the bed.

She nudged Nik. "Nik, wake up!"

He rolled onto his back yawning and stretching his arms over his head. She licked her lips. Those pecs and biceps just invited her tongue to explore and play. She looked up to find him watching her, a smug grin on his face.

"See something you like?"

Turnabout was fair play so she rose a little in the bed to turn toward him, letting the sheet fall, baring her breasts. The smug grin disappeared and he lunged at her, bearing her down to the bed beneath him, and taking a nipple into his mouth. Oh! Heat ran in a straight line from her nipple down the middle of her body. It was as if he touched her in both places at once. She hated to do it but she had to know what was going on so she pushed him back.

"Look at the bed. Look at where we are. How did we get here? Why don't I remember?"

He lifted his head, looked, then shrugged his shoulders. Wrapping his arms around her, he bent his head, touching his lips to hers, then deepened the kiss. She opened to him, loving that he was here in her bed. When he raised his head, he said, "Probably something my mother did."

"Hmmm?" What was he talking about?

"You asked how we got here. Probably with my mother's help."

"She really is your mother?"

He nodded, "She's my mother. We were on her island. You really did drive a chariot pulled by white horses."

She closed her eyes. How could she believe the unbelievable? Yet, how could she not trust her own experience? *What if, MJ?* Opening her eyes, she searched his. What she saw in them brought tears of relief and surrender. With joy, she leaped from her tower of facts and research, of isolation and others' expectations knowing he would catch her. Because he loved her.

"I love you." She wrapped her arms around his neck and pulled him to her.

"I love you, MJ, now and forever," he said before he claimed her mouth with his.

If anyone understood forever, he certainly should. She smiled beneath his lips as they sank back onto the rose-petal-covered bed, letting their bodies whisper and share all the poetry their mouths were too busy to speak.

Chapter 35

T he late afternoon sun sparkled off the water, and made gems in the sand of the beach. The sky was clear and cloudless, the blue expanse broken only occasionally by a circling gull.

The arbor they'd set up was entwined with—what else—sea roses in honor of Erato. How did you deal with a mother-in-law who was also an immortal? But if all she did was whisk them away to an island every time she and Nik had a disagreement, or scatter rose petals on their bed, she wouldn't worry.

"Are you ready?" Neri asked her, reaching out to twitch at the fluttering fabric of the simple gown she'd chosen for the wedding. She looked at her reflection, loving the simple, Grecian-like lines of the satin and silk organza gown that left her shoulders bare, with a skirt falling in folds from the gathers below her breasts. Perfect for exchanging vows on the beach.

Because they couldn't wait, she and Nik decided on a beach wedding at the end of the summer. The beach also made it easier for the few immortals who wanted to attend, like his mother, to do so.

A circlet of small shells with an elbow-length veil attached rested on her head, nestled among the soft curls of her hair. The veil, also of silk organza, fluttered behind her with every step. She took one last look in the mirror.

"You look like a fairy princess." Neri gazed over MJ's shoulder at her reflection.

MJ turned and gave her a hug. "Thank you for coming, for being here and being my Maid of Honor."

Neri hugged her back. "Are you kidding? I wouldn't miss this. I'm so happy for you. It will be my delight to tell anyone from the university who asks, how happy you are."

MJ nodded. "I am. I just wish…"

Neri nodded. "I'm sorry about your mother. I'm glad though you are finally doing what you want to do. I'm thrilled you're writing."

"Can you believe it? Nik says the publisher thinks Gran's last book will be a huge seller because it is her last one, which will also boost the sales of her previous one. He also likes my novel. I'm doing it, Neri."

Her friend gave her another hug, longer this time. "You are, and you deserve this. Don't cry and mess up your makeup."

They laughed, then MJ tilted her head. "Uh oh, I hear music. I better get out there before Dad or Nik come looking for me."

Neri handed MJ her wedding bouquet and they left the bedroom. Her father stood by the French doors to the deck, waiting for her. He turned and smiled broadly when he saw her.

"You look beautiful, daughter mine."

"Thank you. Thank you for being here, even if—"

"Ah, where else would I be? I'm proud of you. Your Gran would be so happy for you." He took her free hand and tucked it into his bent arm. "It's plain to see Nik loves you and cares for you. I can trust him with my special girl."

MJ blinked back tears. Her dad opened the door and stood back to let Neri exit first. After a few moments, he gestured to the open door.

"Shall we, daughter mine?"

"One more thing, Dad."

"What is it? Hurry. That man of yours won't wait."

"Isn't it time you lived your own dream and started writing again?"

He led them through the door onto the deck. "You know about that, do you? Well, I was inspired recently by a young woman I know." He turned his head to wink at her. "I'm returning to my own land of make believe."

She squeezed his arm. "I'm so glad."

He became serious and slowed his steps. "I'm sorry, darling, your mother isn't here. I don't understand her."

She squeezed his arm again. "Hush, Dad. I'm sorry she's not here, for her sake. I wish she could be happy for me, but I won't let her spoil my day with her absence."

He swallowed, then said softly, "I'm happy for you, darling girl, and if your Gran were here, she'd tell you the same."

MJ couldn't speak past the lump in her throat. She blinked quickly and stepped into the aisle between the guests standing and smiling at her and her father. She smiled at them as she passed, grateful for the few friends and students who were there. Then all she could see was Nik, standing in front of the arbor waiting for her next to his friend, Alek.

Nik watched her walk up the aisle created by the standing guests.

He'd witnessed so many mortal weddings, never imagining he might be the groom in one. Now he was. Because of her.

He glanced over at his mother who'd donned the age-appropriate form of a mortal mother of the groom. Even so, she was vibrant with beauty. She had approved the idea he and MJ had of a writing retreat and school they planned to open on the island. In this way, the two of them together could continue Nik's work of awakening others to their *merika*, their creative spark. She beamed at him. He smiled back at her and tried to ignore the fact Morpheus stood next to her. He hoped the immortals behaved themselves.

"No wonder you deserted us, bro," Alek whispered to him. "She's fine."

"More than fine, Alek. So much more."

When her father placed her hand in his own, he nodded to the older man, an acknowledgement of respect and gratitude for her father. It couldn't have been easy for him to come in spite of his wife's own refusal to attend. He pulled MJ to him and turned to the celebrant, hoping Hermes didn't mess this up.

He'd never hear the end of it.

Thalassa watched in anger and disbelief as that insipid mortal woman walked to Nik, taking his hand and turning to Hermes, the traitor, to exchange mortal vows.

She wanted to scream out her frustration, watch all the mortals cower and cover their ears. She wanted to scream so high and long that the water rose up and crashed down on the beach, destroying the happy scene.

She didn't dare. Not with Hermes and Erato there as witnesses. That made her more furious. Nik was never going to be hers again. No matter what she did, or how long she waited near this beach, he wouldn't be hers. He was a mortal man now...one she could easily overpower.

As they joined hands to say their vows, she could see strands of creative energy extend from their joining, connecting with other creative strands, strengthening each other.

Bah! She sank below the water, banishing them from her sight. Eventually, she would banish them from memory if she worked hard enough at it. Banish the memory of the light and love radiating from them in golden waves.

She needed to get back to her sisters. She'd been gone too long. And now they needed a new plan.

After all, she smiled, there were other fish in the sea.

Her groom was so handsome in his tux, his dark hair blowing slightly in the breeze, his eyes focused on her, his smile wide.

She was so lucky. So very lucky. To have found a man who helped her claim her courage and creativity, and who was her every fairy tale dream come true. She shifted her gaze to the celebrant and almost stopped breathing. Wasn't that... ? He looked like the host at the White Horses. In fact, she was sure he was. Nik told her he knew just the person to perform the ceremony, so she'd left that up to him. But a restaurant host?

Her father gave her hand to Nik who pulled her in close to him. She nudged him and nodded at the celebrant who oddly had eyes of different colors.

"Are you sure this will be legal?"

The celebrant smiled and winked at her. "In this world and beyond."

Oh, he was that kind of celebrant.

"We are gathered here today to celebrate the union..."

As the words rang out, picked up by the wind, MJ looked up at Nik and saw only him, only his love for her in his eyes.

Thank you, Gran. For my happily ever after.

CHECK OUT MORE GREAT BOOKS FROM ROWAN PROSE.

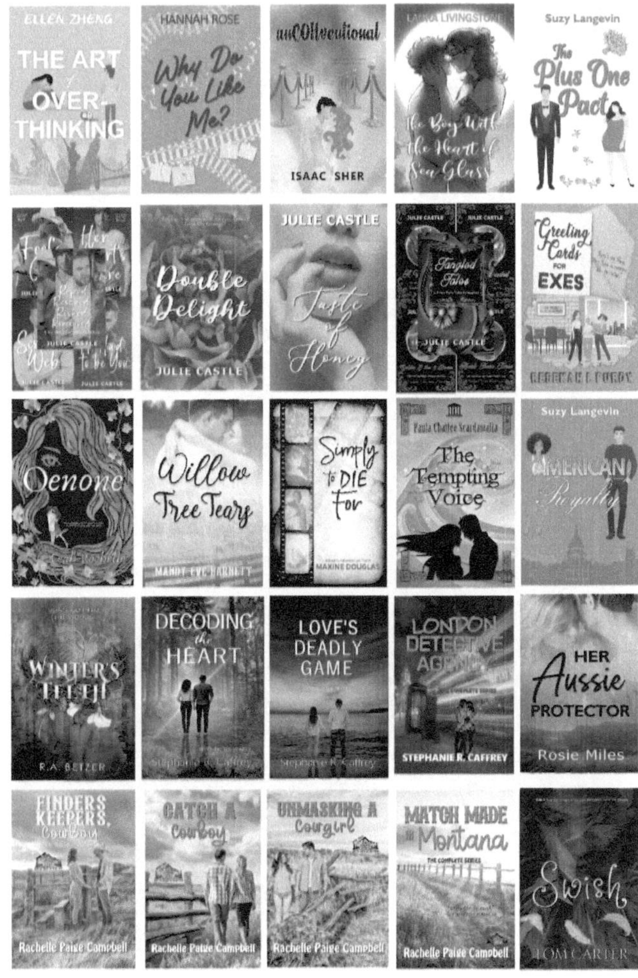

Besides being an author, Paula Chaffee Scardamalia is a book coach who loves helping other writers write their stories or life discoveries using her experience and knowledge as well as intuitive tools such as dreams and the tarot. She's the author of "Enchanting Creativity, Tarot for the Fiction Writer," the award-winning "Weaving a Woman's Life: Spiritual Lessons from the Loom," and her fantasy romance novel, "In the Land of the Vultures." Divine Muse-ings is her weekly newsletter on writing, creativity, dreams, and tarot. She lives with her husband in an 1840s Greek Revival farmhouse, constantly in need of TLC, in the foothills of the Catskills.

www.ingramcontent.com/pod-product-compliance
Lightning Source LLC
Chambersburg PA
CBHW021344310726
48971CB00001B/274